The Raven Cc

CW00498477

Fire-Walker Book Two

By Emma Miles

Copyright Emma Miles 2019

Chapter One

Letters

From Lady Rosa Cainridge, Northold, Elden, to Kesta Silene, Fulmer Hold, Fulmer Isle.

Dearest Kesta,

Northold is far too quiet without you. At least I am still here and not summoned back to Taurmaline. I imagine her Majesty is too busy with her pregnancy to think of me. You will be pleased to hear that I have been spending time with Merkis Tantony. The Thane has let us take his ship out onto the lake a few times. He hasn't kissed me yet and I wonder do I dare be as brave as you say, should I kiss him first?

I have not seen much of the Thane. He has gone back to spending most of his time in the Raven Tower although he is often summoned away to Taurmaline. I visit your horse, Griffon, when I can and have taken a short ride out on little Nettle from time to time. Nerim, the stablemaster, tells me that the Thane goes out riding in the forest on Griffon. I think he is missing you more than I although he will not talk about you when I have tried. Tantony tells me to leave it alone. You never explained why you left, I understand if you prefer not to say, but I cannot help but wonder.

Will you ever visit here do you think? I would love to see you. Perhaps I might be able to visit the Fulmers one day?

With fond wishes

Rosa.

***

From Dia Icante, Fulmer Hold, Fulmer Isle, to Thane Jorrun, Northold, Elden.

Thane Jorrun,

Kesta mentioned that you have had no formal training in your magic and have learnt most of it from books. I cannot teach you the secrets of the Walkers, however there is no reason I cannot offer you training in elemental magic if you so wish. If your king will spare you, you are most welcome to come and stay here in the Fulmer Islands.

Dia Icante.

***

From Kesta Silene, Fulmer Hold, Fulmer Isle, to Lady Rosa Cainridge, Northold, Elden.

Yes, Rosa, kiss him! Tantony is an old stick in the mud and may never do so himself.

I am glad you are still in Northold. I hope you are not too lonely? It's good that you are riding Nettle, I know you were not that fond of riding. I'm surprised Griffon allows Jorrun to ride him, he doesn't really like people.

Tantony is right. Please leave it, Rosa. Jorrun and I chose our lives. There are reasons why we can't be together that he isn't willing to fight against.

I have never written a letter to a friend before, I'm not at all sure what to say. That will amaze Tantony!

Catya is doing well. Heara encourages her into mischief far too much. She has asked me to say hello.

I can't come to the Raven Tower but would love it if you could visit me. Bring Tantony.

With love

Kesta.

***

Thane Jorrun of Northold, Elden, to Dia Icante, Fulmer Hold, Fulmer Isle.

Icante,

I thank you for your generous offer however I will not be able to leave Elden for the foreseeable future.

Jorrun.

***

Lady Rosa Cainridge, Northold, Elden, to Kesta Silene, Fulmer Hold, Fulmer Isle.

Dearest Kesta,

I have the most wonderful news! Tantony has asked me to marry him! My only fear is that Her Majesty will refuse her permission. You will come to our wedding if it happens? I couldn't bear for you to not be there. We could hold it in Cainridge or Taurmouth if it is too painful for you to visit Northold?

I am worried about the Thane though. I have taken over young Catya's duty of taking his food to the Tower, but I have not seen him in days. He barely touches his food. Tantony tells me the Thane is very quiet when he sees him. I know you told me to leave things, but I don't like to see him like this.

You are well, I hope? Please give my love back to Catya, I hope she is behaving. Tell her I hope she is still studying her letters!

Fondest regards

Rosa.

***

Dia Icante, Fulmer Hold, Fulmer Isle, to King Bractius, Taurmaline, Elden.

Your Majesty,

After the success of our collaboration against the necromancers of Chem, I would like to invite you to Fulmer to discuss a possible exchange of ambassadors. It would be good if our two countries continued with a more open dialogue and a closer friendship. I understand you might be too busy to come yourself at this time, perhaps you might send your advisor, Thane Jorrun, with a delegation to represent you initially?

In faith,

Dia Icante.

***

Kesta Silene, Fulmer Hold, Fulmer Isle, to Thane Jorrun, Northold, Elden.

Stop being the Dark Man. You don't have to be anymore.

Please give my love to Azrael.

***

Kesta Silene, Fulmer Hold, Fulmer Isle, to Lady Rosa Cainridge, Northold, Elden.

Dearest Rosa,

Congratulations to you and Tantony, I'm so happy for you! If the Queen will not give you permission to marry could Jorrun intervene with the King? If not then you must both elope here to the Fulmers!

I am well enough.

You wouldn't believe the change Heara has brought about in Catya, she has really come out of herself.

Do you see anything of our little fire-spirit, Azrael? I do miss him.

With love

Kesta.

***

King Bractius, Taurmaline, to Thane Jorrun, Northold.

Jorrun, attend me at Taurmaline as soon as possible. I have a mission for you in the Fulmers but I want your word in person that you will make no attempt to stay there. I will, however, expect you to bring your wife back with *you. As I have already said you are embarrassing yourself and Elden by allowing her to run wild. Be here.*

***

King Bractius, Taurmaline, Elden, to Dia Icante, Fulmer Hold, Fulmer Isle.

Icante,

Thank you for your kind invitation, as you suspected I am too busy here at present to visit you, however I would be honoured to do so in the future. Considering his ties to your islands, Jorrun will represent me and be with you for two weeks along with Merkis Vilnue, with whom you have worked before. I cannot spare my sorcerer for longer. I look forward to a lasting friendship between our two countries.

Bractius, King of Elden.

Chapter Two

Kesta; Fulmer Islands

Kesta shifted on the short-cropped grass, hugging her knees to her chest. She could feel the vibration from a small waterfall that plunged down from above to her left, and far below waves threw themselves at the cliff. The sun was warm against her skin but the wind off the sea still had a chill to it. Kesta glared out across the ocean, watching as the two-masted ship drew closer to Fulmer bay. Her teeth clenched tighter as pins and needles tingled in her chest and she realised she was tapping her feet.

With a loud sigh she stood, her eyes still on the ship. She hadn't wanted to be here for the Elden delegation, but her mother had insisted. She told herself she'd be polite, then find excuses to get out of the way. Tearing her eyes away, she turned and climbed slowly up the cliff to the path above and made her way toward the hold, her feet feeling heavy. There were a lot of people coming and going across the causeway from fortified Fulmer Hold, carrying supplies for the welcome feast. She caught herself scowling and drew in a deep breath to compose herself. It was the Elden's king she hated, not the people, in fact she quite liked Merkis Vilnue who was coming here as their ambassador. Her mother's closest friend, Heara, certainly liked the Merkis. Kesta grinned.

By the time she got close to the beach, the Elden ship had already sent out a row boat toward the shore. Her mother was easy to spot. Although not as tall as Kesta, Dia wore the authority of the Icante, ruler of the islands, without the need of any crown or ornament. Kesta's uncle, Worvig, stood to Dia's left and her father, Arrus, to her right. Although much quieter than his brother, there was something about Worvig that always made Kesta feel safe.

Kesta's eyes lifted toward the rowboat and she drew in a sharp breath, her foot slipped off the edge of the path and she raised her arms to keep her balance and prevent herself falling. It couldn't be! She swallowed, eyes wide, breathing hard as her heart raced. He was unmistakable. Taller than the men around him and as poised as a stag, dressed as always in elegantly tailored black. The Dark Man of Elden. Her husband.

But why was he here? For a moment hope leapt inside her, but one look at his face and it sank, pulling her shoulders down with it. He was angry. He didn't blink as his piercing eyes regarding the people waiting on the shore, his movements were stiff, his bow overly formal. Kesta watched as they exchanged words, unable to hear them from where she stood. Merkis Vilnue joined them, the sandy-haired man showing his teeth in a cheerful smile through his red-tinted beard.

Her mother turned, indicating with her hand, and the group began to make their way across the beach toward the path. Kesta leaned back, but she found her feet wouldn't move. Why was he here? She rubbed at her chest with the heel of one hand, her heart throwing itself against her ribs. Her nostrils flared, and she dug her nails into the palms of her hands.

Her mother only glanced at her as they approached, deep in conversation with Vilnue. Her father's cheeks looked a little red beneath his dark beard and Kesta narrowed her eyes at him. Only Worvig met her eyes, and he gave her a nod. She looked past them and was immediately caught in Jorrun's intense gaze, her breath stilled in her lungs and her face flushed, even as the blood seemed to drain from her lips. He didn't blink, didn't look away, but his feet faltered and he stopped.

Kesta wanted to kiss him so badly she felt dizzy.

'Silene, would you show Thane Jorrun around the Hold?'

Kesta swallowed, tearing her eyes away from Jorrun to look at her mother. Dia had used her title, not her name, so it was an order from the Icante, not a request from her mother. Kesta cleared her throat and forced out the words. 'Yes, Icante.'

Dia nodded, and the group moved away toward the Hold, leaving Kesta and Jorrun alone on the path. She watched the Eldemen unloading on the beach for a moment, forcing herself to breathe, before she turned back to Jorrun.

His eyes travelled over her face, even with his amulet blocking her *knowing,* she could feel the anger radiating off him. Then the stiffness left him and his eyes softened.

'You didn't know, did you?'

'What?' Kesta cleared her throat again. 'That you were coming? No, no one told me.'

He sighed, looking out over the sea before turning back to her. 'You'd better show me around then.'

She nodded, waiting for him to step up beside her, before proceeding along the path. They both spoke at the same time, Kesta asking about Azrael, Jorrun about Catya.

'Go on,' Jorrun prompted, the slightest of smiles ghosting his face.

'Catya is settling in very well,' she told him. 'She's certainly committed to learning from Heara. She'll be really pleased to see you.'

He nodded once. 'Azrael ... he misses you. He nags me, as always.'

Kesta laughed at that, glancing up to see that Jorrun's eyes were fixed on her. She rubbed at her nose, looking around her. 'Well, this is obviously Fulmer Hold. The only way to get to the Hold itself is along that high causeway there.' She proceeded to describe the area and then told him a little of the

Hold's history. She introduced him to a few people they passed, but other than an occasional polite greeting, Jorrun didn't speak. Whenever she looked up, he was watching her.

They entered the great hall and Kesta was almost bowled over by a warrior who was carrying out an empty crate.

'Sorry, Kes!' he called back over his shoulder without stopping.

The hall was a bustle of activity, garlands of flowers and leaves were being strung up around the walls and food was hastily being set on the tables. Looking across to the opposite end of the long room, Kesta saw that her mother's group had settled to talk together. She stopped, her eyes narrowing as she watched them. Why hadn't her mother warned her that Jorrun was coming? Was she behind this, or was it Bractius?

She clenched and unclenched her jaw, now wasn't the time or place to confront her about it. 'I'll show you where your room is.' She glanced over her shoulder at Jorrun.

They squeezed their way past the tables and the busy hold folk to a large double door at the back of the hall. She didn't bother to acknowledge her mother's group. She pushed through the doors and pointed at the stairs, one set going up, another heading down into darkness. 'Up there is my mother's room, and mine. Guest rooms are down here, with the storage cellars.'

Jorrun made no reply, so she headed down the stairs. Kesta raised her left hand and used her magic to call flames there, she doubted that Jorrun needed the fire to see by any more than she did, but automatic politeness was comfortable to hide behind. At the first door they came to she let her magic dissipate and she pushed it open, taking a few steps across the room. It was a generous size, with a long narrow window high up in one wall that let in a shaft of light. She jumped when the door closed behind her, but she didn't turn, her eyes were fixed on the bed. Jorrun's steps were barely perceptible as he moved closer. Her heart was racing again and she bit down hard on her lower lip, trying to steady her breathing.

'Kesta.'

She turned and his hands reached out to tangle in her hair, his mouth found hers and she closed her eyes.

***

Kesta woke slowly, blinking at the darkness in the room. She turned her head slightly to see Jorrun was sitting up in the bed, knees drawn toward him and his head in his hands.

'Jorrun?'

He started, his hands dropping to the blankets as he turned to look at her, his black hair mussed as though he'd been running his fingers through it. 'Kesta, I'm so sorry! I can't believe I le—'

'Jorrun, shut up.'

He stared at her, eyes wide and mouth open. 'Bu—'

'No, Jorrun.' She sat up. 'We haven't done anything wrong, *you* haven't done anything wrong. Even if this was Elden and not the Fulmers, we're married for spirit's sake!'

He shook his head, looking everywhere but at her. 'I don't want you caught up in Bractius's plans, I'm meant to be protecting you.'

She snorted. 'I can protect myself, I seem to be saving you, more often than not.'

He glared at her and she grinned.

His expression softened and his eyes travelled over her face. 'Kesta, our situation hasn't changed.'

She stiffened. 'Did Bractius order you here?'

Jorrun rubbed at his beard. 'He did. Although it was actually your mother who instigated it.'

Kesta's eyes narrowed and she sat back. 'Really.' She could feel him watching her. She swallowed. 'How long are you here?'

'Two weeks.'

Her chest muscles clenched. Such a short time.

'Jorrun.' She turned to look at him. 'Give me these two weeks. Please. Forget Bractius, forget Elden, forget Thane Jorrun and Kesta Silene. Let's just be us, for two weeks, until you have to go back.'

He gazed at her unblinking. 'I'm not sur—'

'Can't we even have that much? Something just for us after everything we did for Bractius and Elden?' She moved closer, resting her hand against his chest.

He placed his hand over hers, stroking her fingers with his thumb, and she could feel the rapid thud of his heart. The skin around his eyes creased as he regarded her. 'At the end of the two weeks I'll have to leave. I ... I don't want to go through arguing about all this again, hurting each other. I want you to rule the Fulmers after your mother. I want you to be happy, here, where you're free.'

She clenched her teeth, stopping herself from saying that she wanted him to be free, too.

He swallowed. 'We can have these two weeks.'

She hadn't realised she'd been holding her breath until she let it out. She quickly tried to hide behind humour. 'Well, I don't know about you, but I'm starving. Let's go up and get something to eat.'

They quickly dressed and headed up to the great hall.

'It's very quiet,' Jorrun said with a frown.

Kesta pushed the doors open a little and peered in. There were maybe a dozen people still in the hall, several of them snoring. The central fires had died down to smouldering ash and much of the food had been eaten or cleared away.

'It's later than I thought.' Kesta raised her eyebrows. When she turned to look at Jorrun, she saw he was blushing. She shook her head, in a way it was quite sweet, but she was still shocked at how conservative Elden men could be.

'We missed the welcome feast?'

'No one will care, Jorrun.'

'I care,' he replied stiffly. 'They'll think I'm rude.'

'They'll think you missed your wife.' She watched as his cheeks reddened further. 'Let's get some food and go back downstairs.'

***

They spent little of the two weeks in the Hold, instead exploring the islands and visiting some of Kesta's favourite hiding places. As agreed, Jorrun didn't bring up his concerns about Bractius again, but she could see how much it worried him in the tensing of his shoulders, the way his eyes would grow distant and his brows knot together in a frown. As much as she tried not to think of it, Kesta's own happiness was also dogged by a shadow of anxiety.

Catya was overjoyed to see Jorrun, and he watched on in amazement as the previously introverted girl chattered away to him unselfconsciously. She showed him the fighting skills she'd learned and tracked for him through the forest that surrounded the Hold. Dia left them alone for the most part, only insisting they join her on the morning of the Elden delegation's leaving as Jorrun's authority was needed to close some trade matters.

'By the way, has there been any news from Chem?' Dia asked as they concluded their business.

Jorrun held her gaze as he shook his head. 'Nothing at the moment.'

Kesta narrowed her eyes. Why did she have the feeling he was evading the truth?

Dia made a small noise in her throat, obviously thinking the same thing. 'Another boat landed on Dolphin Island last night, more Borrow refugees.'

Jorrun leaned forward. 'What news do they bring?'

Dia sighed. 'The same. The islands are cursed. They seek sanctuary, food, rest.'

'You've granted it?'

'For now.' Dia gave a slight shake of her head.

A man appeared in the doorway and waved a hand toward Merkis Vilnue.

'Looks like we're ready to sail.' Merkis Vilnue looked around at them all.

Kesta froze. She'd been determined not to get upset, but pressure rose up from her chest to push against her eyes and throat. She couldn't look up, but she could see in her peripheral vision that both Jorrun and her mother were watching her.

Jorrun stood slowly to shake the hands of Arrus, Worvig, and Dia, and thank them for their hospitality. Kesta held her breath as he touched her cheek lightly and kissed her forehead. He walked away across the hall without another word. Kesta raised her hand to her face, still feeling the ghost of his touch.

'Kesta?' Dia demanded.

She turned to see her mother glaring at her with her arms folded. Kesta scowled. 'What?'

Dia's eyes widened. 'With me, now!' Dia grabbed Kesta's arm and almost dragged her out of the doors at the back of the hall. 'What's going on?'

Kesta shrugged stubbornly, avoiding her mother's mis-matched eyes. 'Nothing's going on.'

'Well something should be!' Dia placed her hands on her hips. 'Why is he leaving? Why are you not going with him?'

'Because nothing has changed!' Kesta all but shouted, her throat hurt and her vision blurred.

Dia stared at her open-mouthed. 'You had two weeks! Did you not talk to each other?'

'Not about that.'

Dia rolled her eyes and blew out air loudly. 'You two are idiots! I can't believe you couldn't find a solution. I told you that I'd support you against King Bractius if Jorrun came her—'

Kesta threw her hands up in the air. 'Jorrun and I have been through all that, mother! If he comes to stay here, it could mean war. If I go there, we risk any child we might have being ruled by that awful man. Not to mention I'd have to endure the way he treats Jorrun.'

'From what I recall, there were a lot of 'ifs' in your argument that might never happen.'

'But the whole point of 'ifs' is they could.'

Dia narrowed her eyes. 'The way I see it, the only thing stopping the two of you being together is that you're too stubborn, and he's too rigidly noble! That and the fact he won't stand up to Bractius, which he certainly ought to.'

18

'Bractius is his king.'

'I'm your Icante but that doesn't stop you arguing with me.' She raised an eyebrow.

Kesta tutted. 'It isn't the same at all. It's complicated.'

Dia pursed her lips. 'If you say so. I've never known you to give up, why aren't you fighting for him?'

'Because he isn't fighting for me.' Her eyes widened and she stared at her mother, breathing hard. Where had those words come from? Was that what she really believed?

'I don't think that's true,' Dia said slowly. 'From what I know of him, I would say he's fighting his own feelings to keep you safe, to do what he thinks is best for you. By the way, his ship is leaving.'

Kesta took a step toward the stairs, every instinct demanding she run up them to look out of her window, but clenching her fists she stopped herself.

'I thought so.' Dia sighed loudly. 'I'll get you one more chance, after that I'm done with helping you both and you're on your own.'

'We don't need any help,' Kesta retorted.

'You need your heads knocked together,' Dia murmured. With a last sharp look at Kesta, her mother made her way up the stairs to her room.

***

Kesta pushed her food around her plate, not even seeing it. She'd thrown herself into working, training hard with Heara and Catya and had even gone sailing alone around the islands with the excuse of looking out for Borrow refugees. Nothing had quelled the churning of her stomach or lifted the heavy darkness in her heart.

Someone knocked on her door and she sighed. She slowly pushed herself up off the chair and went to open it. A young boy stood there with a thin letter in his hand.

'Silene.' He nodded.

She murmured her thanks and took it to her desk. Even a letter from Rosa didn't raise her spirits. Then she looked at the handwriting and the air caught in her lungs, she nearly missed the chair as she sat. She lifted it to her face to breathe in the scent, but it only smelt of parchment. She broke the seal, scanning the words. Her vision blurred as her eyes filled with water and she rubbed them with her fingers so she could read the letter again.

My Kesta.

I have been told off by your mother. Again. She is right though, we need to talk. I was wrong, we should have done so. Will you come to the Raven Tower?

I miss you.

Jorrun. X

Chapter Three

Kesta; Kingdom of Elden

Kesta reached up to brush away the wisps of her dark hair as the wind teased it across her face. The earthy smell of the silty lake brought a tingle to her chest muscles and she breathed in deeper. It was a warm day, a few clouds casting shadows on the grey-green water, riding up over the small waves. Her smile grew and her heart beat faster as the ship moved out onto the lake and she saw a familiar shape reaching up beyond the trees. The Raven Tower. It looked dark, but sunlight glinted off the westward window, even from here she could see two ravens circling lazily. She stretched out her fingers, hands down by her sides, using her magic to call up a wind to fill the sails and shorten the distance to the shore. One of the warriors gave a low sound of alarm at the ship's sudden speed, but Kesta responded by increasing it further, her smile turning into a grin.

She couldn't wait.

It had been less than three weeks since she'd seen him. Less than three weeks since they'd parted for a second time, intending that this time it would be forever. She swallowed, looking down at the deck as grief mingled with the butterflies in her belly. This third time might really be the last. She had to remember that nothing had changed. Her skin tightened in a blush and she almost lost her concentration on her magic. Well, Jorrun had relented in one thing. She bit at her lower lip and turned her eyes back to The Tower. She was just here to talk.

Kesta ceased her magic, her hand going to her throat, her eyes still on the Raven Tower until the trees obscured her view. As they neared the narrow wharf, she spotted a familiar figure striding out to meet them. Ceasing her magic, she crossed the deck to the prow.

'Kurghan!'

The bearded carpenter lifted his hand in a wave. She leapt across from the ship onto the wooden planks of the wharf as soon as the gap was narrow enough, not waiting for the warriors to tie up. Kurghan grabbed her arm to steady her as she landed, then shook her hand with a grin.

'My Lady.'

'It's good to see you.' She looked him up and down. 'Are all your family well?'

'They are, lady.'

Movement caught her eye and looking up she saw Rosa and Tantony making their way down the path from the Hold toward her. She drew in a deep breath at the sight of her friends and for a moment the prickling and churning of her stomach calmed. They both looked so well, their eyes bright and their postures upright and confident. Kesta touched Kurghan's arm to excuse herself and hurried to meet them.

'Kesta Silene.' Rosa gave a curtsy and Tantony bowed.

Kesta growled at them and stepped forward to grab Rosa in a hug and then kissed Tantony's cheek.

'You've trimmed your beard, Merkis,' she teased.

Tantony's hand went up to his face and he coloured slightly beneath his greying whiskers.

Rosa linked her arm through Kesta's and turned her toward the Hold. 'Catya didn't come then?'

'No, I couldn't tear her away from her training with Heara.'

'She really is serious about being a bodyguard?' Rosa raised her eyebrows.

'She is.' Kesta sighed silently. 'And what about you?'

Rosa and Tantony looked at each other, sharing a smile. 'The Queen has finally responded to my request to marry.' Rosa squeezed her arm. 'She has agreed.'

Kesta drew in a sharp breath and turned to hug her friend again. 'When?'

Rosa glanced at Tantony. 'We were hoping to do it while you were here; so, soon. Unless …' She watched Kesta hopefully, but Kesta looked away toward the Hold's gate.

'Let's go in.' Tantony placed a hand on Rosa's shoulder.

They made their way through the gate of the outer ring of the Hold, a tall earthwork with wooden ramparts. Beyond were the thatched houses that nestled safely between the Hold's defences. Kesta's eyes narrowed as she glanced around at the buildings, she'd have to persuade them to change the roofs to slate. The warriors guarding the main gate stood up straight to salute Kesta. That was new. She paused to nod in return. When she reached the inner ward, beyond the high stone walls, her smile returned at once as she gazed around to see the results of the work she'd started months ago. The herb and vegetable beds were flourishing, geese wandered the edges of a small pond and the foundations and shell of a large barn were in place, several men working on nailing up planks for the walls.

'What do you think?' Rosa asked.

'It look—' her voice caught in her throat as she saw him standing across the ward outside the Raven Tower. Her stomach flipped and her blood rushed to her cheeks.

'Go on,' Rosa said. 'We'll see you later.'

She nodded without taking her eyes off Jorrun. He didn't move as she approached, not even a smile, but the spark in his blue eyes made her lips tingle and her heart beat faster.

'Silene.' He gave a slight bow.

'Thane.' She raised an eyebrow in response.

He took his hands out from behind his back and pushed open the door to the Raven Tower. Kesta stepped in and Jorrun followed her, closing the door behind them and sliding a bolt across.

She stared at the bolt, her mouth slightly open. Had that been here before? She had never known the Raven Tower to be actually locked.

He brushed the back of her hand with his fingers and she turned to face him. A smile lit his face and electricity surged through every muscle of her body. She slid her arms around his ribs and he kissed her as though his life depended on it. He stepped away, leaving her feeling suddenly cold and breathing hard. Taking her hand, he led her up the narrow winding steps of The Tower. She glanced around his room, turning to run her fingers along his dark beard. 'Tantony has trimmed his, but you've let yours grow.'

He grabbed her hand and kissed her wrist. 'Kesta, we are meant to be talking.' His voice still held a hint of the Chemman accent he'd picked up again from spending time with his half-brother. She loved how he almost purred his 'r's.

She grinned at him and perched herself on the edge of the table. He'd obviously made some effort to tidy up as the highest room of the Raven Tower wasn't as cluttered as it had previously been. There were still more books than there was space for, some balanced precariously on the windowsill above his small bed pushed awkwardly up against the curved wall of The Tower room. Azrael was making slow, looping circuits of the room, excited she was here.

'Settle down, Bug,' Jorrun scolded gently.

The fire-spirit hissed at him and came to hover near Kesta. Her smile faded as she regarded Jorrun's serious expression. For a while he looked at everywhere except her and her heart sank.

'Kesta.' He took in a deep breath and regarded her unblinking. 'Why did you not tell me *walkers* often can't have children?'

She started, her mouth opened for a moment before she could reply. 'Well, I ... it's common knowledge, isn't it?'

'Not to me, not to Bractius. Not until your mother told me in her letter.' He turned away from her.

She folded her arms across her chest. 'It can be difficult for us, but not impossible, obviously. And often the children of *walkers* have no magic themselves. I was one of the few exceptions.'

He looked at her over his shoulder. 'So, what I fear from Bractius might not even happen.'

'But it might.'

He looked away again and a sudden suspicion entered her mind. She jumped to her feet and clenched her fists. 'Are you saying you don't want me because I might not be able to have a child?'

He spun about and placed his hands on her arms. 'Of course not! It just means maybe we are worrying about something that may never happen.' He sighed. 'But then we should consider it might and we'll have to plan ahead about what we'll do regarding Bractius.'

'Hold on a moment.' She placed a hand flat against his chest. She took in several fast breaths as she looked up at him. 'You were adamant we couldn't be together. You broke my heart, Jorrun!'

He closed his eyes. 'And my own, too. I thought I was doing the right thing. I *was* doing the right thing.'

Azrael crackled and spat. 'Foolissh human! You made yoursself sick!'

'Bug!' Jorrun held a finger up warning the fire-spirit to silence.

Kesta cocked her head to one side. 'Sick?'

'He didn't eat, or sleep.' Azrael sounded almost delighted. 'Couldn't even read or do hiss magic!'

Jorrun growled. 'Bug!' His shoulders sagged and he turned his pale eyes back to Kesta. 'I missed you. I *really* missed you.'

She stood on her tiptoes to kiss him but he placed two fingers over her mouth. 'Kesta, our situation hasn't changed. Bractius won't allow me to live on the Fulmers. I thought you didn't want to live here under his command? That you wouldn't allow our children to be manipulated by the Elden throne?'

She set her heels back on the floor and sat again on the table, her eyes still on his. Was she willing to stay in Northold? As happy as she'd been to return to her family and home on the Fulmers she couldn't deny she'd been totally miserable. As such an independent person she'd been furious at how much she'd pined for Jorrun. But even thinking about the way Bractius used Jorrun made her clench her teeth. She knew she'd find it hard to tolerate.

She bit her lower lip. 'What if I was free to come and go between here and the Fulmers?'

'I would never stop you going.'

'Would Bractius?'

He pulled at the end of his beard. 'He might, or at least try to make things awkward.'

'If we did have a child, my mother would protect it in the Fulmers.'

Jorrun looked away, sighing and rubbing at his face with his hand. 'Then we would risk war, or at the least animosity. We've been through this.'

'But as you said, it might not even happen.'

He turned to look at her. 'But as you said, it might.'

She growled. 'We're not getting anywhere.'

His eyes searched her face.

'I would have to be able to go back to the Fulmers whenever I wanted, within reason.' She licked her lips. 'I understand I would have duties to Elden as your wife.'

'I don't want you to give up your duties to the Fulmers. Your mother is an inspirational leader, you will be too. I don't want you to give that up for me.'

Kesta took in a breath. 'If we have a child, I won't allow it to be forced into a political marriage against its will. Is that something you can promise me?'

He swallowed, lines creasing his forehead. He glanced at Azrael and then looked out of the window, Kesta noticed his hands were shaking. That was Bractius's doing! Kesta had to restrain herself from leaping to her feet as anger rose in her. She wanted to snarl. Both Bractius and his father before him had ensured that Jorrun had been isolated all his life, dependent on them. They'd taken a powerful, but emotionally vulnerable boy, sent his brother away, and ensured they had his complete loyalty. She turned to Azrael and met the Drake's fiery blue gaze. Thank the spirits Jorrun had him.

Jorrun cleared his throat. 'I can promise to support you against Bractius when it comes to a child.'

She took in a deep breath and looked deep in his eyes. His evasive answer would have left her furious before. She pressed her nails into her palms. They could do this. Even so, she was afraid to let her hope rise in case it was shattered. 'We could take a risk, just see what happens?'

He nodded. 'We could. But could you live like this? Would you be happy here in Elden? Can you deal with Bractius?'

She stood and slid her hands around his back. 'As long as I know I can go back to the Fulmers whenever I want, then I can deal with him. I need to be with you.'

He smiled and bent to kiss her.

Azrael darted around their heads. 'Excuse, me!' he spluttered and darted away up the chimney.

Jorrun laughed. Kesta's heart swelled at the sound. She felt as though a mountain had been lifted from her shoulders.

'Come on.' He squeezed her hand. 'Rosa has spent the last few days organising a welcome feast for you and we should join them.'

'I should probably get changed.' She looked down at the dark-green trousers and tunic she'd travelled in.

His eyes narrowed. 'Actually, quite a lot of the women in the Hold have started wearing trousers, not to mention continuing to shoot bows.'

She grinned at him and he shook his head. 'You haven't stopped them?'

He shrugged. 'Why? I believe we are the best defended Hold in Elden even if we are getting a reputation for strangeness.'

'Well what do they expect from the Dark Man and a *Fire-Walker*?'

He snorted. 'I'll meet you in the Hall. All of your things will have been taken to the Ivy Tower.'

She felt a moment of nostalgia at the thought of her old room. 'All right, I won't be long.'

***

As much as she wanted to spend time familiarising herself with the Ivy Tower, she went straight to her travel chest and took out the green dress Jorrun had bought her shortly after their marriage. The leaf necklace he'd given her was already reassuringly heavy against her skin and she ran a finger over the intricately made silver links. As she quickly brushed her hair, she couldn't resist going over to the east window to look across to the Raven Tower. Someone had set a candle in a silver holder on her windowsill. She smiled and a delightful tingle shivered across her skin. When she'd stayed here before it had taken Jorrun a while to trust her enough to allow her to enter the Raven Tower. In order to preserve his privacy, they'd agreed she would only visit if he invited her by lighting a candle in his window. She hadn't considered calling him across to her tower with a candle of her own. She would definitely be lighting it later.

Holding up her hem she hurried down the stone steps and through the door into the great hall. Her eyes widened at how crowded it had become in the short time she'd been up in her room. She spotted most of Kurghan's family, familiar warriors, and folk of the Hold. There were two noticeable absences however, and she frowned..

Jorrun was talking with Tantony and Rosa and he paused on seeing her. As much as she wanted to greet him with a kiss, or at least a touch of his hand, she'd learned in their two weeks in the Fulmers that, although he was affectionate in private, in public he was incredibly reserved. She settled for a smile.

'I think you must be the only woman in Elden who, when she says she won't be long, actually means it,' he said with a straight face.

Rosa tutted, but Kesta grinned. Her smile faded as she looked around the room again. 'Is your brother not here?'

Jorrun's face grew serious and he bent to reply softly. 'Osun has returned to Chem, I'll tell you of it later.'

She nodded, hoping the relief didn't show on her face. The other person she hadn't been looking forward to seeing was the warrior chieftain, Adrin. It was possible he was on duty or had chosen to avoid the feast. She decided to ask Tantony or Jorrun later.

She spent very little time actually sitting down at the high table that evening, there were so many people to catch up with. Aven, Kurghan's sister, caught her up with gossip about the families of the Hold while Kesta patiently nodded and smiled. Several of the warriors wanted to know if she'd secretly been away fighting Chemmen and pestered her to tell them again of her exploits in Mantu and Chem. Reetha, the cook, insisted on taking her out to the herb beds to discuss how things were progressing and other matters of the household. Then she unexpectedly grabbed both Kesta's hands and squeezed them, tearfully exclaiming, 'Bless you, for coming back to us!'

She made it back to Jorrun's side and sat back in her chair with a loud sigh. He watched her with amusement before pouring her some wine. 'You are the most patient person I've met one moment, and then explosively impatient the next.'

She narrowed her mis-matched green eyes as she looked up into his blue ones, trying to judge whether he was baiting her or paying her a compliment. She picked up her wine and took a sip while she contemplated how to respond.

His face became serious. 'Do you really think you could be happy here? The people of Northold clearly love you.'

She looked around at him, he didn't blink as he regarded her face.

'As long as I can go home.'

He looked away and she wondered if she'd hurt him by pointing out that she didn't think of Northold as her home. Although in many ways it was, the larger part of her heart was here. If only Northold was on the Fulmers and not in Elden.

She reached under the table to rest her hand on his leg. 'Do you have to work tonight?'

'A little.' He turned back to face her, his own hand covering hers. 'I must speak with Osun. Will you light the candle?'

She grinned. 'Of course.'

***

Kesta was delighted to find Rosa waiting for her at the table in the receiving room when she went down for breakfast. The older woman's warm smile vanished immediately when she saw Jorrun with her; she stood so quickly she banged her leg on the table. Jorrun looked Rosa up and down without a word and then proceeded down the stairs.

Kesta laughed. 'Don't look so scandalised, Rosa, we are married remember.'

Rosa turned and picked up her chair, sitting down slowly. 'I know, but I didn't realise ... I though—'

'I'm going to stay.'

'What?' Rosa stared at her with her mouth open.

'I'm staying, Rosa, here at Northold, with Jorrun.'

Rosa's hand went to her mouth. 'Truly?'

Kesta smiled and nodded. Rosa almost knocked her off her feet when she ran across the room to give her a hug.

'It won't be all the time.' Kesta managed to pull herself free. 'I'll be going back to the Fulmers often.'

'That doesn't matter.' Rosa blinked rapidly, her eyes filling. 'You and Jorrun are meant to be together. It's so good to see you both happy.'

Kesta snorted. 'We'll see.'

Rosa scowled at her and poured the tea. Nettle and peppermint. Kesta took in a deep breath, absorbing the subtle familiar scent and ...

'Thyme bread!' She sat at the table and grabbed up a still warm roll.

'So, what are we doing today?' Rosa sat down and continued with her own breakfast.

Kesta laughed. 'It's so good to be plotting with you again at the morning table! As much as I would love to go and worry Tantony in his office, I've promised to go riding with Jorrun.'

'Griffon will be happy to see you.'

'And I him. I'm glad he wasn't neglected while I was away, not that stablemaster Nerim would have. Would you like to do something this afternoon, or are you busy?'

'No, I'm looking forward to spending some time with you. Perhaps ...' Rosa tried to keep a straight face but there was a gleam of mischief in her eyes. 'It is a while since I had a knife fighting lesson.'

Kesta grinned. 'Okay, fighting it is, as long as you haven't been neglecting your letters!'

Rosa laughed. 'Never!'

Kesta put her cup down and grabbed a handful of hazelnuts from a bowl. 'I'd best get going. I'll see you later.'

She hurried down the Tower steps and out into the great hall. She greeted several people who were tidying up after the previous night and those who'd come in for breakfast. Two warriors lay snoring on the floor beneath the benches.

Outside it was warm, the sun already above the trees and the wall of the Hold. She drew in a deep breath and closed her eyes, taking a moment to enjoy the kiss of the sun and the light touch of a gentle, cool breeze. She walked across the soft grass of the ward, kept short by a few grazing sheep. When she'd first come here, she'd thought the Hold had been badly neglected, left to go wild; only when she'd known Jorrun better had she realised it was down to his aversion to keeping anything caged or enclosed.

She opened up her *knowing* as soon as she entered the stables, allowing the emotions of those around her to flow in. She smiled as she felt concentration from Nip. The young stable boy was mucking out a stall and humming quietly to himself. She felt a touch of anxiety from Nerim; the scarred, one-eyed stablemaster was mixing a treatment for one of the horses that had become unwell. She heard a snort and felt excitement, Griffon had smelt her. She hurried to his stall, and the gelding pushed his way out to nudge her and blow air against her clothes the moment she drew back the catch. Behind her she heard the clatter of Nip dropping his rake.

'My lady?'

She turned and smiled at the curly-haired boy with the soft-grey eyes, trying to keep her balance as Griffon continued to nudge her.

'It's all right, Nip, I'll ready him myself.'

He gave a quick smile and a bob of his head. 'Your tack is still in its place, lady.'

Kesta gave Griffon's hooves a quick check before fetching her saddle. She had to adjust the stirrups and she paused to regard the bridle with a sigh. On the Islands *walkers* rarely used a bridle and never a bit, instead they used their *knowing* to work with a horse. Here in Elden though, she'd been wary of showing too much of her magic and frightening people. Griffon was used to such a harness, but even so …

'Something on your mind?'

She gasped, spinning around to see the only person who could hide from her *knowing* standing right behind her. He looked far too smug about scaring her for her liking, and she growled at him. 'You should be an assassin, sneaking about like that!'

The corners of his mouth lifted slightly and amusement lit his eyes.

She narrowed her eyes at him and picking up the harness took it back to its shelf.

'Would you help me find a horse that wants to go out?'

She turned back to him. 'You don't have a horse of your own?'

He shook his head. 'There are horses belonging to the Hold, but I rarely ride. It's usually quicker to travel by water from Northold.'

She looked at Griffon and he followed her gaze, reaching up to stroke the horse's head. 'He made me feel closer to you and seemed to like the company.'

She swallowed, reaching up to place her hand over his. She didn't need her *knowing* to understand the loneliness he must have felt. 'He is an intelligent horse that needs stimulation. You can ride him if you like?'

34

He lifted his hand from Griffon to take hold of hers. 'No, he likes the connection he has with you. I can ride another horse.'

Nerim came out from where he was working and gave them a nod before going about his business.

'So, you would like a horse that enjoys being ridden rather than one that goes along because it is forced?' She looked up at him.

'If there is such a thing.'

She nodded and made her way slowly along the stalls, stopping to say hello to Rosa's pony, Nettle. Jorrun leaned against the wall and watched her, his arms folded. Several of the horses showed an interest in her and the majority were keen to go outside although more for the grazing and freedom than for any interest in being ridden. She halted outside the stall of a brown mare who regarded her with suspicion but who was restless and longing to stretch her legs. There was intelligence there, but without the sharpness of Griffon's mind. The mare was mildly intrigued by Kesta, but not interested in making any kind of connection with her.

Kesta sighed. 'We should perhaps look in Taurmaline if you want to find a horse willing to be a friend, like Griffon, but in the meantime this mare would enjoy going out.'

Jorrun nodded and went to look for his saddle. Nip darted out from where he'd been observing to help him.

They headed down to the lake and then followed the road toward the river bridge for a while before Jorrun turned his mare off the main way to follow a smaller track into the forest. They rode in single file, Griffon getting annoyed at the mare being in front. As used to Jorrun's long silences as she was, Kesta began to suspect something was wrong. His shoulders and back were tense and he barely looked at the forest around them.

He turned off the track, glancing over his shoulder to give her a brief smile. Soon the forest became too overgrown to ride through easily and they dismounted. Kesta could hear water and they came to a rapid stream that fed a wide pond, green with duckweed and lilies. Kesta looked around, breathing in the scents of the forest and smiling at the simple beauty of sunlight on the water. She drew in a sharp breath as a doe stepped forward to drink, her ears flicking and her tongue tasting the air. Jorrun came to stand beside her but out of the corner of her eye she could see he was watching her rather than the doe.

'What?' She turned to face him and the doe leapt away.

Jorrun smiled and leaned forward to kiss the corner of her jaw below her ear. 'Come and sit,' he said, his smile vanished to be replaced by a frown.

He sat on a fallen log and she sat beside him. She guessed this must be somewhere he often came alone to think. He looked out across the pond and licked his lips before pulling at his beard. She waited, a stone settling in her stomach. Whatever this was, it wasn't good.

'I spoke to Osun again this morning,' he said eventually. 'He's been checking on the situation in Chem and meeting up with his old contacts. There aren't enough strong covens remaining to fill all the Seats. Weaker houses led by those with minor power and limited finances are vying for position. The strongest remaining coven is led by a man called Feren. Feren Dunham. He's my father's uncle.'

Kesta shifted on the log. 'Go on.'

'It's likely Feren will be unopposed in taking Arkoom Seat and being elected Overlord. All we did could end up being for nothing.'

She studied his face but he didn't look around at her. 'But?'

He glanced at her and snorted, one half of his mouth twitching upward in a smile. 'But. Osun has a plan. It's actually reasonable, if dangerous, and already he's working on gathering support and resources. He suggests another Dunham taking a Seat and challenging Feren for Arkoom.'

'You.' She felt nauseous and held her breath waiting for his response.

He turned to regard her, his eyes unblinking, intense. 'That was his suggestion; however, I've already said no. Bractius would never agree to my going if it was for me to rule in Chem in any way – even if it benefited him. The plan would be for Osun to take the Seat of Navere, our father's old Seat. It has never been known for someone without 'blood' to hold a Seat. Never. I would go there to fight for him, to take the Seat and hold it until he's established.'

Kesta wanted to protest but he raised his hand as soon as she opened her mouth.

'There is another part to the plan, Kesta. Osun will need a coven formed of magic users to back and protect him. We hope to do something else that has never been known in Chem. We'll build a coven of women. We'll buy and free women with magical ability and hope they'll stay and fight with us. As I said, it will be dangerous, it will be revolutionary. There has never been a better opportunity though.'

Kesta stood up and turned away, folding her arms tightly around her body. 'And who will train those women?'

He stood also and walking over quietly placed a hand on her back. 'I hoped *we* would. I know it's a huge thing to ask, Chem was a living nightmare for you and won't have changed. Navere is not as bad as Arkoom, but it's bad enough. You would have no freedo—'

She raised a hand and stepped away from him. Her stomach was churning and her skin felt as though it was on fire. She pulled at the neck of her tunic, her other hand curled into a fist. They'd only just agreed to be together, and now he wanted to leave, leave for a place that she hated with every ounce of her soul. The only reason she'd ever want to go back to Chem would be to burn the place to the ground.

Then she thought of Milaiya, of how desperately she'd wanted to save Osun's slave from Chem. There were hundreds, thousands, of women just like her, all suffering the same mistreatment. This would be a chance to free them, probably their only chance. Could she say no, knowing that she'd be leaving them to their intolerable lives? And Jorrun would go anyway, even if it meant leaving her behind, he wouldn't walk away from doing what was right.

She turned around and looked him in the eyes, chin raised. 'When do we go?'

He stared at her open-mouthed, a smile struggled and then failed on his lips. 'Kesta, at least think about it, please.'

She shrugged. 'What's there to think about? It needs doing, so we'll do it.'

He stepped forward and kissed her, not giving her time to take a breath. 'I don't deserve you!'

She scowled at him and then leaned her head against his chest and slid her arms around him listening to his heart. 'You didn't answer my question. When do we go?'

He breathed in deeply and sighed. 'That will depend on if we can convince Bractius of the benefits to him and to Elden. We're going to have to put it to him very carefully.'

Kesta grinned. 'Oh, I think I can come up with some convincing arguments, just ask Tantony. Oh!' She stepped back and looked up at him. 'Rosa and Tantony's wedding.'

He winced, and then smiled at her. 'They have waited long enough. They can get married the day after tomorrow.'

'We should probably ask them.'

'What's the point in being a Thane if I can't give orders now and again?'

She shook her head but laughed, anyway.

Chapter Four

Dia Icante; Fulmer Island

Worvig burst into the hall and spotting Dia, skidded to a halt.

'Another boat!'

Dia passed her scroll to her apprentice, Pirelle, and with a quick shake of her head strode across the room to join her chieftain. 'Where?'

'Just a mile down the coast.' Worvig was red-faced and breathing hard. He was a large man, taller and broader than most islanders, as was his brother, Dia's husband. The lines about his hazel eyes increased as he frowned. 'Just women and children by the looks of things.'

'Even so.' Dia indicated to one of the warriors guarding the Hold. 'Get thirty men, quickly, and follow.'

'Yes, Icante.' The man turned at once to obey.

'Where's Heara?' Worvig glanced around them.

'Out training Catya.' Dia pursed her lips. 'She'll be along no doubt. Arrus?'

'Stayed to watch the boat.'

Dia nodded. 'Come on then.' She broke into a run and, with a groan, Worvig caught up and matched her pace.

Over the last three months, several ships of varying sizes had arrived in the Fulmer Islands carrying refugees from the Borrows. Some of them had fled to the coast of Chem after the conquest of the Borrow Islands only to be attacked there and driven out or captured as slaves. Others had spent days at sea before returning to their ruined homes. Few of the survivors, it seemed, were able to endure it there for long.

40

They reached the small cove where the boat had set in. Arrus and two other warriors were standing amidst the seaweed of the high tideline. The boat was partially pulled up onto the beach but only one person had gotten out, a woman about ten years older than Dia with iron-grey streaking her otherwise brown, curly hair. Her eyes were a pale hazel, and she watched Dia without fear. Dia made her way across to Arrus who gave her a nod and relaxed his stance a little. With a glance over her shoulder Dia saw the rest of the warriors were on their way.

She touched Arrus' arm and took a few steps toward the boat. Raising one hand she called flames to her fingertips. Several of the women and children in the boat cried out in alarm.

'Just so you know,' she said to the Borrowwoman.

The woman nodded and Dia extinguished her flame.

She already knew the answer, but she asked anyway. 'I am Dia, Icante of the Fulmers. Why are you here?'

'I am Grya, Matriarch of Nisten Isle.' She indicated behind her with her head. 'We seek safety.'

'Your men have raided the Fulmers for years, killing and enslaving our people. Why would we help you?'

'Because you are a mother.'

The words hit her like a stone to her temple, like a slicing open of her heart. Dia swallowed, forcing the muscles of her face to relax to hide her emotions.

'We'll give you food and allow you to rest here for one night, but you must go back to the Borrows.'

Grya turned as if to spit but stopped herself. 'The Borrows are cursed. The birds and animals have fled. Those that can't leave suffer illness and nightmares. We've tried to tolerate the land, but it's impossible.'

'I've been told the effects of the blood spells will pass. They have done so here and in Elden.'

'We can't live on the sea until that happens.'

The two women regarded each other. Dia sighed. 'Our resources are not limitless. You will work for your food and shelter. You will live by our laws and be judged by them. You must return to the Borrows when it's safe to do so and let none of your descendants attack here again. Is that acceptable?'

Grya stepped forward and reached out her hand. Dia saw Arrus's hand go to his sword. She waved her husband away. Calling up her *knowing* she wasn't surprised by the mixture of hope, exhaustion, and desperate fear she felt from the people in the boat. Grya was a different matter. There was a lot of pride and confidence there. The woman would bear watching.

She crossed the distance between them and took Grya's hand firmly. 'You'll stay outside the Hold, but we'll ensure you have the materials to build reasonable shelters. This man here is Worvig Silene. He and these warriors will escort you to the Hold.'

'Thank you, Icante.' She winced as though the words brought her pain.

Dia looked her up and down before making her way back up the beach.

'We can't keep taking them in,' Arrus complained under his breath with a scowl.

'No, we can't,' Dia agreed. They climbed up over the rocks to the coastal path. 'I think it's time we made use of our new Elden Ambassador, Merkis Vilnue, see if he can get Bractius to accept a few Borrow refugees.'

Arrus grunted. She looked up at him to see his eyebrows were pinched in tightly over his green-flecked eyes.

'I thought you liked Vilnue?'

'Vilnue won't be the problem,' he replied. 'If we ask Bractius to assist with our refugee problem, he'll want something in return.'

'You're probably right.' She slipped her arm through his, for a man in his late-forties he was still solidly muscled.

'Have you decided who you'll send as our ambassador?'

'I considered Larissa, but I'll wait and see if Kesta decides to stay in Elden before I choose a *walker*. If I sent Larissa, I'd want your brother to go with her.'

Arrus drew in a long breath. 'Worvig won't want to leave here. As for our Kesta, she won't leave Jorrun again unless the fool makes her.'

Dia smiled to herself. She had asked Kesta a simple question not long after they'd returned to the Fulmers. If Kesta could live her life again, or be born anew in another life, would Jorrun be the one she prayed to be with, or would she seek another? Her daughter had replied with no hesitation: *I would seek Jorrun.* It had taken several attempts on her part, but she'd finally given her daughter and Jorrun the opportunity they needed; now they just needed to take it. She couldn't help feeling some concern about them, they were not people destined to live quiet lives.

Looking up she saw her best friend and bodyguard hurrying toward them. Heara looked embarrassed.

'Icante, I'm sorr—'

Dia waved a hand at her. 'I can handle a few women and children, Heara.'

Heara frowned. 'How many?'

'Just under two dozen,' Arrus replied. 'We're keeping them here, this time.'

Heara looked from Arrus to Dia. 'I thought we were keeping them away from Fulmer Hold?'

Dia opened her mouth and sighed. 'We can't keep passing the burden on to the other holds. If they cause trouble they'll be off the islands, no excuses.' She touched two fingers to her mouth, gazing up at the Hold that stood on a narrow peninsular high up on the cliffs. 'We may have to be careful of Milaiya. It might not go down well if the Borrowwomen run into a Chem woman.'

They had already had to send the former slave across to Otter Hold when Jorrun visited. Dia was sure the Thane would have been too polite to say or do anything to the woman wh'd tried to kill his half-brother; however, she hadn't wanted anything to get in the way of him and Kesta.

'Shall I speak to her?' Heara offered.

Dia shook her head. 'I'll do it. Where is Vilnue?'

Heara grinned. 'In the great hall.'

'Very well.' Dia gave Arrus's arm a squeeze. 'See what you can find to help our guests build shelters.'

She went into the hall and was greeted by laughing and cheering. A group had gathered in a corner to watch what sounded like a fight. Her apprentice, Pirelle, was attempting to intervene, however it was Vilnue who shoved his way past the men and grabbed up two children by the collars to separate them. Dia's heart sank when she saw who they were, although she wasn't surprised.

A voice spoke softly at her shoulder. 'The boy told her Elden women are stupid and weak.'

44

She turned to look at Milaiya, she had a scarf tied about her long, copper hair, but had adopted the Fulmer preference of wearing trousers and a tunic. She had a habit of not meeting people's eyes and lowering her head when anyone spoke to her, she clearly still felt vulnerable without her veil.

'Thank you.' Dia nodded. 'Will you meet me in my room? Nothing to worry about, but I have some news for you.'

Milaiya gave her a bow, drifting away with her water urn cradled in her arms.

Gritting her teeth, Dia strode toward where the crowd were still gathered. On seeing the Icante's face most of them quickly remembered they had other places to be.

'Well?' She demanded, looking from Catya to the boy, Gilfy, who both still struggled in Vilnue's grip.

Catya glared at her but said nothing. The boy, on the other hand, pointed a finger at Catya. 'She started it! She said—'

'Islanders take responsibility for their own actions!' Dia raised a hand. 'It doesn't matter what someone says or does, it's up to you to choose how you react. There are some things that can only be solved by fighting, but a difference of opinion is not one of them!'

Both of them stop struggling and Vilnue let them go, looking at Dia with raised eyebrows.

Dia sighed. 'Catya, go and find Heara. Gilfy, Arrus Silene will have some work for you.'

'Yes, Icante.' The boy sloped away.

Dia continued to regard Catya. The young girl had plaited her long brown hair back out of the way making her large blue eyes more prominent. Her face muscles were relaxed and she waited patiently for Dia to speak. She wondered if the girl had learnt how to control and hide her feelings so well from watching Jorrun, or from a need to master her own emotions so early on in life.

'You have nothing to say?'

'No, Icante.'

'You do not wish to defend your actions?'

Catya turned away with a frown as she thought for a moment. She looked back up at Dia, the frown gone again. 'I felt I had to prove my side of the argument by demonstrating the truth.'

'Which is?'

'That I'm a better fighter than him.' Her fingers curled momentarily into fists, but quickly relaxed again.

'I see.' Dia took in a deep breath and breathed out slowly.

'Actually, he said he was stronger than her,' Vilnue interjected.

Catya scowled up at him.

'Well, that's a different matter.' Dia stepped forward and put a hand on the girl's shoulder. 'Catya, Gilfy *is* physically stronger than you, will probably always be stronger than you and you have to accept that. It doesn't mean you can't be a better fighter though; but if you can't understand the difference between physical strength and skill, then you *won't* be a better fighter. You need to find a different way to fight that negates his strength, as I'm sure Heara is teaching you. Part of that is knowing when to walk away. Most of the time it's not necessary to prove what you know is true. The truth stands up for itself. Do you understand what I'm telling you?'

Catya nodded, her eyes wide and unblinking. 'Yes, Icante.'

'Good. Then go and find Heara.'

Catya bowed and darted away and out of the hall at a run.

Dia turned to regard Vilnue and Pirelle. 'I've agreed to allow some Borrow refugees to stay outside the Hold. We'll need to find work for them; we should concentrate on trying to increase our food resources. Pirelle, could you please see if any of them have any particularly useful skills?'

'Yes, Icante.'

'Vilnue.' Dia hesitated and studied his face. Since he'd been assigned to the Fulmers to help fight against Chem, Dia had come to rely on the Elden Merkis as much as she did her own chieftains, more than some even. His sandy hair and greying beard held touches of red, a colour rare among Islanders, it was what had first attracted her best friend to this Eldeman. 'How likely would your king be to assist us with Borrow refugees?'

Vilnue shifted his feet and glanced away. 'To be honest, I'm not sure. It's not a situation we have encountered before. There have been a few people from the Borrows over the years who've arrived in ones and twos looking to settle, which they have done with no difficulties I'm aware of; but the numbers were very few. Would he help?' The Merkis scratched at his beard and shrugged. 'All I can do is make him aware of the situation and ask.'

'Please do so.' Dia nodded, although she got the impression Vilnue already thought the answer would be no.

Vilnue gave a bow of his head and headed for the doors at the back of the hall to the private rooms where he'd been quartered. Dia took a look around to reassure herself everything had settled before she followed him and climbed the stairs up to her own room. Milaiya was waiting for her.

'Come on in.' She held the door open and the Chem woman took slow, stilted steps into the room. She didn't get a lot of sunlight in the room as it faced north, north-east, but the long window looked out over the sea. She indicated a chair and Milaiya sat at once, her hands folded in her lap.

'Are you happy enough here, Milaiya? You are not too alone with Kesta gone?'

'I am happy, Icante,' she replied without looking up.

Dia narrowed her eyes and called up her *knowing*. She wasn't surprised to find Milaiya was feeling apprehension and sadness. The former slave had tried her best to adjust, but the Fulmers were a huge cultural world away from Chem.

'People have been treating you well?'

'Yes, Icante.'

'Unless it's a formal occasion, please call me Dia.' She studied the woman's bowed head, her hair shone like brass where the light caught it. Milaiya's confidence had been shattered, but she still had her pride. 'I wanted to warn you we have some refugees from the Borrows who'll be staying outside the Hold. Just women and children. I'm sure they would hold no blame against a woman from Chem for their situation, but you may wish to be cautious around them, just in case.'

Milaiya looked up, her brown eyes wide. 'I'll be careful, thank you. I … I certainly understand how anger can … can make you act in vengeance without thinking.'

Dia nodded, pleased the woman continued to maintain eye contact. 'If you have any concerns, if there's anything you need or wish to share, please talk to me. Not as an Icante, but as my daughter's friend. As my friend.'

Milaiya looked down again and swallowed. 'Thank you, Dia.'

'You are enjoying looking after the ponies?'

'Oh, yes!' Milaiya's face became animated and a smile lit her eyes. She leaned forward. 'And the farrier has been teaching me to care for the hooves!'

'Has he.' The farrier, Faine, was maybe a couple of years younger than Milaiya and single. Dia didn't think he was the sort of man to take advantage of the former slave, but it would be worth keeping an eye on. 'Would you be interested in spending some time with the blacksmith also?'

Milaiya's smile widened. 'Yes, please. I love learning all these new things.'

Dia's own heart lightened, and she reached forward to squeeze one of her hands. 'I'll see to it then. Would you like to stay and drink some tea?'

Milaiya hesitated and Dia waited.

'Yes, please.' Milaiya glanced up at her from under her lashes.

***

When she was alone again, Dia went to the window and gazed out across the sea, placing one hand against the cool glass. She caught her own reflection, her frown increasing the lines around her eyes, before her gaze went further, toward the horizon. Far down below the waves shushed rhythmically against the base of the cliff. Her thoughts turned to her daughter and Dia hoped that she was happy, that she and Jorrun had had the sense to find some kind of compromise with which they could live. She couldn't quite throw off the knot of anxiety in her stomach. She spoke into the empty room. 'Doroquael, are you here?'

There was a pop and hiss and shadows danced across the room. Turning she saw the fire-spirit hovering near the fire grate.

'I'm here, Dia.'

'You heard we have more refugees from the Borrows?'

Doroquael made a crackling sound that may have been words In his own language. 'I heard. How many now?'

'Nearly two hundred in all.' She moved away from the window and sat on the bed. 'It will put a huge strain on our resources, but could mean if the Borrows ever recover, they won't attack us as they used to. Is there any way for your brothers to know when the spells the necromancers cast will fade and the land feel at peace again?'

'There are no Drakes on the Borrowss.'

'Because of the spells?'

Doroquael grew larger and brighter, but quickly shrank again. 'No. The Borrows belongs to the ssea, it's not a place Drakess can live. We can vissit from our own realm, but not sstay long.'

She tucked her feet up under her on the bed and leaned against the footboard to gaze at him. 'Are you saying the Borrows are ruled by water spirits?'

'Yes, those of the ssea.'

'Do such spirits exist around our islands? I've never felt one.'

Doroquael made himself small. 'No. These islands belong to *fire-walkers.*'

Dia looked down at the woven carpet that covered some of the wooden boards. 'I wonder if I could talk to them, though, if they could do something about this blood curse?'

'Don't talk to them, Dia!' Doroquael darted about in a mad circle. 'They are dangerouss!'

She made a noise in her throat, neither agreement nor denial. It was something to think about. She stood up and made her way over to the wash stand and leaned over to splash water on her face. Two green eyes stared back up at her. She drew back, heart hammering, her hand going to her chest.

'What iss it?' Doroquael demanded, darting closer.

Swallowing, Dia took a step forward. She tensed, holding her breath before she bent her neck and peered back into the bowl. All she saw was her own reflection, one blue eye, one brown.

Chapter Five

Kesta; Kingdom of Elden

Kesta tensed, drawing in her *knowing* as tightly as she could, she tried to uncurl her fingers, to release the knot in her chest, but the crowded streets of Taurmaline made her feel like she couldn't breathe. Jorrun walked slightly ahead of her and kept glancing back at her over his shoulder. She had an overwhelming urge to call up her flames and clear the streets. Jorrun touched her arm and nodded toward a set of steps leading up off the main way. She followed and found they were in a narrow lane leading between tightly packed terraced houses. Her muscles relaxed when she saw how few people were using this route.

Jorrun slowed his pace to walk beside her. 'It takes a little longer this way, but it's quieter.'

'Thank you.' She looked up at him, her heart easing.

Even the smell of the city set her teeth on edge. For such an overpopulated place the streets themselves were clean, but the scent of the many human industries blended together into something overpowering for someone used to living in harmony with nature. Tanners, butchers, fishermen, and the sewage that was allowed to run out into the lake all stung her nostrils. The noise was incessant and almost hurt her ears.

Jorrun touched the back of her hand. 'I didn't realise you found crowds so difficult.'

She gave a shake of her head. 'I'm just not used to it.'

She could sense him looking at her but she didn't look up, sometimes she found his gaze overwhelming.

When they came to the castle Jorrun was admitted at once and a page ran ahead of them to the king's audience chamber. It somehow seemed smaller, warmer and less intimidating than the first time she'd come here, pushed to her knees by uncouth guards who didn't know who she and her father were.

On seeing Jorrun, Bractius quickly dismissed everyone else from the room. He poured himself some water, spilling a little over his pale-red beard as he drank quickly. He wiped at his mouth with the back of his hand, glancing at Kesta with his light-brown eyes. 'My apologies, it's been a long morning with no moment to myself.'

'What's happening?' Jorrun frowned, regarding his friend without blinking.

Bractius waved a hand dismissively. 'There's a lot of work to be done repairing Mantu and Taurmouth and not enough funds. I'm reluctant to raise taxes and put pressure on our people after they've just faced invasion. It's not easy keeping a balance between putting too much burden on everyone, but easing the suffering of the heroes and victims of the Chemman attacks. But I take it you have news for me?' He turned to Kesta. 'I'm happy to see you back with us. Your mother is well and the Fulmers in order?'

'They are, your majesty.' Kesta gave a slight curtsy, and she heard Jorrun's quiet snort of amusement.

'I'll come straight to the point,' Jorrun said.

'Do I need to sit down?' Bractius raised his sandy-coloured eyebrows.

Jorrun opened his mouth, then closed it and nodded.

Bractius walked over to his throne and sat slowly in it. So, he was being the king today rather than Jorrun's friend. From the way Jorrun's face muscles relaxed, and all expression vanished, Kesta knew Jorrun had seen the same thing. He chose to remain standing and Kesta took a step closer to him.

'I've received some extremely useful reports from Osun,' Jorrun began. 'And also, some concerning ones.' He told the king of everything Osun had warned him about and then began to outline Osun's plan. Kesta watched as the King's frown deepened and he leaned toward the right arm of his throne. Bractius opened his mouth, but Kesta quickly stepped forward and called up her *knowing*.

Jorrun stopped speaking, trusting her to interject.

'Your majesty. Taking Navere, one of the major sea ports of Chem, would be a huge achievement for Elden. Imagine the trade that could be established, the wealth and opportunities, not to mention the strategic significance.' She took another step forward. 'And healthy trade would deter the desire for animosity and future war. If we can completely eliminate the last of the Dunhams, and with them the desire for revenge, and instead open a dialogue with more liberal and peaceful Seats, we lose Chem as an enemy and instead gain an ally. And think also of the significance of training female magic users who are grateful and loyal to Elden.' She bit her lower lip and she and Jorrun gazed at each other for a moment before she went on. 'If you want to restore magic to Elden and introduce it to your royal line, then there are descendants of Elden women – like Osun's own mother – who possess the blood and the potential.' A part of her felt nauseous and her temperature rose at the thought of offering other women up as bait to protect herself and Jorrun's children from Bractius's manipulation. 'There is a lot to be gained if we succeed.'

'If.' Bractius looked from her to Jorrun. 'There is every chance you will fail and I will lose my sorcerer.'

'It's possible,' Jorrun replied slowly. 'It is a risky and ambitious plan, I'll admit, but surely worth the gamble? There is much to be gained. And with Chem's internal conflict it's unlikely they will even consider another attack on us any time soon.'

'And you now have the Fulmers at your back,' Kesta continued. 'Even if, spirits forbid, something happens to Jorrun, the Fulmers would offer you any magical aid you might require against Chem.'

Bractius sat back against his throne and studied their faces. 'It is a lot to consider. It's not just about losing my only sorcerer, I'd also be losing my most trusted advisor, although he has been conspicuously absent from court of late. Let me think about this. Stay in Taurmaline and eat with me tonight. We'll discuss it again in the morning when I've had time to consider the possible consequences to your plan.'

Jorrun bowed. 'As you command, your majesty.'

***

Jorrun led her through the castle to the rooms he used in Taurmaline. As with everywhere Jorrun stayed, they were cluttered with books, maps, and strange objects carved from stone, wood, and even bone. The room felt cold despite the season and was eerily quiet, the sounds of the busy castle left beyond the thick stone walls. Kesta slid her finger through the dust that had settled on the table.

'I haven't been here for a while.' He winced. 'And the servants don't come in here except to change the bedding.'

'Don't apologise, the room is so very ... you.' She took in a deep breath and smelt the lingering scent of jasmine and cinnamon. 'Do you think he'll agree?'

Jorrun went over to the window, he pulled at the end of his beard, a deep frown on his face. 'I think he'll be tempted by the benefits, but his controlling nature will make it hard for him to let me go. I ...' He turned to look at her. 'I think he is losing his trust in me.'

Kesta considered what she'd picked up with her *knowing*. 'There was fear in Bractius, but under the circumstances I can understand him being wary of the consequences. I didn't feel any bad feeling toward you, only caution. I did get a sense of his isolation though.' She looked up at Jorrun and saw the sadness and concern grow in his eyes.

'It was different when we were younger, before he was king.' Jorrun picked up a small figurine of a cat and held it in his open palm. 'We were never allowed to be just boys, but we tried.' He turned to Kesta and grinned, she couldn't help but respond in kind. 'After ... after what I'd been through, I found it hard to feel safe, to relax or have fun, but Bractius was always rebelling. He never feared the consequences of his actions. He was the heir to Elden, protected. He felt invulnerable and always talked his way out of any serious punishment. A lot of the time it seemed like us against the world. He was the adventurer, the dreamer and the charming rogue. I was the conscience, the voice of reason and the loyal older brother.

'Then we were posted out to Mantu to serve as warriors and put our training to the test. Bractius was given a small command. He made some bad decisions and people died. He witnessed death and true battle for the first time and was not prepared.'

Jorrun put the cat down carefully on the table. 'He never got over it. He hates not being in control, he is extraordinarily thorough in his thinking. He became ruthless in that he learned the necessity of sacrificing anyone for the good of Elden and for the security of his throne.'

'That must have been hard for you, losing your friend to the throne.' Kesta watched him as he ran his fingers over the books on the table. He glanced up briefly.

'I still had Osun, although he was across the sea.'

She swallowed and looked away. He knew she couldn't forgive Osun for what he'd done to Milaiya.

'We are going to have to spend a lot of time with my brother.' Jorrun moved closer to look down at her.

She nodded. 'I know. I promise I won't make things difficult; but I'm doing it for you and for the women of Chem, not for him.'

He placed two fingers under her chin and looked into her eyes. 'Thank you.'

She snorted, then took his hand and squeezed it. 'I do know when to be diplomatic.'

He gave a ghost of a smile and it rankled her that he didn't agree with her statement.

'I'd best see if I need any of these books for Chem.'

***

The main hall was exceptionally crowded, although the guests seemed mainly to be made up of warriors rather than Jarls, Thanes, and their ladies. To someone who ate no meat, the smell of cooked flesh was overwhelming and she wrinkled her nose at it. Smoke escaped from the huge fireplaces to curl out across the room and voices competed to be heard. Already the atmosphere was somewhat raucous and Kesta tensed. The page who'd led them down pulled out a chair for Kesta to the King's left, she hesitated, exchanging a worried frown with Jorrun. To the left of the king was normally always Jorrun's seat. Bractius noticed their arrival and stood.

'Ah, Jorrun! Come sit beside Ayline!'

Jorrun squeezed Kesta's hand and then moved around the king to give the queen a polite bow. She was a small young woman and the swell of her early pregnancy was noticeable. Ayline watched Jorrun as he sat, her hand on her belly as though to draw his attention to what was obvious. With a sigh Kesta gritted her teeth and sat down. The chair to her left scraped back, and she turned, forcing a polite smile for her dinner companion.

She froze, tension locking her spine.

Adrin stood grinning down at her, his long blonde hair tied back in a neat tail and his face clean shaven. She hadn't seen the chieftain since he'd left to fight the Chemman, just after she'd punched him in the face for trying to force a kiss from her. She turned quickly to look down the table at Jorrun, he was engaged in polite conversation with the Queen.

'Lady Kesta, how good to see you.'

She forced her teeth apart. 'Adrin. I wasn't aware you were in Taurmaline.'

'As one of the King's most favoured Merkis where else would I be?' He sat, glancing across to Jorrun to see if he was watching.

Kesta swallowed and reached for a goblet, one of the servants darted forward at once to fill it with wine. This was going to be a long evening, especially as she needed to keep the king on side and not lose her temper.

'Ah! Adrin!' Bractius reached across in front of Kesta's face to shake hands with the warrior. She had to restrain herself from biting his arm. She supposed a king was entitled to be bad mannered at his own table, but even so her skin grew warm and the tension in her body spread down to her toes. 'Of course, you two know each other?'

Kesta nodded, not trusting herself to speak.

'I had the pleasure of meeting Lady Kesta when she first came to Northold.' Adrin gestured the servant back over and began filling his plate as he spoke to the king.

Kesta sat back and sipped at her wine, half listening to the conversations that went on around her. She recalled the words Osun had said to her months ago to describe Arkoom and wondered how he would describe this place. She supposed in reality it wasn't all that different here than the hall of her own home, it was just that she knew and trusted the people there.

'Are you not eating?'

It took a moment for Kesta to realise Adrin was addressing her.

'Here, get some of this nice red meat in you.' He tipped a slab of venison onto her plate, the sauce splashed up and caught her face. She leapt up, knocking back her chair and calling power instinctively to her fingertips. She tore her eyes from the meat to glare at the grinning face of Adrin. Out of the corner of her eyes she saw Jorrun was also on his feet.

She took in several breaths, trying to calm herself, aware a hush was falling over the hall. She withdrew her magic and glanced at Jorrun. Wiping her face with her fingers she gritted her teeth and sat back down, beckoning one of the servants over.

'Would you kindly remove this?' she asked.

Jorrun also slowly sat and Bractius looked from one of them to the other, Adrin was smiling down the table at Jorrun. 'Is there a problem?' The king demanded, his brown eyes hard and his brows lowered.

'I'm sure the Merkis meant no insult.' Kesta held Bractius's gaze a moment longer before turning to Adrin. '*Walkers* don't eat meat.'

Adrin sat back, mouth open. She didn't need to use her *knowing* to know it was all an act. She clenched her fists under the table and drew in a long breath. The servant gave her a clean plate, and she nodded her thanks.

'I've been craving nothing but liver.' Ayline announced.

Kesta sighed and swigged back her wine. She picked up an apple and reaching down to pull her dagger from her boot, she proceeded to cut it into pieces, looking at Adrin as she did so.

Adrin snorted. 'I heard you'd left Jorrun and gone back to the Fulmers.'

She put the apple down and looked him in the eye without blinking. 'I would never leave Jorrun.'

'Ah yes.' Adrin leaned back in his chair and threw a piece of beef into his open mouth. 'You came to Mantu to free him when he was trapped by a sorcerer, then left me to liberate the island.' He grinned, looking up at the ceiling.

Kesta realised smoke was rising up from between her fingers and she withdrew her hand quickly from the table. Four scorch marks marred the wood. There was little doubt that, had she not killed Karinna Dunham, Mantu would have fallen to Chem. Even so, she still carried guilt that she'd returned to Taurmouth at Jorrun's command rather than remain to see Mantu's people freed. Knowing Adrin had claimed all the glory for the small island's liberation made things infinitely worse. Siveraell, the fire-spirit, had probably had more to do with it than this arrogant man. She reached for her goblet, then changed her mind and poured herself some water instead.

Bractius had turned to speak to Jorrun about the repair work being done to the harbour, Ayline was pouting into her cup, a frown marring her perfect skin. Kesta turned toward them, trying to find a point at which she could politely join the conversation.

Adrin touched her arm and revulsion shivered across her skin. She wanted more than anything to turn and punch the man again.

'Listen, I didn't mean to upset you, I was just having a laugh. I thought you had a sense of humour.'

'Sprits,' she said through gritted teeth. If this was a test of her patience and ability to control her temper, she really wanted to fail. She caught Jorrun's eyes and he smiled at her. She released the air from her lungs and smiled back. She closed her eyes momentarily and then turned back to Adrin. 'Perhaps our humour is different in the Fulmers. So, you are based now at Taurmaline?'

Adrin narrowed his eyes, his smile shrank but still ghosted his mouth. 'I am. I've replaced Vilnue now he is an ambassador to the Fulmers.'

Kesta let the Eldeman talk, occasionally forcing a smile or nodding at his words. He didn't seem to notice or care about her own lack of conversation. He seemed more than happy to talk at length about himself and his victories. Ayline seemed to be leading most of the conversation between herself, Jorrun, and the king, interrupted now and again by the others in the hall who came up to speak with Bractius.

When the King announced that he was going to bed, Kesta slumped in her seat, before standing quickly to give a curtsy. It was mere seconds after he and the queen left the hall that Jorrun stood and walked over to take her hand.

'Let's go.'

His grip was tight, and she looked up at him in surprise, he never normally touched her in public.

'Stay and have some wine, Jorrun!' Adrin showed his teeth in what was supposed to be a smile. 'I haven't had a chance to speak with you this evening.'

Jorrun's eyes narrowed and he glared down at the warrior. 'Address me as Thane.'

Jorrun almost pulled her up off her seat as he headed for the door. Behind them, Kesta heard Adrin laughing and she ground her teeth together so hard her jaw hurt.

She almost had to run to keep up with Jorrun as they headed toward his rooms.

'You're angry with me,' she said.

'What?' He looked down at her, his frown deepening before it vanished. 'No. No, of course not.' He squeezed her hand gently. 'I'm proud, though amazed, at how you kept your patience. Personally, I wanted to reach down his throat and rip his spine out!'

She stared up at him open-mouthed. The only person she could recall him being that angry with was herself. He pushed open the door to his rooms and dropped the latch behind them.

'Why do you think Bractius seated us like that?'

He looked across to the window and swallowed. 'It could mean nothing, or it could mean several things. It's usual in Elden to mix guests at dinner.' He turned back to look at her. 'Kesta, something happened between you and Adrin when you first came to Northold, didn't it?'

'I ...' It was hard to hold his gaze when he barely blinked. He reached out and tucked a strand of her black hair behind her ear. 'The day he was due to leave for Taurmouth he confronted me and tried to force himself on me.' Her face flushed with anger and un-warranted embarrassment. 'I think he thought he'd managed to charm me. I guess at first he had although I hate to admit it. I thought you knew? You came running out of The Tower ...'

He looked away and she saw his hands had clenched into fists. 'Both Azrael and I sensed you using your magic, he got there in time to see you reminding Adrin of who you were. You should have told me, I'd have killed the man.'

Kesta bit her lip. Her first thought was that Jorrun's brother had done worse and yet he'd done nothing about that. 'I dealt with it,' she said quietly and he turned to frown at her. 'And back then I didn't know, or trust, you.'

He sighed. 'Now he is high in the king's favour and I not so much so, he thinks he's safe to get some petty revenge. I also worry what mischief he'll cause for his own ambition if we go away to Chem.'

'Surely Bractius will see through him?'

'I hope so.' He forced a smile. 'Come on, let's go to bed.'

***

They were kept waiting for the king for almost an hour the next morning. Normally, Jorrun would have been admitted immediately to sit in the chair to the king's left, assist him with his audiences, and play the part of the sinister 'Dark Man'. Kesta realised she was tapping her foot and stopped herself, glancing up at Jorrun. She wasn't surprised to see he was perfectly composed, his face and shoulder muscles relaxed. Even his eyes, that she knew could convey so much, gave nothing away.

The doors opened and a man dressed in richly embroidered fabric hurried out, he started when he saw Jorrun, but barely paused. Jorrun and Kesta were invited in and he strode across the room to stand only three feet in front of the throne. Bractius leaned back and held Jorrun's gaze as he approached, he waved a hand at the guards and they left the room. Jorrun placed his hands behind his back, folding his fingers together.

'Thank you for seeing us.'

'Of course.' Bractius looked from Jorrun to Kesta and stood. He frowned, looking down at the floor, before stepping forward to place a hand on Jorrun's shoulder. 'If your plan works, it will be excellent for Elden.'

Both Jorrun and Kesta turned to stare at Bractius in surprise.

'But there are things to consider.' The king removed his hand and paced across the room. 'First, do you absolutely trust Osun?'

'Of course!' Jorrun replied without hesitation. Kesta looked down at the floor.

Bractius snorted. 'And do you really believe he can take Navere and hold a Seat in Arkoom?'

Jorrun took in a deep breath. 'With myself and Kesta I have no doubt we can take Navere. Osun and I know it well. Arkoom and the Seat of the Overlord will be a different matter. It will take time and planning.'

'How much time?' Bractius stopped his pacing to frown at him.

'We could be talking a year or two.'

Kesta swallowed. The king's frown deepened.

'That's a big investment of our time.' Bractius moved back to his throne but his gaze was on Jorrun's empty chair. 'We would have to explain your absence of course. Last night's dinner and your exclusion from assisting me this morning will make people think you are out of favour. Not ideal, but it will mean it will be a while until people think too much of your absence from court. We'll make them believe you are still at the Raven Tower for as long as possible. If it's discovered you're not there, I will tell people that you are visiting the Fulmers and then Mantu. Until you're ready to make your move in Navere, only the three of us in this room will know what you're really doing.'

'Let me understand you.' Jorrun held up his hand. 'You do want us to go to Chem and take the Seat of Navere?'

'Yes.'

Jorrun tilted his head slightly to one side and Kesta reached up to take his arm.

'You're right, Jorrun, we need to strike while they are in disarray and we have the advantage. After their attack we don't have the men or the resources to mount a military action against them. If we can put our man in the Overlord's seat and make Chem an ally, then we have defeated our enemy with little cost to us. I have your word you will return to me though? That you're not planning to take a Seat for yourself?'

Jorrun shook his head. 'You know me better than that.'

'Neither of us would want to stay in Chem any longer than we had to,' Kesta added.

Bractius' eyes narrowed and he looked her up and down. 'But if your plans succeed Chem will change.'

'I hope it does.' She raised her chin. 'But I already have two homes I'm finding it hard to choose between, I'm not looking for a third.'

Bractius barked out a laugh. 'As honest as ever.'

Jorrun shifted his feet ever so slightly and glanced at her.

'Let's not rush into this.' Bractius rubbed at his bearded jaw. 'Come back at the end of the week, Jorrun and sit in on a few audiences with me. We'll make some more plans then, and see what news Osun has for us. Shall we aim to have you away in two weeks?'

Jorrun gave a slight bow. 'As you wish it.'

Kesta swallowed, her heart beating faster. They were going back to Chem.

Chapter Six

Osun; Covenet of Chem

Osun walked along the pens. His hand went instinctively to his nose but he couldn't block out the stench of urine, sweat, and blood. The smell of human misery always made his skin crawl and it was harder to keep his facial expressions under control. He had to force himself to meet people's eyes, to pretend ignorance and apathy. He ground his teeth, looking at the colourful signs that hung from poles beside each pen. Some areas had shelters, even seats, most were just fenced off squares of dust and despair. He spotted the man he wanted and strode over.

'Drogda!'

'Osun! What brings you to Navere?' The man was short and burly, his sleeveless tunic showing off his muscles.

'I'm looking to purchase myself a good fighter and I know you train the   best.' Drogda's grin widened as Osun looked over the chained men. All of them stood upright and relaxed, eyes down, but for one. A young man sat at the back, his knees drawn up with his arms leaning across them. Unlike the other slaves he looked straight at Osun, although there was no spark of defiance in his grey eyes. Bruises mottled his face, black turning to yellow and green. He couldn't have been much more than sixteen.

Osun realised Drogda was talking to him.

'This one here is excellent with a spear and can care for horses.'

Osun didn't even look at the slave Drogda was indicating.

'What about this boy?' Osun asked.

Drogda spat and Osun winced. 'Best fighter I ever trained but he's flawed.'

'Flawed how?'

'He refuses to kill.'

'Then how is he still alive?'

'Oh, he'll kill in the ring to save his own sorry skin, which is surprising as he seems determined to die by my whip, but if you order him to make a kill, he'll drop his weapon like a brainless fool!'

Osun frowned. 'Is he disobedient in any other way?'

The boy sat up straighter and met Osun's eyes again. Something tingled inside Osun's ribs, like an itch, like pins and needles. He knew those eyes, they frightened him but he couldn't look away.

'I suppose not.' The slaver unhooked his whip and tapped his left palm with it, narrowing his eyes at Osun.

Osun made his way past the other slaves to stand over the boy. 'What's your name?'

'Cassien, master.'

'Why won't you kill when commanded to?'

The boy swallowed, glancing away before looking back. 'I won't kill someone who doesn't deserve it, master.'

'It's up to your master who deserves to die!' The slaver kicked Cassien hard in the ribs. Osun opened his mouth to protest but stopped himself. Cassien himself made no sound but slowly sat up again.

'Do you understand the difference between obedience, and respect?' Osun asked the boy.

He nodded. 'I do.'

Drogda's face turned bright red at the boy's omission of the word, 'master' and he let go of the end of his whip, Osun stepped in and gripped his forearm. 'I'll buy this slave.'

Drogda looked incredulous, then avarice lit his eyes. 'Are you sure, master?'

Osun held the boy's gaze. 'I'm sure. Of course, I'll expect a discount for the fact he is – as you say – "flawed" and for his condition. Did you break any bones?'

'Of course not!' Drogda scowled. 'I put a lot of years and training into this   boy   ...'
They negotiated a price and with his heart aching for his lost gold Osun handed it over. He gritted his teeth and shook his head at himself, no doubt he would regret this moment of foolish, weak sentimentality.

The slaver unlocked Cassien's chains from the wall and handed the end to Osun with a grunt. 'Good luck to you.'

Osun didn't reply but led the boy out of the skin market towards the part of Navere where craftsmen traded.

He found a blacksmith and instructed him to remove all of Cassien's chains. The blacksmith raised an eyebrow but went about it without question. Cassien didn't say a word but watched Osun as he examined the swords that were for sale. Osun tried the hilt of one that was far superior to the sword belted around his own waist but decided he'd spent too much already. He pointed to one that was plain and serviceable. 'I'll take this as well. And I'll need a servant's collar.'

Cassien did react at that, spinning about on his toes to face him with his mouth open.

'Didn't say it was for you now, did I?' Osun tried to look stern.

Cassien closed his mouth quickly.

Osun took the large ring of copper from the blacksmith, handing over his gold slowly. He held the servant's collar out for the boy. 'Put this on and follow me.'

Osun set off at a fast pace, his long stride making the shorter boy have to almost run to keep up. They were close to the inn when the boy plucked up the courage to speak. 'You don't even know me, why would you free me?'

'I haven't freed you, I still expect you to work for me and I won't pay you other than the food you eat.'

'But if I'm a servant I could go and work for someone else who pays me better.'

Osun turned and looked him up and down. 'Know anyone who'd pay you? You've already forgotten to call me master.'

Cassien opened his mouth and then closed it again. He bowed his head a little. 'Sorry, master.'

'Can you cook?'

'What?'

'Are you deaf?'

'No, master. I'm a trained fighter, why would I cook?'

'Perhaps because you'd like to eat?' Osun sighed. 'Never mind, we'll manage.'

He made his way to the entrance of the Narwhale Inn. He couldn't help a shudder as he looked around the now busy market place and remembered the dead men raised by Adelphy Dunham who'd clustered here only months before. He was sure he could still catch wafts of the awful smell they'd emitted. He caught the innkeeper, Gulden's attention and asked him to bring hot water and food up to his room and to arrange a bed for his servant. Gulden looked Cassien up and down with a narrow-eyed frown but nodded. For pride's sake Osun had taken the same room as he had months before, but luckily for him Gulden had genuinely appreciated his patronage and advice during what had been an awful time for the inn. Gulden had given him a very fair discount and a brandy with every meal.

When they entered his room, Osun put down the sword he'd purchased and turned to look at the boy.

'I have some things to do out in the city. Take a bath and eat. Tomorrow I'm heading to Margith and all I need from you is for you to help me get there alive and assist with the horses.' He went over to his clothes and picking out a clean blue shirt and trousers, he threw them at Cassien. 'They might be a bit long; can you use a needle?'

'I can stitch a wound.'

Osun stared at him for a moment, then sighed. 'Good enough. We'll talk when I get back. Don't leave!'

***

Osun went first to the temple. He followed the narrow walkway that hugged the dark cliff, holding onto the rope and occasionally pressing his back to the stone to let someone else pass. The wooden planks were slippery and moved under his weight, far below the sea surged loudly between the rocks. Fat candles were wedged into crevices at the cave's entrance, the wax of many years making the false face of a glacier. The smell of incense mixed with refreshing, natural brine. He drew in a deep breath before entering the deep caverns in which the priests of the gods dwelt. Unlike Arkoom, and a few of the other major cities, the fire-spirits hadn't burned down the temple of Navere. Even so, it couldn't have been more different than when he'd visited the temples before Elden and the Fulmers had beaten off Chem's attack.

Then, the Gods of death and war had been in ascendancy, now no one seemed to be visiting their alcoves and it was his own god, Domarra, god of prosperity, and the god of health, Seveda, who were receiving all of the visitors. A few worshipers furtively left gifts and prayers in the alcove of the god of magic, Warenna.

After the temple, Osun went to the docks and to an inn where he knew he would hear gossip. He ordered a simple meal and a light ale. It wasn't long before he heard what he needed. A man called Cepack was presently holding the Seat of Navere. He smiled to himself and swallowed back his ale, placing a coin on the table and leaving half of his meal untouched. His last stop was a messenger company that prided itself in expediency and privacy. He handed them a letter and a gold coin and then returned to the Narwhale Inn.

When he opened the door to his room, he found Cassien had dressed himself in Osun's old clothes and was in the middle of running through some sword exercises. Cassien put the weapon down guiltily.

'Keep it,' Osun said. 'I bought that for you. You're no good to me unarmed.'

'Actually, I can fight very well without a sword.' The boy seemed to notice Osun's expression and quickly added, 'master.'

Osun drew his own sword. 'Let's see what you can do.'

Cassien opened his mouth, his grey eyes widened a little. He swallowed and said, 'Master, I don't mean it as boasting but I'm very good. I wouldn't want to hurt you.'

Osun grinned and swung his sword. Cassien's came up to meet his and they danced across the carpet, the chime and scream of metal on metal was loud in their ears. Osun noticed Cassien's bruises were hampering him and he suspected that despite Drogda's reassurances, something might be broken. Not the boy's spirit though. He reminded him … Osun's feet momentarily faltered and he pushed away the emotions that churned in his stomach. Cassien reminded Osun so much of his younger, half-brother, Jorrun.

'Halt!' Osun stepped back and lowered his sword. He realised he was slightly out of breath.

Cassien lowered his sword also and gave a low bow. 'Forgive me, master, I shouldn't have assumed you didn't know how to fight.'

'Never assume, Cassien.' Osun sheathed his sword. 'Few of us ever show who we really are. Some pretend to be greater, other's hide their light. I've lived my life being whatever I had to be. Your integrity is … rare. I admire it but I'm surprised it hasn't gotten you killed. Take yourself down to the servant's quarters. We leave early tomorrow.'

Cassien went tentatively to the table and picked up the sheath for his sword. Osun saw his jaw move as he debated what he wanted to say. 'Master?' He looked up. 'Who are you?'

'I was a merchant. Now I have other business. Do as I've instructed you, please, Cassien.'

Cassien almost started at the word, 'please'. Osun wasn't surprised. It was almost non-existent in Chem.

Cassien gave another bow and left the room.

***

Osun stood back and let Cassien ready their three horses. He'd bought one of good quality for himself to ride and two sturdy working horses for his new servant and his supplies. Osun had considered returning to his guise as a merchant but had decided the need to move quickly was more urgent than the need for more money. He had quite a lot hidden away but he had to hope his brother would supply the funds for what they needed.

It took seven days to reach Margith. The roads that had been safe under the rule of the Dunhams were now practically lawless and dangerous. The patrols that once kept them safe now worked for different factions and often, for themselves. Osun knew the roads well though and kept them from the places where he expected the worst trouble. He spoke to Jorrun several times on the journey using his scrying bowl and blood amulet. He only had a small supply of his brother's blood, having burned what he'd stored previously before returning to Elden. He didn't hide what he was doing from Cassien, he just moved a discreet distance away. He wasn't surprised when the boy asked him about it.

'Are you a sorcerer?'

Osun smiled and shook his head. 'My father was a powerful necromancer and my mother of good blood, but I was born "bloodless." This is a simple magic that I can perform because my brother is very powerful.'

'Who is your brother? Master,' he added quickly.

Osun drew in a breath and regarded the boy. 'You might get to meet him sometime. I'm sure the two of you will get along, you're both stubbornly moralistic considering the land we live in.'

'You sound as though you know other lands.'

Osun ran his fingers through his curling black hair. 'You ask too many questions. It's a good job I freed you, you make an appallingly bad slave.'

Cassien laughed. Most of the bruises had faded from his face but he still moved as though his bones hadn't healed. His face grew serious. 'I guess I couldn't live as a slave. I think I wanted to die.'

Osun cleared his throat and looked away. He'd seen many people like that in his lifetime, none who had lived as long as Cassien. He scratched at his beard, looking anywhere but at the boy. He wasn't any good at this kind of thing and resented being forced to feel sympathy. He hadn't survived by being soft-hearted. 'Haven't you got that fire started yet?'

Cassien threw his flints down. 'I can't seem to manage fires.'

Osun breathed out loudly. 'Why did I waste my gold on you? Keep trying, you'll never get the hang of it if you don't.'

Cassien made a loud 'huff' but picked the flints back up.

***

Osun slowed his horse as the sharp, black walls of Margith came into sight. It was hard not to wince at the serrated stone, hard not to imagine how it would slice your skin, how much blood must have been shed to raise it. He shuddered but turning his eyes to the gate he smiled when he saw his old acquaintance was on duty. The young man with the bushy blonde beard recognised Osun at once.

'Where's your wagon, brother?'

Osun grimaced. 'Stolen, brother. The roads just aren't safe since Dryn Dunham was murdered. I'm having to start again. Got myself a good bodyguard this time.'

The guard whistled. 'Sorry to hear that, brother. Will you be in the geranna house later?'

'Aye, will I see you?'

'I'll be there, brother.'

'Um.' Osun hesitated. 'I'm embarrassed to say, I don't think I ever asked your name?'

'Well.' The guard frowned and put his hands on his hips. 'I don't recall that I gave it. I'm Ralden.'

'Ralden.' Osun gave him a wave and rode on through the gate. He chose a cheap but clean inn near the market place and left Cassien to deal with the horses. He stopped at one of the stalls where a young man was selling a mixture of ornaments and jewellery. He recognised a piece he himself had sold.

'Are you Farkle Warne's son?' he asked.

The young man nodded.

'I'm Osun, your father should be expecting me.'

'Oh, yes! He is already at Gunthe's.'

'Thank you.' Osun gave him a nod and hurried on toward the temple district. He turned off down a narrow ally before he got to the main street, the small sign showing a plate and cup the only indication that an eating house resided there.

Taking in a deep breath he lifted the latch and pushed open the door. There were four men within and all of them froze and ceased talking to stare at him.

'Osun!' Farkle Warne stood and the men relaxed. He looked to have lost even more weight than when Osun had last seen him, his face was almost skeletal and had a yellowish hue to it. He held onto the back of his chair with one hand, swaying slightly. 'You can trust these men. Let me introduce you. This is Balten.' Farkle pointed to the man seated to his right. He had brown eyes and dark brown hair that was going grey at the temples. The man nodded, his eyes scrutinising Osun. 'He is a trader here in Margith and part of a group that, well, they protect women.'

Osun's eyebrows went up.

The man sat back, his hand moving to his sword hilt in order to show Osun he was armed. 'I was under the impression from Farkle you were looking for people like me. Of course, I need to know more about you, your aims, and if you are genuine before I tell you anything.'

'Of course.' Osun nodded. He grabbed the back of a chair and dragged it across to the table to sit. The sound brought the establishment's owner to the dividing curtain. The short man peered out and gave Osun a wave. 'Light ale, master Osun?'

'Thank you.' Osun smiled, pleased Gunthe had remembered. He turned to look at the other two men.

'This is Jagner.' Farkle sat down and indicated the man beside Balten. He had green eyes and dark blonde hair cut short to his scalp. 'He is, as far as he knows, the only survivor of the family of Telanis.'

'Telanis!' Osun's eyes widened. 'Do you have power?'

Jagner shifted in his seat, glancing at those around him. This was a dangerous meeting for all of them and Jagner was young, perhaps not even twenty. He would have been a child when his family were all but wiped out by the Dunhams in their bid to take all of the Seats of Chem. He looked up at Osun. 'I have a little.'

Gunthe came out from behind the curtain and placed a mug of ale in front of Osun and a bowl of nuts and dried fruit in the centre of the table. He retreated to his stool in the corner beside a low counter. No one objected.

The remaining man stood to introduce himself. He had a narrow face, a hooked nose and extremely bushy black eyebrows. 'I'm Tembre, of Ifker Coven. I plan on taking Margith.'

Osun nodded up at him. 'I'm Osun. I plan on taking Navere.'

Tembre cocked his head to one side, then grinned and sat back down.

Farkle cleared his throat. 'So, Osun, what is it you want? It was a big risk to you, and to me, to send that letter. Why did you choose to trust me?'

Osun placed his hands on the table. 'We have trusted each other before and – I hope it isn't rude of me to say – other than protecting your son you have nothing to lose.'

'That's true enough.' Farkle winced. 'But I'm not someone of note let alone power.'

Osun raised a hand. 'But you are a man of contacts, as you have proved today.' He looked around the table coming last to Gunthe who watched them silently. 'I want to build up a network of support and information across Chem, our aim to complete the overthrow of the Dunhams that myself and my brother began. We wish to ensure a more liberal and less war-hungry coven comes to the Seats of Arkoo—'

'Who is your brother?' Tembre demanded. 'For that matter, who are you and what do you mean by what you "began?"'

Osun paused. 'I'm Osun Dunham. My brother is Jorrun Dunham, the Dark Man of Elden.'

Both Tembre and Jagner leapt to their feet, young Jagner taking several steps back. Osun remained seated. 'You have nothing to fear from me. I have no power, I'm a bloodless slave who should have died many years ago. Despite that, it was this sword that took the head from my father's body.'

'You killed Dryn Dunham? *You?*' Tembre's laughter died on his lips when he saw Osun's expression.

'Only due to the power of my brother and his wife.'

'His wife?' Balten waved a hand for the others to sit down.

'Yes. She is a *fire-walker* of the Fulmers. Dryn Dunham made the error of underestimating the Fulmers as they are led by women. Kesta is very strong in magic, her mother – the Icante – even more so. The Icante took out Adelphy, Relta, and several other Dunhams all on her own. It was Kesta who killed Karinna and two others on Mantu. Jorrun and Kesta fought Dryn until he was drained of power and then I took his head.' His fists clenched as he relived the moment.

Tembre's eyes narrowed and he leaned forward. 'But you say it's you who will take Navere, you with no blood.'

Osun nodded. 'We do not want another Dunham sorcerer in a Seat. The fact I have no blood of which to speak will be revolutionary. Think of the impact that will have on the ordinary folk of Chem.'

Osun saw both Farkle and Gunthe sit up straighter and exchange a glance.

Tembre snorted. 'They'll be thinking the Seats are up for grabs to just anyone!'

'I think that might be the point,' Farkle said quietly.

'And how do you propose to take Navere?'

'With the help of my brother and his wife. I will hold Navere by teaching the women held in the palace to use their magic. My coven will be formed of women.'

'What?' Tembre almost choked.

'Osun.' Balten reached across to place his hand on the table close to Osun's. 'Let me tell you who I am and the group I represent.'

Osun nodded. 'Go on.'

'The woman I purchased to bear me heirs is called Sellar. I was lucky. She loves me and I love her. She is clever and wise, and I don't know what I'd do without her. We have a daughter, Eona, and we dread what will become of her. There are a few people like us in each city of Chem and we have formed a secret network. We try our best to ensure our daughters are only sold willingly into a good family and to a good man – one from our group. We have an arrangement that if anything happens to any of the men in the group, the others must step in quickly to try to buy their women and keep them safe. If you take Navere and form this coven of women, I can get you support from traders, craftsmen, and even a couple of minor coven members from my network.'

Osun was amazed, he'd had no idea such a group existed. He turned to Farkle. 'You are a part of this group?'

'*I* am.' Gunthe spoke up from his stool in the corner.

Jagner took in a deep breath. 'I've nothing to lose and I'm tired of hiding. I have no idea if I can trust you, after all you're a Dunham, but I'd be willing to go to Navere with you and join your coven.'

All of them turned to look at Tembre, aware that if he didn't join them, they would have to consider him against them. The man glowered from under his huge eyebrows, regarding them all one at a time. 'I don't like this sentimentality about women and I like the idea of giving them power even less,' he admitted. 'But even if I take Margith I'll be on my own. I'll back your plan if you back mine and we support each other in Arkoom. Maybe it's time to do things differently, I don't want to spend the rest of my life watching my back waiting for the next plot. If we can form a stable coven in Arkoom with the support of common people of no blood, fellow sorcerers and, yes, even women, then I'd be a fool to go against it.' He sighed and held out his hand. 'I'm in.'

Chapter Seven

Kesta; Kingdom of Elden

Kesta lifted her face to feel the wind against her skin and closed her eyes. Jorrun placed a hand against her back and then gently teased the ends of her hair through his fingers, making her scalp tingle. The warriors who were sailing his small ship across the lake were talking quietly together toward the stern.

'It will be nice to be out sailing again, just the two of us,' she said without turning. 'Not that I'm in a hurry to return to Chem.'

He gave a snort of amusement. 'From what I recall we were barely talking the last time we sailed to Chem.'

She turned to look up at him. 'That was then. I love being on the sea.'

'Unlike poor Azrael.'

Kesta gazed out across the water, they were drawing close to the small wharf that served Northold, the Raven Tower seemed to watch them from above the walls and keep. 'Will you ask him to come with us?'

'He'll be hurt if I didn't.'

They moved out of the way as the warriors guided the ship against the wooden walkway and they stepped off together.

'Shall I leave you to tell Rosa while I speak with Tantony?'

Her heart sank and she bit her lower lip. Jorrun gave her shoulder a squeeze and headed toward the Hold. She turned to check that the warriors had unloaded her chest.

'Would you bring that to the ivy tower for me?' she asked.

The warrior nodded, slinging his own bag over his shoulder and then picking up the chest to proceed her.

When she entered the great hall, she found preparations were already underway for the wedding. Garlands of green leaves had been strung around the walls and candles were being set on the clothed tables, only one left bare for the Hold folk to use tonight. Rosa was waiting up in their receiving room and she stood on seeing Kesta, putting aside a shirt she was sewing.

'How was Taurmaline?'

Kesta told the warrior to leave the chest and thanked him, then hurried over to hug Rosa. She sighed. 'I hated it as much as ever, to be honest. Your queen looks well.'

'And did Jorrun and the king leave on better terms?'

Kesta regarded her friend. She had only just told her she was staying at Northold, now she'd have to tell her she was leaving and wasn't even allowed to tell her the truth of where. 'Things are better,' she replied slowly.

Rosa narrowed her brown eyes. 'I sense a but.'

Kesta smiled, it faded quickly. 'Bractius has some work for us that will involve our travelling for a while. We're to go to the Fulmers and then to Mantu.'

'Oh.' Rosa looked away but drew in a breath and straightened up. 'Well I imagine there must be a lot to do still after the war. Do you think you'll be gone long?'

Kesta couldn't meet her eyes. 'I don't know. We'll have to find you a maid so you have some female company and someone to plot with!'

Rosa laughed, but Kesta could see she was upset. 'We've got you some presents.' She squeezed Rosa's arm and went over to the chest. She didn't have any money of her own, it wasn't something they traded in on the Fulmer Islands, and she'd had to swallow her pride and ask Jorrun if he would get some things for Rosa. He'd known better than her what Rosa might need and insisted on buying it all. The only thing Kesta had added were a pair of sturdy boots. She held them out for Rosa.

'So you don't ruin your good shoes following me anymore.'

Rosa shook her head as she took them, blinking rapidly and rubbing at the corner of her eye with one finger. 'Thank you.'

'We got you a dress.'

Rosa's mouth fell open.

'It's only fair as you got me mine. Unless you wanted to wear your one that you had in mind?'

'Well,' Rosa pursed her lip. 'I guess it depends on which one goes best with these walking boots!'

***

Kesta stood close to Jorrun as they watched their friends getting married, her arm against his and the backs of their hands touching. He looked down at her and smiled, not able to completely maintain his guise of the severe and unbending Dark Man. Jorrun insisted on Rosa and Tantony taking the main seats at the high table but broke Elden tradition by sitting beside Kesta. As happy as she was, a little trepidation and sadness crept in. She'd only just decided to stay and already she was leaving.

The celebrations went on late into the evening. Jorrun leaned in and kissed her neck, taking hold of her hand. She looked up at him in surprise.

'Come on.'

He stood and Kesta said a quick goodnight to Rosa and Tantony. She followed him up to her room in the ivy tower, past Rosa and Catya's empty chambers. Out of habit she looked out of the window toward the Raven Tower. A faint glow told her Azrael was at home in Jorrun's room.

'He's decided to come.' Jorrun stood behind her and followed her gaze. 'Not that I thought he would stay. I don't think he'll ever lose his fear of the sea, but he can't bear to be left behind.' Jorrun ran a lock of her hair through his fingers, sending a pleasant shiver down her back. 'You seemed sad today, are you worried about Chem?'

She snorted. 'I'd be stupid not to have concerns about going there. I'm not worrying about it though, I'll leave that until I get there. I'm sad about leaving Rosa; I know she can manage perfectly well without me, but I'll miss her. I already miss Catya.'

He slid his arms around her. 'Just think how many others there are waiting in Chem for you to take under your wing. Do you want to stay here while I go back to Taurmaline?'

She broke free from his hug and looked up at him. 'Would you mind?'

He frowned, although there was mischief in his eyes. 'I thought you might be at least a little reluctant to be without me.'

She scowled. 'You know very well I'll miss you, but I'll have plenty of time with you in Chem, locked away in your palace. I don't have much time with Rosa.'

He looked over her head and out of the window, a smile growing on his face.

She narrowed her eyes. 'What?'

'Mmmm, just thinking about Chem, where you have to do as you're told and aren't allowed to talk back.'

She pushed him hard in the chest. 'We'll see about that, Jorrun Dunham!'

He grabbed her hand and grinned although the humour faded from his eyes. 'I want to leave the name Dunham behind me,' he said quietly. 'Here and on the Fulmers it doesn't matter so much as we only carry single names and titles. But in Chem they use family names.'

She swallowed and looked into his eyes. There was only one name that came to her mind. 'Raven.'

His eyes widened a little and he placed a hand against her cheek. 'Jorrun Raven.'

***

Kesta spent every moment she could with Rosa although she tried not to be selfish and take Rosa away from her new husband too often. They went out riding together and worked in the gardens, Kesta telling Rosa of her future plans, leaving out the fact it would be Rosa who'd have to carry them out. Kesta spent her nights in the Raven Tower, keeping Azrael company and reading through some of Jorrun's books. Her eyes fell on a silver-tipped quill and, after several minutes of internal struggle, she gave in and wrote a letter to her mother, telling her only that she and Jorrun had work to do and that she might not hear from her for some time.

Only five days after Jorrun had departed for Taurmaline, one of the Hold children came to tell her the Thane's ship had been sighted returning across the lake. As much as she wanted to rush out and meet him, she knew he'd want to keep up his stern appearance. She chose to wait for him at the door of the Raven Tower. She wondered how many people at Northold were still fooled by his act, not many, she guessed, but they were all too loyal to say anything.

She found it hard to keep her composure as he came striding across the grass. She couldn't seem to decide what to do with her hands and her stomach fluttered. He tilted his head a little to regard her, reaching out an arm to push open the door. She went in, heart beating fast, and glanced at the bolt as he closed the door behind him. He didn't slide it across. She met his eyes and saw the Dark Man standing there instead of her Jorrun, his eyes emotionless, relaxed muscles giving away nothing. The butterflies in her stomach died.

Then he laughed and slid the bolt across and she growled at him, standing on her tiptoes to kiss him. She bit his lip but not hard.

'Jorrun Raven, do you enjoy making me angry?'

'Did you miss me?' He smiled smugly.

'No!' She glared up at him.

He took her hand and they climbed the steps. 'Will you be ready to sail for Chem tomorrow?'

She shrugged. 'I can be ready whenever you need me to be.' A stone formed in her stomach. 'How was Bractius?'

Jorrun frowned, raising his hand to acknowledge Azrael as they entered his room. 'He seemed tired. In good enough spirits though. He has definitely come around to our plan and was full of enthusiasm for trade deals and the prestige this will bring him.'

'How does he feel about you going?' She carefully moved a couple of books aside and perched on the edge of the table. She saw Jorrun's jaw muscles move as he clenched his teeth.

'He seems happy enough being without my counsel now he has his new friend Adrin to keep him entertained.'

She reached out to take his hands. 'Surely he will see through him? You and Bractius have been friends since childhood.'

Jorrun gave a slight shake of his head. 'The trouble with Adrin is there isn't actually much to see through. As charming as he is, he doesn't have the patience to hide his nature for long. Aside from that, he and Bractius are actually quite alike.'

Concern for Jorrun flowed through her and she squeezed his fingers. She wanted to reassure him they could always go to the Fulmers, but she knew how much he cared about Elden and the king. 'Shall we have a quiet dinner in the ivy tower tonight, just us, Rosa and Tantony?'

He nodded and smiled though lines still creased his forehead.

'You should come too, Azrael.' She smiled at the fire-spirit. Although he still hid in The Tower, so many people in Elden had now seen or at least heard of fire-spirits since the invasion from Chem he was hardly a secret anymore.

'Not a word to them about Chem though!' Jorrun warned.

'Of course!' Azrael buzzed, he made himself narrow and more human looking.

***

It was quite hard to spend the evening with Rosa and Tantony and not give anything away, Kesta's instinct was to trust and confide in them. Knowing it might be a very long time until she saw them again gnawed at the edges of her happiness. She took comfort and strength from the fact her two friends were so happy and that Jorrun was so relaxed and so much himself with them in the privacy of the Ivy Tower. Azrael also revelled in the fact that he didn't have to hide and took every opportunity to show off.

She struggled to sleep that night and found herself looking at the darkness in the windows and at Jorrun who slept beside her. He stirred, a frown forming. His breathing became more rapid and beads of sweat formed on his forehead.

'Jorrun?' She pulled herself up a little and leaned toward him.

With a gasp he sat up, pulling up his knees and bending over, breathing hard as though he'd been running. Kesta touched his shoulder and he flinched, raising his arm as though he meant to strike her, or ward off an attack.

'Jorrun what is it?' Kesta reached out with her magic and lit the candles that stood across the room on the table.

He looked up at her, his eyes huge and fearful, still struggling for breath. She wanted desperately to touch him again but didn't dare. He swallowed, his eyes slowly narrowing, his breath coming easier. He turned away, his face flushing slightly.

'I'm sorry, Kesta.'

'What's happened?' She moved a little closer.

'A dream.'

'A nightmare, you mean!'

He nodded, glancing at her. 'I ... I thought I was trapped again.'

'Oh, Jorrun.' She tentatively reached out to stroke his hair. She realised he'd never talked about it before and she'd never asked. Guilt washed through her. 'What was it like?'

'I don't want to talk about it.'

She bit her bottom lip, gently touching his hair again and kissing his shoulder. 'Not now then, but you should talk to someone when you're ready. It obviously still has a hold on you, talking might loosen its grip.'

He slid back down in the bed and turned to look at her. 'When did you become wise?'

'Oh, I've always been wise.' She grinned, and he smiled back, her muscles relaxed a little. 'I'm sorry I never asked about it, what you went through.'

He gave a small snort. 'I wouldn't have answered.' He was quiet for a while and she studied his face. 'Maybe in the daylight.'

She nodded and moved to snuggle against him and lay her head on his shoulder, his skin felt too warm. 'I've never known you have a nightmare before. Is it because we are leaving for Chem tomorrow?'

He didn't reply, so she watched the candle flames dance and waited.

'I think it might be,' he admitted at last. 'Leave it for now, Kesta. Please.'

She nodded against his chest and gave him a squeeze.

***

When they went down for breakfast, they found Rosa waiting in the receiving room. Jorrun brushed aside Kesta's hair to kiss her neck and went on down the stairs without a word.

'Oh, I didn't mean to chase him away.' Rosa's brows drew together anxiously.

Kesta shook her head and smiled. 'He has a lot to do before we leave, anyway. I'm glad you're here, I shall miss our breakfasts together.'

Rosa watched her as she poured some tea and sat down. 'So, what's really happening?'

Kesta's mouth involuntarily opened a little and she picked up a thyme bread roll to try to hide her surprise. 'What do you mean?'

'I mean, I know you and Jorrun are going away, but I don't believe it's just some tour of the islands.'

Kesta put some butter on her bread, glancing up at Rosa while she tried to think of what to say. She put the bread and her knife down on the table and sat back in her chair with a heavy sigh. 'Rosa, I can't tell you.'

Rosa narrowed her eyes and nodded. 'It's something dangerous?'

'Rosa.' Kesta leaned across the table toward her. 'I came back from Mantu, I came back from Chem. I even came back here from the Fulmers when I thought I never would. I'll be back, please, try not to worry.'

'Well I can't not worry.' She folded her arms over her chest. 'But if you say you'll be back then I believe you mean it. Just please look after each other.'

Kesta nodded. 'Of course.'

She forced a smile and quickly changed the subject, wanting to know what Rosa was planning to do with the Hold once she was gone. A man came up the Tower stairs and politely interrupted them, asking Kesta where her belongings were that she wanted taking down to the ship. Kesta took the hint and followed him down to the great hall and out into the ward. Rosa walked quietly at her side.

Jorrun was already on-board his small ship when they arrived at the wharf, standing on the gangplank talking with Tantony. Jorrun took Kesta's travel bag from her and Tantony helped the man take her chest aboard.

'Ready?' Jorrun asked her, his gaze intense and unblinking.

Icy snakes moved about in her stomach, but she nodded and turned to Rosa, hugging her fiercely. She kissed Tantony's cheek and then stepped off the gangplank so Jorrun could pull it in.

'Whatever you're doing, take care,' Rosa said, looking from Kesta to Jorrun.

Jorrun's eyes narrowed slightly but he nodded.

Tantony gave them a shove away from the wharf and Kesta set the sail while Jorrun went to the rudder. Both of them called up wind at the same time and Kesta laughed.

'Go on.' Jorrun nodded, letting his dissipate.

90

They moved quickly out onto the lake and away from Northold. The bridge across the river had been repaired after the Chemman attack and men hurried to wind the winches and lift it to allow them through. The Taur took them swiftly north through Elden. Many of the towns that inhabited the riverside were still abandoned, nature already seeking to claim back the wood and stone of devastated buildings. With both of them using their magic they reached the harbour town of Taurmouth just after noon only a day after leaving Northold. Many of the burned-out buildings had been demolished and a few new homes had begun to grow upward from the ground. Sunken ships no longer blocked the harbour and several new wharves, their sanded wood bright and clean, hosted the ships that had returned.

They didn't stop, sailing outward onto the sea.

As night fell, Jorrun fetched some pillows and blankets from the cabin and laid them out on the deck. They'd been propping the door open so Azrael could come and go as he pleased although the poor fire-spirit was too afraid to leave his lantern for long. Kesta was taking a turn on the rudder but Jorrun held his hand out toward her and called her over to where he'd made their bed under the stars.

'Shouldn't one of us keep watch and make sure we don't drift?' She took his hand and followed him anyway.

'It will be fine for a while.'

She instinctively called up her *knowing* and she felt in his fingers the anxiety thrumming through his body.

He glanced at her. 'Don't forget I know when you call your magic.'

She winced and withdrew it at once. 'I'm sorry, I didn—'

He turned to face her, raising a hand. 'Please, use it.' He looked away, his breathing coming faster. Slowly his hands moved up to the amulet he wore around his neck to protect himself from the knowing of *fire-walkers*. He lifted it over his head and looked down at it in his hands. Kesta held her breath but found herself too afraid to call back her magic.

Jorrun closed his fist over the amulet and sat on the blankets. 'I haven't dream-walked since Karinna caught me.'

Kesta drew in a sharp breath and quickly sat beside him. Although the wind still pushed at the sail, with neither of them using their magic, the ship lost some of its pace and the sea took charge, rocking them gently. Kesta waited but he didn't speak. She reached out and took one of his long-fingered hands between hers.

'If anyone else caught you, I'd kill them too,' she said firmly.

He smiled. 'I believe you.' He drew in a breath but was silent again, lying back on the deck. Kesta stretched herself out beside him and waited. 'It …' He gazed up at the stars, his chest rising and falling. 'Being confined, being trapped, that was bad. But … it was what he did to me. Your soul, your thoughts, they are safe. They belong only to you. Having someone … having someone rip you open inside and trample through everything that's private and …' His words caught in his throat and Kesta rolled over onto her side to place her hand over his heart.

'I'm here.' She opened her *knowing*, not to feel his pain, but to reassure him with her love.

He nodded, placing a hand on hers, his breathing gradually slowing. She felt his nausea, his terror. 'I've faced death before. I took beatings as a child that would have paralysed a grown man with fear. Having someone control my mind, my soul, like that though, Kest—'

'You don't have to dream-walk again.' She pushed herself up to look down into his storm-blue eyes.

'But I do.' He didn't blink as he looked back up at her. 'If I don't, then I will always be afraid.'

She shook her head, and he reached up to place a hand against her cheek.

'Kesta, will you let me walk your dreams?'

She sat up. He was terrified of someone ravaging his most private thoughts and yet wanted her permission to walk through her subconscious mind. She studied his face and he didn't look away.

She nodded. 'All right.'

'It won't be safe to do it on the ship. If we find somewhere secure in the Borrows, we can try there.' He propped himself up on his elbow to look at her. With a wave of his hand he sent a gust of wind toward the cabin door to close it and leaned over to kiss her.

***

'A ship!' Kesta ran barefoot across the sun-kissed deck and squeezed around the side of the cabin to stand at the prow.

'Chemman?' Jorrun demanded from where he sat at the rudder.

Kesta shook her head. 'Looks like a Borrow ship, a large fishing vessel.'

'Many on board?'

'I can't see from here.' She called up her *knowing*, but it was too far to feel anything either. Jorrun had returned to wearing his amulet and she felt its familiar reaction like an icy blast of emptiness. From the cabin she felt poor Azrael's utter misery and the metallic tang of his alien mind. They drew closer, the islands of the Borrows growing larger against the horizon.

'I think there are children.' She strained her eyes to make out the figures. If they both maintained their courses, they would pass close, but not meet. 'There seem to be maybe two men and three women.'

'Okay, we'll see what they do.'

Kesta sensed a slight fluctuation in his control over the wind he was sending into their sail. He was more nervous than his steady voice suggested. The Borrow ship cut across their path and she made out the features of the people on board. They looked haggard, their skin pale, despite the summer sun, and tight across their skulls. Two of the men held bows and one of them nocked an arrow to it. Kesta drew fire to her left hand and held it up so those on the Borrow boat could see.

'Kesta?'

'Letting them know who I am,' she replied.

One of the other men moved to touch the aggressive bowman on the shoulder. Reluctantly he let his bow go slack. Kesta let her flames dissipate and nodded. The man nodded back. She tried again with her *knowing* and was in time to feel the tension on the Borrow ship easing.

'It's fine,' Kesta called back to Jorrun. She slipped back past the cabin to check the sail. 'They have no interest in us, just surviving.'

'Bractius mentioned the Fulmers have been taking in more refugees. I think things will be very different between the Islands and what remains of the Borrow folk in the future.'

She turned to look at him and nodded. 'We can hope.' She made her way forward and continued to scan the horizon. The nearest island of the Borrows was so close now she could make out the individual trees and bushes. 'Do you know the names of the Borrow Islands?'

'Yes, I have maps if you want to see them.'

Three gulls came flying out to investigate them, their shrill cries almost drowning out Jorrun's reply. Kesta's stomach begin to tighten and she almost withdrew her *knowing*. The last time she'd passed through here she'd felt the taint of blood magic on the land and the awful effect it had on the animals. The gulls gave her hope things had improved.

Then she felt it, like insects crawling inside her skin. Like whispers just beyond hearing. Her stomach reacted as though she'd smelt something foul, although all she could smell was the sea and the varnish of the ship; and Jorrun's jasmine and cinnamon soap. She turned and wasn't surprised to find him right beside her.

'What do you feel?' he asked.

She sighed and withdrew her *knowing*. 'It's still bad. Not as sharp, but like a nagging pain deep in your bones that you can't quite ignore.'

'I wish we could repair it somehow.' He gazed across the water, shielding his vision as he turned westward, his eyes themselves the colour of the sea.

'At least we can stop it ever happening again.' She curled her fingers up, her nails digging into her palms.

'We'll sail straight through and chance the crossing to Chem.'

'But ... we were going to stop so you can dream-walk.'

He looked away and swallowed, then met her eyes with his brows drawn in tight. 'It can wait. And the Borrows are uncomfortable for you.'

She studied his face and he shifted his feet. She placed a hand on his chest. 'Jorrun, I'll be fine here for a short while and poor Azrael could really do with a break from the sea. You found the courage to tell me what was worrying you and asked me to help. Let me help.'

He met her gaze unblinking, she felt his heart beat beneath her fingers several times before he nodded. 'All right. We'll stop just long enough to sleep a while.'

***

Kesta perched on a rock and watched as Jorrun built a small fire and made them a bed from their blankets. Sea spray caught her arm and the side of her face as a particularly large wave crashed below her. Azrael was making happy loops across the coarse grass a little further inland and Jorrun paused to smile at him. 'Daft bug!'

Kesta pushed herself up off the rock and made her way over to him. 'Don't you need to make a star out of elemental representations to dream-walk?'

He narrowed his eyes at her. 'Have you been in my books?'

She grinned. 'Of course! I had to read something to Azrael.'

He couldn't help catching her smile. 'I don't actually need anything but myself to dream-walk,' he admitted. 'The trance herbs help, but to find dreams close by I don't need assistance. What you saw in The Tower that time … when … Well that time I was trying to *walk* a long distance and find someone who had similar blood to mine. That required what you call "elemental representations" to boost my ability.'

'So, you just need me to sleep?'

'Yes.'

'But I'm not tired.'

'I can do something about that.' He took a step forward and her skin flushed as her heart pumped her blood faster.

'Azrael is watching.'

'I meant trance herbs, Kesta.'

She growled at him and he laughed at her blushes.

'Come on.'

She kicked at the back of his knee as he moved away, but he just laughed more. She hoped it had eased some of his fear.

She lay down on the blanket closest to the firewood but didn't close her eyes. Azrael came closer to keep a look out for them and Jorrun started the fire, throwing in a handful of the trance herbs. She shifted, unable to get comfortable and realised it wasn't the ground that was bothering her, but the slow oozing stain left from blood magic. She shuddered.

Jorrun lay beside her but his shoulders were drawn up and there were lines of worry above his nose. She took his hand and twinned her fingers between his, closing her eyes and taking in slow, deep breaths of the herbs.

She wasn't aware she was dreaming at first. She was in the crowded streets of Taurmaline trying to find the market, but whichever way she went she ended up back at the castle. There was a tightness across her chest and she picked up her pace, the crowd seemed to thicken and it became harder to draw in air.

Come this way, Kesta, it's quieter.

Her heart muscles eased, and she changed direction and found herself on a forest path with low evening light striking through the leaves. Part of her felt apprehension that this wasn't the way to the market, but she continued.

What do you need at the market?

'Elemental representations.'

She felt Jorrun's amusement and realised at once she was dreaming. She looked around to find him, her ears becoming aware of the shush of waves and the crackle of the fire, but her vision was still locked in the forest. Something moved and she focused between the foliage. The sunlight was in her eyes but she could just make out a man. A young man with green eyes. She felt ... *malice.*

She woke and sat up with a gasp, looking quickly around to take in the rugged Borrow coast, their tethered ship, and their steadily burning fire. Her hand went to her chest and she felt her heart racing and her ribs expanding and deflating rapidly. Above her thin clouds ghosted across the stars.

Jorrun stirred beside her and his eyes fluttered open. Azrael came to hover near them, the size of a raven with his long tail trailing behind him.

'Are you all right?' she asked Jorrun, her still tight muscles made her voice hoarse.

He sat up slowly and turned to look at her. 'I'm fine. It was fine.'

'Wasn't I supposed to be unaware of you though?'

He took in a deep breath. 'Yes. I'm used to dealing with anxiety dreams, they're very common, but you did make me laugh.' He grinned and she scowled at him. 'Seriously, though, I used to be good at being undetected. Karinna has ... he's destroyed my confidence.'

Azrael hissed and darted around his head. 'Jorrun, even with your confidence sshattered you took down Dryn Dunham!'

'But it nearly cost me everything,' he said quietly, glancing at Kesta.

Kesta swallowed. 'You can practice on me if you like. If I'm aware you may be in my dreams, then it might be harder for you to stay undetected and make it challenging enough for you to improve again?'

'If you're sure? I don't want to be too intrusive.'

'Just don't laugh at me!' She jabbed a finger in his leg. 'I can't help what I dream!'

He couldn't help but break into a smile and he struggled for a moment to become serious again. 'Thank you for having so much trust in me.'

Kesta glanced up at Azrael. As much as she loved the fire-spirit it was sometimes inconvenient to have the elemental chaperone about all the time. 'Shall we get some proper sleep or do you want to get going?'

'Let's sleep and let Azrael have a bit more time on land.'

She nodded. Azrael replied by making himself huge, pulling a terrifying face, and shooting off across the island.

'Be careful, crazy bug!' Jorrun yelled after him.

***

When Kesta woke again, Jorrun was quietly packing away their camp with Azrael bobbing along beside him. It was still dark and their fire had gone out. She stretched and then sat up.

'Is everything all right?'

Jorrun nodded and walked over to her. 'Azrael spotted another boatload of Borrowmen landing on the other side of the island, he thinks they just stopped for supplies but it's best if we go.'

She hugged herself tightly, feeling a deep chill in her bones. 'I'm more than happy to go.'

'Blood magic,' Azrael spluttered and spat. 'I almosst want to be back on the ssea!'

Kesta picked up her blanket and checked around her that they'd left nothing behind. She climbed up into the ship. 'Are we not taking the small boat again?'

Jorrun shook his head. 'We're going to sail into Navere.'

'What?' She stared at him.

'Osun has everything arranged.'

She clenched her teeth together at his name but went to the sail and prepared to set it when Jorrun was ready. 'Don't start keeping things from me when you're back with your brother, Jorrun.'

She heard him sigh. 'I won't.'

She wanted to retort that it seemed he already was, but she bit her tongue.

Chapter Eight

Dia; Fulmer Islands

Dia watched as Catya twisted and ducked, Heara's stick whistling over her head and then slicing at the girl's legs. Catya jumped, then danced back. As Heara swung the long stick again Catya backflipped then immediately cartwheeled to try to get past her instructor. There were several gasps and Dia found herself smiling. The audiences that stopped to watch Catya train were getting bigger. She hadn't seen anyone this good since ... well, since Heara and her desperately missed dead twin, Shaherra.

'Icante!'

She turned to see young Gilfy running toward her with two letters clasped in his hand. The boy scowled toward Catya.

'Thank you, Gilfy.' Dia took the letters and leaned back against a tree. One of them had the royal seal of Elden on it. The other was sealed with unmarked wax and tied about with twine. Her name was written in her daughter's handwriting. She almost dropped the king's missive in her haste to open Kesta's letter.

Jorrun and I will be away for a while. Please don't worry.

She tensed, holding her breath as she read it again. Her first thought was they'd absconded from Elden together, but if that were the case, then surely, they would have come here? There was nowhere else they could go excep–

'Chem.'

Tucking Kesta's letter under her arm she ripped open the King's, her eyes darting over his scrawling script.

My dear Icante,

I hope Vilnue has settled well on Fulmer Isle? I received his request for assistance regarding refugees from the Borrows. As you know I am still dealing with repairs to Mantu, Taurmouth, and the Taur valley, however I would be glad to help. Let me know what you need most urgently and I will endeavour to supply it.

You may have heard from your daughter? She and Jorrun are presently travelling at my behest and dealing with some urgent matters. With my sorcerer gone I humbly request your choice of envoy be one that can serve in a magical capacity should the need arise.

Your friend

Bractius.

'Humbly request!' Dia folded the letter over roughly with one hand. No wonder he was so eager to help her with the refugee situation!

But where was Kesta and what was she really doing?

She glanced towards Heara and pushed herself away from the tree. Gilfy was still there, his arms folded across his chest.

'Gilfy, go find Silenes Arrus and Worvig, tell them I want to see them at once in my room.'

The boy's eyes widened and with a nod he ran off.

Dia made her way back to the Hold more slowly. It was hardly a new sensation to wish she'd never gotten involved with Elden. The irony of it was still bitter, they'd gone to Bractius for help but had ended up saving him.

As she passed through the great hall, she spotted Pirelle seated at the table teaching Milaiya how to read and write. Despite their attack from Chem, despite the fact her daughter had been there to kill off their necromancer lord, she'd never before been curious about what happened in that country beyond the barricade of the Borrow Islands. Perhaps it was time to learn.

She went into her room and calling flame to her fingers she lit a candle.

'Doroquael?'

The candle spluttered and the fire-spirit emerged like a butterfly climbing from its chrysalis. 'Dia! I wasss talking with a Drake who has come up to vissit from the fire realm.'

'I hope I didn't call you away from anything important?'

'We were discussing the blood cursse on the Borrowss.'

'Anything?'

'Ssorry, Dia, we don't know enough about blood magic.' Doroquael made himself small and flew a circuit around the room. 'There has been a meeting of Drakes from Elden and Drakess from Shem.'

Dia took two steps closer to the fire-spirit. 'And?'

'Shem is in chaoss. The Spirits there are very pleased, but I'm worried.'

'Why, spirit?'

'Many things can be born from chaos.'

'Things?'

'A multitude of outcomess. Chem's fate affects us all, like a weight on a sscale.'

She frowned, sitting on the edge of the table. 'I thought destroying the Dunhams was a good thing?'

'Potentially.'

'But also, potentially bad?'

Doroquael burned a dark, almost invisible blue.

'And what of Elden?'

'Azrael has gone.'

'Gone?'

'He left the Raven Tower and the Elden Spirits know only that he iss with Jorrun and Kessta.'

The door flew inward and Arrus strode in with his brother on his heels. They were alike in build but Arrus's eyes held a hint of green and his brown hair contained more grey than Worvig's. Dia stood and gestured for them to close the door behind them.

'I saw a boat had come in,' Worvig said. 'You have news?'

'Letters from Kesta and Bractius.' She handed them to her husband and Worvig read them over his shoulder.

'What does this mean?' Arrus demanded. 'Where has Kesta gone?'

'I wish I knew.' Dia sighed. 'I intend to find out. It seems I will need to send Larissa to Elden as our ambassador after all. Worvig, I hate to ask, but will you go with her?'

Worvig screwed up his face and looked down. 'If I have to. I'd rather you chose someone else.'

'The only other people I'd send to protect Larissa are Heara, and you, Arrus.'

Arrus straightened up and opened his mouth to protest.

'I'll do it.' Worvig raised his hand and sighed. 'Spirits know I have no wish to leave the islands. I'll only do it temporarily though, until you find a permanent escort for Larissa.'

Dia nodded. 'Agreed. I'll have Heara start training someone up for the role, Catya will have to wait. In the meantime, I'll be going with you just for a few days. I want to ask Bractius to his face what Kesta is doing.'

'I should come,' Arrus said, but Dia could tell by his expression he already knew she'd refuse.

'Then who will rule the islands? I need to choose another Silene to replace Kesta.'

None of them made eye contact. She'd been putting it off, not wanting Kesta's absence to be something acknowledged and set in stone.

'Who?' Arrus asked.

'Pirelle isn't ready.' She glanced up. 'I'd go for Larissa if I didn't need her to go to Elden. Everlyn proved herself against the Chemman, but she is a quiet woman who might not settle well into a command role.' She shook her head and sighed. 'I'll see how Pirelle manages with you to guide her while I'm away.' She touched her husband's arm.

Worvig snorted. 'Give it a few years and I'd lay money on Catya being your best bet for Silene, though she's no islander.'

'She's incredibly focused and determined, not to mention intelligent,' Dia agreed. 'Time will tell, but I think she has her heart set on being an Icante's bodyguard!'

And who will be that Icante with Kesta gone? Dia wondered.

***

Those few of the Islanders who visited Elden normally headed for the closest large harbour, Burneton, however they'd learned that to get to the capital it was much quicker to head further east to Taurmouth and follow the river inland. They had taken one of their longships, giving Dia the excuse for bringing several warriors without it looking like she was either posturing, or felt she needed protection. In reality, it was a little of both.

As they sailed across lake Taur, a raven came out to meet them. Dia watched as it circled them and flew back toward The Tower that peered over the trees at Northold. She was tempted to go there to get answers, perhaps Kesta's friend, Rosa, knew something; however, knowing Bractius he would take some offense at her visiting there first. Several dark specks emerged from The Tower, growing in number. The ravens flew toward the ship, their guttural caws deafening. With a laugh, Dia raised her arms and several of the birds came down to settle on them.

'They adore you!' Larissa's mis-matched blue eyes were wide and unblinking. 'I've never seen a reaction like that before from a flock of corvids.'

Dia sent her warmth and appreciation out with her *knowing* and tried to impress that she would visit them on her way back. One of the ravens pressed into her mind the image of a dark, fruit cake and quickly all the others tried to follow suit, fighting to sit on her arms and tell her their favourite treats. One of them showed her an eyeball and with a lurch of her stomach she lowered her arms and mentally pushed them away.

'Soon,' she called up to the circling birds.

Dia looked down again to regard Larissa. It wasn't just because she was a strong *walker* that Dia had chosen her as her envoy. Larissa was beautiful, her eyes not too strange, her red hair striking, her face small and delicate. She was used to getting a lot of attention and wasn't easily fooled. She listened and observed and turned down advances in a way that left men still feeling good about themselves.

'I think it must be their relationship with Jorrun that makes them particularly open to friendship with a human,' Dia mused. 'They love that I can communicate much more clearly. It might pay you to befriend them also.'

Larissa nodded, watching them chase each other over the lake. 'We should agree on a way for me to warn you of trouble in case my letters are read.' She rubbed at her chin. 'If I mention the ravens, then whatever I write directly after will be the opposite of what I say. On the next line pick out every other word.'

Dia's apprehension grew, at the same time she felt proud of Larissa for her cleverness and caution. 'I hope there will be no trouble. We have no reason to fear Chem for the present and any scheming of Bractius' will be no more than him trying to gain as much as he can while giving as little as possible in return!'

Larissa laughed. 'It's going to be an interesting experience.'

'Look after Worvig for me, he's going to hate it.'

Larissa's smile faded. 'I'll help him settle as best I can. I'm glad you chose him, I feel safe with him to back me up.'

As do I, Dia thought.

***

The harbour was busy and they had to wait to let two supply ships out before they moved across to the landing dock that the harbourmaster waved them into. One of the King's stewards was waiting to meet them and greeted them with a flurry of elaborate bows that made Larissa laugh and Worvig scowl. With eight of their warriors escorting them, pushing through the crowds to the castle wasn't a problem. They were taken straight to the throne room, the warriors standing back as Dia, Worvig, and Larissa approached the King. Both Worvig and Larissa bowed, Dia just giving a polite inclination of her head. The Queen was seated in a smaller throne to the King's right, Jorrun's stark chair was glaringly empty. Dia met Ayline's eyes and smiled at her. The young woman didn't look well, her pale skin making the dark shadows under her eyes all the more striking.

'Welcome!' Bractius held out both his hands dramatically and stepped down from his throne to greet them. He kissed Dia's cheek and shook Worvig's hand.

'Your majesty, this is my husband's brother, Worvig Silene. You remember Larissa?'

'Of course!' Bractius beamed, showing his straight, white teeth through his beard. 'You are to be our envoy from the Fulmers?'

'I am, your majesty.' Larissa smiled up at the king.

Dia caught movement out of the corner of her eye and glanced up at the Queen. Ayline's hazel eyes had narrowed and she all but glared at Larissa. There was no doubt Ayline was a pretty girl, but there was something almost artificial and forced about it. Would she consider an effortless beauty like Larissa a threat? More than likely. It would be a good idea to warn Larissa although her fellow *fire-walker* had probably already realised.

'And how is the Queen?' Dia asked.

'Oh.' Bractius looked over his shoulder. 'Her majesty is well, aren't you, my darling?' He held out a hand toward her.

Ayline forced a smile and pushed herself up from her throne. She held out her hand to daintily take the King's, her other hand going to her belly. 'Welcome again, to Taurmaline.'

'How are you finding your pregnancy?' Dia asked with genuine concern.

Ayline's eyes narrowed again and she looked up at Dia through her lashes. 'I've had some sickness, but it is to be expected.'

'Larissa and I have some skill with midwifery, if yo—'

'I have my own midwife.' Ayline's eyes had hardened but her smile remained fixed.

Dia nodded, smiling in return, but she called up her *knowing*. She took a step back at the ferocity of the Queen's emotions. Luckily only Larissa seemed to notice her reaction. There was anger toward the King that bordered on hatred, and resentment toward her and Larissa. Underneath it all was a nagging nausea that seemed to emanate from the Queen's spine. Dia immediately felt sorry for the young woman. She wondered if, in all her ambition to secure the King and her lofty status, she'd truly realised what her life would be.

'And your journey here was good?' Bractius was still focused on Larissa.

'It was,' Larissa replied. She turned to the Queen. 'How is the spirit of Elden since those awful attacks? It must have given the people so much courage to see how resiliently their Queen endured the siege?'

Ayline's eyes widened. 'Oh, well, one must lead by example. It was quite terrifying but I trusted my husband to save us.' She smiled up at Bractius and he patted her arm. Anyone watching would have believed there was real affection between them.

Worvig shuffled his feet and Dia found it hard to maintain eye contact.

'I've been collecting unwanted clothes and useful items for your refugees,' Ayline went on, her enthusiasm growing.

'That's incredibly kind,' Larissa said with seeming sincerity.

Dia shut off her *knowing*, finding this deceptive dance depressing. Diplomacy was a part of an Icante's job, but she certainly didn't envy Larissa the task she'd assigned her. In a way it was as well Kesta had left and Larissa taken her place, she doubted her daughter would have had the patience to put up with Ayline. She had to bite her lower lip to stop herself smiling at the thought of it.

'How is the refugee situation?'

Dia realised Bractius was addressing her.

'No more have arrived since my letter,' she replied. 'Not surprisingly they are reluctant, afraid even, to approach us for help. Those that do are incredibly brave, or terrified.'

'I'm surprised they don't go to Chem, surely it's much nearer?' Ayline frowned.

'For women, Chem means enslavement. Most will risk the sea, the Fulmers, or even the stain of the blood magic on the Borrows, rather than that.'

Ayline visibly shivered.

'Right, shall we get you all settled in, then?' Bractius adeptly changed the subject.

Dia gave a slight bow. 'Thank you. If you could spare me a moment there is a matter I would like to discuss with you.'

'I thought there might be.' Bractius raised an eyebrow. 'Let me walk you to your room myself.'

Ayline stared at them both. Dia's instinct was to soothe the Queen, but she was itching to know news of her daughter. 'Thank you, I would appreciate it.'

Bractius beckoned over his stewards and they hurried forward to guide Worvig and Larissa. The king offered his arm and Dia took it, feeling a little uncomfortable. Instead of taking Dia up to the guest room in which she'd stayed previously, he took her to his private study. Maps adorned the walls as well as portraits of those Dia assumed to be previous kings. Bractius spoke the instant he closed the door behind them.

'Before you react, bear in mind this was Jorrun and Kesta's plan, they came here to convince me of it!'

'Convince you of what?' Dia's eyes narrowed.

'Only they and myself know of this, no one else. They have gone to Chem.'

The words kicked hard at Dia's heart, she closed her eyes. 'I feared as much. Go on.'

'They have an ambitious plan to get rid of the last of the necromancers and set Jorrun's brother, Osun, up on the throne of the Overlord. I think they want to form some kind of democracy.' The King's lip curled in distaste. 'Still, if it works, they will turn Chem into an ally and trade partner and eliminate their threat forever.'

To Dia, a democracy in Chem seemed like an excellent, if impossible concept. She could understand why a king might find the idea so concerning though. On the Fulmers the next Icante was always chosen from among the *Walkers* by the ruling Icante. Chieftains were elected by each Hold, but the Icante got to choose her own Silenes.

She drew in air and considered her reply. 'I'm not sure how to feel about that. Scared for my daughter, more than anything.'

'Of course.' Bractius patted at her arm, his gaze somewhere across the room. 'I was reluctant to let Jorrun go, but it made sense. Apparently, there is another Dunham, Feren I think he said, in line to step in as Overlord. If nothing is done, we are hardly better off than before.'

'Yes, we certainly don't want to allow another necromancer to take charge. Have you heard anything?'

Bractius pulled at his beard and turned to look at her. 'Nothing yet, but they would have only been in Chem maybe four or five days. It would be difficult for them to send word.'

'Doesn't Jorrun do some kind of long-distance scrying?'

Bractius stood up straighter and lowered his voice. 'That's Chem magic and involves blood. Jorrun refused to take any of my blood with him in case it falls into the wrong hands.'

Dia's intestines grew cold. Jorrun used blood magic? Kesta had never told her that. Did she know?

'All we can do is wait and trust them.' Bractius folded his arms across his chest and regarded her.

Dia nodded, forcing herself to breathe more slowly. 'I appreciate you telling me. Would you like Larissa to know so you have someone to confide in? I realise the more people who know a secret, the more at risk it becomes.'

'I'm grateful for the sentiment of the offer.' He looked across the room, his eyes meeting those of a portrait. *His father*? Dia wondered. 'For the moment I'd prefer to leave it as the four of us. I must admit it's a relief to speak to you of it.'

'Thank you for telling me. Despite everything … I'm glad we started talking with Elden.'

Bractius nodded. 'We would be in a different world now if we hadn't. Come on, I'll walk you to your room.'

Chapter Nine

Osun; Covenet of Chem

'Trouble!' he called out, reining in his horse.

Cassien pulled his own mount up sharply and jumped down to draw his sword. Jagna was slower to react and turned his horse around further up the road. Osun cursed, they were almost within sight of Navere.

The six men pursuing them slowed to a walk. From their leather armour and lack of any identifying marks Osun guessed they were ex-guardsmen, probably from a Dunham Coven. The way their apparent leader stared at him and halted his horse confirmed it. 'Who are you?' The man demanded, leaning forward over his horse's neck with his reins held in one hand.

Osun sat up straighter. 'You know who I am.'

The man narrowed his eyes, Cassien pushed his horse away from him to give himself more room. The man spat and Osun sighed. Why did so many men feel the need to do that?

'I know what you are.' The man looked at him unblinkingly. 'I want to know who.'

The ex-guardsmen all looked up as Jagna called flame to his fingers. 'Answer enough for you?' The young sorcerer called out.

The man sat back in his saddle, his horse moving uneasily beneath him. He regarded Jagna and then turned back to Osun. 'Very well, "master", we'll be on our way.'

He gestured at his men and turned his horse around, heading off the path before breaking into a gallop.

Jagna let his flames die away.

Osun nodded at the young sorcerer. 'Thanks.'

'I could have taken them, master,' Cassien grumbled. He retrieved his horse, their supply horse still tied to its saddle.

'Bandits?' Jagna asked as Osun caught up to him. He looked shaken.

Osun nodded. 'Undoubtably.' He had to stop himself glancing at his belt. He carried a fortune there not in gold, but in diamonds, everything he had to buy women with blood for his coven. 'Let's get on.'

It wasn't the first time they'd met trouble on their way back from Margith. They'd been attacked one night while camping by a river some three miles from the road. Cassien had proved his worth by dispatching the thieves before Jagna had even struggled out of his blanket. The sooner the Seats were settled the better it would be for the whole country.

'We should get off the road,' Jagna suggested.

The young man had spent so much of his life hiding and trying to go unnoticed that travelling on the open roads with Osun had made him a nervous wreck. Osun supposed he couldn't blame him, after all, Jagna didn't know him, didn't know Osun could hide himself in plain sight by playing whatever part was required.

Cassien, on the other hand, seemed to have chosen to trust him completely. Perhaps it was just the nature of being a slave. It made Osun feel uncomfortable.

'Osun?' Jagna frowned, glancing around. His horse snorted and tossed its head.

'The road is safer,' Osun replied. 'We'll attract more attention if we try to sneak into Navere.'

Jagna slumped a little in his saddle, but he turned his horse to fall in beside Osun.

As always, the gates to the harbour city were open wide, the guards going about their business despite the chaos in the ruling Seats. Seabirds called sharply, large numbers of them perched on the granite walls, many more following the boats out on the sea. The guards paid Osun more attention than they did when he'd come through with his wagon as a merchant, but didn't stop him. Osun felt a surprising amount of sympathy for them, at times like these it was probably best to keep out of any potential trouble and just wait to see who came out on top. With any luck it would soon be him.

They stopped outside the Narwhale Inn, Gulden coming out himself to greet them and order about his slaves and servants.

'Osun! Good to see you again so soon.' Gulden took the reins of Osun's horse as he dismounted. 'I have three letters here for you.'

'Thank you for keeping them for me,' Osun replied. 'I'll need a room for my friend here and somewhere for my servant.'

'Of course.' Gulden frowned a little at Osun's formal manner. 'I'll fetch your letters.'

'This is a bad place,' Jagna muttered. 'I can feel blood magic.'

Osun waved a hand at him and scowled. 'Adelphy kept his undead here, they're long gone.'

He followed Gulden inside the inn, it was busier than usual and Osun felt a moment of annoyance. Despite the crowded dining room, Gulden made Osun his priority and going to a strongbox took out the three letters.

'Your usual room is taken, master Osun, but I can try to move the occupan—'

'No need.' Osun made a slashing gesture with his hand. 'We'll probably only be here a few nights this time and I know all of your rooms are comfortable and clean.'

Gulden's chest swelled a little, and he straightened his back. 'Well now, master Osun, that's good of you to say.'

'I wouldn't put a friend in a bad position for no good reason.' Osun glanced about the room, noting those that were there to see if there might be any potential trouble. Jagna was shifting his feet, his back to the wall, hands twitching. Osun's jaw tightened and he sighed. 'Where's that room, Gulden?'

'Oh, this way!' Gulden gestured at a slave and handed her two keys. He almost snarled at her. 'Quickly!'

The woman bowed and made her way to the stairs without making eye contact with anyone. She wore a thick, black veil and her long brown hair was tied back in a neat plait. She stopped at one door and unlocked it, going inside and stooping in a low bow with the key held out on her palm. Osun took it and, after a quick look around, handed the key to Jagna.

'And my room?' he demanded.

The slave straightened up and led him along the corridor to open another door. Osun snatched the key from her at once. 'This will do. Cassien, find out where your room is and then come back at once. I have work for you.'

'Yes, master.' Cassien raised his eyebrows in a way that would have gotten him a knock about the head from most masters, but he bowed and Osun chose to ignore it. The slave beckoned at Cassien for him to follow her and closed the door.

Osun breathed out, his muscles relaxing. He went over to the window and looked down at the marketplace. Cattle stood miserably in pens and various goods sprawled beneath brightly coloured awnings. He was relieved to see the slave pens were across the other side of the market and barely visible. He straightened up and turned away, his fingers curling up into fists and his eyebrows drawing in across his nose. Empathy could get him killed.

He looked down at the letters crumpled in his hand and walked slowly over to the bed to sit down. He'd barely had time to read them all when someone knocked at the door.

'Come!'

The door opened and Cassien stepped in, closing it again behind him. Osun turned back to his letters.

'Why do you do that?' Cassien asked.

Osun span about and put the letters down as hard as it was possible to do so on a soft bed.

'Master.' The young man added, although he gave a shake of his head.

'Do you want me to beat you to death?' Osun demanded angrily.

Cassien's eyes widened.

'I might not be cruel, but that doesn't mean I'm soft!' Osun stood up and approached the window, his hands behind his back.

'I'm sorry,' Cassien stuttered. He actually sounded as though he meant it.

Osun turned to him. 'It isn't just me you have to think of! Your impertinence reflects badly on me and could cause me trouble also. Don't make me regret helping you.'

Cassien swallowed, his grey eyes going to the floor. 'I'm sorry, master.'

Osun took in a deep breath and sighed it out loudly. 'Now, what was your impertinent question?'

Cassien shuffled his feet and didn't look up. 'You are hard to understand, master. It's like you are … thirty different people. How you are with me, how you are with Jagna and that innkeeper, all different. And when you scry in the bowl, you are different again.'

Osun regarded the young man, barely more than a boy although he had a man's build. 'I won't chastise you for being observant, in fact I'd encourage it, but watch your tongue and your attitude. If you want to stay alive and have a chance to be a part of something that will change the future of Chem, then stay quiet, behave as you should, and do as you're told. If you want to end up dead in the bottom of a fighter's pit, then carry on the way you are! I'd be happy to get some of my gold back.'

'Yes, master.'

'Yes to what?' Osun threw his arms up.

'Yes, I'll behave!' Cassien raised his voice a little to say through gritted teeth. 'Master.'

Osun shook his head. 'How are you even alive still?'

They both jumped when there was another knock at the door. Osun glared at Cassien until the boy realised what he was supposed to be doing and went to open the door. Jagna pushed his way in, glancing around the room and going straight to the window to look down at the street.

'So, what's our next move?' Jagna asked, scratching at his chin where his stubble had grown almost as long as his severely cut hair.

Osun narrowed his eyes and regarded the young sorcerer. 'My brother is close and should join us tomorrow night. Balten has arranged for one of his order to be on the docks and sign Jorrun's ship in, no questions asked. He has also given me the address of a house near the harbour, presumably a safe house we can stay in. I'll check it out tonight.'

'I should come too, master,' Cassien said.

Osun nodded.

'When do we take Navere from Cepack?' Jagna asked.

'That will be up to my brother. I'll check out the palace and temple tomorrow, get an idea of what we're up against.' Osun hesitated, studying Jagna's face and green eyes. 'Be careful when you meet my brother's wife. She's from the Fulmers and you might find her ... startling.'

'I can deal with a woman.' Jagna scowled.

A laugh escaped from Osun, he couldn't help it. He'd been shocked when he'd first met Kesta, then utterly transfixed by her openness and her fighter's grace. Then jealousy had come creeping into his heart when he saw the relationship she had with his brother, despite their denial of it, a longing had overwhelmed him for something he hadn't even realised was missing from his life. He could certainly understand Balten and his friends. Kesta's opinion of him had crushed him and brought a flood of emotions he barely recognised, emotions he didn't want to feel. Guilt. Remorse. Admiration had turned almost to hatred that long, quiet talks with Jorrun on their way back to Elden had calmed. He was nervous of seeing Kesta again. He doubted she'd forgiven him or ever would. He told himself her opinion didn't matter. But it did. He'd considered what his mother would have thought of his behaviour towards Milaiya and his previous slave; what Jorrun's mother, Naderra would have thought. No matter how many times he'd told himself he was a Chemman, that it was the way things were and he'd done nothing wrong, shame still burned him and he felt sick with it. Admitting it to Jorrun had eased it a little, but the ghost of it still clung to him.

He glanced at the door, the walls of the room seeming suddenly too close.

'Just be warned,' he told Jagna. 'You've never met anything so fierce.'

He burned the letters in the fireplace and then left Jagna in his room. Cassien followed him out of the inn and into the marketplace.

'I like the sound of your brother's wife, master,' Cassien said behind him.

Osun snorted. 'Yes, you would.'

The address Osun had been given didn't take him to the harbour but to a cobbler's shop on the edge of the poorer part of the city. A few boots hung from long nails beside the small, grimy window.

Osun hesitated to take hold of the rusty door handle.

'Allow me, master.' Cassien stepped forward and pushed the door open, causing a small bell to give a dull, unmelodious thud. Osun waited as Cassien looked around, the young boy nodded and he followed him inside.

The shop was dark and cluttered with tools and materials. One wall was filled with shelves from floor to ceiling that housed wooden lasts. A man stopped his work to look at them, his hammer still clenched in his hand. He looked to be in his forties and was as scruffy as his shop.

'Help you?' he muttered, looking from Osun to Cassien.

'I need two left shoes,' Osun said.

Cassien looked at him as though he'd gone crazy.

The cobbler looked him up and down. 'I think I have your order, what was the name?'

'Osun.'

The cobbler put down his hammer and disappeared into a back room. Cassien swayed from one foot to the other, his hand near his sword.

Osun frowned at Cassien and the boy stopped fidgeting.

The cobbler returned and held out a key to Osun. 'House with the black door on Net Lane. Someone will deliver your shoes there in a couple of days.'

Osun took the key and nodded. 'Thank you.'

As curious as he was, Osun chose not to hang about. He headed straight for the docks and the narrow lane that ran alongside where the fishermen gutted their catch. Cassien wrinkled his face in disgust at the stench and swore when he slipped on some fish guts. There were still some women working alongside their masters despite the fading light. Osun watched one of them deftly using a sharp knife and shuddered, his hand moving to where a scar marked his chest.

They found a black door, but Osun checked the whole lane to be sure there were no others. It also gave him the opportunity to check who was about. As he put the key in the lock, one of the female slaves looked up at him for two heartbeats.

Interesting.

It was dark inside, only a tiny shaft of light leaking in through the closed shutters. They stepped in and let the door bang shut behind them. Osun waited, letting his eyes adjust and straining his ears for any sound. Cassien was eerily silent beside him. When he was confident no one else was around, Osun opened the shutters.

'It's bigger than it looks!' Cassien exclaimed.

The room went back a long way with a fireplace halfway down one wall. There wasn't much in the way of furniture, just a long table and six uncomfortable chairs. There was a door at the far end and Cassien un-bolted it and looked out into a small, paved yard.

'There's an outhouse!' he called in to Osun.

'Come back in and lock the door.' Osun headed for the stairs, his hand on his sword hilt.

There were two bedrooms on the next floor and an attic room with a straw mattress. Osun found a chest and opening it, found some reasonably clean blankets, candles, and flints.

It would do.

'Cassien, can you find your own way back to the Inn?'

'What? Why? Are you staying here?'

Osun raised his hand and Cassien actually flinched.

'Master,' the boy added quickly.

'No, I have work to do. There are a couple of ale and geranna houses I need to visit. I need to know what's been happening in Navere.'

'Then I should come, master, you pay me to protect you.'

Osun snorted. 'I don't pay you and people don't go drinking with their servant!'

Cassien reached up to unclasp his servant's collar.

'What in the gods' name are you doing?' Osun stared at him incredulously.

Cassien stopped, shrugging. 'My job, I thought.'

'Gods, why did I ever buy you! Get yourself back to the Inn, boy, and try not to get into any trouble!'

Cassien let his arms drop to his side.

'Go on!' Osun aimed a kick at him, but the young man dodged it and went out the door with a last hurt look in Osun's direction.

Osun waited a moment before leaving himself, making sure he couldn't see Cassien lurking anywhere before locking the door and placing the key in the purse on his belt. He smiled to himself when the same woman as before glanced up at him ever so briefly.

He headed away from the harbour and toward the richer part of the city, to the main street that eventually followed the high cliff to the caves in which the gods dwelt in their temples. He slowed his steps as he came to the palace. A high wall hid most of the grounds, but the upper stories loomed above them, dark shadows against a blackened sky. Light shone in only four windows and from what he remembered they were the rooms normally occupied by the Coven Lord. Four guards stood at the iron gate, all of them upright and alert, the whites of their eyes showing in the light of the flickering oil lamps. Osun passed them by and turned off the main street, heading toward the noise and brightness of a geranna house.

The door was propped open and smoke from pipes swirled out along with the sickly smells of geranna and sweat. He pushed his way to the bar and took a coin from his purse.

'Spiced or plain?' The barman barely glanced at him.

'Spiced.' Osun winced at the thought of it, he hated the sickly fruit liquor in any form, but it was a necessary evil. He exchanged his coin for a dirty looking horn and moved to the end of the bar. Leaning against the wall, he let his eyes glaze over and concentrated on listening. He let the conversations wash over him, waiting to pick up on any keywords. It was nearly two hours before he heard mention of the palace. He waited until after the conversation had ended and drained his horn. He tried not to let his excitement show as he made his way back out.

The temperature had dropped and he gave an involuntary shiver. As tempting as it was to head straight back to the inn and contact Jorrun, he needed more to back up what he'd heard. He made his way back toward the main street but turned off down a narrow alley. The slight scuff of a shoe was the only warning he got. Osun drew his sword, turning on his toes as he did so. Two men with scarves over the lower parts of their faces blocked the alley, one with a dagger raised, the other with a club resting nonchalantly against his shoulder. The man with the dagger shifted from one foot to the other, glancing at his companion and then looking Osun up and down.

'Your purse!'

Osun frowned at him, lowering his sword a little and improving his stance. 'You confront a man carrying a sword, with only a dagger and a piece of wood, and expect him to just hand over his hard-earned money?'

The left side of 'dagger's' face twitched and he shifted his feet again. 'There's two of us!'

'Thanks, I *can* count.'

Dagger man'sface turned red. Osun moved before he did, hacking off the man's hand and then stabbing him through the stomach. The man with the club had barely moved, but as his companion crumpled, he backed away and raised a hand.

'Shall we both go on our way, brother?'

Osun ground his teeth at the thief addressing him as 'brother,' but he stepped back and lowered his sword again.

'Time was when no one would dare attack anyone in Navere,' he said.

The thief shrugged. 'Times change. Guard's don't care, half the time they don't even know who they're serving, or, more importantly, who's paying.'

'I thought Navere had a new lord?'

The thief snorted. 'Today it's Cepack, who knows who it will be tomorrow? Place has gone to hell since Dunham was murdered and someone burned the temples of Arkoom. A man has to look to himself these days.'

'I'd have thought there'd be plenty of work going?' Osun tensed, waiting for the man to spit. He didn't.

'I'm no servant!'

'Never said you were. There's always need of mercenaries though.'

The man swayed a little. 'Dangerous work, these days, and I'm not stupid. You sign up with a lord and next day someone's trying to overthrow him. Sign up with a merchant and you're hit several times on the road. Dunham scared the shit out of me with all those dead people and blood magic, don't get me wrong, but at least there was stability.'

'Things will settle again.'

'Aye, when all the sorcerers have killed each other! And who will run things then?'

Osun smiled. 'Maybe we will, *brother*.' He sheathed his sword and turning his back, continued along the alley, listening hard to be sure the man didn't follow. He couldn't help a quick look over his shoulder as he got back to the main street. The alley was empty.

He quickened his pace and headed straight toward the palace, running his fingers through his hair to muss it and breathing harder though his mouth to roughen his throat and redden his face. The guards saw him coming and stood up straighter, all but one of them putting a hand to their swords.

'I've just been attacked by thieves!' Osun called out to them. 'Just a few yards from the palace!'

'And?' one of the men demanded.

'And?' Osun's mouth fell open and he stared at them. 'Well, aren't you going to do something?'

'You're alive, aren't you?' one of them muttered.

The first man who'd spoken scowled at his colleague. 'Not our job, I'm afraid, master. We have orders to guard the palace so that's what we do. Try the city guard house, but I wouldn't hold my breath if I were you.'

'What in the Gods' names has become of this city?'

'That's just the thing.' The guard made a swift sign against evil. 'Someone burned down the houses of the Gods and the gods didn't reply. No Dunham, no gods, no fear, and no law.'

Osun let the air out of his lungs and his muscles sagged. He was responsible for this, him and his brother and the fire-spirits who'd risen against the blood magic of Chem. They'd never really thought through the consequences, just assumed they would make things better.

'Thanks,' he muttered.

***

He'd intended to try another geranna house, but he felt too unsettled and headed straight back to the marketplace and the security of the Narwhale Inn. As soon as he turned into the market square, he spotted Cassien walking up and down outside the inn. The boy stopped on seeing him, took a couple of steps toward the door, then thought better of it and waited, head down but watching Osun anxiously.

'Something happen?' Osun demanded.

'Oh! No.' Cassien shook his head. 'I … I just wanted to be sure you got back to the inn.'

Osun sighed. He unbuckled his sword and handed it to Cassien. 'Clean this up then get to sleep. I have a lot to do in the city tomorrow and will be up early.'

Cassien drew the sword a little and his eyes widened at the blood.

'Now!'

Cassien jumped, then with a slight bow, hurried off to his room.

Osun made his way more slowly to his own room and, after locking the door behind him, he took his scrying bowl out of his bag and poured in some water and three drops of blood. It was less than five minutes until his brother's face appeared in the water. Relief surged through Osun.

'Brother, where are you?' he asked.

'The Borrows,' Jorrun replied. 'How are things with you?'

Osun pursed his lips and drew in a deep breath. 'Our plans are going relatively well. Navere is in disarray, the city itself seems to be lost to the coven, Cepack is concentrating on protecting his own hide. If we strike quickly, I think we can take the palace with a minimum of resistance.'

'We'll talk about that when I arrive. I should be there tomorrow night.'

'Come straight to the harbour, to the fisherman's wharf. I'll have my servant meet you and take you straight to a safe house.'

'Into the harbour? Are you sure, Osun?'

'Very.'

'All right. I'll see you soon.'

Chapter Ten

Kesta; Covenet of Chem

Kesta's heartbeat was loud in her ears as the lights of the harbour drew closer, reflected in the dark waters. She leaned out over the railing, her *knowing* cast out wide, watching the narrow walkways for any signs of people.

Jorrun called out from the stern where he controlled the rudder. 'Kesta, you'd best not use your magic just in case anyone senses it.'

Reluctantly she called her *knowing* back. Her shoulders and neck ached with tension and her stomach had tightened into a hard knot. Why oh, why had she said yes to coming back to Chem? She looked back past the cabin to Jorrun's barely perceptible shape. He was why. And Milaiya.

The ship turned abruptly, heading across the harbour towards its eastern end.

'We'll be there in a moment, you'd best get your disguise on.'

Kesta snorted. 'Disguise,' she muttered under her breath. She ducked into the cabin and pulled the Chemman dress on over her tunic and trousers, tucking her dagger into her boot. 'Nearly there, Azra,' she reassured the fire-spirit before pulling the hood down over her head. When she went back out on the deck, it was so dark she could barely see anything through the gauze that covered her eyes. Light flared out and she realised someone had uncovered a lantern on the docks. Jorrun drifted them in toward it and she hurried to take down and secure the sail.

'Can I ask your name, master?'

Kesta looked up to see the person holding the lamp was maybe five years younger than her with a muscular build, dark brown hair, and wide grey eyes.

128

'Raven,' Jorrun replied, jumping out of the ship to tie up. 'Jorrun Raven.'

The boy's eyes narrowed a little and his shoulders sagged. 'This way, master.'

Kesta ducked back inside the cabin to get Azrael's lamp and Jorrun held out his hand to help her onto the wooden gangway. The boy watched her intently as though he expected her to do something crazy any moment. He started when he realised they were waiting and turned to lead them along a path that followed the waterside. It stank of decomposing sea creatures.

The boy stopped outside a house with a black door, knocked twice, then opened it and stepped straight in. Kesta desperately wanted to call up her *knowing*, but Jorrun's previous warning stopped her. He touched her arm, glancing at her, and stepped into the building to look around. He nodded for her to follow. A single candle stood upon a mantlepiece and the boy strode forward to place his lantern on a table in the centre of the long, narrow room. She realised someone was seated there and her hands twitched, wanting to reach for flame.

'Osssun!' Azrael came hurling out of her lantern, singeing the glass as he morphed through it. The boy threw himself back, falling over a chair and almost landing in the fireplace.

'Azra!' Jorrun chastised the Drake.

Osun leapt up and hurried to the boy, reaching out a hand to help him up. 'It's all right, Cassien, Azrael is a friend. He's a fire-spirit.'

Kesta put her lantern down and pulled her hood up off her head. Cassien's eyes caught hers as he stood and he froze, his mouth open.

Osun sighed. 'Cassien, this is Kesta. She is a *Fire-Walker* from the Fulmers and my brother's wife. Kesta, this is my ... this is Cassien. The two of you should get on amazingly well.'

Kesta reached out a hand and the boy visibly flinched, looking at Osun with his eyes wide again. She lowered her arm with a slight shake of her head.

Osun looked at his brother and his eyes softened, a smile pulling at his mouth. 'This is my brother, Jorrun.'

Jorrun strode forward and grabbed his brother in a hug. Osun was slow to respond, but he placed his hands briefly against Jorrun's back. Kesta looked away.

Jorrun pulled out a chair and sat, the others followed suit except Cassien who stood rooted to the spot until Azrael darted to the candle, whereupon the boy almost ran to stand beside Osun's chair.

'Sit down.' Osun gave him a shove.

Cassien flushed and pulled out a seat away from the fireplace.

Kesta swallowed, glancing at Osun before turning to Jorrun. He met her eyes and then asked Osun, 'So, what's our situation?'

Osun scratched his cheek just above his beard. 'Tomorrow someone will visit us here who belongs to the group who contacted me in Margith. They call themselves the Order of the Rowen, I don't know why. They will back anyone who will change the status of women and protect their families.'

Kesta sat back and looked at Osun. He coloured slightly, and she realised she was staring.

'Rowan was the name of a woman who, according to legend, refused every advance and evaded every trick of the gods Monaris and Warenna.' Jorrun leaned forward over the table and Kesta smiled to herself. Jorrun loved his history. 'In the end Monaris lost patience and killed her.'

Kesta's smile vanished. Osun glanced at her and shifted in his chair.

'The name makes sense, then.' Osun nodded slowly. 'Anyway, their representative here in Navere will speak with us tomorrow. Jagna is still in the Narwhale Inn, he doesn't know about this place and very little about you. I'll bring him tomorrow and you can see what you think. He isn't particularly powerful but it will help our status to have the backing of an old, if almost non-existent, family.'

'And the palace?' Jorrun asked.

Osun nodded. 'I'm sure we can get in the way we got out when we were children.'

Cassien made a sound as though he were about to speak, but quickly clamped his mouth shut. Osun ignored him and went on. 'I thought we could take a look together tonight?'

Jorrun nodded.

'Oh.' Osun glanced at Kesta, then got up and went over to a hessian sack near the foot of the stairs. He pulled something out and returned to the table slowly. 'I ... I thought walking Navere at night with Kesta might draw too much attention and ... well, I thought there might be a way for her ...' He gritted his teeth and made himself look at her. Kesta drew her hands down under the table, clenching them into fists. She was aware Jorrun was watching her, barely blinking. 'Lady, I got you these.'

He placed the objects down on the table and withdrew as though he expected them to come to life and attack him. Kesta took in several slow, deep breaths, before reaching out. She lifted a piece of dark brown fleece to find it had been twisted into the shape of a beard, with two wire hooks to fit over her ears. Underneath it was a leather eye patch. A laugh burst out of her.

Osun's eye's widened and a smile twitched at his mouth before vanishing quickly.

Jorrun was smiling, but he shook his head. 'It's a lovely idea, but that won't fool anyone.'

Osun sat down. 'Maybe at night, with a hood ...'

'Maybe, brother,' he said softly, placing a hand on the table.

Osun nodded, glancing at Kesta. 'There's also some food and some oil for Azrael.'

Cassien jumped when the fire-spirit crackled loudly on the mantlepiece. 'Thank you, Ossun. Jorrun, I need to go and speak with the other Drakess.'

'Of course, be careful,' Jorrun frowned.

The fire-spirit darted away from the candle and shot away up the chimney. Kesta realised Osun was watching her and she made herself meet his eyes again. He drummed his fingers silently on the edge of the table, opened his mouth, chewed at his lip, then spoke, his eyes averted again. 'How is Milaiya?'

Kesta froze, her breath caught in her throat, making her cough.

'Shall we go and take a look at the palace?' Jorrun stood quickly.

Osun looked startled, his face coloured. 'Well, yes, all right.'

Kesta's skin grew warmer. Pressure built in her sternum. She drew her arms up and pressed them tightly against her abdomen, trying to hold in her rage. She could feel the three men looking at her and she felt as though something exploded inside her chest, her vision blurred and she shot to her feet, knocking back her chair. Seeing the stairs through the flashes of red she all but ran to them, grabbing the loose rail to pull herself up. She pushed through a door and found herself in a small bedroom.

How dare he!

Without thinking she drew fire to her hands, letting her power build. She blasted flames into the small fireplace, letting them rip through her with her anger. The stones of the chimney cracked, soot blackened the floor and walls.

'Kesta! Stop that now!'

She turned, her power subsiding, breathing hard, every muscle in her body tense. Jorrun let the door close behind him. She expected to see anger, but there was sadness and disappointment in his blue eyes.

'We talked about this.' He reached a hand toward her.

'How could he ask about her?' She clenched and unclenched her fists, not caring about how loud her voice was.

Jorrun closed his eyes briefly and she saw his shoulders rise in a sigh. 'He's trying, Kesta. He can't change what he did but he's sorrie—'

'Sorry?'

'—than you know. You got a glimpse of what Chem was like. In the next few months you'll see worse, you'll see what life is like for children like he and I—'

'Stop making excuses for him!' Her throat was so tight it hurt, but she forced her words out anyway. 'He had a choice. He could have been like you. Your own king ordered you to behave like a Chemman, to have a child with me and you refused. You refused because you knew it was wrong.'

Jorrun opened his mouth and looked away. She saw the muscles of his jaw move before he went on. 'He was forced to come back here when he was only sixteen. The only way to survive in Chem is to not care, to have no empathy. Kindness here ...' He swallowed, blinking rapidly. He shook his head. 'You might as well throw your heart to the sharks.'

'This isn't about kindness. This is about simple right and wrong.'

'How do you know what's right and wrong?'

She let out a scream of frustration. 'Stop it, Jorrun. Or do you want me to hate you too? There is no excuse. None!'

'What do you want me to do, Kesta? What do you want me to say? Do you want me to kill him? Would that be enough?'

'You killed the man who hurt Catya.'

'She was a child, even a Chemman wouldn't touch a child.'

'But a woma—'

'I'm not saying that!' Jorrun's cheeks and neck had reddened and he raised his voice for the first time. 'It was wrong, he was wrong, he understands that now. He can't take it back. He can't do anything to make amends to Milaiya. But he is trying to make things right for the other women of Chem. It was his idea to come back, to see if now was the time. Kest—'

'Just go away.' She could feel pressure building behind her eyes and nose.

'All right.' He nodded. 'Would you like me to leave Cassien downstairs?'

She turned away, gritting her teeth hard and folding her arms over her chest. 'No.'

She heard the door close and span around to see he'd gone. Just like that. She stared at the door, mouth open. She forced air out through her nose, feeling light-headed, she swayed on her feet. Why did he always take Osun's side? She glanced around the room, there was nothing but the bed, nothing for her to take her fury out on. She needed to be outside.

She went to the window and forced it open, letting in the cold night air. It was shockingly quiet for a city, not at all like Taurmaline or vile Arkoom.

There was a small yard down below and a row of taller buildings opposite, blocking her view of everything but a few stars. She studied the walls surrounding the yards, wondering how far she could travel along them through the city without being seen. She couldn't help thinking back over what Jorrun had said, but she shook her head stubbornly. She couldn't forgive Osun. Never.

She made her way quietly down the stairs. The house was empty, the two lanterns and candle still burning. She saw the ridiculous false beard on the table and drew power to her hands, summoning wind. She'd intended to blast it against the wall, table, and all, but with a growl of frustration she let the wind dissipate. Without Osun, then who could they set up as Coven Lord? Who else could they trust to make the changes they wanted, to turn Chem into a better place? The answer was Jorrun. Without Osun, Jorrun would have to take the Seat. She would lose him to Chem.

She sat down in one of the chairs, leaning her forehead against the table. Could she live here if it meant saving all those women?

Could she endure being around Osun?

Yes. If she had to …

But she didn't want to.

***

A quiet buzzing sound slowly seeped into her thoughts and she lifted her head up groggily, realising she'd dozed off. Looking around she saw Azrael had returned and was sucking the oil from one of the lanterns.

'Would you like a bowl?' She yawned.

'Kcssta!' The fire-spirit flipped over and did a loop around her head.

'Come on, let's go up.' She blew out the candle and left one lantern on the table, turning down the wick a little. She checked the door to the street and found it was locked. She lifted Azrael's lantern and took it up to the bedroom she'd instinctively fled to. It was cold with the window open, but she didn't trust the bed to be clean and so lay on top of it, placing the lantern on the floor nearby.

'Did you find the other Drakes?'

'Yess.' Azrael came to hover near the bed. 'They have been watching over the Sseats and the remaining sorcerers. Three there are that possess the power to trap a sspirit. Feren at the Sseat of Harva. Veron of Sseat Letniv and Backra who holds the Sseat at Darva. You and Jorrun are stronger than all of them unless they unite. But ...'

Kesta sat up. 'But what, Azra?'

The fire-spirit made himself small. 'Don't you feel it Kesta?'

She frowned and shook her head. Tentatively, she called up her *knowing*. She felt the distant emotions of the inhabitants of the city, intertwining into an undercurrent of anxiety, fatigue, and fear.

Azrael hissed. 'Look deeper, Kessta!'

It was hard to relax, but she let herself go, sinking into the feel of the sleeping city. It crept in slowly, subtly, something more alien even than the metallic feel of a fire-spirit. A presence: watchful, impatient.

She gasped, drawing back her *knowing* quickly.

'What was that, Azra?'

The fire-spirit made himself smaller still. 'I don't know, but it isn't something good!'

Kesta put her fingers to her lips. She could taste blood in her mouth.

Chapter Eleven

Ayline; Kingdom of Elden

Ayline watched from the tower window, her eyes fixed on the departing longship far below and a feeling of satisfaction built deep inside her. The lake appeared more brown than grey today, the waves larger and more frequent, white foam making hypnotic patterns on the slick, silty shore. Raising her eyes she could just make out the distant forest.

'Do you see that? The witch is going.'

She rubbed at her rounded stomach, shifting a little to sit more comfortably. She loved coming up here. Aside from the fact the views across the harbour and lake were amazing, few people came up to the highest room in the castle and it was incredibly peaceful. Dust covered the floor and the furnishings and white webs criss-crossed in varying states of repair. The busy spiders fascinated her and she watched them as often as the life far down below.

She often wondered who this room had belonged to. Nothing hung on the walls. The chest and drawers were empty. A long unused four-posted bed with a sagging mattress took up most of the space. The only thing that was clean and polished was the chair on which she sat.

The longship moved out onto the lake, growing smaller. If only Larissa had gone too. Bractius was paying the ugly islander far too much attention for her liking. She screwed her face up as she pictured the older woman's light-brown skin, her garish red hair, and those odd eyes. She couldn't understand why people were so captivated by her.

'It's because she is a witch!' she hissed.

Bractius should have been doting on *her*, not distracted by whatever woman turned up at court. He had been delighted at the news of her pregnancy, but the novelty had soon worn off. Days of sickness had left her feeling exhausted and resentful to the point she'd begun to wish she hadn't sought to get herself pregnant. That had in turn brought waves of guilt. It wasn't the baby's fault. Admittedly, it had initially been a ploy to keep her place secure and ensure a hold on her husband, but as it had grown her feelings had changed. The baby had become real.

'My little one.'

She rubbed at her belly again.

She jumped as the door opened, her mouth falling open. No one ever came up here! A servant walked in, carrying a basket of candles.

He stopped in his tracks with a gasp. 'Your majesty! I … I … a thousand pardons!' He stooped in a bow. 'I thought this room was empty.'

He was young, maybe a year or two younger than herself, with thick black hair and a rather handsome face. She swallowed down her anger at the intrusion, intrigued. In the back of her mind she vaguely recalled seeing him around, but only recently.

'What are you doing here?'

The young man remained in his uncomfortable looking bow. 'I'm replenishing the candles in The Tower. I … I sometimes come in here to look at the view. I didn't think anyone else came here.'

'Well, I do.' She retorted imperiously. 'For goodness' sake, stand up straight, you look ridiculous!'

He did so, keeping his eyes downcast. Her back twinged and she shifted in her chair.

The servant immediately darted forward to grab a pillow off the bed. He beat it against his leg and then the bed, dust flying up everywhere.

'Would you allow me, your majesty?'

She nodded, lifting her chin and looking out of the window. She leaned forward to allow him to arrange the pillow behind her on the chair. When she leaned back, the relief was immediate. She looked up and caught his eyes. They were stunning. The colours sharp and almost unnatural, ringed by a dark line that emphasised their brilliance. His long lashes blinked over them and she blushed, realising she was staring.

'Thank you, servant. What's your name?' She looked out of the window rather than at him.

'Inari, your majesty.'

She swallowed. An intriguing name.

'Well, Inari, be aware I do come in here, and I do so for privacy.'

'I'm sorry, your majesty. I won't come agai—'

'I didn't say that, did I?' She spun about and immediately found herself captivated by his eyes again. 'Your job is to replace the candles, but I don't see any in here. See to it.'

'I will, your majesty.'

'Good, now go.'

The young man bowed and left without another word. Ayline's hand went to her throat and she felt her pulse fluttering beneath her fingers. She hadn't been that attracted to a man since, well, since she'd first seen Thane Jorrun.

***

Ayline smiled and chatted her way through dinner with her ladies. With the Fulmer guests gone there was no formal gathering tonight in the great hall and she'd chosen to eat in her own rooms. They were discussing Worvig, some of them insisted he was clumsy, unfriendly, and rough looking. Others argued he looked strong and was intriguing. She glared down at her plate, tearing a piece of bread into small pieces. Worvig was no use to her and of little interest. She was bored with talking about trivial things, she wanted to talk about defences and repairs, about the impact of the war on the people. The very things that the blasted witch, Dia, had spoken of at dinners. When she'd tried to talk of such things with Bractius, he'd just brushed her aside.

She stood up. 'I'm going for a walk.'

The room hushed.

'Would you like me to come with you?' one of the ladies-in-waiting asked timidly.

'No.' She dropped her napkin on her chair and made her way through the corridors. The lamps had been turned down and the castle felt almost eerie. Her feet took her instinctively to the lake tower, and she held on to the bannister as she ascended the narrow, uneven steps, occasionally hearing voices beyond the oak doors.

She was slightly out of breath when she reached the last door at the top. She opened it and peered in. She gasped, her mouth shifting in to a delighted smile. The room was as dusty as ever, but her old wooden chair had been replaced by a comfortable, cushioned one. A small table had been set beside it on which stood a candlestick, a bowl of fruit, a flask, and a cup. Wood had been placed in the grate despite the fact it was early summer and flints were set on the mantle. She walked over to the table, careful of her step in the darkness, the only light coming from the moon that shone through the window overlooking the lake.

She uncorked the flask and sniffed. It seemed to be cold chamomile tea. There was a sweet smell to it though. Honey.

She poured some into the cup and took a careful sip. The flavour was soothing and smooth. It would have been better hot, but she sat back in her chair, snuggling into the cushions, and looked up at the stars.

Inari.

Where had he come from, she wondered, *who could his family be?* No one of consequence if he was a servant. She clenched her jaw and shook her head violently. Daydreaming about a servant wouldn't get her what she wanted.

She'd been born into a family with money, a few connections, and huge ambition. Almost from her birth she'd been schooled to behave and think like a queen. Her parents had hoped for her to marry well and improve their influence, it was her own pride that had set her sights on the greatest prize in the kingdom. Her only moment of doubt had been when she'd seen the Dark Man. Like many she'd been captivated by his power, his mystery. She'd spent many nights imagining what it was he was doing up in his forbidden Raven Tower. But wife to a Thane, sorcerer though he was, didn't fulfil her ambition and Jorrun had turned down the title, even, of Jarl and was frustratingly uninterested in women.

Bractius had been easy to win.

Her victory had been hollow. Her prize had been a loveless marriage and only the illusion of power. Manipulating the lives of her ladies had amused her for a while, but she'd grown tired of it. Then the witches had come to Elden, and she'd caught a glimpse of women with real power, women with true freedom. She gripped the arms of the chair hard. First Kesta had come and stolen Jorrun from her, embarrassing her by making changes to

Northold that all the men admired. Then Dia had saved them all from Chem. Not that Bractius would admit it. She'd tried, asking to be allowed to sit in on the King's audiences and councils, but he'd laughed indulgently and dismissed her.

A dark and dangerous thought crept into her mind. Had a queen ever ruled Elden?

She placed her hands over her belly. If something happened to Bractius, could she rule until her child was old enough? What if it was a girl?

She placed a hand over her mouth as though to still her thoughts, staring at the brightness of the moon.

Would she dare?

'No, baby, I can't.' She stroked her abdomen, but a smile slowly crept onto her face.

***

She awoke with a gasp, breathing fast and clutching at her blankets. Her skin was so flushed she was sweating and she sat up, looking around to be sure no one had observed her. Her fingers went to her lips, her eyes wide. She'd dreamed of him, Inari. It had been an incredibly intimate and passionate dream – and so real!

Shaking herself she went to her dresser and splashed water onto her face. Almost immediately her stomach cramped and nausea rushed up from her stomach, making her retch. She gripped the edge of the wash stand, taking slow, deep breaths until it passed.

'Lerra!' she bellowed.

Moments later a girl of about fourteen fumbled at the door and hurried in. Her blonde hair was mussed and she rubbed at one of her brown eyes. Ayline had taken her on from the Thane of a less affluent Hold, after all, the ladies-in-waiting needed someone to look down on and do the least favourable chores for them. Lerra slept in the chamber just outside the Queen's suite so she could be there the instant she needed her.

'Lerra, find me something to wear that will make me look alluring despite my condition, then I need something plain but not disgusting for breakfast.'

'Yes, your majesty.'

The girl hurried over to the huge closet that took up the entire length of one wall and began searching inside. Ayline sat down at her dresser, gazing into her bronze mirror as she waited. She picked up her brush and slowly eased out the tangles in her chestnut hair, her gaze fixed firmly on her own eyes.

'How about this one, your majesty?' Lerra held up a green gown of shining taffeta with a low neckline. It was one that laced at the back and would possibly still fit. 'We should probably get someone here to measure you for some new dresses,' she suggested, her eyes downcast.

'Yes, get Helled up here this afternoon. Come on, then, let's see if I can get into that!'

Ayline winced and scowled as Lerra did up the laces, but it wasn't as uncomfortable as she'd feared. She joined her other ladies-in-waiting at their communal table. There was some plain porridge and Lerra added some apples spiced with cinnamon, pouring a little hot milk from the kettle on the fireplace over the top of it.

Ayline ate in silence while the ladies talked around her. They were subdued and she knew they were concerned about her mood, but she didn't care. She jumped when one of them dropped her fork and had to force herself to unclench her teeth so she could make herself take another bite of the

143

tasteless food. She couldn't seem to shake off the remnants of her vivid dream.

'Will you be sitting in on the King's audiences today?' One of the ladies asked.

She swallowed back her porridge. 'No, I have something else to do.'

Some of the ladies exchanged glances and Ayline ground her teeth. She forced a smile onto her face. 'Would you be darlings and see if you can gather any more resources for the Borrow refugees? Perhaps you could write letters to your homes and let them know of our noble cause?'

She tried not to roll her eyes at their eager responses. Their so-called noble cause was no more than Bractius's way of keeping the Fulmers onside without having to put his hand in Elden's treasury.

'Thank you, ladies.' She stood and looked around at them all with a smile. 'I knew I could rely on you.'

She pushed away from the table and left her quarters without another word.

There were more people about in the hallways in the daytime, all of whom stopped in their tracks to bow to her. As she came to the stairway to the tower, she took a quick look around to ensure no one was watching, before going through the door and heading up.

She opened the door to her tower room cautiously, only to find it empty, however her breath caught when she saw a vase of flowers standing on the old, dusty chest. She walked over and touched the edges of the petals gently with the backs of her fingers. She realised the cup and flask had been changed. When she uncorked it and took a small sip, she found this one was peppermint with just a hint of fennel. She sat in the chair and waited, picking up an old, withered apple and taking little bites. It was rather dry and grainy but the baby seemed happy with it.

It was only about half an hour later that she jumped as a soft knock sounded at the door. She tensed, straightening her spine and holding her breath.

The door creaked open and she turned to see Inari tentatively looking in.

'Come in, boy,' she said.

He stepped in and closed the door. 'I'm sorry to disturb you, your majesty, I came to see if you needed a fresh candle yet.'

'Not yet,' she replied, looking out of the window and raising her chin. She tried to ignore the fact her heart was racing. 'Are you responsible for the changes in this room?'

There was a moment before he replied. 'Yes, your majesty. I wanted you to be comfortable.'

'I see. It could do with a clean, but I like the spiders.'

'Not many people appreciate the beauty of spiders, your majesty.'

She narrowed her eyes, wondering what he meant by that. 'I preferred the chamomile tea.'

'Of course, your majesty. I'd heard peppermint was good for pregnancy.'

'What would you know about pregnancy?'

'I've been asking for advice, so I can best know how to be of assistance to you.'

She turned to look at him, he cast his eyes to the ground quickly in a deferential manner. 'My pregnancy is none of your business.'

'Yes, your majesty.'

She shifted in her chair.

'Is your chair not comfortable, your majesty?' he asked in concern.

'It's adequate,' she replied. 'It must have been heavy to bring up all those stairs?'

He shrugged. 'It was no more than my duty.'

She rolled her shoulders against the ache there.

'I could ...' He looked away, his face colouring a little.

'What?' she demanded. 'Speak!'

'Would you like me to rub your shoulders and back?'

Her mouth fell open a little at his impertinence and heat rose to her cheeks. 'Not many would be bold enough to suggest touching the Queen!'

'My intent is only to be of help, your majesty, not to offend.'

She held her breath, looking out of the window toward the lake. 'Very well. You may try.'

He walked slowly up behind her and her pulse quickened, it was an effort to breathe slowly. His fingers settled so lightly on her shoulders that she barely felt them at first, then he seemed to gain confidence and they dug in deeply into her tense muscles. She let out an involuntary groan of pleasure and bit her bottom lip in embarrassment. Looking up she caught his reflection in the window; he was looking right at her.

He really did have the loveliest green eyes.

Chapter Twelve

Jorrun; Covenet of Chem

Jorrun drew in a deep breath before unlocking and opening the door. The room was empty, only one lamp lit, the flame dancing a little despite being behind glass. The house smelt damp, almost sandy. He listened for a moment before making his way quietly up the stairs. The cold draft under the door worried him, it wouldn't have surprised him if Kesta had left out a window. When he saw her on the bed his muscles relaxed. He sighed when he saw she wasn't using the blankets, the chill air was lifting the hairs on his arms.

He made his way back down and into the narrow lane, checking no one was around before heading to his ship. He took the blankets off the bed and picked up both Kesta's and his own travel bag. He started at the sound of two cats fighting somewhere in the docks. Trying not to hurry, he made his way back, not wanting to appear anxious or vulnerable should anyone be watching. He dropped the bags by the fireplace and went to lock the door before going back up the stairs. Kesta hadn't moved. He carefully covered her in a blanket, the fact she didn't stir made him suspect she was awake.

He rubbed at his beard with the back of his hand, tempted to speak. He clenched his jaw instead and made his way back downstairs.

Osun and Cassien had both been subdued as they'd left the safe house. Osun frowning and pulling at the button on his jacket, Cassien glancing wide-eyed from one of them to the other. Jorrun wondered how much the young man had heard and understood. He'd tried to draw Osun out in conversation, concerned that, having had his attempts at friendship so violently rebuffed, Osun would resort to being surly and even spiteful again.

It had taken Osun a measure of courage to confess his feelings regarding Milaiya to him on their journey to Elden while Kesta recovered. Jorrun had kept his own emotions to himself, letting his brother speak. The truth was that to say he was disappointed in Osun was an understatement. Had Osun abused Milaiya in Elden, had it been anyone but his brother, Jorrun would have reacted in the same way as Kesta.

He sat down at the table, rubbing at his temples with two fingers as a headache began to nag there. He didn't want to have to take sides between Kesta and Osun, his heart and conscience wouldn't hesitate to choose her, but for the sake of every other woman in Chem they needed Osun. They needed his knowledge, his contacts, and they needed him to take the role of Overlord if he were ever to escape this cursed land for good. And he couldn't bear to hate his brother even though he hated what he'd done. His nostrils flared and he felt heat rise to the skin of his cheeks, he forced his hands to lie flat on the smooth wood of the table.

'Jorrun?'

He opened his eyes to see Azrael wriggling through the hole he'd melted in the glass of the lantern.

'Won't you ssleep?'

'I can't sleep, bug.'

'I hate it when you and Kessta fight.'

'I don't like it much, either.' He sat back, regarding the fire-spirit, and sighed. 'It will be all right, Azrael. So, what did you discover?'

Azrael told him everything he'd told Kesta.

'I don't feel anything.' He frowned. 'But then I don't have yours or Kesta's ability. Could it just be the undercurrent of fear in the land because there is so much uncertainty?'

148

Azrael changed his shape to form two shoulders which he enlarged in the imitation of a shrug. Jorrun couldn't help but laugh.

'Well, tell me if anything changes, crazy bug.'

'I will, stubborn human!'

***

Jorrun paused in his reading, hearing the creak of the door upstairs, and immediately his heart pulsed faster. She came down the stairs as quietly as a hunting cat and he pretended to be concentrating on the words in front of him.

'Good morning,' Kesta placed a hand on his shoulder and kissed his cheek. Jorrun let out the air he'd been holding in his lungs. 'Thank you for the blanket. Did you not sleep?'

She stalked over to the chair opposite him, leaning back and folding her arms.

She was still angry.

'I've been too on edge to sleep. I think it's just being back in Che—'

'Look, Jorrun.' She unfolded her arms and leaned towards him. 'I'll never be able to forgive Osun, but I understand that we need him. And that he is your brother. He took me off guard asking about Milaiya but I'll try harder.'

'I'm angry with him too, Kesta, but if you condemn him you have to condemn nearly every grown man in Chem.'

She swallowed, her face reddening a little and her fingers twitching into fists. She held his gaze. 'Is it really that bad here?'

'It is.'

They stood up at the same time and he pulled her into a hug. The tension in his heart eased.

'Of course, you realise I do condemn all Chemmen,' she said, her breath warm against his neck.

He laughed. 'Good. So do I. Kesta.' He stepped back to look down at her, anxiety was like a claw climbing up the inside of his ribs. 'I should warn you of what we are likely to find when we enter the palace.'

Her brows drew together and her green eyes, emerald and spring-leaf, gazed up at him unblinking. 'Do I need to sit?'

He nodded. 'Azrael, come out and listen too.'

The fire-spirit made them both jump by appearing not from the lamp, but from out of the chimney.

Jorrun sat down and Kesta followed suit slowly. He kept hold of the ends of her fingers.

'When a coven is taken over, the new members of the coven first make sure they eliminate any potential enemies and remove anyone who might seek revenge for their fathers.' He drew in a deep breath. 'They slaughter any male child over the age of three.'

Kesta drew her hand away, her olive skin turning ashen.

'They then ...' He closed his eyes, his words catching in his throat. He couldn't say it. He felt sick even thinking about it.

Kesta moved to kneel before him, placing one hand on his knee and reaching up to touch his cheek with the other. 'It's okay, don't tell me.'

He was so glad she wasn't using her *knowing*, he didn't want her to have to feel what he was feeling.

He opened his mouth and forced himself to look down at her. 'The women in the palace will have been through probably the worst time in their lives. When we arrive and take the Seat, they will expect the same from us. Kes, they'll need you and your *knowing*.'

She nodded, blinking rapidly.

'What of me?' Azrael demanded, chasing his tail in a loop.

Jorrun smiled, although his nose and throat itched and pressure built behind his eyes. 'You, bug, can be incredibly comforting when you want to be. You shall guard the ladies for me.'

Kesta grabbed for the table as the room seemed to shudder, Jorrun had drawn power to his fingertips before he realised what it was. Something he hadn't felt since he was a young boy. The candle toppled from the mantlepiece and Kesta scrambled to her feet. Azrael made himself large, pulling faces frantically at every corner of the room. The room stilled. Kesta turned to speak, but it came again, the table and chairs rattled against the floor, dust fell from the stone walls. Kesta drew her dagger and turned to look at him, she froze on seeing his expression, her fear turning into annoyance.

'Why are you laughing at me?' she demanded.

He tried hard not to grin, but his face muscles just wouldn't obey. The room juddered to stillness. 'I've never seen anyone try to fight an earthquake before!'

'An earthquake?' she growled and sheathed her dagger.

'Chem is volcanic.' His chest still tingled with the need to laugh, but he didn't dare. Instead he turned to Azrael who was still contorting his shape. 'Calm down, bug. Earthquakes are relatively common and we ...' He stopped. It had been a long time since he'd ever thought of Chem as something he considered 'we.' 'In Chem they still have an occasional volcano erupt. The quakes are unsettling but most of the time nothing to fear. There hasn't been a bad one in many years.'

'I'll give you something to fear.' She made to stamp on his foot, but he withdrew it in time.

'I'm sorry.' He managed to straighten his face, his jaw ached.

She shook her head at him then strode forward to kiss him. 'I love it when you laugh.'

'I am here, you know.' Azrael protested.

'Sorry, Azrael.' Kesta squeezed Jorrun's arm and stepped back. 'So how did it go last night? Did you find what you'd hoped at the palace?'

He turned to look toward the door. It hadn't been easy returning to his old prison, his childhood hell. He might have been young at the time, but the night of his escape was still burned into his soul. His mother had gone *walking* in the flame, but she never awoke, falling dead against the carpet. His first thought, even at his age, had been, *she is free*. Azrael had emerged from the fire, Osun placing himself between Jorrun and the fire-spirit with nothing more than a broom to defend them, but the spirit had told them to follow him, that he was sent by Naderra.

They'd followed the fire-spirit along the corridors, Jorrun holding onto Osun's hand so tightly he must have hurt him. He still remembered how the corridors had fractured into rainbows in his vision. They'd fled the palace out into the streets of Navere, Azrael telling them they had to get far away. Jorrun had stopped and turned toward the south, smelling the sea. Without a word he'd summoned the last of his strength to run to the docks, choosing a small boat and climbing within. Azrael had gone crazy then, cursing and darting about, but Jorrun had stood firm. They were leaving Chem, they were going south. Osun had stared at him for some time, his posture changing, his back straightening before he'd bowed and said, 'Yes, master.' They hadn't given Azrael any choice, fire-spirit or no, only to go with them or burn the boat out from under them. Azrael had relented on the condition they grab him a lamp and oil.

They'd untied, pushing away from the dock and allowing the north wind and the sea to take them where it willed. Osun hadn't teased Jorrun as his nose and eyes had run, only cleaned his face silently, as though he were a much younger child and not one who had seen ...

'Jorrun?' Kesta asked gently.

He shook himself. 'I'm sorry. Yes. It looked as though the way we escaped will be the best route in. Azra, will you check it for us later?'

'Of course!' He buzzed.

***

Osun arrived about an hour after sunrise. Young Cassien was carrying a basket laden with food as well as a kettle and a bucket of water. Jorrun couldn't help but watch Kesta's reaction. She glanced only briefly at Osun, but darted forward at once to help Cassien.

'Jagna is just running an errand for me and will be along shortly. We brought breakfast,' Osun announced.

'That was kind of you,' Kesta replied without looking at him.

Jorrun relaxed a little, it was a start.

Kesta lit the fire and Azrael came back out from up the chimney, Cassien didn't seem to know who to follow the most with his wide-eyed stare, Kesta or the fire-spirit. Osun and Kesta silently helped Cassien lay things out on the table, Jorrun realised he was standing there staring and filled the kettle to set it on the fire.

He took in a deep breath. 'I want to take the palace tonight.'

They all turned to stare at him.

'Tonight?' Osun placed a bowl of nuts slowly on the table. 'Do you not want to wait and see what help the Rowen Order can offer?'

He shook his head. 'Kesta, Azrael, and I can take the palace. Brother, are you ready to take charge of the Seat?'

Cassien's mouth fell open and he dropped the cup he was holding.

Osun visibly paled. He nodded once. 'I was hoping to set a few other things in place first. I don't know anything about running a palace, let alone a city.'

'Jorrun and I both have experience of running a Hold.' Kesta looked up at Jorrun rather than Osun. 'So, we can help.'

'Can we wait and see what the Order have to offer, before you decide for sure?'

'All right.' Jorrun looked down at his hands, his stomach muscles tightening. He needed it done, his demons faced and over with. But Osun was right, they shouldn't rush it. He realised Kesta was watching him, even without her *knowing* she could tell when something was wrong. He placed a hand briefly against her back as he moved past to take the kettle off the fire.

'Master,' Cassien spoke quietly to Osun, his voice tentative. Jorrun didn't look up, taking the kettle to the table. 'What's happening?'

Osun folded his arms over his chest. 'You don't need to get involved, boy. I'll see you get a safe job.'

'I never said that.' Cassien raised his voice. 'Look, I'm not stupid, I've pieced it together, but I don't know why or who you are. You freed me to fight for you, I'm happy to do it. And I know I'm just a servant, but it would be helpful if I knew what I was in for.'

Kesta touched Jorrun's hand and said quietly, 'Osun was right, I do like Cassien.'

'Tell him, Osun.' Jorrun looked up at his brother.

Osun sighed. 'If you're determined to stick your nose in, then all right. Since you're useless at being a servant, you might as well be one of us. Jorrun and I are the sons of Dryn Dunham. We have come to take his Seat, but intend to give freedom to and protect the women of the Palace. That's as much as you need to know for now.'

'I knew it!' Cassien clenched his fists, his eyes alight. 'I knew you were a good man!'

Osun flushed, both he and Jorrun glanced at Kesta to see her reaction.

Her shoulders rose as she took in a deep breath. Lifting her head she turned to Cassien. 'Shouldn't you be taking that collar off?'

His grey eyes widened, and he reached up for the clasp on the copper collar.

'Come on, let's eat.' Kesta pulled out a chair. 'We don't know when we'll get another chance.'

Cassien didn't hesitate to take advantage of his new-found status. He sat opposite Kesta at the table, trying not to be rude and look at her eyes too much. Jorrun smiled to himself, he couldn't blame the boy, he'd struggled not to be transfixed by her when he'd first seen her.

'Um, I've heard tales about the Fulmers.' Cassien pushed at his food.

Jorrun looked around the table, there was no meat at all, so Osun was still trying despite Kesta's outburst.

'If the tales you heard are anything like the book on Fulmer magic I read in Elden, then they'll be wildly inaccurate.' Kesta grinned. 'First of all, I'm not a witch.'

Cassien leaned forward across the table. 'But you have magic?'

She nodded. 'I'm not as strong as Jorrun, nor indeed, my mother, the Icante, but yes I do.'

'And women really rule the islands?'

'They really do.'

'An—'

'Cassien, let the lady eat,' Osun interrupted.

Jorrun looked at his brother. Even in Elden, Osun had been unable to form any attachments to people. As far as he could recall Osun hadn't shed a tear when his own mother had been killed by Karinna, instead developing a cold anger that had burned for years. Jorrun's mother's death had been different, Osun had sobbed quietly, somehow still keeping his dignity. Osun's half-hidden concern for Milaiya had been a breakthrough, his attempts at friendship with Kesta gave Jorrun hope. But this; something in Cassien had allowed his brother to care in a way he hadn't with anyone except … except himself. Jorrun looked harder at Cassien. His naivety, his courage, his refusal to be shaped by Chem. The boy was just like him. Osun had found himself a new little brother.

'I don't mind, Osun.' Kesta turned to look at him, her nostrils flared but she held his eyes.

Someone knocked at the door. Cassien stood, glancing around the table.

'Go on,' Osun said.

Cassien drew his sword and went to the door. Jorrun felt Kesta call power and found his own fingers twitching.

'My *knowing* suggests it's one person, nervous,' she said. 'No aggression or deception.'

'Let them in!' he called to the boy.

Cassien nodded and opened the door.

A young man with severely short-cropped blond hair and the wisp of a beard stood there, his green eyes glanced across all of them in the room. Jorrun heard a small gasp from Kesta.

'It's Jagna,' Osun said, standing.

The man stepped in and Cassien closed the door behind him.

'Problem?' Jorrun asked Kesta under his breath.

'No, nothing.' But she shifted in her chair.

Osun introduced everyone, then asked the Chemman sorcerer, 'How did it go?'

Jagna winced. 'If I'm honest, not that good.'

'Jagna went to speak with the man who sheltered him when his family were slaughtered,' Osun explained. 'He was a weak sorcerer of family Delphan, who allied with the Dunham's rather than face death.'

'I don't think we can trust him.' Jagna gave a shake of his head. 'He put his neck on the line for me for the sake of his friendship with my father, but was quick to get me out of his home. He'll turn with the tide, he is still a coward. He also ... well, I don't think he will ever back a plan that gives power to women.' He turned to look Kesta up and down. Jorrun felt his hackles rise in a way they hadn't with Cassien.

Osun sighed. 'Never mind. Thanks for trying, and for not betraying us.'

Jagna drew himself up. 'I'm not a betrayer!'

Osun waved a hand at him. 'No, but you don't have much reason to be loyal to us as yet and what we are attempting is rad—'

'There are people outside,' Kesta warned them. 'Three, I think.'

Cassien got up and drew his sword again, moving quietly to the door.

'What do you feel?' Jorrun asked Kesta.

She closed her eyes, fine lines wrinkling above her nose. 'Anxiety, close to fear in the case of one. Excitement. No aggression.'

Cassien relaxed his stance a little, changing his grip on his sword. Even so he jumped when someone knocked firmly. Cassien looked to Jorrun, and he nodded. Azrael moved to attach himself to the candle on the mantle.

Standing back as much as he could, Cassien opened the door.

Two men and a woman stood there. One man in his early fifties with neat grey hair and a short-clipped beard, the other in his mid-twenties with dark brown hair. The woman was perhaps early forties with the short veil of a worker, her hair pinned back in a bun. All of them had brown eyes and wore the threadbare and practical clothing of labourers.

A small smile came to Osun's lips when he saw the woman.

Jorrun stood. 'Come on in.'

They did so cautiously, their eyes going mostly to Kesta. Jorrun turned to his brother, it was important that he start to take the lead.

'Will you introduce yourselves?' Osun asked. 'The lady I have met, gutting fish out in the lane there.'

The veiled woman turned quickly to look at the oldest of her companions.

Osun raised a hand. 'Don't worry, you did nothing wrong. I've survived by not missing the smallest of things.'

'What gave me away?' She tilted her head slightly.

'A woman in Chem does not look up at a man she doesn't know without the incentive of fear, or the backing of courage. From the fact you speak to me now, you confirm you have been given courage.'

She swallowed and nodded.

'Let me introduce everyone.' Osun went around the room, missing out Azrael.

The older man spoke. 'As you know, we are of the Rowen Order. My name is Anador, my wife is Loruth, and this is our son, Marda. We are just fisher folk, but we'll be your contacts in Navere for the moment. Balten sent word that you would need resources?'

'Sit, please.' Osun offered his own chair so there were enough for them all but himself to sit down. Jorrun watched with admiration at how easily Osun adapted to what he needed to be, to put the family at ease. There was a frown on Kesta's face as she concentrated on the emotions in the room.

'The resources I actually need are people.' Osun rubbed at his beard. 'I will need good clerks and administrators who I can trust to get this city back on track. I need to know who among the guardsmen I can rely on to restore order and law. Are they things you think you can find?'

The three from the Rowen Order looked at each other. It was the son who spoke. 'Maybe. We'll see what we can do.'

Osun nodded. 'We may not be here tomorrow, but one of us here will come back to this house to meet you when we can.'

Anador chewed at the inside of his lip, regarding all of them. He nodded. 'Very well. We will start spreading the word and see what people we can find for you. If ... When you take the palace, will you take our women there to keep them safe?'

'Of course!' Osun's brows drew together. 'As safe as we can. It might be worth waiting until we're certain we are secure though.'

Anador glanced at his wife. 'We'll get going then. Gods be with you.'

Jorrun saw Osun wince, his brother never did rely on the gods.

They waited until the fisherfolk had left, then Osun turned to Jorrun. 'What do you think?'

'I think I still want to take the palace tonight. The longer we wait, the more chance of us being discovered or betrayed.' He held his brother's gaze.

'They felt honest enough to me,' Kesta said. 'But I think you're right, the more people they go to, the more chance of betrayal.'

Osun sat down on one of the now empty chairs. 'All right. Let's do it. Jagna, if you want to sit this ou—'

'No way!' The Chemman's face reddened a little. 'I've spent too much of my life hiding. If I'm going to join a coven, then I need to fight for it, same as the rest of you.' He looked at Kesta as he finished speaking and Jorrun wondered if he resented a woman having more power and more involvement than him.

'Let's get some rest and meet here this afternoon,' Jorrun suggested.

Osun looked from him to Kesta, his eyes narrowed.

Kesta bit her lower lip, then stood slowly. 'Osun, before you go Jorrun and I wanted to show you that book we told you about.'

Jorrun looked at her, trying to hide his confusion. Osun understood a moment before he did. 'Ah, yes, thank you, Kesta.'

'Come on up.' Kesta went to the stairs and ran lightly up. They followed her into her room. 'Sorry,' she said quietly. 'That was the best I could think of. The two of you need to speak alone without offending the others, particularly Jagna?'

Osun smiled and nodded.

'You reacted when Jagna came in, is something wrong?' Jorrun asked her.

She shook her head, but frowned a little. 'No. It was silly, really, but his eyes startled me, they reminded me of a dream I had. He seems genuine to me, but I was surprised I could read him. Does he not have an amulet?'

'No, he was a boy when he was hidden away from the Dunhams and never obtained one,' Jorrun replied. 'Do you think we can trust him?'

She shrugged. 'As far as I can tell, yes, but it's not impossible to fool a *walker*. I'd better go back down.'

Jorrun watched her as she left the room and then turned to his brother. 'We can do this, Osun. We dreamed of avenging our mothers and we did it. We can change Chem.'

'I never wanted this, though.' Osun looked scared. 'The height of my ambition ended with owning my own shop! You would be better at ruling than me.'

Jorrun felt guilt crawl across his skin, knowing he was being selfish. 'Osun, I've seen you become whatever it was needed for you to be, it is better that it's you. Imagine people's reaction if the Dark Man of Elden took the Seat? Another Dunham sorcerer. No. It needs to be a bloodless slave. We need to turn Chem upside down and give the country back to those that deserve it, including the women.

'We need to be the Coven of the Raven.'

Chapter Thirteen

Kesta; Covenet of Chem

Both Jagna and Cassien's eyes followed Kesta as she returned to the downstairs room. She forced a smile, feeling incredibly self-conscious. She picked up a piece of coal and encouraged Azrael to come down off the candle to try to take their attention away from her.

'What's this book then?' Jagna asked. Kesta could feel his suspicion.

'The night Osun killed Dryn Dunham, we found a book.' She sat down and turned one of the cups on the table around slowly with her fingers. 'It was covered in strange symbols, writing that none of us recognised.'

Cassien gasped. 'So, it really was Osun who killed Dryn Dunham?'

'Can I see the book?' Jagna asked. 'I lived with a scholar for a while, I might recognise it.'

She managed to maintain her smile, hoping Jorrun still carried the book everywhere with him. She went to the stairs and shouted up, 'Jorrun! Jagna would love to see the book!'

She returned to her seat, her heart beating just a little faster.

Only moments later she heard the door above open and footsteps coming down the stairs. She breathed out, her muscles relaxing, when she saw the small green book in Jorrun's hand.

Jagna stood up at once, Jorrun tilting his head slightly to regard him as he handed it over.

'What happened to it?' Jagna demanded, barely looking up as he examined the deep, narrow hole that ran through several pages.

'It saved my life from a dagger,' Kesta told him.

162

He looked up at her, eyes wide, then went back to examining it. 'I think it's from the Borrows.'

'The Borrows?' Kesta moved closer to Jorrun. 'Do they even write?'

'Rarely, and they use old runes like this. Of course, I can't be sure, and I can't tell you what it says I'm afraid. Look at the cover.' Jagna ran a finger over it. 'Here in Chem we mostly use leather, but this is plant fibre, probably hemp, like they use in Elden,'

'And the Fulmers,' Kesta added.

'That, I didn't know.' He looked directly at her and she glanced away, closing down her *knowing*. Sometimes it was best not to know what people were feeling.

He handed the book back to Jorrun.

'Come on, let's get back to the inn,' Osun suggested. 'It's going to be a long night, tonight.'

Jorrun gave him a brief nod.

When the others had left, Jorrun sat at the table, looking down at his hands folded in his lap. Kesta sat beside him.

'You're worried?'

He looked up at her. 'I'd be stupid not to be.'

She drew in a deep breath and let it out slowly. She could try to reassure him, but he was a clever man and would have thought through everything himself already, many times over. 'I'm very proud of you.'

He turned to look at her in surprise.

'No, really.' She felt her face warm. 'We could have considered saving Elden and the Fulmers enough and walked away, but you want to save Chem too, a country you have every reason to hate. And I love that you're willing to deal with the consequences of your actions and fix the mess we made.'

He looked away and sighed, a frown forming above his blue eyes. 'I wanted chaos, I wanted a chance for those who could change things to come forth. I hadn't accounted for the suffering people would experience in the meantime because there was no one to show them the way.'

'Can there be a revolution without someone having to pay for it somewhere?' She placed a hand on his leg.

'Fire burnss.' Azrael drifted in front of him. 'But from ashess new things grow.'

'Not comforting for those who are burnt.' Jorrun snorted.

'How about … you can't make an omelette without breaking eggs?' She grinned at him.

He looked up and smiled, shaking his head. 'Thank you, both of you.'

'We'll make sure we do things properly,' she said. 'Set up a firm foundation we can feel confident in leaving.'

He opened his mouth but didn't reply. She wished she hadn't closed down her *knowing*, to use it now would be too obvious. 'Go and catch up on some sleep, I'll tidy this lot up.' She nodded toward the table.

He sighed. 'All right.'

***

Kesta considered going up to get some sleep herself but, despite her restless night, she found herself unable to sit still. Had she been anywhere but Chem she'd have gone out for a long walk. She really needed to be outside. She went to the yard door and opened it, looking out at grey stone and wooden fencing that was green with slime. The sound of gulls was incessant and the smell of the docks strong. Underneath it was the scent of the sea and she raised her face to feel the warm wind against her face. The light grew brighter behind her closed lids and she smiled.

'Are you missing Elden, yet, Azrael?'

She opened her eyes and looked up at the fire-spirit.

'Thiss was my home for decadess,' he crackled. 'Well, asss much as any place above the ground and away from the fire realm could be. We ussed to wait for the pressure in the volcanoess to build and come shooting up. Whoooosh!'

Azrael shot up into the air, spinning like a mad thing, then drifted down like a falling leaf, his fiery arms behind his head. Kesta laughed in delight, but her joy faded. 'Do you miss the fire realm, Azra? What possessed you to make a bargain that would leave you trapped here for eternity?'

He came to hover not far from her face, making himself small again. 'A plea from a soul we all loved.'

'Jorrun's mother, Naderra?'

Azrael dipped briefly. 'Yesss. And two boys we thought might change the world.'

She blinked at that. She loved Jorrun and certainly respected and admired him, but to think of him as someone who was destined to change the world was somewhat overwhelming. As for Osun … And Doroquael had come through from the fire realm for her mother, Dia. Did the fire-spirits presume a great destiny for the Icante also?

She regarded the little fire-spirit, looking into his flaming blue eyes as he gazed back. What were the fire-spirits up to?

'I hope you two aren't up to no good.'

Kesta jumped, gritting her teeth. She hated that he could creep up on her.

'Of course not.' She turned and smiled at Jorrun, trying to hide the fact he'd startled her, but of course he knew.

'Did you not get any sleep? I thought you might come up.'

'I'm fine. Come on in, Azra.' She waited until the fire-spirit had bobbed in and closed and bolted the door.

'I'm going to the ship to get the rest of the things we might need; would you like to come?'

'Oh, I'd love to!' She went over to the table and picked up the fleece. 'Which do you think, the beard or the hood?' She turned around to see he was smiling, but shaking his head.

She rolled her eyes. 'Oh, all right, the hood then.'

She pulled it down over her head and folded her arms across her chest.

Jorrun opened his mouth and sighed. 'It won't be for long.'

They stepped out into the lane and Kesta let her shoulders drop and lowered her head, opening up her *knowing* to warn her of any trouble. It was hard not to give into the temptation to look around. As before, women lined the wharf, sorting and gutting fish, packing some of them in salt. It reminded her of the dead warriors she'd seen being transported from Chem months before and a shiver ran down her spine. She recognised Loruth. The woman from the Rowan Order didn't pause in her work or acknowledge them in any way.

Jorrun's ship seemed untouched and he unlocked the cabin, checking it was clear before holding out his hand to invite her in. As soon as the door was shut, she pulled off the hood and drew in air as though she'd been holding her breath the whole time.

'What do we need?' she asked.

'Once we enter the palace it's unlikely we'll be able to leave for a while.' His eyes glanced over the objects on the cluttered table. 'We'll have

166

to stay and hold it until we're certain it's secure, so take anything you deem essential, but bear in mind we'll be climbing and fighting our way into the palace.'

She shrugged. 'I need nothing but my dagger.'

He turned to look at her, his eyes searching hers, although he had returned to his usual habit of hiding his feelings behind a relaxed and expressionless face. 'It's hard to know whether it would be safest to leave things here or in the safehouse.'

'Then let's divide things between the two.'

He nodded but his attention was still on the table.

'Jorrun, are you worrying about your books?'

He looked up at her, a slight smile playing on his lips and a little colour touching his cheeks. 'You know me too well.'

'Bring the most precious ones and we'll see if we can find somewhere to hide them in the house. We can always get Cassien to come and get them later. I'm surprised you risked bringing any.'

'You don't go anywhere without your dagger, I don't go anywhere without my books.'

She touched his arm and smiled to herself.

He picked out about a dozen of them, then changed two. He also selected several packages of incense. Kesta opened the cabin window while she waited, wishing she could stand out on the deck. It would be months, possibly even years, before they sailed this ship back across the sea to Elden.

She realised Jorrun had stopped packing. His shoulders rose and fell in a sigh.

'Come on,' he said. 'Let's go.'

A fishing boat was coming in as they stepped across onto the wharf, a trail of seabirds screaming behind it. The light was starting to fade and Kesta's stomach muscles tightened a little.

They hadn't long returned before the others knocked at the door. All three of them now wore swords and Cassien was wearing a leather jacket with a patch of chainmail sewn onto the breast and a narrow strip of it along the length of the spine. He held himself a little taller, a little surer. Kesta smiled, glad for the young man. Then nausea flipped her stomach over at the thought Osun might be doting on this boy to compensate for what he'd done to Milaiya.

No one seemed comfortable sitting down. Gritting her teeth and taking in a breath, Kesta eased her own nerves before calling up her *knowing* to subtly send out calm.

Jagna leapt to his feet. 'What are you doing?' He stared at Kesta, drawing his own power.

Jorrun stepped forward to put himself between the Chemman and Kesta. 'She is taking the edge off our nerves.' His eyes were hard, the Dark Man was back.

Jagna looked past Jorrun to glare at Kesta. 'Don't use your Fulmer magic on me!'

She drew back her *knowing*, but Jorrun glanced over his shoulder and reaching into his shirt drew out his amulet and pulled it up over his head. 'I'd give this to you, Jagna, but it belonged to my mother. Kesta.' He turned and faced her. 'I for one would be grateful for any courage you can lend me.'

'You have more than enough of your own.' She smiled, ignoring Jagna's glare. 'I was just trying to help everyone relax. It's a while until we go to the palace and this much tension so early on won't help any of us.'

'I don't like magic being used on me,' Jagna grumbled, but he sat down.

'I can understand that.' Kesta nodded, not calling back her *knowing* but altering her tone and posture subtly. Jorrun took her cue and sat down.

'Tell me about the palace.' Kesta forced herself to look at Osun.

'Of course.' He leaned forward, a frown on his face, before looking up to speak. 'It's a long time since I was there, but I was able to access most areas of it when I was a child. There is a huge library.' He grinned at Jorrun. 'There are secret cupboards in it that hide stairs to take you up to the higher levels. The gardens aren't as big as Arkoom ...'

Kesta watched as the others in the room began to settle in their chairs, Azrael perching on his candle. She had to admit Osun had a lovely voice, soothing and melodious. She got up and quietly put out the leftovers from their breakfast while they listened, Cassien and Jagna eventually joining in to talk of Navere. She didn't like how quiet Jorrun had become. He looked down at the amulet in his hand, turning it over occasionally.

'It's time,' he said without looking up.

The others slowly ceased their conversation as his quiet words sunk in.

Darkness had crept up on them, kept away by Azrael's soft glow.

Kesta nodded at Jorrun and went upstairs to put her trousers and tunic on under her dress, sliding her dagger into one of her long boots. She rejoined the others quickly, wanting to put on the false beard to make them all laugh. One look at Jorrun's face changed her mind. She pulled the hood down over her face without a word.

Jorrun turned to the fire-spirit. 'Azra, you know where to meet us.'

Azrael detached himself from the candle and disappeared up the chimney.

***

Osun and Jagna took the lead as they left the safehouse and headed along the lane, Jorrun stepped in beside Kesta and Cassien walked at the rear. There were no lanterns lit as they made their way through the streets, the only light coming from the windows of the buildings around them.

'Shall I use my *knowing*?' Kesta asked under her breath.

Jorrun drew in a breath, chewed on his lip and narrowed his eyes. He shook his head, breathing out. 'It will be best if we use no magic as we get closer to the palace.'

She didn't reply, not wanting to draw attention to herself if anyone were watching their strange group.

They passed few people, most of them armed and in a hurry to be off the streets themselves. They received curious stares but no one was interested in paying them too close attention. Looking up, Kesta saw the towers of the palace rising up above the city, almost invisible against the high cliffs that hemmed it in on the western side. Her heart fluttered and her breathing came just a little faster. She lost sight of the palace as the buildings grew taller and the streets narrower and then it was suddenly before them again.

Osun led them along the high wall. She knew from their plan that they were looking for a servant's gate. Osun stopped abruptly and turned to look at them. 'The gate is just around the curve of the wall. As we have discussed there will be two guards on the outside, two within. We need to take out the two outside without warning those inside. If we all go together, they'll sound the alarm straight away. Azrael is waiting to take the two inside as soon as we dispatch those outside.'

'It needs to be me,' Jorrun said.

'No!' Kesta interrupted him quickly. 'Me. If any of you approach, they will be on guard. A woman alone will draw more curiosity than fear. It could give me the extra seconds to kill them.'

'They would be as suspicious of a hooded figure as of a man.' Jorrun shook his head.

Without hesitation Kesta drew the hood up over her head and dropped in on the ground.

'But your eye—'

Kesta put a finger to his lips. 'I'll keep my head and eyes lowered.'

'She would have the most chance,' Osun agreed.

Jorrun frowned, but nodded, not blinking as he held her gaze.

'I'll be quick, so be ready,' she told them. She took her dagger out of her boot and twisting her arms behind her back, she pushed the blade through the material of her dress so it rested against the small of her back. She bent forward, tipping her head over and mussing up her long hair. Without looking back, she headed along the wall, taking slow, staggering steps, as though she were injured. She dearly wanted to call on her *knowing* and she realised for the first time how much she'd come to rely on her magic. She saw the guards from under her lashes and they reacted almost at once.

'What's this?' One of them moved away from the gate, taking a few steps towards her.

'Shove her inside the gate or let her go,' the other guard said in a bored tone as she slowly advanced. 'Not our job to be dealing with lost property.'

'Finders, keepers, I say.' The first man hitched his belt up a little and stalked toward her. Kesta cursed. If they separated it would make things harder for her to kill them both without a sound.

'Well be quick!' The second guard said in annoyance.

Kesta grabbed her dagger and spun on her toes, extending her arm to slash through the guard's throat as she passed. The second guard cursed, grabbing for his sword and turning to raise his fist to the gate. She threw her dagger and it caught him in the shoulder as he turned. Beyond the gate there was a muffled scream, quickly cut off. Kesta sprang hand over feet, landing beside the guard to grab her dagger and force it into his spine. He collapsed, his nails scoring down the wood of the gate. She wanted to throw up. Her breath came in gasps, but she grabbed his hair and pulled back his head to expose his throat so she could cut it.

She staggered back. Jorrun took hold of her shoulders and crushed her in a hug, kissing her forehead. 'Well done.'

'He might have been a good ma—'

'Don't think about it,' Jorrun growled against her ear.

The gate opened a crack. Cassien drew his sword and, gesturing for the rest of them to stand clear, he pushed it open with his foot. Azrael immediately shot through the gap.

'All clear,' he hissed.

They dragged the dead guards through and closed the gate. Kesta couldn't bring herself to look at the two Azrael had killed. Although they were not burning, there was an awful smell of cooked flesh. Cassien went to push the large bolt across but Azrael made himself large to head him off.

'Don't touch the metal, Casssien! It will sstil be hot.'

The young man's eyes widened, turning crimson as they reflected the light of the fire-spirit. 'Thank you.' He used the hilt of his sword to knock the bolt into place.

'Right,' Osun said. 'Our next step is the palace. Let's get across these gardens as quickly as possible.'

Kesta took the lead and no one objected. Like all Fulmer women, she'd been taught how to track and scout. She was nowhere near as good as the likes of Heara, but she was still good. Twice she glanced over her shoulder toward Osun and he pointed in the direction she needed to go. The gardens were eerily empty, the only thing that stirred was the gentlest of winds. They drew close to the granite walls and she slowed her steps, feeling more than seeing, as Osun came up beside her.

'Look at the corner of this building,' he whispered close to her ear.

It took a moment for her eyes to adjust, then she started and turned to look at Osun, 'Isn't that foolish? Who would be so careless?'

Osun raised his eyebrows. 'Like putting in a gate for servants? It's vanity, Kesta, and arrogance.'

She nodded, her eyes following the line of gargoyles that decorated the sharp corner of the palace. They went all the way to the roof, past several balconies and windows.

Osun took in a deep breath. 'Up we go.'

Cassien stepped forward but Osun stopped him. With a nod, Jorrun made his way to the wall and began to climb. Kesta didn't like it, all her instincts screaming at her to protect him, but she had to respect his ability and it made sense for a magic user to go first. Osun followed next with Cassien. The thought of having Jagna behind her made her feel uneasy, so she gestured for him to proceed her.

Jorrun passed the first two windows and the first balcony, reaching out an arm as he got to the next. Kesta held her breath as he pulled himself across, hanging for a moment before pulling himself up and climbing the rail. His silence was uncanny.

The others followed, Jorrun helping to pull each one across and up. His eyes met Kesta's, sharp in the moonlight, as he took her hand and she trusted his strength to take her weight as she sprang from the gargoyle to the balcony.

The doors were open a little. From the flickering light within, they knew Azrael was there to meet them. It was Osun who pushed the doors open and they stepped into a room that had been ravaged. A bed frame remained and a dark coloured fabric lay discarded near the door. There was a chest with every drawer pulled open and a tapestry hung crookedly from one nail.

'The palace has been looted.' Osun turned to Jorrun.

He gave the slightest shake of his head. 'It's of little matter, the value of the palace for us is in its people.'

'You might not think so when it comes to administrating the city,' Osun glowered. 'The more we spend on defence, the less we have to buy women of blood.'

Jorrun glanced at Kesta. 'We'll deal with that when we come to it. Let's take the palace first.'

Osun nodded. 'I have no doubt Cepack will have taken the Overlord's quarters for himself. I imagine he will keep his coven close.'

Jorrun turned to look at Kesta, she tilted her head and held his gaze.

'It might be worth risking your *knowing*,' he murmured. 'Although there is a good chance they will have amulets.'

'No.' Osun stepped toward the door and touched the handle. 'No magic until we have to. We take the rooms two at a time, as quietly as we can. Cassien, you stick with Jorrun. Jagna, you and Kesta come with me.'

Although she longed to fight beside Jorrun, Kesta couldn't argue with Osun's division of their strength. Jorrun was watching his brother, an almost distant look in his eyes. Despite being the elder, for most of their lives it had been Jorrun who'd taken command and taken the lead because of his power and their upbringing. It was hard to tell how Jorrun felt at Osun stepping up without hesitation.

Jorrun nodded and Osun stepped through the door and into the corridor.

'Let's take the coven out first, quietly as we can,' Jorrun whispered.

Osun responded by going to the door opposite. Kesta quickly stepped up beside him, flexing her fingers ready to call up her magic, then thinking better of it she took her dagger out of her boot. The room was empty. They tried another and Kesta drew in a sharp breath, her heart beating faster, as she heard noises from the room Jorrun had entered. The next room they tried, they found someone sleeping in the bed. Osun and Jagna looked at each other. With an aching heart, Kesta crept over to the bed and forced her dagger down into the soft part of the sleeper's throat above his collar bone. It wasn't as silent or as quick a death as she'd hoped, the man choked on his own blood, face red, eyes bulging. She covered her face with her hands, praying for the sound to stop.

She jumped when Osun touched her arm.

'Let's just go,' he said.

She didn't argue.

Jorrun and Cassien had already moved on to another room, when they came out, Jorrun's skin was pale and he could barely look at her. They tried the next room. Again, someone was sleeping, but this time he was not alone. Kesta pointed at the woman and Osun nodded, Jagna holding back in the doorway. Kesta crept around the bed and placed a hand over the woman's mouth as Osun drew his dagger. The woman woke at once, lashing out and trying to scream. The man opened his eyes and sat up, drawing his power at once. Osun stabbed at him, but the man caught the blow on his arm, spraying blood across the bed. Hating herself, Kesta removed her hand and punched the woman hard in the head. She caught the man's arm, allowing Osun to stab him through the heart.

Kesta drew herself up, eyes wide, she could feel power being summoned by at least three different people.

'That's it,' she panted, looking from Osun to Jagna who still stood frozen at the door. 'No more element of surprise.' She leapt off the bed and called her own power to her hands.

They met Jorrun and Cassien back out in the corridor just as a blonde-haired man burst out of his room, bare chested and red-eyed from sleep. Jorrun didn't hesitate, but threw him down the corridor with a blast of air. There was no time to follow before two more men appeared and the ornate door to the Overlord's room exploded outward in splinters. Kesta ran to put herself at Jorrun's side, calling up a shield. Azrael followed Cepack out of his room, making himself as wide as the doorway. A small blast of flame passed close to Kesta's shoulder, hitting Cepack's shield with no effect. She didn't need to turn to know it had come from Jagna. Kesta continued to shield while Jorrun blasted flame at the men of Cepack's coven. They advanced together, side by side, pushing them back down the hall. Azrael darted in to engulf one of the men, his screams hurt deep inside Kesta's brain, it was impossible not to hear, or feel.

The remaining man scuttled toward Cepack, attempting to emulate Kesta and Jorrun, but Kesta increased her power and swept away his shield. The man tumbled down the corridor to be met by Azrael. She couldn't help it, she closed her eyes.

Cepack's blast hit her hard, only Jorrun's quick reactions halting the fiery-blue missile he'd hurled at her. She reacted instantly, directing a whirlwind at the man that lifted him off his feet and sucked the oxygen from his lungs. She stopped, her own chest heaving, he crumpled to the floor in a heap of broken bones. The moment their magic died in the corridor, Osun darted forward to make sure all of their enemies were dead with his sword.

They all looked at Jorrun, who turned to his brother.

Osun nodded. 'Upstairs,' was all he said.

Jorrun looked as though someone had walked over his grave.

They found the stairway and hurried up, Osun taking the lead. They heard shouting and a steady, loud pounding. On reaching the upper corridor they saw two men trying to break into one of the rooms, the door was a double one and more ornate than the rest in the corridor. Both Osun and Cassien ran forward to engage the guards with their swords. Jorrun took a few steps and then froze. A door was open and Kesta stopped at his side to look in. It was a small room and bars stood across the window. There were two beds and layers of dust covered everything. On the floor a small wooden animal lay, perhaps a stag that had lost its antlers.

'Kesta! Get him away from there!'

She looked up to see Osun and Cassien had finished off the guards. Osun was staring at his brother, breathing hard. She reached up and grabbed Jorrun's jaw, turning his head so that she could look into his frightened eyes.

'Jorrun! Come on.'

He shook himself and took her hand, letting her pull him toward Osun.

Osun took in a deep breath, his eyes fixed on hers. He gave one, curt nod. 'Kesta, this part is yours.' He stood back and ushered Cassien out of the way. Kesta regarded the sturdy doors, feeling her fear rise even though she knew there was no danger on the other side. Calling up her power she blasted the door open. Slowly, the shards of wood settled and she stepped into the room on the balls of her feet.

Several women were hiding there. All veiled, all wide-eyed, some crying. A baby bawled, red-faced, its mother crooning and jiggling it despite her own terror. There were two other babies and to Kesta, their silence seemed unnatural. Two small children peeped at her from behind a long curtain at the back of the room, a thin defence against sword or magic. Some of the women bore signs of injury, bruises turning now green and yellow, one had an arm in a sling and a nasty cut on her cheek.

She couldn't call her *knowing*, couldn't help them that way, she could barely breathe. She tried to speak, but choked, emotion crushing her larynx and chest. She raised a hand and called flame to her fingertips.

Several of the women gasped. Some scuttled backward, but one got slowly to her feet. She had dark curly hair and one of her brown eyes was lighter than the other. Her face, her neck, her hands, were all covered in tattoos, runes that made Kesta nauseous. Kesta drew in a deep breath, forcing herself to speak.

'You're safe,' she said. 'You are free. Stay here for now while we secure the palace.'

She tried to retreat from the room in in a dignified manner, but she almost tripped on her own feet. She turned in the corridor and collided with Jorrun, throwing her arms around him. He hugged her back hard.

Chapter Fourteen

Dia; Fulmer Islands

Dia woke with a start, someone was banging on the door. Arrus groaned and turned over. With a sigh, Dia grabbed a robe and went to the door to open it. Pirelle stood there with a lantern, her eyes red and wide.

'I'm sorry, Dia, but the watch has raised the alarm. There's a ship approaching, a large one. It looks to be of Borrow make but is bigger than their warships or any vessel we've seen.'

'A moment.'

She went back to the bed and gave Arrus a shove before dressing quickly and slipping her dagger into her belt.

'What?' Arrus demanded, sitting up and blinking.

'Borrow ship,' Dia replied. 'A big one, hurry up!'

She held a shirt and trousers out for her husband then went to the door, shifting her weight impatiently from one foot to the other as he splashed water on his face and grabbed his sword. Heara was waiting in the great hall, wide-eyed Catya on her heels.

'Vilnue is on his way,' Heara said as they strode out of the Hold.

Dia nodded. 'Rouse the warriors, get them down on the beach before I reach it.'

'At once.' Heara loped away, Catya running behind her.

'Surely they wouldn't dare raid us.' Arrus shook his shaggy head.

Dia glanced at him and then looked down at the shelters of the Borrow refugees as they hurried across the high path between the Hold and the rest of Fulmer Island. Several warriors came running to join them. Instead of heading straight to the beach, Dia held up a hand for everyone to wait while she stepped off the path and headed for the mis-matched shelters. She hesitated only a moment beside one before calling out, 'Grya, come out!'

There was a rustle of material and a head appeared. The Borrow matriarch blinked up at Dia before disappearing. It was only a few seconds later that she emerged fully dressed.

'Come with me,' Dia commanded.

They went on to the beach, more warriors joining them. Dia could make out the shape of the Borrow ship with its serpentine prow and twin masts, almost as big as the best ships of Elden. A Fulmer scout hurried up the dunes toward them, hampered by the sliding sand.

'It's too big to come in and land, Icante,' he panted. 'They have not launched a boat and there seems to be a man standing out on the prow, he doesn't move.'

Dia turned to Grya.

The Borrow woman nodded. 'The man stands there to let you see him, so you can decide who he is. It means he has come to talk.'

'I've never seen a Borrow ship of such size,' Dia admitted. 'Do you know who it is?'

Grya shifted her feet and moved her jaw. 'I only know one such ship. It belongs to The Bard. Temerran. He left two years ago to cross the ocean.'

'The Bard?' Dia stiffened, sensing trouble.

Grya turned to look at her. 'We have no magic on the Borrows except in song. If the sea has called him home to the Borrows, then there is trouble.'

'Trouble?' Dia blinked. 'If he came for the decimation of the Borrows, then he is too late.'

Grya drew in a deep breath. 'If he is come, then it is for worse than that.'

Dia snorted and shook her head, glancing at her husband. The people of the Borrows had all but been wiped out, their islands made uninhabitable, what could possibly be worse than that?

Grya continued to stare at the ship, barely blinking, her fingers folded together before her. Dia felt something with long, tickling legs crawl up her spine to the nape of her neck.

'Set torches in the sand,' she commanded. 'Light the beach so they know to land.'

Arrus didn't disagree, but he placed his large hands on his hips. She couldn't blame him for his concern, this was something completely unknown to them. The Fulmer Islanders had bards, those who could sing and pass on the old tales, but she got the impression Grya meant something else by the term, something more foreboding.

They didn't have to wait long after the torches were lit before the man moved away from the prow. Moments later a small boat was lowered and rowed toward the shore. Grya became restless, taking several steps forward onto the sand. Dia felt her own nervousness growing, but she forced herself not to move nor step closer to the shelter that was her husband. Heara stood at her back, little Catya her eager shadow. No one moved as the boat hit the beach, two men jumping out to drag them up the sand. A third man stood up in the boat, he was slim and quite tall, maybe a little under six feet. The torchlight caught his hair, like flame, as unusual a colour in the Borrows as the Fulmers.

He jumped out of the boat and took a few steps forward. Dia lifted her chin and walked out to meet him, Arrus at her left and Heara at her back.

The man was dressed in green trousers, long boots, and a brown shirt that was unbuttoned at the top. He wore no weapons that she could see, but a flute was tucked into his belt. He raised a hand in greeting, glancing at them all, his eyes finally resting on Dia. His green eyes as dark an emerald as Kesta's right eye.

Dia sucked in air and bit her lower lip. Hadn't she seen those eyes before?

'Icante, thank you for allowing me on your island.'

His voice was deep and rich, seeming to vibrate within Dia's bones. His skin had been roughened by wind and sea, but he seemed to be about ten years younger than Dia herself.

'Why have you come?'

His face broke into a grin, but it slowly faded when she didn't respond. 'You are quick to the point.' He cocked his head to one side. 'The sea called me home. I found the Borrows empty, a curse upon the land. I came to the only place I knew that could lift a curse.'

'Not to Chem?'

He looked down at the sand and then back to capture her eyes. 'Chem is the place that lays the curses, is it not?'

'That is so.' Dia narrowed her eyes. 'But we know nothing of blood magic here, if I did, I'd have healed your lands and sent your people back and away from my islands.'

Temerran's brows drew in toward his nose. 'Yes, you have taken in the people of the Borrows despite everything.'

Grya took that moment to step forward and the Bard held out his arms to hug her. She stepped back and he kissed both her cheeks. 'Matriarch Grya, you have survived.'

183

'And not many others.' She shook her head, her face crumpling.

Dia looked away, embarrassed by the strong woman's show of grief.

'So.' Temerran looked up, studying Dia, Arrus shifted at her side. 'The flame shelters the sea. Who would have imagined that?'

Arrus growled. 'It was not us who made war between our people.'

Temerran held up his hands. 'Let us not bring up the past or we won't move forward. Icante, it's late – or early! Let me return to my ship and we will move out away from your Hold. Later, when it's light, would you talk with me to see if we can find a solution?'

'Time, it seems, will be the best solution,' she replied.

'Although not ideal for the Fulmers, or for us. There may be another way.'

She drew in a deep breath and sighed. There was no harm in talking and yet … and yet she couldn't trust this man. 'We'll meet on this beach tomorrow.'

Temerran bowed, but Dia turned her back and gestured for the others to follow. Arrus commanded several of the warriors to remain on the beach. As they followed the path back up to the Hold, she looked down and saw Grya was still talking with the Bard on the sand. She felt her hackles rise.

Heading straight to her room she told Pirelle and Heara to follow. Calling flame to her fingertip she lit a candle and called out to Doroquael who appeared at once, growing out of the candle flame. When Dia turned around to address them all she realised the girl, Catya, had come too. She rolled her eyes but didn't object. Perhaps someone from Elden might offer a different perspective. It gave her an idea.

'Heara, fetch Vilnue in and get Milaiya too.'

Heara frowned, but nodded, darting out through the door.

184

'That seems a good idea,' Arrus said, pouring himself some water. 'Anyone else want any?'

Dia raised a hand in dismissal, wandering toward the window that looked out across the sea. Doroquael was drifting about the room and Dia realised that she herself was pacing. She pulled out a chair and made herself sit down. The door opened and Heara ushered Vilnue and Milaiya in before her. Vilnue already knew what was going on, but Milaiya looked frightened, glancing around at the others in the room. Catya's presence seemed to ease her fears a little.

'Okay.' Dia placed her hands together and tapped at her lips with the tips of her forefingers. She looked up at the fire spirit and Doroquael came to an immediate halt. 'As far as we were aware, the Borrows has no magic, yet tonight I spoke with a Borrowman whose very words were magic. Furthermore, he admitted he speaks with the spirits of the sea. Tell me, Doroquael, how can this be?'

Doroquael made a popping sound like driftwood on a fire. 'We knew the Borrowss was the land of the ssea spirits, they surround the islandss but cannot walk upon them. Sea spiritss are wild, fierce, they care little for mortals. A bard would be different though, a bard might leave them enraptured.'

'We have bards.' Arrus frowned. 'Keepers of tales, writers of official records. They don't have magic.'

'All words have a certain amount of power,' Pirelle disagreed. 'Even our bards can calm or lift a room.'

'No.' Dia stood up and grasped the back of her chair to lean on it. 'This was different power. It was almost, but not quite, elemental.'

'Jorrun would be the best person to ask,' Catya spoke up. 'He has hundreds of books and knows lots of old things.'

Dia gripped the back of the chair harder. She hadn't told the girl Kesta and Jorrun were far out of reach and now was not the time. It might be possible for Rosa to find something in the Raven Tower, however. 'I'll write to Northold, that's a good suggestion, Catya, but it will be several days before we hear back. Vilnue, Milaiya, do you know anything of this bard?'

'I'm sorry.' Merkis Vilnue shrugged. 'We have entertainers, musicians, in Elden, but I've never heard claim of a Borrowman Bard.'

'Milaiya?'

The freed Chemman slave was chewing furiously at her thumb. 'There are folk tales of sea spirits.' She glanced up, blinking rapidly. 'From the tales they are cruel and unpredictable.'

'They are asss like to harm a Borrowman as help them,' Doroquael hissed.

'And bards?' Dia prompted the girl.

She shook her head.

Dia sighed in frustration. 'I suppose I must listen to him tomorrow. If there is a way to heal the Borrows faster and send them all back there, it won't be a bad thing.'

'Until they come back and raid us again.' Heara huffed.

'That is always a risk.' Dia let go of the chair and made her way over to the wash stand. She looked down into the water, seeing only her own reflection. 'Thank you for your thoughts, everyone. Try to get some sleep and we'll speak again in the morning.'

They left slowly, Doroquael squeezing out through the gap in the window and Heara staying until last, one hand on Catya's shoulder. Heara looked from Arrus to Dia. 'Get a message to Everlyn,' she said. 'You should have a *walker* with battle experience with you.'

'Very well,' Dia nodded.

When her friend and bodyguard left, Arrus made his way back to their bed, but Dia crossed the room instead to the desk.

'Will you not try to sleep?'

She pulled a clean piece of parchment across the desk. 'Not yet. I won't be able to settle until I've written these letters.'

Arrus sighed loudly and she heard the creak of the bed as he got in. 'Perhaps this bard is a good thing? If he takes away the refugee—'

'I don't trust him.' She glared down at the empty paper.

But why was it she didn't trust him? Was it because he had power when no one in the Borrows should have? Or was it just because of his green eyes?

***

Dia chose those who'd met in her room the previous night to come with her to the beach. As before, the Borrowman Bard had two men row him ashore, but he walked alone across the sand, the sea breeze playing with the long curls of his red hair. Grya hurried forward to meet him and he took her hand, kissing both cheeks. Dia could hardly blame her for standing with her countryman even if it might jeopardise aid to her people.

'You had time to consider my words.' Temerran looked up at Dia.

Dia took in a breath, holding his gaze. 'Of course, although as I said last night, I'm not sure there is anything I can do.' She gestured for the Bard to follow and they all moved along the beach to where some blankets had been set out in a circle. 'I've sent for assistance from a friend in Elden, but it will take time before I hear back. When you said there might be another way, did you mean there is, or that you hoped we might find one?'

He looked down at the sand and smiled to himself. 'A little of both, actually.'

They stood beside the blankets, none of them yet sitting down.

Temerran ran a finger down the flute in his belt. 'I know little of Fulmer magic, nor do I expect you to tell me of it, but I believed you can change emotions.'

She nodded, not wanting to give away any more than she had to.

'Do you think you could change the feel of a land?'

She almost laughed, but she saw in his face how serious he was. 'I've not been to the Borrows but my daughter described to me how it felt to her. She seemed to think the evil feel of it was the residue of so many blood spells cast. *Walkers* can influence the emotions of people and animals, but not the land itself. I could give calm to bird and beast, courage to your people, but until this stain on the Borrows fade, anything I do will only be temporary, if it would even be effective at all.'

'I see.' Temerran's shoulders sagged a little and he turned to look out across the sea.

Dia felt pity stir in her heart. 'Let's sit,' she said.

Arrus and Vilnue placed themselves to either side of Temerran and Grya, Heara remained standing close behind Dia. Milaiya had her arms folded tightly around her body, looking down at her covered knees. Dia regretted bringing the former slave, the poor woman was clearly uncomfortable.

Temerran drew his flute from his belt and placed it on the blanket so he could sit cross-legged. 'I have supplies on my ship and treasures from another land far across the ocean. I must keep some for the men who risked their lives to sail with me, but the rest I give to pay the debt of the Borrows.'

Dia swallowed, Arrus sat up straighter. 'If you have food to help feed your people then by all means, let them have it,' Dia replied. 'But we wish for no treasures.'

Temerran raised a hand. 'I hope I did not offend.'

Merkis Vilnue cleared his throat. 'Icante, I hope I'm not stepping out of line?' He turned to face the Bard. 'I could set up trade deals with Elden so you can exchange your goods for things that might be of more use to your people.'

'I have questions.' Heara interrupted before Temerran could respond, her hand on her hip near a dagger hilt. 'As far as we are aware the Borrows has no overall leader, only separate tribes that are often at war with each other. Then you step up out of the sea claiming they are your people.'

'I didn't mean that in the respect of owning them.' His green eyes lit with his smile, but Heara wasn't charmed. 'But more of belonging to them.'

'Heara has a point though.' Dia sat back to study him. She wondered if he would feel it if she called her *knowing*, it would be worth the risk. 'Tell us more of who you are and what your position is among the Borrows.'

He smiled. 'I'll tell you, and gladly, if you will afterwards introduce me to everyone here. I see several people not of the Fulmers and I'm intrigued.' His eyes went last of all to Doroquael.

Dia felt a moment of discomfort, she should probably have introduced everyone to him before they began speaking, but her suspicion had gotten the better of her. 'Of course, let me introduce them now. To your left is my husband, Arrus Silene. Behind me is my bodyguard, Heara, with her novice, Catya, who is from Elden. This is Milaiya, our guest from Chem.' She saw him

189

start at that. 'Pirelle, my apprentice, Merkis Vilnue, our ambassador from Elden, and Doroquael of the fire realm.'

'Such a wondrous group!' He looked around at them all. He leaned toward Milaiya, placing a hand flat on the sand before him. 'My lady, do you not know anything of the curse?'

Milaiya shook her head vigorously.

'No woman in Chem is allowed to know anything of magic,' Dia replied for her.

For the first time a little frustration showed on Temerran's face. He glanced at Doroquael and opened his mouth to speak. Seeming to think better of it he sighed and looked down at his hands that now lay palm up in his lap. Dia carefully called up her *knowing*.

'Well then.' Temerran settled himself and looked up to make eye contact with them all. Dia felt his confidence, excitement, and curiosity, only the slightest touch of nervousness flowed beneath it. 'As you say, the Borrows is made of many clans and although some of them make alliances, for the most part they are very competitive. Resources are scarce, not much grows on the islands. Even wood to build ships and houses is something to be fought over.

'The first bard came into being many generations ago. No one knows for sure from where he came. He carried news and tales, he could read and write – not just the old runes – and so wrote official records for each clan. He took no side, refused to divulge the secrets of each island. There were times a clan would try to bribe or force him to their cause, but to those he never returned and they lost his services and were damned in the eyes of the other clans.

'Each bard would choose an apprentice from out of the clans, a boy who could be trusted, one without ambition to rule. Most importantly, one who could learn the magic.'

He was using it now, Dia realised. It wasn't like the magic of a *walker*, or the elemental magic used by Doroquael and the Chemmen. With their magic she could feel the air charge as though lightning were about to strike. Temerran's magic was a subtle tingling sensation deep within her chest. He looked at her, his eyes wide and bright. 'It's magic of the soul.'

She drew in a sharp breath, had he read her mind?

'Of the soul?' Pirelle cocked her head. 'My understanding is magic is of the elements or of the blood.'

Doroquael drifted higher, burning brighter. 'He referss to magic of the sspirit, I think. Like a fire-walker's *knowing*.'

'Ah, of course.' Temerran gave a slight bow. 'You think of spirit as one of the building blocks of the universe, like fire or water. We bards think of the spirit, the soul, as something else, something divine.'

Dia frowned. 'I think I understand. So; you have been away from your people?'

Pain crossed his face. 'A vain adventure and costly to the Borrows, it seems.'

'No!' Grya scrambled onto her knees to touch his arm. 'You are not to blame.'

Dia swallowed, looking away, Temerran's guilt was crushing. 'Would you have had the power to defend the Borrows from Chem?'

He looked up. 'Magical power? No. But I might have united the clans to make a stand.'

'Then they would have just taken longer to die,' Heara muttered.

'You may be right,' Temerran reached out to touch his flute. 'Icante, would you sail with me to the Borrows?'

'What?' Arrus demanded. 'You appear from nowhere, with magi—'

'I'll consider it,' Dia said quietly.

'Dia!' Heara stepped forward almost hissing in her ear.

She stood, glaring at her husband and her friend, before turning to address Temerran. 'If we do, we'll take our own ship. Grya and her people will remain here as our hostages until my return. We will wait, though, until I hear back from my friend in Elden. She may obtain information to help us with the blood curse. You, and you alone, will stay within Fulmer Hold until we sail, but you will go nowhere but your own room without one of my warriors. Is that acceptable?'

Grya looked from her to Temerran, her eyes wide.

Temerran stood. He took in a deep breath and held out his hand. 'I accept.'

Chapter Fifteen

Ayline; Kingdom of Elden

Ayline winced, Adrin's exaggerated laugh seeming to jar her bones. She'd found him charming and exciting at first, but it soon wore off when she realised how shallow and narcissistic the man was. She glanced up to see both her husband and Adrin fawning over the red-haired witch who was seated between them. Worvig was sat to Ayline's right and when she looked at him, she saw he was as fed up as she was. There was water in his cup, rather than wine, and he tore a crust of bread in two, his jaw muscles moving. She had to admit he'd proved to be more pleasant to talk to than she'd assumed. He was quiet but knew a surprising amount about a large range of subjects and he listened to her. Really listened.

She started as a soft voice spoke close behind her. 'Your tea, your majesty.'

The sound of Inari's voice set pins and needles dancing inside her chest. She refused to turn and look at him, lifting her hand off the table slightly in acknowledgement. She watched as his muscled arm, with its soft dark hair, reached past her to leave the cup. She held her breath, wondering if he'd gone but refusing to look around.

She'd stayed away from the lake tower since the day he had massaged her shoulders, her daring and desire crushed by fear of the consequences. If she were caught being inappropriate with any man it was very likely she'd face execution. Likely her child's legitimacy would be put into question as well, and therefore its life. It hadn't stopped her dreaming of Inari, though, dreams that left her feeling hot and set her heart racing. Despite avoiding The Tower, she seemed to bump into him everywhere. He always behaved with perfect propriety, unlike Adrin. Bractius seemed to find it amusing when Adrin turned his barely hidden, bawdy flirting on her, it was as though her husband thought it were impossible anyone would really find her attractive now she was over four months pregnant. Bractius certainly had no interest in her himself, not that he had for quite some time.

'Are you well, your majesty?'

She looked up to see Worvig was watching her and realised she was glowering. She forced a smile and rubbed at her belly. 'I'm fine, it was just kicking a bit.'

Worvig shifted in his seat, watching her hand.

'Do you have children, Silene?' she asked.

'I don't.' A frown settled over his dark-hazel eyes. 'I guess I never got around to it. My niece was child enough for me.'

'You're close?'

She tried to keep her expression pleasant as she thought of the demon-eyed woman who had stolen Jorrun.

'Yes.' Worvig's face broke into such a warm smile she couldn't help but genuinely respond in kind.

She gasped as Bractius' hand came down heavily on her shoulder. 'Ayline, Larissa would like to visit the Raven Tower tomorrow, I'm busy, would you take her?'

She opened her mouth, trying to find a good excuse to say no. The last thing she wanted was to spend time with the witch.

'I'll take her, I used to serve there, remember?' Adrin grinned at Larissa.

For a moment the Fulmer woman looked annoyed, but she hid it quickly.

194

'I can go,' Ayline found herself saying. With Jorrun away on some secret trip, would they let her up into his forbidden tower? She shivered.

'Good.' Bractius slapped her on the back a little too hard. Worvig smiled at her in sympathy.

'Will you come to The Tower also, Silene?' she asked politely.

He shrugged. 'I guess I may as well see it and it would be good to be out in the countryside for a while.'

She picked up her cup and sipped at the tea. It was chamomile and sweetened with honey. She forced aside her sudden longing for the green-eyed servant.

No one stopped her when she excused herself, claiming tiredness; at least her pregnancy was good for something! Lerra immediately darted forward from where she'd been hovering at the back of the hall.

'Lerra, I want to take some fresh air. Go to my room and fetch a warm cloak, meet me in the gardens.'

'At once.' Lerra curtseyed.

Ayline waited until the girl was out of sight, but instead of heading for the gardens she turned down the corridor that led to the lake tower. It was harder to take the uneven steps upward than the last time she'd done so and she wondered how much longer she'd be able to manage them before her ungainly shape and extra weight made it too difficult. The thought of not being able to go to the tower room actually hurt, despite the fact she'd been avoiding it.

She opened the door slowly, the candle on the table by her chair had been lit but as far as she could see there was no one there. Her eyes widened when she saw the bed and her skin flushed and her muscles tightened. The old, sagging mattress had been replaced by a new one and clean, soft, blankets were stretched neatly across it. The floor had been swept and a soft fur rug lay before the fireplace. There were still cobwebs in the corners and around the glass of the window. Ayline smiled. She took slow, careful steps toward the window and looked out over the lake. The sun had almost set, lighting the clouds in gold and red.

'It's a beautiful evening, your majesty.'

She spun around to see Inari standing in the doorway, his basket of candles balanced over one arm.

'You changed the bed.' She nodded toward it.

'You asked me to clean the room, your majesty.'

She raised her chin. 'I did.'

'You haven't been for a while.' He stepped into the room, letting the door close behind him.

'I've been busy.' She took a step back.

His eyes ran slowly over her, from the hem of her long dress up to her eyes and hair, she felt herself blush but didn't look away.

'You are always beautiful, but the evening glow from that window really suits you.' Inari moved to the foot of the bed and put down the candles. 'Someone should paint you, right there, with a crown upon your head and Taurmaline below your feet.'

She held her breath, her heart beating fast. He stalked closer and she tensed leaning back a little as he lifted a hand to touch her cheek with his long fingers. 'You forget your place!' Her voice came out with no conviction, even to her own ears.

'Oh, I know my place.' His green eyes were very, very close. 'It is under your command, your majesty. I'm your most loyal subject. My fate is yours.'

196

'Our fate will be the executioners block.' She drew in a breath and stepped away, meaning to get past him and leave. He was faster.

'You have more courage than that, my queen. Besides, who will know but us?' He put his hands behind his back and moved aside. She looked toward the door, but couldn't seem to bring her feet to move.

'Not tonight.' He leaned forward, his breath tickling her ear. 'Lerra will be panicking about where you are. Come late at night, I'll watch for you.'

She stared at him wide-eyed, shocked and thrilled by the boldness of his invitation. She grabbed a handful of her skirt and hurried to the door without a word, clumsily fumbling at the handle and darting outside. She sucked in air, leaning against the wall as she descended, forcing herself to slow down and not risk a fall.

How could a servant be so daring? She needed to find out more about him, but who could she ask without stirring suspicion? She stopped.

Was she really considering this?

She could lose everything, including her life. It hardly seemed worth it. And yet …

An ally, a place to start, someone who treated her as she deserved. She placed one hand on her abdomen and continued down the stairs.

***

Worvig held out his hand and Ayline didn't hesitate to take it, letting him steady her as she stepped down the gangplank and onto the narrow wharf. Her former lady-in-waiting, Rosa, stood waiting to greet her, her rough-looking husband at her side. Larissa seemed to know them, and she recalled the Icante and her party had insisted on leaving the luxury of Taurmaline castle to come here and wait for Kesta to return from Chem. Rosa didn't bat an eyelid when Larissa kissed Tantony on the cheek. She winced at the vulgar familiarity, no lady of Elden would great a man not of her family in such a way.

'This is Worvig Silene,' Larissa introduced the large Fulmer warrior.

Merkis Tantony's face broke into a wide, toothy grin. 'Silene, I'm honoured to meet you at last.'

'Is that so?' Worvig looked genuinely confused.

'I owe you thanks for ensuring Kesta and I got on and off of Mantu in one piece. She accredited her rather unorthodox fighting style to you.'

'Oh!' Worvig smiled uncomfortably. 'Well, yes I guess I did teach her a move or two.'

'Your majesty.' Rosa gave a curtsey. 'Please come inside and have some refreshment?'

Ayline glared at her through narrowed eyes and she was pleased when the older woman's face reddened. The woman had been away from court for a while and Ayline felt a need to assert her dominance and remind the plain, dull woman who she was.

'Actually, I want to see inside the Raven Tower.' Ayline gritted her teeth angrily when Rosa and Tantony glanced at each other.

Rosa opened her mouth to speak, 'Oh, wel—'

'I'm not making a request.' Ayline all but snarled. How dare they question her!

'Your majesty.' It was Tantony's turn to redden a little. Neither Worvig nor Larissa lifted their gaze up from the ground. 'Thane Jorrun commands tha—'

'*Thane* Jorrun does not command the Queen!' Ayline clenched her fists and took a step toward the Merkis.

He glanced at Rosa again, but nodded quickly. 'This way, your majesty.'

Behind her she heard Rosa invite Larissa and Worvig into the Hold. The two ladies-in-waiting who had accompanied her started to follow their queen, but Tantony halted.

'I'm sorry, your majesty, but your ladies will have to wait outside The Tower, them I cannot allow.'

She felt a moment of outrage, followed by concern at going into The Tower alone with the Merkis, but she waved a hand to dismiss the ladies.

Tantony pushed the door open and gave a slight bow. Ayline swallowed, looking into the darkness. She straightened her back and walked quickly past the Merkis, her shoulders dropping and her feet faltering when she saw the room. It was disappointingly empty, just a table and a stone stairway leading up.

Tantony looked at her expectantly. Clutching the front of her dress to lift it a little she ascended the steps. It was ridiculously dark, only three candles lit in sconces along the entire length of the stairway. She wondered if Tantony had done it on purpose to scare her, but then she remembered he hadn't known she'd wanted to come here.

'What's in here?' she demanded, stopping at the first door.

'Jorrun's library, your majesty.'

She tried the door and found it unlocked. It was even darker within the room than out on the stairway, there didn't even seem to be a window! She refused to be afraid and stepped in, running her hand along the spines, although in truth she could barely make out what they said.

She didn't even glance at Tantony as she spun about and went back out to the stairs. She began to climb again and couldn't help but think of the Lake Tower back at Taurmaline. Would Inari be waiting tonight?

'That's the rest of Jorrun's library.'

She realised she was standing outside the next door. She narrowed her eyes at Tantony, sure there had been some sarcasm in his voice. He really was a scruffy looking man. She went into the room and a smile of malice crept to her lips. Rosa really did deserve a husband as dull as she was.

She snorted, at least this room had a window, although it was as uninteresting as the one before. Tantony kept his eyes lowered and his head bowed as she passed him again.

As soon as she opened the third door a mixture of scents wafted out to greet her. Now this was more interesting. Her eyes widened, taking in the shelves of jars and bottles and the hundreds of carefully carved drawers that no doubt hid interesting things. She completely forgot about the Merkis as she peered at labels and opened drawers. She picked up a jar that contained a beautiful crimson powder that seemed to shimmer despite the darkness. She pulled out the cork stopper and bent her head to sniff the contents.

Tantony cleared his throat loudly. 'Best not, your majesty, you don't know what it might do.'

Her lip curled upward and she had to stop herself snarling at the impertinent man. She put the jar down though, not bothering with the stopper.

'So, the last room is the Thane's?' She raised her eyebrows.

'Yes, indeed.' Tantony shifted his weight from one foot to the other. 'Jorrun is an extremely private ma—'

'Show me!'

Tantony opened his mouth, then quickly closed it again and swallowed. He gave a small bow. 'This way.'

She almost pointed out to him there was only one way to go, stupid man, but she bit her tongue.

She took the last few stairs quickly, but when she reached out her hand to open Jorrun's door she saw it was shaking. She pushed the door open and blinked at the light from the three leaded glass windows. Most of the room was taken up by a table and the fireplace, a small bed was pushed awkwardly against the curved wall beneath one window. There was still a faint trace of the jasmine and cinnamon soap Jorrun used, but her nostrils also caught the musty, reptilian smell of the ravens up above. She could hear their claws as they skittered about in their loft, the sound made her skin itch. She went over to the table and shoved at some of the scrolls there. She felt disappointed, she'd expected something more ... well, more exciting.

She picked up a couple of the books, leafing through them without actually reading them, not wanting Tantony to know what a waste of her time this had been. Not the potion room, though, she would like to see more of that.

She screwed up her face and gave a dramatic shudder. 'However does he stand the stink of those creatures and that awful noise they make? Take me back to the great hall, Merkis.'

'At once.' Tantony bowed.

***

Her temper didn't improve when she entered the great hall, it was so rustic and plain. The Hold women were darting about, clumsily laying out food that she no doubt wouldn't be able to stomach. She couldn't understand why Jorrun didn't employ proper servants. Her own ladies-in-waiting had seated themselves with Larissa and Rosa, all of them were laughing and appeared far too comfortable together for her liking. Worvig sat a little apart from them and it was he who noticed her first. He got quickly to his feet and bowed, at least one of the fools here had manners, even if it was the rough Fulmer man.

Her ladies-in-waiting almost fell over their own skirts scrambling to their feet. She chose to ignore them and made her way to the high table where she sat in Jorrun's seat.

Lunch was intolerable. Rosa tried to entertain her with dull talk of Northold and questions about court she couldn't be bothered to answer. Worvig and Tantony went off together, talking about Mantu. Had the King been here they wouldn't have dared wander off without permission.

'Would you like to take a walk around the ward and see how Kesta's projects are coming along?' Rosa asked.

Ayline realised she was talking to her. 'No, I would not. I have no interest in cabbages and potatoes.'

'Would you mind if I sho—'

She gave a loud sigh of exasperation. 'Do what you wish, but I will be on the ship back to Taurmaline within the hour.'

'You do not wish to stay?' Rosa looked at her in surprise. 'It will be very late by the time you get back to Taurmaline.'

Ayline put her knife and fork down loudly on her plate and sat back to stare at her former lady. How could she seriously think she'd want to stay here? Rosa's face turned a bright red.

Larissa stood and gave a low and long curtsey. 'Your majesty, we will be quick, please excuse us.'

The two women hurried from the hall and Ayline watched them with her eyes narrowing, they seemed to walk rather closely together, as though they were good friends or conspired about something. She shoved her plate away.

'Someone get me some chamomile tea!'

One of the Hold women heard and darted off at once. Ayline rubbed at her temples. Her two ladies had gone very quiet, picking at their food although eating little. She didn't care. The whole day had been unbearable and had just highlighted how little power she really had. She had to take authority, demand the respect she deserved. But where should she start?

***

She spent the journey back shut away in the cabin, forcing her two ladies to stay out on deck in the cold and the dark. She hoped they were miserable. Eventually she fell asleep.

For once she didn't dream of Inari and the tower but instead of the throne room in Taurmaline. She herself was seated on the throne and something heavy sat on her head, warm and comforting against her brow. Several men, dressed in the finery of princes, knelt before her, awaiting her command for them to stand. Glancing to her left she saw Jorrun was seated in his stark, black chair, his skin like marble and his eyes like glass. A familiar voice whispered in her ear.

'Start with the King. When he cedes you power, all will follow his example.'

She turned quickly to come face to face with Inari, his green eyes wide, his mouth almost close enough to kiss, but the dream took her out and away from the throne room. She heard a strange sound, reminiscent of the ropes of the rigging, but terror gripped her stomach when she saw the scaffolding in the castle ward. Three figures hung from it, swinging still, the red hair of one unmistakable. Larissa, Dia, and that ugly witch, Kesta. Her fear turned into delight.

'Will you come to the tower?' A voice spoke softly in her mind.

'Yes!' Deep in sleep, she smiled.

Chapter Sixteen

Jorrun; Covenet of Chem

He'd expected her anger, feeling Kesta shaking against his shoulder was so much harder to bear. He held her tightly, wishing there was something he could say, consumed by guilt that he'd brought her here.

'Azrael, guard those women!' Osun commanded.

Jorrun looked up and caught his brother's darker eyes. Osun gestured down the corridor and he nodded.

'What next?' Jagna looked pale, his chest rising and falling rapidly.

'We ensure the palace guards will take our command, or we kill them,' Osun replied.

Kesta pushed herself away from Jorrun's chest and he let her go. She glanced up at him quickly, the skin of her cheeks and around her eyes was red. 'How many are we likely to face?' she asked.

'From the information I gathered, not that many.' Osun pressed his lips together in a thin smile. 'A lot of them had served Dryn for many years and either took the chance to leave when he died, or stayed and died when Cepack took the palace. I'd be surprised if there were many who feel loyalty to Cepack.'

'And yet two of them were prepared to kill the women for him.' Kesta's nostrils flared and her fingers curled tighter around her dagger.

Jorrun cleared his throat. 'It's not an unusual order. Killing the women stops the new coven from potentially gaining strength for the future.'

'We need to get going,' Osun prompted.

He led them back down the corridor and Jorrun found himself trailing at the rear. He couldn't help it, his feet faltered when he came back to the door. The small room had been his home, his defenceless haven for the first eight years of his life. During the day he'd been made to attend lessons, learning to read and write and how to fight, how to obey and how to endure pain. His nights were spent with his mother, learning about life, how to care, how to love and how to perform magic. Whenever they could avoid the guards their small sanctuary was shared with Osun and his mother, Matyla.

Sometimes the guards had come to take his mother away. He never asked but he knew where she was being taken, he saw the bruises on her skin. He'd never seen his mother fight them, although she did in her own way, with her quiet dignified strength; the same strength that helped her survive two miscarriages and a stillbirth. They didn't speak of what happened downstairs in the palace, but the other women did, and Jorrun was a curious child, always needing to understand the world. He learned early to hate men, sometimes the women too, not understanding until he was much older that they couldn't change the way things were, not on their own, that defying the masters meant death – or worse.

Jorrun had never known safety, never lived without a creeping shadow of fear on his soul, but this room, with his mother, was the closest he'd come to it. His mother never lied but she did hide things, trying to protect his innocence for as long as she could, trying to keep from him her own despair. Osun, on the other hand, told him everything, showed him everything, brought him the only small wonders available to a coven boy.

'Jorrun?'

He turned to see Kesta looking up at him, her green eyes full of concern. It was difficult to shake off the tendrils of the past that had rooted him to the spot but he forced himself, calling on the shield he had made for himself; the Dark Man.

He hurried to catch up with the others, passing Cassien and Jagna to walk at his brother's side. When they got back down to the level of the Overlord's residence, they found three guards examining the bodies of the coven. Jorrun called power ready.

Osun stepped forward. 'Stand where you are and lower your swords!'

Jorrun felt pride at the strength and command in his brother's voice although he locked his emotions down tight in his chest. He lifted a hand to let blue flames dance across his fingertips.

The guards glanced at each other, two lowered their swords, the third dropped his completely.

'Good.' Osun took a few steps closer to them. 'Do you have a captain here?'

'Yes, master,' one of the guards spoke up, his eyes glancing over them all.

'Wake him and get him to meet me in the audience chamber.' Osun didn't wait, but went back to the stairs and made his way down to the ground floor. Two other guards stood at an ornate door, they took one look at the group advancing on them and dropped to their knees.

'Very wise,' Osun remarked. 'Anyone in there?'

'No master,' one of the guards stuttered.

'It's all clear as far as I can tell,' Kesta spoke behind Jorrun.

Cassien stepped forward past the guards and gave the doors a shove. Jorrun watched the young man's face as his eyes searched the room. Cassien's shoulders fell a little as he breathed out. 'All clear.'

Jorrun moved the instant his brother did, *his* shield, *his* sorcerer now instead of Bractius's. He could barely bring himself to look around the audience chamber, it was hard not to see his father seated in the chair even though he knew he was dead. His vision blurred and he dug his nails into his palms to try to focus his mind. He'd been a small child the last time h'd stood here, so terrified that he'd almost wet himself, his back twinged at the memory of the burning bite of the whip. He realised he was breathing hard through his mouth and clamped his jaw shut, forcing himself to calm down. Behind him someone closed the doors.

'What now?' Jagna demanded.

Osun walked over to the large bronze chair with its red leather cushioning on which their father had once sat. Jorrun found himself holding his breath, a part of him couldn't bear the thought of his brother sitting there in that awful seat.

'We must establish ourselves here and protect each other.' Osun looked around at them all. 'Kesta, can you please join Azrael after I've spoken to the captain of the guard? The two of you will need to protect those women.'

'Of course,' she replied at once.

'The rest of you will, I fear, have to protect me. We will take turns sleeping, just one of us at a time, no one should walk the corridors alone if it can be help—'

The door creaked open and a man walked in, wearing the livery of the palace guard but with two wide blue stripes across his red jacket. He halted, his spine straight, his eyes travelling across all of them and widening on seeing Kesta.

'I have questions for you.' Osun moved around to stand beside the coven seat. Jorrun raised his left hand to let blue flames dance at his fingertips once again.

'Master.' The captain bowed neatly.

'Why did you remain when Dryn Dunham was slain?'

The captain's mouth opened and his jaw muscles moved as he considered his reply. 'My duty is to protect the palace. I had no desire to become a mercenary or beg on the streets for work. I knew sooner or later another coven would come.'

'You did not slay the women when Dryn Dunham died.'

Jorrun's flame flickered despite his composure, he saw Kesta step forward out of the corner of his eye.

'No, master.' The captain shook his head. 'For a start, there were still Dunham Coven members here after the Overlord's death. In truth the order was given, but when Lord Cepack came, my priority was protecting the palace, not slaughtering helpless women. I ... I've not been captain long.'

'Yet when we came there were guards trying to do that very thing.' Osun stalked slowly forward, Jorrun increased the size of his flame.

'Yes.' The captain looked down at the flagstone floor. 'There are those among the guard who would be happy to carry out such an instruction.'

'Kesta.' Osun raised a hand.

Jorrun held his breath as Kesta moved toward the captain. She called up a wind that was so perfectly controlled it lifted the captain of the guard off his feet while still allowing him to gasp in air.

'I suggest you remove such men from your ranks or Lady Kesta here will remove them in a terminal fashion.' Osun turned his back on the man and went back to the seat. 'No woman in this palace will be harmed in any way; none. Do I have your word on that?'

The captain nodded vigorously, his hands trying to clutch in vain at empty air to try to steady himself.

Osun raised a hand and Kesta allowed the man to fall in a heap on the floor.

'How do I know I will have your loyalty?' Osun demanded.

The captain struggled back onto his feet, his eyes not leaving Kesta. 'I guess you'll only know that in time, master. If you want the loyalty of the men, though, giving them the wages they're owed would be a start.'

Osun glanced at Jorrun and he let the fire at his fingertips subside. 'Get this ugly chair here melted down and sell the metal.' Osun's lip twitched in a brief snarl. 'Use that toward the wages. And take this.' Osun opened the purse at his belt and took out a small diamond, the captain's eyes widened. 'Sell this too. If you steal it, or cheat me, it won't be just be my coven on your heels, but your own men.'

He shook his head. 'I won't cheat you, master.'

'I should hope not. I want the servant's entrance in the palace wall bricked up immediately and I require all the ledgers pertaining to the running of the palace. See that the captain of the city guard is here to attend me first thing. Go and instruct your men.'

The captain bowed and started to back out of the room. He stopped at the door, glancing up but afraid to speak.

'You have a question?' Osun tilted his head slightly.

'Yes, master. I wondered … what coven do I have the honour of serving?'

'I'm Osun. You serve the Coven of the Raven.'

As soon as the captain left the room, Osun sagged against the chair. 'I don't know if I can keep this up, brother you're more used to command than m—'

'You were amazing!' Cassien sheathed his sword, his eyes all but glowing.

Jorrun opened his mouth to speak, but turned quickly away, keeping his posture rigid. He could feel Kesta watching him but refused to look at her.

'Thank you, Cassien.' Osun drew in a deep breath. 'The rest of this night will be long, and tomorrow longer. If word gets out that such a small coven has taken Navere there is a good chance we can expect others trying their luck. We must show our strength and power at every opportunity.' He looked at Kesta and she didn't look away. 'Kesta, you must win the trust of the women and start their training as soon as possible.'

'I'll go there now,' she agreed. 'I'm worried about leaving Azrael on his own anyway.'

'Jorrun, make sure she gets there safely. Could you check on the library on your way past, see if it has been looted? If you can remember the way into the passages check there also, Dryn's coven may have hidden things of value in there.'

Jorrun bowed and went over to the door to open it, behind him he heard Kesta say, 'Take care of yourselves.'

When they stepped out into the hall, he saw the guards had been doubled, the four men straightening up as they passed them by. Jorrun had been to the library three times in his life. The first time when Osun had snuck him in there while fulfilling his duties as a slave. The second time he'd made his way in alone in the early hours of the morning only to be caught there by Dryn himself. The Chemman Lord had hit him so hard around the head his ears had rung and he'd almost vomited. His father had given him a warning, a last chance, to stay in his room unless summoned. Too restless, too curious, and not scared enough, Jorrun had found himself going back to the library only two months later on a night they'd come to take his mother away. Nearly four glorious hours he'd spent there, touching the books, breathing in their smell, feeling their mystery. He'd been caught on the way out. Dryn hadn't said a word when Jorrun had been brought before him, he'd just held his hand out for the whip. Two guards had held him up by the arms so his father could mete out his punishment, they hadn't let go of him even after he had passed out from the pain and the fear. He was seven years old that last time he'd come to the library.

He realised he was standing in front of the door. Kesta reached out a hand toward him, concern on her face, but he flinched away before she could touch him. He put out both hands, shoving the doors open and striding in. The smell was unmistakable. Paper, parchment, wood, leather, and dust with the subtle lavender smell of the polish that was used on the gleaming wooden shelves and tables. He gasped in a sharp breath, tensing every muscle as his emotions tried to escape.

'Jorrun.' Kesta stepped around to stand before him. 'Why are you being the Dark Man? We don't need him, we need *you*. Chem needs you, those women upstairs need *you*. They need a good man, one to trust, not one to fear.'

He gritted his teeth, unable to meet her eyes. As she raised her hand, he stepped back.

'Jorrun.' She placed her hands on her hips. Her anger was easier to bear than her pity.

'*I* need the Dark Man.' The words burst from him and pain lanced his heart. He gasped and turned away, clutching at the front of his shirt with one hand, trying to hold everything back by drawing on his anger.

Kesta stepped around him and stood on her toes, sliding one arm around his waist and the other around the back of his neck to make him look at her. Her strength took him off guard, her *knowing* was open and she drew his pain from him like pulling poison from a wound. Things he'd thought he'd left behind, that he had refused to face or acknowledge, all forced their way up to the surface of his mind, blinding him, overwhelming him so that he could barely breathe. His helplessness, his confused naïve feelings of betrayal all came flooding back. No matter what Dryn had done to him, he had clung desperately to his sense of right and wrong. Hatred and terror were all he recalled of his father. The familiar smell of the palace, the garish opulence of it, made him feel sick. His fingers dug into the fabric on Kesta's back and he closed his eyes as the room swam away from him. He tried desperately to draw in her warmth, breathing in deeply the scent of her hair. His soul seemed to twist inside him and with a shudder tears overflowed his eyes even as bile pushed upward from his stomach.

'I love you,' she said into his neck. 'You're safe, let it go.'

He took several breaths before he could speak. 'I can't afford to be weak now.' Her hair caught against his wet cheek as he shook his head.

She stepped back, placing a hand to the side of his jaw, his grip on her clothing didn't lessen. 'Facing your demons doesn't make you weak, it makes you whole. If you carry on as you are, fighting a battle on the inside as well as the one we face, then you'll destroy yourself and we'll lose. You had the courage to walk dreams again despite the damage that Karinna caused. You can face this too, Jorrun, you can.'

He swallowed. 'I thought killing my father would have put an end to this, but being here … it even smells the same.'

She stood on her toes again to kiss him slowly and for a moment the pain in his chest eased. 'I can't even imagine what it's like for you to be back here, in this place.' She lowered herself back onto her heels and he looked down into her mis-matched eyes, desperately hoping for salvation somewhere in her words. 'I've seen the scars on your back, but I know only a tiny amount about your life here.'

'I got those scars because of this place, because I refused to stop visiting the library.'

He was amazed when she laughed, but the knots in his soul released a little more.

'Jorrun, only you would take a whipping to see some books.'

He closed his eyes and smiled, letting himself feel her amusement – tinged still with anxiety for him. 'Books – stories – were my only escape and I had so few of them.'

'But because of you, hundreds, maybe thousands, in Chem will find something close to real freedom and at the very least not experience the life you had to endure. Stop being so hard on yoursel—'

'But I can't afford to break down now.'

'But if you don't deal with it now, break down is exactly what you'll do! By all means hide it from everyone else, but not from me and not … not from Osun. He will understand more than me, he may even need to talk to you too.'

He nodded, lifting his gaze to look around at the multitude of book spines. When he turned back to Kesta she was smiling again although she blinked rapidly at the moisture in her eyes.

'You'll have all the time you want to look at them soon.'

He reached out to catch a tear as it fell from her lashes and then tapped the tip of her nose with his finger. 'And I'd best have a quick look at those passages and then get you up to Azrael. I don't like leaving Osun without someone much stronger than Jagna for long.'

Kesta frowned. 'Cassien's loyalty I do not doubt, but I'm still a little unsure about Jagna.'

Jorrun paused beside one of the bookcases. He was sure it was this one, but it had been so long ago. He ran his fingers along the spines of the books. 'What of the captain of the guard?'

Kesta perched herself on one of the tables. 'There was fear, anger, a lot of pride too. He seemed more pleased than upset by Cepack's death but that doesn't mean he'll think any more highly of us.'

'As long as they give us a moment to establish ourselves.' He pulled out a large brown book and reaching behind it found the lever. The bookcase swung slowly out toward him. He heard Kesta gasp.

'How did you know where to find that if you were not allowed in the library?'

'Osun was allowed in.' He glanced at her over his shoulder. 'He found himself many jobs as a slave while they were waiting to see if his blood would show. He could all but make himself invisible.'

She hopped down off the table and came to stand beside him, her closeness made him feel safer. He couldn't see much in the darkness, but it was clear the stairway was empty. He called a small, yellow flame to his fingertips and the shadows leapt back. Cobwebs spanned the passage, heavy with dust, it was clear no one had found the way up to the upper tiers of the library in many weeks.

'Is that the only way up to the balcony?' Kesta asked.

'There is another passage up on the other side. I never got to go up there as a child.'

'Shall we go?'

He looked down at her. He wanted to more than anything and having someone to share the experience with made it even more exciting, but they had an important duty to think of first.

'Not now.' He gently squeezed her arm. 'We should get you to Azra and I need to get back to Osun.'

She nodded, looking down at the carpeted floor. 'We won't have much time together for a while, will we?'

He reached out and lifted her chin with two fingers. 'I will make time for you, no matter what. I really need you, Kesta, to keep the nightmares away.'

She took his hand and squeezed it hard. 'Don't worry, they won't dare stand up to me!'

He smiled, not quite able to laugh. 'I can well believe it. Come on, let's check on that crazy bug.'

They stepped back into the library and he pushed the hidden door closed, ensuring there were no scuff marks on the carpet to give it away. He checked the second passage quickly, only to find it just as empty as the first. If any of Dryn Dunham's wealth had been hidden away, it wasn't here.

They could hear nothing when they went back out into the hallway and he felt Kesta call up her *knowing*. It was tempting to touch her, to feel the comfort of her confidence, but he refrained; he needed to shake off his ghosts and regain his own faith in himself. They reached the floor on which the coven's residences stood, the bodies of the sorcerers still littering the floor. Kesta's steps slowed as they passed and he moved ahead of her as they went up to where the women were kept. The door to his old room stood closed as he had left it, but still it seemed to call out to him.

'I'll be all right from here,' Kesta said.

He tore his eyes away from the door to look at her, becoming aware of a strange sound coming from the women's common room. Kesta saw his frown.

She smiled. 'That's Azrael singing.'

'Singing?'

'Yes, Milaiya taught him to sing. I'd better see what he's up to.' She slid her arms around his waist to hug him hard. 'I'll see you soon.'

'As soon as I can,' he promised. He watched her walk away up the hall with the assuredness of a cat. She paused to look back at him before disappearing through the ruined doorway.

Jorrun shivered, somehow the corridor seemed darker.

Chapter Seventeen

Kesta: Covenet of Chem

She felt a moment of doubt as she turned back to look at him; he looked so vulnerable alone in the hallway despite being such a tall man. His eyes were like windows to a bright stormy sky, the sun silver behind black clouds. Had she done the wrong thing in taking away his defence of the Dark Man? Perhaps she should have waited until they could have more time together. Her heart ached for him and at the thought they would mostly be apart, either he, Azrael, or herself would always need to be either with Osun or with the women of the palace.

Azrael's singing broke back into her thoughts and gave her an idea. Forcing herself to break eye contact with Jorrun she turned and stepped into the room.

Azrael stopped speaking and the women all turned to look at her. They'd gathered in a semi-circle on the carpet, the two small children seated at the front.

'No, please go on, Azra.' She waved a hand toward the fire-spirit and sat herself at the end of the row of women. As Azrael continued his tale, she took the opportunity to study the women. Their ages ranged from about fifteen to their late twenties, none of them old enough to have remembered Jorrun. Only one of the women appeared to be over thirty and she was the one covered in tattoos. Kesta couldn't make out the runes, but they covered every inch of the woman's body, including her fingers and palms. The woman looked back at Kesta, studying her mis-matched eyes with her own oddly coloured ones.

The woman spoke as soon as Azrael came to the end of his tale. 'I'm Calayna.'

'Kesta.' She nodded in reply. 'Did Azrael explain to you why we're here?'

'He did. It won't work.'

'Why do you say that?'

'The men will never allow us to be equals.'

'Hmph.' Kesta looked down at her hands and then stood up quickly. 'Well, we'll be off then and leave you to go back to the way things are.'

Several of the women cried out in alarm.

Kesta raised her eyebrows and turned to Calayna. 'Seems like they want to give it a try to me.'

Calayna raised her chin and held Kesta's gaze, showing a surprising amount of pride for a slave. She pointed to her face. 'This is what happens here to a woman who develops magical ability.'

'I imagine it was very painful.'

Calayna looked away. 'The spells cast were worse than the needle.'

Kesta sat back down on the carpet below where Azrael hovered. 'No one will be forced to use magic, not everyone will be able to, but either way, while we are here, no one will be allowed to harm you. If you help us, we'll be able to establish a permanent sanctuary here and possibly change the lives of women across Chem. I'm quite strong.' She lifted a hand and let flames dance across her fingertips, listening to the gasps and sighs of the women. 'My husband and Azrael here are stronger, but the three of us are not enough to guard you forever.'

'Only three of you took the palace?' One of the women asked, looking fearful.

'We have two Chemmen with us also; Jagna who is a sorcerer of limited power and Cassien who is excellent with a sword. Our ...' Her words caught only briefly in her throat before she went on. 'Our leader is a man who was born here in Navere palace, the son of the now dead Overlord. Osun has no magic, he was once considered no more than a slave, however it was he who took Dryn Dunham's head off his shoulders. We had originally intended to leave our victory at that and go home, but Osun feared the chaos that followed would mean greater suffering for the slaves of Chem rather than freedom. He insisted on coming back here to take a look.' She shrugged. 'It's up to you if you want to help or not.'

She called up her *knowing* then to better gauge their reaction and immediately regretted it. Calayna stood and began clapping, slowly, loudly, the expression on her face one of contempt. Her emotions hit Kesta like darts and she sat back, gasping, one hand going to her chest.

'How very noble.' Calayna's lip curled. 'Less than a month after the Overlord's death the first coven came to take Navere. Those of us you see here are alive because the guards didn't have time to slaughter us all. Only weeks after that, Cepack came. He sold our daughters to raise money, he had Sirelle and Jollen's sons killed. They were five and seven years old. I'm sure you can see what they did to *us*. When you killed Dryn Dunham, you took away our safety and protection.'

Kesta couldn't breathe. Jorrun had tried to warn her, but she hadn't wanted to hear it, didn't want to feel it. Well she was feeling it now, and she didn't need her *knowing*. The eyes of every woman was on her and she felt her skin burn. The impact of their actions on these people was inexcusable. And yet ... and yet she'd had to save the Fulmers. She gritted her teeth and wiped angrily at her eyes with the heel of her hand. 'I have no excuses. We

220

came here to save my people, to stop them having to go through what you have. We thought we'd helped you, as much as we could, anyway. Osun … Osun was the one who came back to check.' She raised one hand to rub at her temple, Azrael turned anxious loops around her.

'But you did come back.' One of the women moved closer on her hands and knees, tentatively touching Kesta's shoulder.

Kesta drew in a deep breath and breathed it out slowly. She looked up at Calayna, the woman blurring before her. The tattooed woman regarded her with her arms folded across her chest.

Kesta recalled something Jorrun had said to her and she straightened her spine. 'We can't change what has happened, but we can do something now and we can try to change your future. We can't do it on our own though, as strong as we are, we are too few. We have to try though, we have to make a start somewhere.'

'What if we can't do magic?'

Kesta turned to the woman who had moved closer to her. She was about sixteen and had blonde hair and brown eyes. Kesta couldn't help but wonder at her heritage.

'What's your name?' Kesta asked.

'Vilai.'

'Not all of you will be able to.' Kesta regarded them all, coming last to Calayna. 'Your magic they have stolen from you.'

Calayna looked away, her resentment like stinging nettles against Kesta's skin.

Kesta swallowed. 'This has been a traumatic night for you. Why don't you try to get some sleep and we can talk more in the morning? Azrael and I will guard you.'

'The servants will be waking soon,' Velai warned her. 'They will be afraid, too.'

'I'll speak with them. Would you feel safer in your rooms or do you want to bring your bedding and all stay in here?' She glanced around the ornate common room. 'To be honest, it would be easier for us to protect you if you're all together in here.'

Calayna's arms dropped to her side. 'We'll stay in here.'

Kesta nodded. 'Is there any way in and out of here other than the stairway?'

'None,' Calayna replied.

'Good. Azra and I will guard the stairs until you're all settled.'

She waved at the fire-spirit to follow her and they went out into the hallway. The palace women hurried behind them, grabbing bedding and returning to the fragile safety of the common room.

'Azra, I have something to ask you,' Kesta said quietly, ensuring no one could overhear. 'I'm worried about Jorrun and even ... and even Osun. This is a difficult place for them. With only the three of us strong enough to protect the palace, fatigue on top of the emotional burden will be huge. Is there any way ... the fire-spirits, your fellow Drakes helped us before?'

Azrael made himself smaller and hovered at her eye-level. 'I will ask, Kessta, of course. The Drakes helped before becausse of the threat of blood magic. Mossst have no interest in human affairs ordinarily and they are alsso restricted by the fact they cannot long leave the fire realm – unlike earth-bound Azssra. Ssome may come though, but their shifts to help will be short.'

'If they can give us a break to rest, any help will make a huge difference.'

222

Azrael bobbed. 'I'll be gone but a moment. Keep a careful watch, Kessta!'

Without another word, Azrael darted into one of the oil lamps on the wall and vanished. Instinctively she reached for her magic, but refrained from calling it, instead gripping the hilt of her dagger. She returned to the common room and found the women settling in to sleep, all but Calayna who was placing two chairs near the damaged door.

'One of us will keep watch with you,' she said without looking up.

Kesta sat in the chair, focusing her *knowing* cautiously. The woman's hostility had subsided a little and was more recognisable now as fear. What terrified her most was hope.

'What came first?' Kesta asked softly. 'Did you find magic or did your eyes change?'

For a moment she thought the woman wouldn't answer. 'I was sixteen when the guards first came to take me down to Dryn. I was terrified. Some of the other women had advised me not to fight, I hadn't meant to, but something happened inside my head.' She leaned forward and momentarily covered her eyes with her hands. 'The room caught fire. The master – Dryn – he laughed. The next day … the next day they tattooed me with blood. It took hours. Days.'

Kesta shuddered, feeling sick.

'I've carried three daughters and two sons. One son was born dead, the other slain for possessing no magical blood. I have no idea where my daughters are.'

'We'll tr—'

'Don't you dare!' Calayna hissed. 'Don't you dare promise what you can't give!'

'Lady, you don't know me! No one will hurt you again while I live.'

Calayna held her gaze for a long time before looking away. Kesta didn't need her *knowing* to feel the woman's thoughts. In Chem, there was every chance Kesta wouldn't live.

***

Kesta's eyes were starting to sting when she heard noises in the hallway. She stood at once and went to the door. Two guards were preceding a group of servants carrying trays along the hallway, they slowed on seeing her.

'We're reporting to someone named Kesta Silene.'

Kesta lifted her chin. 'That's me.'

The two men glanced at each other. 'Where's your master?'

Kesta placed a hand on her hip and sucked at her bottom lip. She gave a short, snort of a laugh deep in her throat. Without warning she called up her magic and hurled both guards against the wall. One of the servants dropped their tray.

'Listen.' Kesta took several steps forward toward the men. 'I don't have the patience to keep telling you Chemmen. I. Don't. Have. A. Master. Got it? Now, did you actually want something?'

She ceased her magic and allowed the men to fall to the floor.

'We're to help you guard this floor,' one of them mumbled as he pushed himself up onto his knees.

'Well, you'd better get on with it, then.' She pointed back down the hall toward the stairs and then regarded the servants, all of them older women but for one in her late teens. 'Don't be frightened, please. Come on in.' She turned to see Calayna and Vilai watching her from the doorway, the younger girl's eyes were wide and shining.

Kesta moved out of the way while the servants set out their food. She cleared her throat. 'You may speak,' she said. 'When you're ready, when you feel comfortable. In this palace there is no restriction on women. If anyone hurts you, tell me.'

A few of the servants lifted their eyes, but none spoke yet. Kesta told herself to be patient, recalling how long it had taken her to win Milaiya's trust. As the servants left and the women settled down to eat, Azrael emerged slowly from one of the lamps. He let the women see him, before drifting across the room to Kesta.

'Eight Drakes will help us, Kessta! They cannot sstay long at a time but it will give us rest. I've been down to tell Ossun.'

'That's amazing, Azra, thank you.' She had to stop herself immediately heading down the stairs to look for Jorrun. She hoped he was all right and longed to know what was happening down in the audience room. 'Are you hungry, Azra?'

'I had ssome oil from the lamps, thank you, Kessta.'

'Take some rest, then.'

She waited for the women and two small children to finish eating, herself nibbling on some dried fruit, before going to sit on the carpet in front of the large fireplace. Vilai and one of the other younger women came to join her, smiling shyly. The others slowly followed, Calayna last of all.

'I'm going to try to teach you how to reach for magic,' Kesta said quietly. 'But remember, it might not be something you can all achieve.' She couldn't bring herself to look up at Calayna's tattooed face.

'I'll mind the children.' Calayna reached out to take one of the babies and gestured for the two infant girls to follow her.

Kesta had to swallow her guilt, she was in no way responsible for what had been done to Calayna. Shifting to sit more comfortably, she straightened her back. 'I'm going to summon flames to my hands. I need you all to try to relax and just focus on the light. It won't be easy, especially in our present climate, but please try.'

She raised both her hands, palms up and agitated the air to let the flames dance above her skin.

'Magic comes from the elements,' she said softly. 'From earth, air, water, fire, and spirit. But the ability to wield it comes from within, from those able to channel it through their bodies and will it into an active form. The place where you control it is within your skull, a muscle deep within, behind and above your eyes. You need to learn to find it and tense that muscle. It will give you an awful headache to start with, but it opens the flow of magic into your body. Try tensing different parts of your brain, see if you can find it.'

She kept her *knowing* open, sending out her own calm to the women. Girls of the Fulmers were taught how to meditate and seek to open their magic, if they were able, from an early age. She remembered her own excitement when she'd felt that first rush of power. It had been nearly a year later that her eyes had slowly changed their colour.

She let flames dissipate and closed down her magic.

'That's enough for now,' she said gently. 'It's all right to try to practice, but please, please only do so when I'm here.'

The women nodded, she felt disappointment from several of them.

'What is it you normally do with your day?' she asked.

'We have weaving and sewing to do,' Vilai said, uncrossing her legs and moving her long skirt to sit more comfortably. 'But there is not much to do with so few children to care for.'

226

Kesta stood up and looked around the room. There were a few books in a case against the wall, two small looms, and a spinning wheel.

'Hmm. I have a little project we can take up if we can get hold of the materials.' Kesta grinned. 'In the meantime, who wants to learn how to kill someone with a dagger?'

***

Kesta was sat quietly listening to one of the women reading aloud from a book when she heard footsteps in the hallway. She leapt up and went to the door, Azrael at her shoulder. Her heart swelled and she took in a sharp breath when she saw Jorrun making his way toward her with Cassien. Several servants followed behind them bringing their evening meal. Cassien glanced away as Kesta reached up to push her fingers through Jorrun's dark hair and kissed him fiercely.

'Did you miss me, by any chance?' He raised an eyebrow and the ghost of a smile creased the skin around his eyes.

She flushed slightly, recalling he didn't like to show affection in public. Instead of apologising she raised her chin. 'Not at all. What's been happening? Come in and meet everyone.'

Jorrun raised a hand. 'I'll catch you up on everything shortly. Cassien has come up to keep watch with Azrael and give you a break. Osun is trying to get some sleep and being guarded by Jagna and two Drake—'

Kesta opened her mouth to protest but Jorrun raised a finger. 'It's fine!' His eyes widened to emphasise his words. 'We need to get some sleep ourselves as there is a lot to do tomorrow. And every day after.' He realised they were holding up the servants and nodded at them to go on in. 'Introduce us, then.'

Kesta had to refrain from taking his arm or hand as they stepped into the room. Glancing up at him she saw he'd stilled the muscles of his face and closed off the emotion from his eyes. She sighed, but she couldn't blame him for wanting to keep his emotions in check on meeting these women. All but the servants stopped what they were doing at once, the palace women scrambling to their feet and then kneeling to bow their heads.

'No!' Kesta waved her hands at them. She grabbed Vilai's arm and tried to pull her up. 'You don't bow anymore! This is my husband, Jorrun, and Osun's bodyguard, Cassien. Cassien was a slave until just a few days ago. Please.' She went over to stand before Calayna. 'Treat them as you have me. Talk to them, talk in front of them, and for goodness' sake get up!'

Calayna looked up, her breathing rapid and her eyes wide as she got to her feet. The other women followed and Kesta introduced them all, pleased she'd been able to remember all the names. Jorrun gave a low bow and Cassien quickly copied him.

'I'm honoured to meet you,' Jorrun said. 'I apologise, but I must borrow Kesta for a while. Cassien and Azrael will keep you safe.'

Cassien smiled nervously.

'Go take a seat, Cassien,' Kesta prompted him. 'But not too far from the door.'

Kesta realised several of the women were staring at Jorrun. Calayna opened her mouth, but stepped back rather than speaking.

'Please speak,' Kesta prompted her.

Calayna swallowed. 'You are a Dunham, Lord?'

Jorrun nodded. 'My father was Dryn Dunham, although I prefer not to think of him as such. My mother was Naderra.'

'I've heard that name,' Calayna frowned. 'In stories from women now long gone.'

Jorrun looked away and his nostrils flared, Kesta could see the speed of his breathing had increased. 'If you will excuse us then.' She smiled at the women and nodded toward Azrael and Cassien before backing out of the room, trying hard to appear as though she wasn't hurrying.

She chose not to push him into talking about anything difficult. 'So? How has poor Osun been getting on?'

He started, looking down at her with narrowed eyes and she realised she'd expressed empathy toward his half-brother. 'It's not been easy.' He gave a shake of his head as they reached the top of the stairs. 'We've taken a look at the accounts of the palace and there's barely enough to feed everyone. It seems several city officials absconded with the tax revenues on hearing of Dryn's death. The palace and city have had little income but for what Cepack looted and sold.' He gritted his teeth. 'Money we'd hoped to use to buy and free women of blood will have to be used to get Navere back on its feet I fear.'

Kesta's heart sank. She sighed. 'It was never going to be easy.'

'Osun ... he is good though, he is already restoring order and begun appointing people from the Rowan Order to strategic places.' He glanced at her as they passed the once luxurious rooms of the coven members and continued down the stairs. 'We might need to make a few more shows of power though, to keep other covens away and give the less cooperative element of Navere reason to obey.'

Kesta nodded. 'I've already had to make a demonstration or two of my power. I'll start working on winning over the servants first thing tomorrow.'

'How's it going with the women?'

She wasn't surprised when he led her toward the library. 'Slowly, but that's to be expected. They've never had the luxury of deciding whether to trust someone or not before. Jorrun, I know our resources are limited, but because of us their children were killed or sold away, can w—'

'Kesta.' He stopped to look down at her, touching his long fingers to the side of her face and stroking her jaw with his thumb. 'We'll try, but we have to prioritise making this place safe. I've had the palace genealogy and slave sales brought to the library so we can have a look and try to trace people's families. We might have to bide our time until we can get them back though.'

He pushed the library doors open, lanterns spilled their warm glow across the central table. Some pillows and blankets had been dropped haphazardly across the chairs and several large ledgers waited on the table. Jorrun went straight to them, moving a lantern closer and seeming to forget she was even there for a moment as he leafed through the pages. He paused, his hand raised above the yellowing paper. Holding her breath, Kesta stepped closer to look past him.

On the top of the page was the name, 'Naderra,' with details of her parentage and blood lines. Beneath were two names followed by the words, 'sired by Dryn Dunham'. Dinari and Jorrun.

'Dinari?' She looked at him, he didn't seem to be breathing.

'I had an older sister.' He turned from the table and sat heavily in one of the chairs. 'I don't even remember her. She was sold when I was six, I think.'

'But … but Osun said your mother was very young when she had you.'

He nodded, his eyes distant. 'She must have been about fifteen when she had Dinari.'

'Fifteen!' Kesta felt her magic rise and her fingers locked into claws.

Jorrun looked her up and down and a little life came back to his eyes. 'We can't kill Dryn again, Kesta, calm down.'

'Calm down?' Her eyes widened even more.

He stood. 'Yes, my little volcano. Save your anger for when we can use it.' He turned back to the window before glancing at her. 'Even in Chem it's unusual for a man to sleep with a woman so young. Not for her sake, sadly, but because there would be a high chance of losing their property if her body isn't developed enough to safely carry a child. Dryn … he was obsessed with my mother. I've sometimes wondered if he even knew she could perform small feats of magic. Seeing Calayna has made me wonder again. My mother's eyes were mis-matched and yet he never had her tattooed.' He sighed and touched the edge of the table. 'These ledgers should tell me what happened to Dinari.'

She turned to the table and began checking the spines and front covers. Jorrun moved to stand beside her although his own search was more cautious.

'This looks like a sales book.' She held a large, blue bound ledger toward him.

He frowned over the pages. 'No, this is for palace slaves and servants.' His hand went to a smaller book with a dark-red cover. She watched him as his eyes moved over the letters and numbers. 'This is it.'

Kesta bit her lower lip and waited, leaning with one hand on the table.

Jorrun had to clear his throat to loosen the muscles enough to speak. 'He sold her to Karinna.'

'What?' The strength went out of Kesta's knees at the same time as Jorrun dropped the book. They were both well aware of what a brutally cruel man Karinna had been before Kesta had killed him. He'd murdered Osun's mother for fun and tortured Jorrun when he'd caught him dream-walking.

Jorrun stood staring up at the beautiful stained-glass window that took up a large part of one of the library walls.

'What …' Kesta tried again, forcing more volume to her voice. 'What city would that be? Is there any way to see their records?'

His shoulders sagged and he glanced at her over his shoulder, she could see in his eyes he had no hope his sister lived.

'Karinna held the seat at Mayliz.'

Her voice came out in a whisper. 'We can try.'

He turned and stepped toward her, enfolding her in a hug that was surprisingly gentle and resting his cheek against the top of her head. 'We can, although it can't be a priority. Come on, we were supposed to be getting some rest.'

He picked up the blankets and pillows, taking them over to the secret passage. 'Take out that large, dark brown book, then feel behind it for the lever.'

Kesta did so, jumping a little as her fingers caught in a spider web. A section of the bookcase sprang toward her and she gave it a tug to widen the gap. Going back to the table she fetched one of the lanterns, turning down the rest, before following Jorrun up the narrow stairs.

***

She awoke to complete darkness; a sense of unease having crept into her dreams. She strained her ears to listen but no sound filtered through the thick stone of the palace. She reached out a hand to reassure herself Jorrun still lay beside her. She gasped, sitting up quickly. The skin of his chest was hot to touch and wet with sweat.

'Jorrun?' She called up her *knowing* and carefully reached out again to touch his cheek with the back of her hand.

She recoiled, scrambling up into a crouch with her back pressed up against the solid balcony. The emotions she'd felt left her nauseous, the taste of blood was in the back of her throat. She drew fire to her fingertips, convinced she'd see a stranger there, someone like Karinna. She let her breath out, almost panting and feeling the slow trickle of sweat down her own back. It was Jorrun, lying so still that had she not felt his heat, she'd have thought him dead. The fire dancing across her palm barely gave colour to his face.

'Jorrun?' She was afraid to touch him again but told herself off for being foolish. She shut off her *knowing*, her stomach still turning backflips despite the tight knots in her muscles. Forcing herself to relax she called his name again and shook his shoulder.

He sat up so quickly she flinched and banged her head against the balcony.

'Kesta, what's wrong?'

She looked into his bright, stormy eyes and sagged in relief. It *was* her Jorrun. She shook herself, feeling stupid for her irrational fear. 'I'm sorry, I think you were having another nightmare.'

He lifted the blanket and she let her flames go out, wriggling beneath the fleece to lie bedside him. He reached out and tucked her hair behind her ear. 'Yes, I think I was having a nightmare, but I don't remember it now.'

She moved to lay her head on his chest and he pulled her closer. She could hear his heart, loud and fast, within his ribs. 'You haven't been dream-walking have you?'

233

'No, not here. Although I'll have to sometime, with Osun here we have no one out gathering information.'

'We have the Rowen Order, I think we can trust them. They would have a lot to lose if they were exposed so they are unlikely to double cross us.'

'Even so, we should both consider using our *walking* to keep ahead of our enemies; we have many now.'

She nodded against his chest.

She listened as his breathing slowed and he drifted back into sleep, but she couldn't find sleep for herself. The iron smell of blood wouldn't leave her.

Chapter Eighteen

Dia; Fulmer Islands

Dia stopped to lean against the wooden pillar and watched the group gathered around Temerran. They were mostly children but Milaiya and Pirelle were also there. She was hardly surprised that he'd won over the women with his pretty face and his charming words, but he had proved equally good at making friends with the warriors, including a couple of late nights drinking with Arrus. She supposed it was all a part of what he was, a bard, but now and again she felt the subtle buzz of his magic behind his words and she found that she couldn't trust him.

The bard seemed to be teaching them how to play a counting and rhyming game with sticks, whatever it was there was a lot of laughing. Taking in a breath, she made her way across the hall to the outer door, not looking up as Temerran's green eyes followed her. Several women sat at a long table, singing as they pounded at the wool they were dyeing. Taking the narrow path away from the Hold, she made her way to the clearing where Heara trained. The shouts and whoops told her that her best friend had attracted an audience again. She knew Heara loved nothing better than showing off, but she worried she was putting too much pressure on the reserved and defensive Catya. She decided it was past time she should intervene.

Heara had set up an assault course out of logs and ropes but it wasn't Catya she had running it, but herself, two Borrowmen, and Merkis Vilnue's warrior. Catya and several Fulmer warriors were throwing clumps of turf at them to try to throw them off balance. Dia sighed. In some ways it was good to see the warriors mixing together, but there was every chance it could end badly. She groaned when Arrus pushed forward out of the crowd to jump up onto one of the logs. With a shake of her head, she strode forward, calling up wind and sweeping them all off of the course and into the mud.

'Hey!' Heara protested, sitting up and pushing her hair back from her face. 'I was winning!'

'Come back and win later,' Dia scowled. 'I need you and Arrus. Now.'

Dia moved away from the crowd to wait for them, already several people, including Catya, had clambered back up onto the logs. Heara sauntered toward her, brushing down her trousers and flicking back her long plait.

'Trouble?' Heara asked, her face serious.

Dia drew in a deep breath. 'Potentially. Do you think it's wise to get the warriors competing against each other like that?'

'It's just a bit of fun, although I'm guessing you don't think so.' Heara frowned. 'I built it for Catya, but they wanted a go. I need to find somewhere more private to train Catya.'

'I'm just concerned it might turn into the Fulmers verses the Borrows.'

'Ah.' Heara's eyes narrowed a little. 'I hadn't thought of it like that.'

'Luckily I don't think it's occurred to them either.'

'What's up?' Arrus put his arm around Heara's shoulders.

'A letter has arrived from Rosa of Northold.' Dia regarded the two of them. 'There's no news still of Kesta and Jorrun but Rosa's sent a book from the Raven Tower, a book about blood magic.'

'Any help?' Heara asked.

'I don't know yet, but as you know our two weeks are up tomorrow.' Dia glanced over their shoulders at the laughing crowd of warriors. 'Let's take a walk.'

'You're not seriously thinking of going are you?' Heara asked as they made their way deeper into the forest.

Arrus turned to stare at her.

'Actually, yes I am.'

'What?' Arrus and Heara both responded at once.

Dia raised a hand. 'I'm going.'

'Then you've thought of a way to remove the curse?' Heara stopped to look at her. 'I thought you'd decided there was nothing to be done?'

Dia gave a slight shake of her head. 'That's probably still the case, but I've weighed up the consequences of me going and failing against those of my not going at all. Sheltering the Borrow refugees has begun a step toward friendship – or at least away from animosity – that refusing to even try to help with the curse might destroy. Even if I fail, they'll continue to be beholden to us, to owe us a debt. If I succeed … well, then no person of honour on the Borrows would even consider ever attacking the Fulmers again.'

Arrus snorted. 'You're assuming they have honour. You don't even like Temerran!'

'It's not a matter of liking him.' Dia frowned. 'I don't trust him. He uses a magic and a skill that manipulates people. This isn't about Temerran, though, this is about securing the future of the Fulmers.'

'Have you spoken to the other *walkers*?' Arrus asked.

She felt a moment of guilt. 'No, only Everlyn. She'll be the one to take my place with Pirelle until I return.'

'It should be Kesta,' Heara muttered.

'Well, we don't know where she is so we can't call her back.' Dia scowled. Concern crept into her heart. She couldn't begrudge her daughter leaving the Fulmers, yet her absence did leave a hole in their small community. With Larissa gone too, the small number of *walkers* seemed to have shrunk and no woman had developed magical ability in nearly two years. 'Listen, I know it's a risk me going to the Borrows, but it's a way to ensure the future security of our islands.'

'Unless it's a trap,' Arrus growled.

'Considering how much the Borrows have been decimated, I don't think they'd risk the lives of all those we have here as hostages, even if they are all from different clans.' Dia looked up at the trees, at the sunlight breaking through the dark-green leaves of summer. 'It will also give me a chance to learn more of the culture of the Borrows and their enigmatic bard. Not to mention the fact that if I do find a way to counter this blood curse, it will be a huge win for us all. I don't imagine Chem would sit back for years to come not considering some kind of revenge. And from what we learned from their attempted conquest, stealing *walkers* might very well be first on their list for rebuilding their power.'

'How do you know Temerran isn't planning to sell you to Chem and make a vast fortune?' Arrus demanded.

'Jorrun seemed to think we had defeated any Chemman who could beat me.' She bit at her thumbnail. Her husband's words had unsettled her more than she wanted to let on. 'I'm going to try.'

'Well I'm coming with you on this occasion.' Arrus prodded her in the chest with one finger. 'No arguments! Chieftain Ufgard can take care of the Fulmers for the few days we are away.'

'Agreed.' Dia nodded.

Arrus took a step back and glanced at Heara. 'Really?'

Dia laughed. 'Yes, Arrus, really. This will be an important and historic voyage for the Fulmers even if I fail to lift the curse. When we get back, though, we really must elect at least one new Silene.'

'Just one?' Heara raised an eyebrow.

'I hope to recall poor Worvig soon.' She sighed. 'We received a curt note from him saying he's had enough of Taurmaline. I'm thinking of sending Dorthai and another more experienced warrior to replace him now Larissa is settled.'

'Marlit would be my suggestion.' Arrus scratched at his beard.

Dia nodded, but her gaze was back up on the slowly moving leaves.

***

Dia rolled her shoulders and stretched her back, reaching out to grab for an inkwell that slid across the table. She glanced out of the cabin window and saw the horizon tilt first one way, then the other. With a sigh she placed a feather inside the pages and closed the book. It had been hard to read, not because of the unfamiliar words and strange sentence structure, but because of its content. Whoever had written this book on magic thought nothing of slaughtering people or animals to gain the required blood for a spell, to them blood was just a resource and its source no different than a candle or an herb. Thus far she hadn't found a single mention of the aftermath of a spell, of any residual effect. She couldn't believe the Chemman sorcerers were unaware such a thing occurred; although it was possible the writer of this book had never experienced death and spell casting on the scale of that used in the Borrows.

She pulled out the letter again that Rosa had sent, the words now so familiar she knew them by heart.

I've had no word from Kesta, I can only hope that she and Jorrun are safe. I hope this book is of use? Please try to return it, I'm sure the Thane will be furious if he finds it gone.

The wind blew a sudden flurry of rain against the window and she jumped at the sound. The summer storm had hit them at midday and showed no sign of letting them go. As comfortable as she was out at sea, even she'd begun to feel a little queasy. The door opened, banging against the wall as the ship tilted and Arrus came stomping in, water streaming from his long hair and beard.

'We've sighted the Borrows.' He wiped at his face with his hand and then grabbed for a towel, feet planted wide apart. He made the cabin feel tiny. 'Temerran's ship has signalled that we turn and let the storm take us west a little.'

The Borrowman Bard had offered to travel with them on their ship as a kind of hostage, but Dia had declined. She didn't feel happy having his strange magic on-board.

'What's Heara up to?' she asked.

Arrus closed his eyes and breathed out loudly. 'She's up in the crow's nest.'

Dia shot to her feet. 'She didn't take Catya up there, did she?'

Arrus' eyes widened. 'Spirits, no! I made sure the girl tied a line about herself and kept her feet firmly on the deck. I'll tell you something, Dia, it's as well your friend doesn't have daughters, they'd be more formidable than a whole Chemman army!'

'Arrus, what would you think of making Heara a Silene?'

'Seriously?' He pulled out a chair and sat himself down, a puddle forming on the planks beneath him. 'There is no one better at what she does.'

'But?'

'But since Shaherra's death she has become somewhat reckless.'

Dia leaned back in her chair and gazed up at the ceiling. 'There's a lot of anger in her and she's finding ways to channel it. Relatively healthy ways when all is said and done. She seems to have naturally slipped into the space left by Kesta, except she's no *walker*. When Larissa comes back from Elden, it's almost certain she will become both a Silene and the elected Icante heir.' Arrus opened his mouth to protest but Dia sat forward and stopped him. 'Kesta has chosen another life and we should be happy for her. I'll appoint Heara as acting Silene until Worvig returns and see how it goes.'

Arrus hunched in his chair, nodding without looking at her.

Dia gave a loud sigh and turned around in her chair. 'I'd better finish this awful book if we're nearly there.'

***

They anchored just beyond a small cove in the rugged island and both ships sent out a small boat toward the shore. Dia raised a hand to shield her eyes against the rain, the wind thankfully warm as it tugged at her clothing and hair. The cliffs were dark and jagged, several rocks spilling into the sea and making their approach dangerous. Arrus had wisely got his warriors to hold back and follow the Borrow boat in, letting them test for a safe channel. Dia grabbed at the side of the boat as they were lifted by the breakers. Her eyes scanned the island. There were a few deep-water birds off shore, but she could see nothing among the low, prickly bushes or the wind-shaped trees.

Arrus and three of the other warriors jumped out of the boat to drag them further up the beach. Catya stood up and Arrus lifted her off her feet, putting her down on the sand. Dia placed a hand on Catya's shoulder to keep her balance and climbed down beside her. Heara was already further up the beach, scanning the cliffs and checking the sand for tracks. Seeing what she was doing, Catya quickly copied.

'This is Samphire Island,' Temerran said as he made his way slowly across to them. His warriors had fanned out to form a protective ring.

'Expecting trouble?' Dia tilted her head.

'It's always wise to be cautious in the Borrows, even for the Bard.' He looked down at the sand with a deep frown on his face. 'This was where the Chemmen attacked first. Samphire had the largest population and the most warriors. I thought perhaps that if this is the place where the blood magic started ...'

'It's as good a place as any to try.' Dia wiped the rain from her face with her hand.

'There's a small copse just up the path here where we'll have more shelter.'

The hairs on Dia's arms prickled and the nausea of apprehension crawled in her stomach. She turned to look at Heara.

'Seems clear.' Heara nodded.

'Your men stay on the beach.' Dia looked at the Bard unblinking.

'Very well,' he agreed at once. One of his men went to protest but he raised a hand to silence him. 'It's this way.'

They trudged through the wet, sliding sand, and followed the narrow gully of a stream further inland. Bushes and small trees formed an arched roof above their heads. Temerran turned off the path and climbed up a steep slope to a hazel grove from the edge of which they could look back toward the beach and see their two ships. Her own Fulmer ship looked old and rustic compared to the Bard's well-built vessel. Heara and one of the other warriors made a search of the area, Catya remained close at Arrus's side.

'Do you feel it?' Temerran asked, his green eyes wide.

'I haven't opened up my magic yet,' she admitted. 'What do you feel?'

He leaned back against a tree, placing one hand flat against the bark. 'It feels like something is buzzing inside my skull so that nothing sounds quite right. Tones are flat. Sounds deadened.'

Dia looked away, glancing at Arrus before calling magic through her blood. She opened her *knowing*. She was struck by cold that went through to her bones and a metallic, iron taste lay like poison on her tongue. The feel of the lives around her was dulled, their emotions sharp but without depth, like the jab of needles.

She drew in a sharp breath as realisation struck her. Raising a hand, she agitated the air to call fire to her fingertips. Small flames danced there, without brightness, without heat.

'What is it?' Temerran asked, pushing himself away from the tree.

'It steals life from our magic as well as the land.' She let the flames die out.

'You're right.' Temerran rubbed at his face with his fingers. 'How can we use that?'

'I'm not sure if we can. I've been reading about their methods, they use blood in Chem to strengthen magic, there is something in blood that gives strength to a magic user, increases their power. They killed hundreds here and used their blood both in making their spells to control the dead, and to increase their own power so they could control more. They took a huge amount of magic from the land.'

'You think that's what this 'stain' is? That the magic has been sucked from the elements of this land?'

243

She shrugged. 'It's a theory. And, of course, death itself leaves a mark for those sensitive enough to feel it. This could be a combination of after effects.'

'It makes sense.' Temerran clenched his fists. 'But is there anything we can do?'

Dia wrapped her arms around herself, suppressing a shiver. 'I wonder if our using magic would make things worse or be ineffectual at best; especially as we don't know what we're doing. I still think time will be our best option, let the land heal itself, but a part of me deeply desires to fight it.'

Temerran's jaw moved as he gritted his teeth. 'Then you understand me.'

'How can you fight something that isn't solid, that you can't see?' Arrus asked.

Dia opened her mouth to reply and her intuition prickled again. '*Walkers* do so all the time, when we use our *knowing*, when we change how people feel. You asked if I could change the feel of the land and I said no, but I wonder if I was wrong. Perhaps even the small lives, the plants, even the stone, could retain a vibration of life and goodness, even as they now sound out the opposite. There is little magic left on the Borrows for us to use, but ...' She spun about to face Temerran. 'Doroquael said the fire-spirits cannot come here because the Borrows belongs to the sea-spirits. They called you back here, is your relationship with them good?'

'It's tempestuous, as it is between them and all mortals.'

'Take me to them.'

'Dia!' Heara moved toward her, her hand on her dagger hilt.

Dia raised her hand. 'This will be done.'

Temerran led them back toward the beach and Dia caught him glancing at her several times. Eventually he held her gaze, holding a branch back out of her way.

'Sea-spirits are not fire-spirits,' he said. 'They can be cruel.'

'Yet they travelled many miles to warn you of what had happened in the Borrows.' Dia frowned. 'They must care.'

'I'm not sure it's caring as such.' Temerran winced. 'Have you ever seen an orca, what you call a magpie whale, or a cat playing with its prey?'

Dia nodded.

'It's closer to that. Their interest in humans is seldom benevolent. As a bard I possess a certain ... influence over them. I cannot calm a real storm but I can a sea-spirit. They were not pleased at me leaving the Borrows and they no doubt saw this as an opportunity to lure me back.'

Dia felt dread creeping under her skin. This might be a bigger risk than she'd anticipated. When they reached the point where the stream met the beach, Temerran halted and looked around at them all.

'It would be best if it was just me and the Icante,' he said.

'Yeah, right.' Heara narrowed her eyes and put her hand on the hilt of her short sword. 'That ain't happening.'

Dia turned her head to hide her smile. 'Heara will come too.'

Arrus quickly placed a hand on Catya's shoulder and the girl scowled.

'Very well.' Temerran nodded.

He stepped out onto the beach and gestured for his men to stay back. Instead of heading directly toward the water, he turned to his right and clambered up onto the pitted rocks. The smaller ones were sharp with limpets and slippery with seaweed. He stepped up onto the higher rocks that stood above the level of the highest tide, holding his hand out to assist Dia. His fingers were warm and rough and he smelt strangely like the petrichor of rainfall. When they'd reached the furthest rock out in the sea, Temerran turned to warn the two women. 'Be wary.'

The Bard turned back toward the sea and closed his eyes, standing completely still. Dia could see his chest rise and fall as he breathed in deeply and through her *knowing* she felt him put himself into a meditative calm. Heara positioned herself so she could watch their backs and see what was happening on the beach.

Dia drew in a sharp breath when Temerran began to sing, his notes had the purity of a morning songbird although deeper in tone, reaching beyond her ears to her soul. She tried to catch the words but quickly realised they were in a tongue she'd never heard before. Dia felt the presence of the sea-spirits before she saw any sign of them, so different to fire-spirits, somehow deeper, slippery, strangely solid. A wave peaked and didn't subside, instead forming into the shape of a woman with hair of constantly streaming water.

'Why have you brought these creatures of fire before us, Bard?' Its voice rose and fell in a breathy rush.

'Spirit, you called me back here and I've come.' Temerran opened his green eyes. 'But the land on which we live is damaged by the blood magic of men. I cannot repair it. This fire queen has come to help.'

Dia tried not to feel flattered by the compliment his words so blatantly evoked. She bowed her head politely, but without subservience. 'Powerful spirit, I'm honoured to be in your presence.'

The spirit rushed upward to tower above them. Dia's eyes widened and she held her breath, but she took her cue from the Borrowman and didn't so much as flinch. Heara took one step back, her fingers twitching although she refrained from reaching for her weapons.

'The whales sing of you.' The spirit rippled, the sunlight shining through its opaque skin. 'That is the only reason I will hear your words.'

Dia bowed again, conceding nothing. 'The necromancers drained the life, the magic, from these islands to cast their spells and left the chill stain of death. I may be able to lift the ill feeling with help from Temerran, but there is not enough magic in me, or for me to channel, and stealing what there is would make things worse. Are you able to give us magic from the sea? Can you give Temerran power?'

The sea-spirit darkened and Dia could feel its wrath. Waves surged against the rock and she couldn't help but raise her arms to shield herself against the briny spray. 'We care not for the land! Where is your strength gone, Bard? You are a people of the sea, live on the sea, raid, fight, you don't need these soft fire-people! Be the storm, Bard!'

Dia laughed and both Temerran and the sea-spirit turned to stare at her.

'You are mistaken spirit. *I* am the storm.' She drew up all the power she had within her and reached for as much as she could around her. It took a huge amount of effort and pain seemed to split her skull in two. Even so she called a tornado to shield herself, both Heara and Temerran having to jump back onto another rock. The sea-spirit shrieked as Dia heated the water and steam rose rapidly to form the anvil shape of a thunderhead.

'I have wrecked ships too, spirit!' Lightning lit the dark cloud above her from within.

'You can't kill me!' The sea churned against Dia's wind shield.

Dia let her fire subside and she smiled sadly. 'Neither would I want to, spirit, but the fates of your Bard, of your chosen people, are in my hands.' Lightning struck the side of the rock on which Temerran stood. 'I want to help them. I don't even ask for anything in return. We are creatures of the land, spirit, we need the land to live and no demands on your part will change that. Help me heal at least one island of the Borrows so your people can thrive again and grow strong.' She realised Temerran was singing again, quietly, his words barely perceptible. The sea around her began to settle to a rhythmic shushing as though it breathed. She dropped her shield, the thunderhead began to drift away with the wind, grumbling as it went.

The spirit sank back toward the water. 'Only once,' it sulked. 'But the Bard must never leave these seas again.'

Dia saw the pain that crossed Temerran's face, but he bowed his head and nodded. 'Agreed.'

'Then lend me the magic of the sea, spirit.' She held out a hand toward it, palm upward and then turned to the Borrowman. 'Sing, Temerran. Sing to me of life.'

She felt the spirit's icy fingers touch her palm and then melt into her skin. Its power hurt, as though water were being forced through her veins, but she drew it in anyway, calling up her *knowing*. Temerran's voice rose, echoing in every crevice of the cliffs, making the muscles inside her chest tingle, filling her heart with emotion that spilled out from her eyes. She gave in to it, closing her eyes and letting her head fall back, her *knowing* flowing out to touch everything that lived, burrowing into the earth, vibrating the stone, pulsing through the twisted, stunted trees and imprinting into the rocky soul of the island.

She dropped to her knees and would have fallen over onto her side had Heara not caught her. The spirit tore itself free and Dia retched sea-water up from her lungs again and again, gasping for air. Dia could hear the spirit laughing and through her blurred vision she saw Temerran jump across to her rock to stand over her.

'That wasn't the bargain, spirit!' he shouted angrily.

A huge wave crashed over the rock, soaking them all, but the spirit withdrew.

Temerran quickly knelt. 'Is she all right?' he asked Heara. 'Get her over onto her stomach!'

Dia vomited again as they tried to lift and turn her, but she finally managed to wheeze air into her burning lungs. She could hear Arrus yelling her name.

'I'm all right,' she said hoarsely.

Heara and Temerran still held her firmly, leaning her forward.

'Get me a blanket!' The Bard's voice carried easily across the water to the beach. 'Icante,' he said quietly. 'The biggest regret of my life is that I never sailed to the Fulmers in friendship to know you and your people sooner instead of believing the ignorance of tradition. I am your servant, lady, now and always.'

'Did it work?' she panted.

Temerran stood and she looked up to see that he was standing with his eyes closed and his arms stretched out wide. 'Can you not feel it?' A smile spread across his face and he turned to look down at her, his emerald eyes bright. 'Life.'

***

They held a celebration on the beach that night, building huge bonfires despite the scarcity of wood on the islands. Any suspicion and animosity between the warriors of the Borrows and the Fulmers seemed to fall away as they shared food and alcohol and Dia wondered how much influence Temerran's song had had on that. The Borrowmen seemed particularly enthralled by Catya and her wild, bloodthirsty tales. Heara was a little more subdued than usual, both her and Vilnue keeping a careful eye on things. Arrus was doing what he did best, making everyone feel at ease and welcome, forging friendships where once there'd been hate. Dia sat quietly watching, the young warrior, Dorthai, hovering nearby in case of trouble without having had to be asked. She nodded to herself, making up her mind that he would be the one she'd send to replace Worvig in Elden.

Movement caught her eye and she saw Temerran making his way toward her. He handed her a cup and stood looking out to sea. 'That is an alcohol made from a plant, a cane, as sweet as honey in the land we sailed to far across the ocean. It might ease your throat.'

She smiled and nodded, too sore still from the sea-spirit's petty vengeance to speak much. He almost seemed to read her thoughts when he continued.

'Yes, I'm sad I won't see such lands again, but there are wonders to be seen here at home as well. Our world is changing.'

She nodded, taking a sip of the dark liquid in the cup and savouring the soothing burn of its warmth.

'Let's make sure it changes for the better,' she whispered.

'Let it be so,' Temerran replied.

Chapter Nineteen

Kesta; Covenet of Chem

Kesta breathed in deeply, savouring the leafy smell and the scent of recent rain. Some of the trees had begun to take on a yellowish hue, and she felt a stab of fear at the thought that the year was waning. Around her the women chattered, the two small children, Perta and Ursaith, running unsteadily across the grass. The palace gardens had become their favourite place to be, a tiny taste of freedom within the safety of the walls. In the six weeks since they'd taken the palace, they'd restored the palace guard to full strength and begun the recovery of the city guard. So far, no other coven had dared attack Navere, but it didn't leave Kesta feeling any less nervous.

'Kesta, can I ask something?'

She turned to see young Vilai looking up at her with her pretty brown eyes.

'Of course.' She frowned, wondering what had made her nervous. Vilai had been the fourth of the women to open up her magic. The first had been Jollen, whose son had been murdered by Cepack. She'd been followed by Rey, one of the oldest of the women, and then Beth who was almost six months pregnant. Only one other had found her power since Vilai, and that was Perta's mother, Estre. There was still hope for the others, all except tattooed Calayna.

'Why can't you eat meat?'

Kesta felt relief at so simple a question. 'As a *walker* I feel the emotions of living things, and that includes animals. They feel the same fear, the same pain, the same hope, love and sometimes even humour as a person does. It is hard to kill and eat something you know felt terror at its death, that you know will be mourned and missed by its mate, by its family. It's hard to kill something whose unique personality you have held inside your own soul.'

'Is it true that Fulmer people …' Vilai's pale skin blushed bright red. 'Is it true they, um, bond with animals?'

Kesta snorted. 'I'm sure you're alluding to something other than 'bonding!' No. We don't. We respect animals, we do our best not to harm them. We see them as our brothers and sisters in this life. Sometimes a *walker* will make a strong emotional attachment to an animal, an exceptional friendship. It's discouraged, though. Such a friendship can take an animal away from its natural behaviour, deprive it of its own kind, and a chance to have young. My mother has a particular affinity with birds and, as I discovered quite recently, ravens in particular love her!'

'Is that why we are to become the Raven Coven?'

Kesta smiled. 'Almost. We have taken the name from my husband's home, from his Raven Tower.'

'Will we give the men our gift tonight?' Vilai asked excitedly.

'Yes, at dinner.'

A buzz of excitement ran through the women and their chattering ceased. It was a moment before Kesta realised what it was that had excited them. Estre called out to Perta, lifting the toddler onto her hip and bidding her shush. Hidden out of sight by a high hedge, someone was singing. His voice was low, but not gratingly deep, the notes as pure as a well-played flute. Kesta couldn't make out the words but the harmonic purr of the 'r's told her it was a Chemman, the women's excitement gave away the man.

'Leave him be.' Kesta shook her head, but little Ursaith ran around the hedge and the singing ceased.

'Hello, little one.'

Kesta followed the others across the grass toward the seat hidden within the high conifer hedge. She forced a smile at Osun who was staring down at the young child with the bemused look of someone who'd never had much to do with children.

'We're sorry to disturb you.' Kesta apologised. She looked around at the other women, none of them looked particularly sorry. She supposed she couldn't blame them, to them Osun was a hero, a kind and daring man; they didn't know his past. She didn't have the heart to tell them, for a start it would destroy their trust and any chance of forming these women into a coven.

Osun brushed a black curl back from his forehead, glancing around at the women until his blue eyes found Kesta and stayed there as though finding a safe harbour in uncharted seas. She almost laughed. This much female attention was probably completely unknown to a Chemman.

He cleared his throat. 'Are your lessons going well?'

'Well enough.' Kesta frowned. 'Should you be out here on your own?'

Osun rubbed at his forehead to hide his eyes. 'I spent most of my life alone. I haven't had a moment to myself in six weeks.'

Kesta's heart burned in sympathy, but she looked away, unable to meet his eyes. She'd barely had a moment to herself either, but at least she had the sanctuary of the library she shared with Jorrun. 'See if a fire-spirit will keep an eye on you,' she chastised. 'How on earth did you manage to give Cassien the slip?'

'He was sleeping. I sent Jagna on an errand.'

Kesta's fists clenched. 'Jagna should know better, as should you.'

She realised all the women were watching her, some wide-eyed and open-mouthed. Although they'd begun to find the courage to speak to Jorrun and Osun, Kesta's behaviour and attitude was still somewhat shocking to them. She gave a slight shake of her head.

'I understand, Osun, I really do, but we can't take risks.'

His shoulders slumped, and he looked down at the grass for a moment.

'You could maybe walk with us for a while, Lord?' Vilai spoke up. She was shaking a little and Kesta had to admire her bravery in breaking a lifetime of conditioning.

Osun nodded and stood up slowly. He glanced at Kesta. 'I guess that will save me from being told off any more!'

Vilai giggled, then placed her hand quickly over her mouth. The bruises that had been there when Kesta had first met her had faded, her wrist had been broken by one of Cepack's men.

'Any news from the city?' Kesta asked seriously. With most of her time taken up with guarding and training the women she had to rely on Jorrun and Azrael to bring her information.

'The market has been back up and trading under official supervision for a week now and we've started to receive more outside traders.' He walked beside her across the lawn. 'I've had a message from a friend in Margith, Farkle, he advises that as yet the sorcerer, Tembre, hasn't made an attempt on that Seat.'

'Nothing from Arkoom?'

'Thankfully, no.' He glanced at her. 'Although the day will come when we are summoned there to sit at council. Without allies there or our coven trained and stronger, we might as well jump straight in the sea and drown.'

'And if we just ignored such a summons?'

Osun blew air out through his mouth. 'We might get away with it for a while, but not attending will alert everyone to the fact we are weak. We can only hope Feren has problems of his own and doesn't dare call a council yet.'

'So, we are pretty much in a race against time as to who can get the most allies or become the strongest first?'

'Pretty much.' He brushed some hair back from his face.

Movement caught Kesta's eye and she halted, grabbing Osun's arm. One of the guards was making his way across the lawn, almost running.

'My Lord, Ladies!' he called out. 'A ship has come into Navere dock! It flies an Elden flag!'

Kesta and Osun looked at each other and grinned.

'Get captain Rece to take two dozen men down to the docks and escort the Elden delegation back here,' Osun ordered.

'At once, Lord.' The guard bowed.

A frown settled on Osun's face as they hurried back into the palace.

'What's wrong?' Kesta asked him.

Osun gave a slight shake of his head and glanced at her. 'Word of this will reach Arkoom. It might push Feren into action.'

'But I thought the whole idea was to show that we had big allies as well as to bring trade and wealth to Navere?'

'It was always a gamble, but then this whole venture is.'

Captain Rece came hurrying out with several of his men behind him. 'My Lord, is this a threat?' he demanded.

'Not at all.'

Kesta noticed the way Osun changed the tone of his voice, how he used it to reassure as well as convey confidence and authority.

'They were invited here by me,' Osun went on. 'They have come to trade and are to be treated as guests.'

The captain's eyebrows shot up, but he bowed and hurried on his way. Rece had proved himself an able and trustworthy man, getting his men into order and adapting quickly to his new situation. Some of the guards they'd had to dismiss for mistreatment of the slaves and inability to accept the authority of the women. Kesta had used her magic on nearly twenty guards to demonstrate her power before the palace had finally settled.

Jorrun was waiting for them in the audience room, his eyes widened on seeing Osun with Kesta and among the palace women. 'I've sent word out to our most loyal traders to get themselves down to the docks,' he said.

'Good.' Osun went to the comfortable chair that had replaced their father's ornate one, but didn't sit down. 'I think it's time we present ourselves as a coven.'

Jorrun nodded and turned to one of the servants. 'Could you please bring more chairs in here, enough for all the ladies?'

The young man gave a nod and darted away.

'What of those of us that have no power?' Calayna asked, her arms folded across her chest.

'Just because you have no magic, doesn't mean you have no power,' Jorrun replied.

'Don't forget I am 'bloodless'.' Osun sat in the chair and regarded the tattooed woman. 'You all have a right to sit in this coven, if you wish to do so.'

Kesta suddenly remembered their surprise. 'Vilai, Jollen, and Rey, please take four guards and go and get that thing we have been working on. Wake Cassien and bring him here also.'

Vilai's face lit in delight and the three women almost ran from the room.

Jorrun's eyes narrowed but Kesta just grinned at him.

'Is Jagna back yet?' Osun asked Jorrun who shook his head.

They were still setting out the chairs to fill out a semi-circle with Osun's seat at the centre when Vilai and the others returned with Cassien, carrying a large piece of dark-green cloth between them. Kesta stood back, watching Jorrun and Osun's faces as the ladies worked together to unravel it and take the edges to hold it up as best they could. Osun's mouth fell open and he glanced at Jorrun, taking a few slow steps toward it. They'd sewn a huge banner, black raven on a green field. The room went quiet, all the women waiting for Osun's reaction. Jorrun moved closer to Kesta and reached out to squeeze her fingers.

'Thank you,' he whispered.

Osun's hand went to his mouth and he cleared his throat. It was a moment before he spoke. 'This is amazing, sisters.'

Kesta drew air in sharply through her mouth. *Sisters.* She regarded Jorrun, he had tensed his shoulders and was blinking rapidly.

'You like it?' Vilai asked timidly.

Osun grinned. 'I love it! Let's get it up in the wall before our guests arrive! Cassien, find a hammer and nails, quickly!'

They had barely settled before Captain Rece strode in to announce that the Eldemen were at the palace. Jagna hurried in just behind him and gave Osun a quick nod before taking a seat. Jorrun had taken the place to Osun's left and Kesta to his right, Cassien sitting somewhat awkwardly between Estre and Calayna.

Kesta recognised the man that led the Elden delegation but couldn't name him until Jorrun did.

'Merkis Teliff, welcome.'

'Thane, good to see you.' Teliff pursed his lips in a smile.

'I believe you know Osun and my wife, these here are our brothers and sisters of the Raven Coven.'

Teliff gestured for one of the men with him to come forward. 'We have letters, and gifts from King Bractius.'

Kesta sat up straight, her heart beating faster. *News from home!*

'We thank you,' Osun replied. 'There should be Navere traders already on their way to the docks to see what you bring. In the meantime, would you sit and join us for some refreshments and give us news of Elden?'

'We'd be delighted.' Teliff gave a bow.

Kesta looked longingly at the chest that contained the letters.

'Jorrun, would you take our correspondence to the library?' Osun said over his shoulder. 'I'll join you shortly.'

Jorrun touched the back of Kesta's hand with one finger. 'Come on.'

He took the small chest from the Elden warrior and carried it to the library. Kesta bit at her lower lip, holding her breath as he placed it on the table and opened the lid. Paper rustled as he looked through it and he handed her a letter sealed with green wax. As soon as she saw the handwriting, she ripped it open, her eyes devouring her mother's words. She barely glanced at Jorrun who was uncurling a scroll.

'Is all well in the Fulmers?' he asked.

Kesta pulled out a chair, almost missing it as she sat down, her eyes running over her mother's words again.

'Kesta?'

She held up a hand, coming back to the end of the letter. 'All is well, I think.' She bit her lower lip again and held out her hand for his. 'Mother has managed to remove the blood curse from one of the Borrow Islands by forging an alliance with a mysterious bard and a sea-spirit! She implies she is worried about Larissa though, what news of Elden?'

He frowned, letting go of her fingers to hold his scroll open again. 'Bractius is vague in his references to Elden's status, but he does mention something strange. He says he has been plagued by nightmares and wishes I was there to correct them, but that Larissa has recommended rosemary under his pillow.' He handed her the scroll and she exchanged it for her mother's letter.

It was Kesta's turn to frown as she read through Bractius' odd message. 'Is he trying to tell us something?'

Jorrun shrugged. 'If he is, I don't understand his meaning.' His face broke into a grin and he waved her mother's letter. 'This is amazing, Kesta. The Borrows and the Fulmers working together. Hope has been born from my father's destruction.'

She stood up, crumpling Bractius' scroll in her hand as she hugged him fiercely, delighting in his relief and joy. His hand tangled in her hair and they'd been kissing for some time before the discreet cough finally registered in her mind. She untangled herself from Jorrun quickly, turning to see Osun standing in the library, his eyes firmly fixed on the floor. Heat rose to her cheeks, and she straightened her tunic and pushed her hair back from her face.

'My apologies, Osun,' Jorrun muttered.

'No.' Osun gave his head a furious shake.

Kesta drew in a sharp breath, coloured light from the stained-glass window caught the moisture in Osun's eyes and on his cheek.

'No, don't apologise,' Osun went on, shifting his feet. 'Do you know what the two of you need to do to change Chem? Nothing. Nothing other than to be yourselves and let others see it. There is hardly a man or woman in Chem who wouldn't long for what you have.' He turned and all but fled the room. Kesta instinctively moved to follow him but Jorrun grabbed her arm.

'Give him a moment,' he said softly.

Kesta stared at the library door, her heart beating hard against her ribs. She couldn't believe how much empathy she was feeling, how much sympathy, for a man she professed to hate.

Chapter Twenty

Ayline; Kingdom of Elden

'I have to go,' she said it firmly, gritting her teeth afterward, but Ayline didn't let go of his hand or sit up from where she lay against his shoulder and chest. The light was already beginning to fade outside the tower window and the cold air stung her bare skin where it was uncovered by the blanket. The baby was quiet within her but her back began to ache and she pulled herself up a little in the bed.

'I can't see you anymore, Inari, it's getting dangerous, people will notice.'

'As you wish.'

She sat up and glared at him. He never argued. She'd lost count of how many times she'd insisted they call off their affair. Somehow, she always found herself making excuses to slip away from her ladies and climb the long steps up the tower.

'Fetch my dress.' She drew her arms up and across her belly. It would be another two months yet until her baby would be born. Part of her dreaded it, part of her couldn't wait, not least because she hated being so uncomfortable.

Inari slipped his trousers on before handing her the ample maternity dress she'd worn to the tower.

'You are the most beautiful woman in all of Elden,' he said.

She narrowed her eyes. 'How do you do that?'

'Do what?' His green eyes were wide and innocent. She kept forgetting he was as young as she was.

'Know what I'm thinking.'

He closed his eye and bowed his head. 'It's because I love you, your majesty.'

Her heart swelled but she tensed her muscles and snatched the dress. 'Don't forget your place, Inari. Did you learn anything useful today?'

'The King consulted with Larissa again about his nightmare—'

'I wish that witch would just die!' Ayline snarled. 'No matter how much I do, Bractius still runs to her for counsel and ignores me!'

Inari helped her into the dress and gently laced up the back of it, kissing her neck when he was done. 'You've succeeded in being involved in all of his audience—'

She snorted and spun about to face him. 'He may let me sit there, but he doesn't let me speak or listen when I do. Perhaps I should find a way to change the colour of one of my eyes or dye my hair red.'

'The problem is Bractius, not Larissa.' Inari's tone was calm and reasonable. 'But with her witch's power she is likely to perceive your intent and learn of what is between us. If she hasn't already.'

Sudden panic struck Ayline and the baby kicked out.

'I can get rid of the witch for you.'

Ayline laughed. 'You? How can a servant get rid of a Fulmer witch?'

Inari's expression didn't change, he didn't even blink. It sent a shiver down Ayline's spine. She turned and headed for the door. 'I won't be seeing you again, Inari.'

He didn't reply. He knew she didn't mean it; and so did she.

***

Ayline watched the new Fulmer delegates as discreetly as she could. It was their first formal dinner since Silene Worvig had returned back to the islands and Bractius had invited them to his private dining room rather than the

262

chaotic great hall. As always Adrin was there, still high in her husband's favour, along with his two closest advisors, Merkis Teliff and Merkis Dalton. Bractius had seated Larissa and Teliff to either side of him, while she was seated at the opposite end of the very long table with the young warrior Dorthai. Everything about the young Fulmer warrior was dark; his eyes, his skin, his hair, his clothing and even his mood. Like Worvig before him, he didn't particularly seem to want to be in Taurmaline.

Larissa laughed, a rich, womanly sound that made Ayline grind her teeth together. 'I'm sure Kesta Silene enjoyed putting those Chemmen in their place very much!'

Ayline realised they were discussing Teliff's recent journey to Chem and she sat up straighter, paying more attention. Ayline had not been privy to his report to Bractius on his return the day before yesterday and her husband had told her annoyingly little. She'd only found out Jorrun was even in Chem by eavesdropping.

Adrin, who was seated to her right, snorted into his ale, but said nothing. She'd come to realise weeks ago that Bractius's favourite chieftain hated both Jorrun and Kesta. She'd suggested to Inari that they use it, but her lover had dismissed Adrin as worthless.

Ayline cleared her throat. 'And did Thane Jorrun find it amusing?'

'Aye, your majesty.' Merkis Teliff bowed in her direction. 'He was very proud indeed. In fact, despite their precarious position, the Thane seemed extraordinarily happy.'

'Why would that be, do you think?' Larissa asked.

'Well.' Teliff gave a shrug. 'I would say he was very much in love with his wife.'

Ayline banged her cup down on the table, realising her error when everyone turned to stare at her. 'Oh, please excuse me,' she said. 'The baby kicked.'

There were several 'ahs' from around the table, but when Ayline glanced up she saw Larissa was watching her through narrowed eyes.

'You say their situation is precarious?' Adrin said, his mouth full of food.

'They've actually done a good job of establishing themselves,' Teliff replied. 'But the women there are only in the early stages of their training.'

'Will you send another ship soon?' Larissa asked Bractius. 'Perhaps we could send them a *walker* and warriors to reinforce their position?'

'I had warriors left there to assist.' Bractius placed a hand over Larissa's momentarily and Ayline's spine stiffened. 'But Osun was concerned that too much help from us would look like an invasion from a foreign power rather than a revolution.'

Larissa nodded, subtly freeing her hand to pick up her glass. 'He is probably right.'

'We'll be establishing a regular trade route though.' Bractius scratched at his beard. 'Taking in the Fulmers and the Borrows also.'

'The Borrows?' Adrin almost spat his food across the table.

Ayline glared at him, but the warrior ignored her. She felt her anger rise. How had she ever thought this oaf was charming?

'Talking of the Borrows.' Bractius' eyes lit up with his grin. 'I have some news for you all. After corresponding with the Icante and, through her, the Borrow refugees, I've invited a rather unusual guest to Taurmaline.'

'Don't tease us.' Larissa pouted.

'The Borrowman's mysterious Bard will be docking at Taurmouth two days from now and he'll be coming here to sing for us!' Bractius looked around at them all to gauge their reactions.

Ayline jumped in quickly. 'Is it safe to have such a man here?' She placed her hands protectively over her belly.

'He owes the Icante a great debt,' Larissa replied. 'And Elden also, for the supplies you yourself collected for them.'

Ayline's nostrils flared and she struggled to find the words to put the witch in her place.

'They are all islanders, all witches, I wouldn't trust any of them,' Adrin muttered.

Dorthai leapt to his feet, his chair scraping back as he slammed his hands down on the table. 'You insult us!'

Ayline stared up at him, eyes wide and mouth open. She couldn't help it, she giggled. Adrin turned to grin at her.

Both Bractius and Larissa stood, the Fulmer woman quickly remembering her place and sitting down again. Ayline couldn't believe it when Bractius' anger was directed at Adrin rather than Dorthai. 'Apologise to our guests, Chieftain.'

'You misunderstand me,' Adrin said, his hands raised, palms upward. 'I was talking of the Borrow folk. They have been enemy to all of us here for generations.'

'The world has changed, Adrin.' Bractius eyed his chieftain and Ayline knew her husband realised full well Adrin was lying. 'We have no enemies now but for those few necromancers remaining in Chem.'

Adrin turned to Dorthai and held out his hand. 'My apologies, man, I have every respect for the Fulmers.'

Dorthai's eyes narrowed, but the young man took Adrin's hand. He didn't so much as blink when Adrin squeezed much too hard and Ayline saw the Fulmer warrior's darker skin whiten in Adrin's grip. Adrin let go and Dorthai sat, bowing toward Bractius.

'Come, let's eat.' Bractius leaned forward to rip the leg off a roasted chicken. Ayline couldn't help but smile as Larissa blanched in disgust.

An idea came to her. 'Husband, would you allow me to see to the arrangements for welcoming our Borrow guests?'

He tilted his head to look at her. 'Yes. Yes, of course, if you would like to?'

'I would love to.' She smiled, excitement making her blood flow faster, her eyes narrowing as she thought over her delightful, if small, chance for revenge.

***

Autumn was the perfect time for holding a feast. Food was plentiful and The Earth Mother provided her own colourful decorations in leaves and berries to string about the hall. Ayline had ordered two rams and a pig slaughtered along with a large array of fowl. She wondered if the witch had felt their deaths, she hoped so, either way she looked forward to seeing Larissa's freckled nose wrinkling in distress at the smell of so much cooking flesh.

Bractius came striding into the great hall with his steward and the Huskarl, Tursac who administrated the household for him. The servants all scampered to get out of their way. Bractius saw her and beamed.

'This all looks marvellous!' He bent to kiss her cheek and squeezed her arm.

She was annoyed at how grateful she was for that small show of affection. 'We are nearly done. Has the ship been sighted yet?'

Tursac shook his head but it was Bractius who spoke. 'Not as yet, but it should be at the lake within the hour.' He rubbed at one of his eyes and then stifled a yawn.

'You did not sleep well again?' Ayline asked him.

Bractius growled in frustration. 'It's those damned dreams. Do you know, last night I dreamt that when the Borrowman Bard started singing, snakes came pouring out of his mouth!'

Ayline drew in a sharp breath. 'Perhaps it was an omen?'

Bractius laughed and she felt her hackles rise. 'Nonsense! If Jorrun were here he would tell you it's a dream brought on by normal, everyday worries. If there was anything about this Temerran to be concerned about then the Icante would have warned me.'

'Unless they are in league.'

Bractius's eyes widened but he snorted. 'You women have such wild fancies. I was just telling Larissa the same.'

'Why, what did Larissa say?'

'Only that my dreams might not be natural. Foolishness, just because her herbs and teas haven't worked. I'm just concerned about Jorrun and what's going on in Chem, it's as simple as that.'

'You're really that worried? I wish you would talk to me about it.'

'You don't need my worries.' He patted her rounded abdomen as tentatively as though it were a temperamental dog that might turn and bite him.

'How many times do I have to tell you I want to be involved?' She flicked his hand away in annoyance. 'You talk to that Fulmer woman, you should be talking to me!'

'Are you jealous, my Queen?' He grinned at her and she felt her temperature rise. She wanted to slap his smug face! Tursac shifted his feet and looked away.

'No, I just want the respect I am owed.'

Bractius's eyebrows lowered over the bridge of his nose, darkening his eyes and his fingers curled into fists. She stepped back, holding her breath.

'This is not the place,' he said through gritted teeth. 'Come, Tursac, let's look over those tythe figures from Cainridge.'

Ayline let out her breath as the king left the great hall. Looking around she spotted an empty-handed servant. 'Don't just stand there. Go and get the glasses and start setting them out!'

***

Ayline sat serenely with her eyes closed while her ladies-in-waiting rushed around the room in a shrill panic. Her maid, Lerra, had such a gentle touch as she pinned up Ayline's hair, it was easy to relax despite the chaos.

'All done,' the girl said quietly.

'One minute and then we go,' Ayline declared, standing up.

One of the women gave a shriek and there was a flurry of fabric. One of the ladies in particular, Sonay, had been getting on her nerves recently, always trying to tag along when Ayline was trying to visit her tower, asking too many personal questions. Ayline narrowed her eyes. Perhaps it was time for a wedding. Sonay was quite pretty and stupidly naïve. Yes, Adrin would do for her very well.

'Let's go!'

Ayline grasped her dress to lift the skirts a little and she headed down to the great hall. Her ladies scattered off to their various seats while she made her way over to stand beside her husband. He barely greeted her, continuing instead with his conversation with Merkis Dalton.

A page came scampering into the hall and a murmur of anticipation travelled about the room. She and Bractius moved to their places at the high table as the herald announced;

'Temerran, Bard of the Borrows!'

Ayline wasn't sure what she'd expected, but it certainly wasn't the elegantly dressed and achingly handsome man who walked in. His curly, copper hair was like fire-light and his dark-green eyes every bit as startling as Inari's. He must have been in his thirties, although his smile brought deep creases to the skin around his eyes. He gave a low bow.

'Your majesties, I'm deeply honoured by your invitation.'

There was a slight accent to his voice that wasn't dissimilar to Jorrun's.

'Welcome, Temerran of the Borrows.' Bractius held out his hands. 'We are glad you accepted.'

The Borrowman's eyes searched their faces and then, strangely, seemed to search the air around them as though hunting for their shadows. Temerran froze, but briefly, his eyes widening and fixed on something behind Ayline. She couldn't help it, she turned to see Inari there, waiting with a decanter of wine.

'Come have a seat beside me,' Bractius invited. 'There's room for your men at the tables there.'

Temerran turned his attention back to the King, his smile hadn't waned in the slightest. 'You honour me. Would you allow me to first present you with my gifts? A personal thank you for the aid you sent the people from whom I was born.' He looked over his shoulder and one of his men stepped forward to hand him a long, flat box. Temerran opened it and lifted it to show its contents around the room. There were sighs and gasps and Ayline shifted in her chair, trying to glimpse what it held.

'For her majesty.' Temerran stepped forward and then went down on one knee. 'Pearls from the deep ocean, although they pale beside her beauty.'

Ayline's face grew warm despite her determination not to fall for such blatant flattery. She longed to see both Bractius's and Inari's expressions. She gave a graceful nod of her head in thanks as a page brought the box to her.

'And for his majesty.' Temerran turned to take a sword in a blue sheath from another of his men. 'A sword forged from the volcanic iron of the Borrow Islands. May it serve you and Elden well.'

Bractius took the sword from his page, drawing it and summoning more murmurs from the guests in the hall. 'It's a good blade.' He nodded. 'Come, man, come and eat!'

Temerran returned the King's grin and hopped lightly up onto the dais, making his way around the long table to the seat beside the King. Larissa was at his other side with Dalton to her left. Adrin had been placed to Ayline's right with Jarl Hadger of Tourmouth and his wife beyond him. She smiled to herself. She'd had Dorthai and the other Fulmer warrior who'd come with him seated at a lower table. Strangely, she'd never have done the same to Silene Worvig, she found herself missing the man's quiet dignity.

She realised she was frowning and forced a smile to her face. She gestured over her shoulder and recognised the scent of Inari without having to look up. 'Take these pearls and have them safely locked away in my room.'

'Yes, your majesty.'

Temerran proved to be genuinely fascinating to listen to. Even Adrin stopped talking to hear the Bard's stories about his adventures on the sea and called in delighted disbelief for descriptions of more of the animals and monsters Temerran had allegedly encountered. She noticed he avoided any mention of raiding or the Fulmers, as tempted as she was to cause upset to Larissa, she bit her tongue.

'Would you be kind enough to sing for us?' Larissa asked.

'Oh, yes, you must!' Ayline said, forgetting for a moment that Larissa was her enemy.

'Well, then I will be delighted.' Temerran stood and made his way over to where the Elden musicians were playing. One of his men brought him over a lyre and the Eldemen politely gave way. At first, he just played a complex and temperate melody that made Ayline think of the view from her lake tower as the sun slowly set beyond the water and the birds flocked to dance spirals above it. Then he began to sing, the first few words in a language she didn't know, but the words made Larissa stiffen in her seat. All at once the tune changed and he was singing a popular Elden ballad. Ayline shook herself, the alteration to the melody had been so subtle she hadn't perceived when it had happened.

Temerran played for nearly an hour, encouraged by shouts for more from the guests in the hall, until Bractius himself intervened to give the man a break. Ayline was loathe to leave when there was so much to learn and observe, but eventually exhaustion got the better of her and she had to excuse herself. She made her way over to Temerran and the Bard offered his arm to steer her away from his audience to where they could speak quietly.

'I don't mean to be rude, but the baby takes all my energy these days,' she said. She found herself frowning at his wide, green eyes.

'There is no need to apologise, your majesty.' He continued to stare at her, his smile fading. 'Be careful, your majesty, there is a darkness around yo—'

'What?' She pulled her hand free. 'What are you talking about.'

'Dark thoughts,' he said. 'Dark words.'

She opened her mouth to protest, to berate him, but no sound would come. Breathing hard, she turned and hurried from the hall, several of her ladies scampering after her. Had they heard?

'Leave me in peace!' she snapped over her shoulder. 'Can't you see I'm tired and going to bed?'

'Is there anything we can do, your majesty?' Sonay asked. 'Some chamomile te—'

Ayline stepped into her room and slammed the door in the girl's face. Lerra immediately scrambled up off her mattress on the floor.

'Help me out of my dress!' Ayline demanded.

The girl did so and Ayline wondered if she noticed the sweat that seemed to trickle down her back. What had that Borrowman meant by dark words? What did he know? Fear locked her spine as she climbed quickly under her blankets. She waved a hand to dismiss Lerra but bade her leave the candles lit. Darkness seemed to press against her bedroom window, the leaded panels of glass seeming a flimsy defence against the night.

***

Ayline awoke to the sound of rapid whispering in her outer chamber. Grabbing her robe she went over to the door and wrenched it open.

'What's going on?'

She froze when she saw Sonay, red-faced and crying. 'Oh, your majesty! It's the worst news! Lady Larissa has been found dead in her bed and the King has ordered the guards gather all the Borrowmen and escort them to the audience room.'

'Help me get dressed, quickly.' She had to rub at her nose to hide the wild grin that wanted to grow there, at the same time as her heart pounded and fear seemed to weaken the muscles of her knees.

As soon as she was dressed, she rushed out into the hall, only to come face to face with Inari, calmly replacing candles in the sconces. One side of his mouth twitched upward into a smile, it wasn't a pleasant smile, there was no humour in his eyes.

'What have you done?' she hissed.

'What you asked.' He regarded her unblinking. 'Removed our enemy as well as destroyed the peace between the Fulmers and the Borrows. Oh, and by the way, I think you'll find your husband's nightmares will stop now the witch is dead.'

'What do you mean?'

His eyes grew hard. 'Use that pretty little head of yours, Ayline.'

She gasped. 'How dare you address me that way!'

He continued to smile at her, his cold, dead smile.

A chill swept through Ayline's heart and grabbing her skirts she all but ran to the audience room.

Chapter Twenty-One

Osun; Covenet of Chem

It was almost eerily quiet after the bustle and energy of the Elden delegation's visit. Beside Osun his clerk's quill scratched away at his parchment and he sighed over the figures. Cassien was sitting by the door reading, he was one of the very few people brave enough to dare borrow a book from the palace library even though he could barely read. Jorrun still slept in there, up on the balcony, refusing to use any of the bedrooms of the palace. Osun could understand why although he preferred not to think too deeply about it.

'Well, things are actually getting better,' the clerk said. 'Even with the increased wages and the need for more food. Did you want to start looking at improvements across the city?'

'No, not yet.' Osun tapped at his lip. 'We'll continue to concentrate on defences and restoring order for the moment. Get me some surveys done though, see what the city needs and we'll prioritise what we can. Did you look through my fath—' Osun gritted his teeth. 'Did you get a chance to look through Dryn's ledgers?'

'I did, master. He was very shrewd in the running of Navere. I ... hope that doesn't offend you?'

Osun stood up and paced across the study, Cassien glanced up from his book. 'How can the truth offend?' Osun replied. 'If what he did worked, we'd be foolish not to learn from it.'

'Very good, master.' The clerk didn't look up, but dipped his pen. Osun narrowed his eyes. The man was one of the Rowen Order, but it was too soon to say if they could trust him or not. 'Get me those reports as soon as you ca—'

Someone knocked at the door and Cassien dropped his book, his right hand going to his sword as he stood to open the door with his left. One of the palace guards stood there, bowing quickly.

'There is a man come from Margith to see you, master,' the guard said. 'Name of Farkle Warne.'

Osun's mouth automatically formed itself into a smile and his heart swelled, his hand moved up to touch his face. *Farkle!* For a moment he couldn't find his voice. He shook his head. 'Show him to the audience room.' He turned to Cassien. 'Who is with me today?'

'Jorrun.' Cassien informed him.

'Good.' He felt less relief than he used to that Kesta hadn't been assigned to him today. She mostly spent her days still with the palace sisters but on occasion took a turn to sit in on audiences with one or two of the other women. They'd tried to get the guards of the palace to address the palace women of blood as 'mistress,' but it had been a step too far too soon for most of them. 'Sister' seemed to sit more comfortably with the Chemmen. A few insisted on calling Kesta 'Master.' It was a start. He turned to the clerk.

'I'll get this finished off,' the man reassured him.

Osun gave a nod and stepped out of the door Cassien held open for him. Two guards remained outside his study, but two others stepped away from the door to follow them along the hall and down the stairs. They entered the audience room through a door at the rear; Jorrun was waiting with Jagna, Jorrun already on his feet. They'd settled on setting three large and sturdy chairs at the top end of the hall facing down its long length to the door. To either side several other chairs fanned out for when all the coven met. Osun couldn't help but smile at the large green banner.

'Osun?'

He waved a hand toward his half-brother. 'The accounts have improved a little,' he mumbled in reply, sitting in the central seat and indicating the guard should let in their guest. Jorrun and Jagna settled in the chairs to either side of him.

The doors opened and a ragged figure stepped in, leaning on the arm of one of the palace guards. Osun drew in a sharp breath and all good humour left him. He jumped to his feet and hurried toward the seemingly old man, evoking a cry of alarm from Cassien. Osun barely heard Jorrun tell the young man to stay back.

'Farkle?' Osun slowed to peer at the man's almost skeletal face. Farkle barely seemed able to lift his feet and his back was bent over as he clutched at the guard. 'What has befallen you?' He turned toward the servant who waited on them only to find Jorrun had already brought one of the chairs down the hall. The guard settled Farkle in it and then stepped back.

Farkle gave Osun a thin-lipped smile that somehow revolted him, although he hid it as best he could. 'My illness has finally got the better of me, master Osun.'

'Please, call me brother as you always have. Why on earth did you travel here if you're so ill?' Osun barely glanced at Cassien who'd brought two more chairs over for Osun and Jorrun.

'My son is settled.' Farkle gave a wheeze. Dread settled like a stone in Osun's stomach as he regarded the man's face. He was dying, painfully slowly, but right there before his eyes. 'My affairs in order. I wanted to see for myself how my old friend Osun had done for himself, see his grand palace and his coven of women!' Farkle gave a shake of his head and a spark of amusement came back to his rheumy eyes. 'Also, I've never seen the sea.'

'What, never?' Cassien exclaimed.

Osun hissed at him to shush. 'Your son is settled? Is there good news then from Margith?'

Farkle nodded. 'Tembre took your advice and used stealth and guile to take Margith rather than risk his small coven in an attack of force. He won over servants, then guards, then one or two of the sitting coven. He now holds Margith and credits it to your careful planning.'

Osun clenched his fists, biting back the cry of triumph he wanted to give.

'He sends gifts as thanks but also a few words. He says he still doesn't hold with giving women power, but, as agreed, he will harm none in his keeping.'

'It's a start.'

Osun looked around at Jorrun, seeing the tension in his shoulders and the lines above the bridge of his nose.

'Forgive me.' Osun sat back a little. 'Farkle let me introduce you to my birth-brother, Jorrun. Jorrun, this is my ... this is my friend, Farkle Warne.' The word felt alien on his lips and was like a wriggling snake in his heart. He didn't have friends, only contacts, but somehow that was suddenly what Farkle was, now, when it was almost too late. It made him feel sick, a strange fear flickering in his soul.

Jorrun gave a bow. 'I've heard good things about you, brother Warne.'

'And I of you.' Farkle nodded back. 'They wait outside.'

'They?' Jorrun had turned pale.

'Three women of Margith palace.'

Jorrun shot to his feet and pointed to one of the guards who hurriedly opened the doors. Captain Rece was waiting outside with three girls. The youngest was about eight with curly black hair and brown eyes, the next perhaps four years older with lighter, straight hair. Between the two of them and holding their hands was a girl close to womanhood with straight black hair and bright blue eyes. Her features were unmistakably Dunham. Farkle fumbled in his jacket to take out a scroll which Jorrun took from him. Osun held his breath, watching his brother's eyes travel over the words, his hands were shaking.

'The girls …' Jorrun cleared his throat and Osun thought his heart would race straight out of his chest. 'Two were sold from here. Rey's daughter, Hylem. Calayna's daughter, Sevi …'

'Jorrun?' Osun demanded, standing up.

'And the eldest girl was sold from Mayliz to Margith. She is my … she is our …' Jorrun seemed to sway on his feet. 'She is our niece, Osun. Kussim.'

Osun blinked twice, unable to breathe for a moment. 'Cass, go and get Kesta. Get all the ladies! Now!'

Cassien almost ran for the door as Osun carefully took the scroll from Jorrun's hands. 'Bring them in, please, Rece.'

The three girls had barely taken a step into the room before they almost fell to the floor to bow, with their foreheads pressed against the cold stone. Captain Rece glanced at Osun, his face gone scarlet as though he expected to be blamed. He grabbed at the youngest girl's arm and tried to lift her to her feet. Osun found it interesting how quickly Rece and some of the other guards had come to see such things as shameful. Perhaps they always had.

'No, stand please, sisters.' Osun changed the tone of his voice to be gentle, without reprimand. 'In this palace you do not bow.'

He felt a surge of pride as Kussim looked up at him, then slowly got to her feet. The two younger girls copied, their eyes fixed firmly on the floor.

278

'We are the Raven Coven,' Osun went on. Jorrun stepped up silently beside him. 'Our coven includes women who have power.'

Kussim's blue eyes flickered up to his again and a frown settled on her face.

'My name is Osun, this is Jorrun. Kussim, we are your uncles.' The last word came out as a harsh whisper as his chest muscles clenched and his throat tightened. All his life he could count the people he loved on the fingers of one hand, now here he was with friends, and a larger family.

Kussim swallowed but didn't speak. Jorrun realised before he did.

'Kussim, you do not need permission to speak here.'

The doors burst open and the guards were almost trampled as the women came running in. Sevi and Hylem were immediately surrounded, leaving Kussim alone facing Osun and Jorrun. Kesta walked into the audience room at a more sedate pace, Azrael hovering at her shoulder. Her eyes sought out Jorrun at once and she quickened her pace.

'Cass gave us the news.' She briefly touched Jorrun's arm, the skin above her nose crinkling in concern. She glanced at Osun, smiled at Kussim and then her eyes widened and her mouth fell open at the sight of Farkle. 'Who is our guest? Have you not offered him some water or better still hot tea or soup?' Even as she spoke, she beckoned over one of the servants and issued him with polite instructions. The man smiled and nodded his head in a bow before hurrying away. Osun immediately felt defensive, he hated how the Fulmer woman could always make him feel guilty and bring up unwanted emotions, like lancing poison he didn't even know was there.

He gritted his teeth but forced himself to politeness. 'This is my friend, Farkle Warne, from Margith. He escorted our girls here.'

'We will have a room ready for you in just a moment, I'm sure you would like some time to recover from your long journey,' Kesta said.

'I was never a good traveller even before my body betrayed me.' Farkle gave a shake of his head and pursed his thin lips. 'I would appreciate a rest, um … *mistress*?'

'Just Kesta.' She smiled and without realising it, Osun smiled also.

He turned to Kussim and saw she was staring at Kesta with eyes so wide they almost bulged. He cleared his throat. 'Kesta, this young lady here is Kussim. According to the records at Margith she is Dinari's daughter and, well, mine and Jorrun's niece.'

Kesta's hands went to her mouth and she turned to look at Jorrun. 'Truly?'

Jorrun nodded, his Adam's apple bobbed.

Kesta reached up to touch Jorrun's face and then she regarded the young girl. 'Welcome to Navere, Kussim, this must all be overwhelming for you.'

Osun wondered if Kesta was using her magic as the girl's muscles relaxed a little and she finally blinked. Kesta's eyes narrowed and she glanced at Jorrun and himself before calling over one of the other women.

'Vilai, would you be kind enough to take young Kussim here up to the sisters' quarters and settle her into a room?'

Both Osun and Jorrun went to protest but Kesta raised a hand. 'There will be time, but not now. This room is very busy, noisy and … strange. Let Vilai settle her in and explain how things are.'

Osun felt a moment of irritation, surprised at how badly he wanted to get to know his niece and learn of his half-sister's fate, but as he watched pretty Vilai, only a little older than Kussim, steer her toward the door, he realised it was the right thing to do.

He drew in a deep breath and turning to Farkle offered his arm. 'Come on then, Farkle, I'll walk you up and you can tell me how your son is doing. You know there will always be a place here for him should he ever need it.'

Farkle lifted a shaking hand and rubbed at the corner of his eye with two fingers. 'Thank you, Osun, you have no idea how much that means to me.'

Osun felt an uncomfortable tingling in his heart and glancing up he saw Vilai and Kussim disappearing around the corner. He had a horrible, itching suspicion that he would soon understand very well how Farkle felt.

***

Osun watched out of the window. Far below he made out the shapes of Kussim and Vilai among the other women as they took their daily walk around the gardens. Some of the trees were now sparsely clothed and a beautiful patchwork of browns and reds was strewn across the long lawns. They'd taken several quiet dinners with Kussim, just himself, Jorrun, and Kesta, but the girl still barely spoke. Osun was hardly surprised, after all, her father had been Karinna and she'd then been sold on to his son, Adelphy, probably to be given to the most powerful of Adelphy's followers. Kussim had no news of her mother, having no means to stay in touch after she'd been sold.

'How is Farkle?' Jorrun asked.

Osun turned away from the window and back to his study. He sighed and rubbed his face with his hands. 'Not good. I've sent a message to his son but I doubt he would get here before his father gives out, even if he set off immediately.'

'I'm sorry,' Jorrun said.

Osun swallowed, looking away from his brother. He waved a hand at him and sat heavily in the seat at his desk. He breathed in and out slowly, trying not to think of Farkle but turn his attention to the matter at hand. 'So, what have we got today then?'

Jorrun regarded him but said nothing.

'Reports from the city guards.' Jagna raised the papers he clutched in his hand. 'As far as I can see there is nothing untoward in them. There are three matters that require your judgement though.'

Osun held out his hand and Jagna handed him three sheets of paper.

'Would you like me to deal with them?' Jorrun offered.

Osun looked up at his brother who was leaning against a bookcase at the side of the room. Jorrun had already managed to alter his loose-fitting Chemmish clothing into something much more elegant and tailored. 'You do have experience with this sort of thing, but I really should do it myself.'

'There is nothing wrong with delegating.' Jorrun stood up straighter and unfolded his arms. 'In fact, I think it's time we started training some of the women in running the palace and city. We should start with Calayna, get her to shadow you, Osun.'

Osun nodded. 'She'd be my first choice for administration and even for matters like this.' He tapped the reports Jagna had given him. 'I'll talk to her this afternoon.'

'There is a matter I wish to discuss with you.' Jagna pulled out a chair and sat at the desk opposite Osun, he glanced toward Jorrun. 'I understand that we are not in a strong enough position at present, but I'd like you to consider taking another Seat and, well, letting me hold it.'

Osun sat back to study his face. The younger man had coloured slightly, but he held Osun's gaze.

'Consider this.' Jagna reached out to grab a map and unrolled it on the desk. 'If we took the city of Mayliz, then we would hold a line right through the centre of Chem, basically have control of the trade routes that cross east to west.' His finger ran down the parchment and he didn't see the look Osun exchanged with Jorrun. Taking Karinna's old seat appealed to them both for more reasons than one.

'It has merit,' Osun replied slowly. 'But as you say we are not in a position to hold both here and Mayliz at the moment. When the women are better able to wield their magic perh—'

'Talking of women,' Jagna leaned forward over the desk. 'How would you feel about some of us taking wives?'

Jorrun took a step forward, fist clenched. 'What do you mean by *taking*?'

Jagna's mouth fell open, but he recovered quickly and waved both hands at Jorrun. 'No, no, nothing like that! I mean by consent. I ... well, Estre and I have an understanding. She's a bit older than me but she's so smart and her magic is, I think, stronger than mine. She would make a perfect companion to me in ruling another Seat and I'm sure she could teach other women as Kesta does.'

'And what does Estre think of all this?' Jorrun's eyes narrowed and he placed his hands palms down on the desk. Even Osun shrank back.

'She is happy with the idea.'

Osun and Jorrun's eyes met. 'Another genuine marriage would be good for the palace and our plans for Chem.' Osun chewed at his bottom lip. 'Get Kesta to talk with Estre, if she's happy then I don't think we should say no.'

Jorrun nodded slowly, removing his hands and straightening up from the table.

'You should think of looking for a wife too, Osun.' Jagna grinned.

Osun flinched. He didn't know why but the idea terrified him. An image of Kesta's face, of the way she'd looked at him after she learnt he'd lain with Milaiya, forced itself into his mind and he clenched his fists under the table. 'I don't have time for that,' he said with a tightened jaw. 'Do we have any petitioners this afternoon?' He turned to Jorrun.

'Three.' Jorrun sighed. 'I can deal with them with Kesta if you want to spend time with Farkle?'

'No, I'd best see them. Would you ask Calayna to join us in the audience room?'

'Of course,' Jorrun nodded, and with a glance through narrowed eyes at Jagna, he left the room.

***

Osun watched the skin trader stride out of the audience chamber, if the guards hadn't been holding the doors open, he was certain the man would have slammed them shut behind him.

'He has a point though,' Calayna said slowly.

'What?' Osun turned to his right to stare at her in surprise. Kesta stopped stalking up and down behind the chairs like an angry cat and came to stand behind Jorrun. 'What point?' she demanded.

The tattooed woman leaned forward to look at Kesta, then Osun. 'Some families have traded in people for decades, their entire fortunes are bound to it and they know no other way of life.'

Kesta snorted and opened her mouth, but Jorrun grabbed her wrist and Osun quickly spoke first. 'I see where you're coming from but don't entirely agree. At the end of the day they are traders and can adapt to sell other goods.'

'You will make powerful enemies,' Calayna warned. 'Changing things within the privacy of the palace is one thing, but trying to alter the entire economic base of Chem is another matter.'

Osun put his head in his hands and breathed out loudly. His head ached.

'Don't give up!' He looked up to see Kesta looking down at him with her wide green eyes. 'We knew this would take time, we just have to be clever.'

'A gradual change would be best.' Jorrun nodded. 'Give a year's notice for the cessation of the skin trade in Navere. Perhaps offer a reduction in trade tax for any new venture they might take up?'

Kesta drew in a sharp breath. 'I have an idea. The slave market could be turned into a trade centre for goods from Elden, the Fulmers, and the Borrows. Give those awful men the first choice to run it, make it something exclusive and exciting to visit.'

'It would draw in trade from the other cities.' Calayna sat up. 'Bring wealth to Navere. Surely the traders would grab such an opportunity?'

'Some would.' Jorrun winced. 'Some enjoy their trade all too much and will miss the feeling of power the skin trade gives them.'

'And you must think of the slaves also.' Calayna dampened Osun's feeling of hope still further. 'What will become of them? There are many masters who might kill a slave or throw them out to starve rather than make them a servant and pay a wage – no matter how low. As for the women, that's a whole different pit of vipers to walk through.'

Osun closed his eyes, all he wanted to do was sit in peace in the garden and drink a horn of geranna or two – and he hated geranna. 'I'm going to have to re-write all the city laws, aren't I? We should all take some more time to think about this.' He opened his eyes and turned to Kesta. 'Your idea is brilliant, though, and exciting. I'll get enquiries made at once and see which slavers would get on board and if they are people we actually want.'

'We'll want a few of the Rowen Order involved in its running,' Jorrun said.

There was a knock at the door and Captain Rece stepped in, breathing fast and red in the face. He gave a quick bow. 'Excuse me, masters, there is a man at the gate, he claims to be a messenger from Arkoom. He is from Dunham Coven, a necromancer of the Overlord's.'

Jorrun shot to his feet, but Osun found himself frozen.

'Let him in,' Jorrun said.

'Should we call all the Raven Coven together?' Calayna asked as Rece hurried away.

Osun glanced at his brother and Kesta. 'No, let's keep our strength, or lack of it, as quiet as possible for the moment, we'll meet him as we are.'

'Let me call Azrael, though,' Kesta suggested.

Osun nodded. 'Although he should stay out of sight.'

'Should I demonstrate my strength if the opportunity presents itself?' she asked.

Osun hesitated.

'It might be good for Kesta to remain a mystery.' Calayna shifted in her chair.

'I'll leave it to your judgement, Kesta,' he decided.

'Could this be a summons to Arkoom?' Kesta had moved closer to Jorrun, their arms touching.

'Let's not jump to conclusions.' Osun realised his pulse was racing and forcing himself to take in slow, deep breaths, he waved over one of the servants. 'Bring some good wine and some light snacks to the audience room.'

The man nodded and hurried away.

It was some moments before Captain Rece brought the man in, time enough for Osun's nerves to have frayed even further. The man wore an expensive dark-green, silk shirt under a calf-skin jacket. A gold chain with a blood amulet hung outside of his clothing and Osun wondered if it were deliberate, he had to refrain from turning to see Kesta's reaction. If he looked really hard there was some resemblance to the Dunham's in their visitor's appearance. He had black hair, but it was curly like a Borrowman's and his eyes were such a dark brown they were almost black. He was quite young, in his early twenties.

Captain Rece bowed and announced, 'Masters, this is Gerant Irren, of Dunham Coven, Arkoom, spokesman for the Overlord.'

'Hmm.' Osun sat back, a slight smile on his face. Not a Dunham then, but a family with close blood ties. 'I don't recall electing a new Overlord?'

The man made no attempt to smile in return but glared at Calayna and Kesta through narrowed eyes. 'Someone had to take control of Chem after the gods deserted us, but as you say, an election has not taken place. Lord Feren Dunham has called a meeting of the covens at the next full moon in just under a month, I'm making my way around the covens to give out the invitation in person.'

Osun swallowed, but managed to keep his polite smile fixed to his face. 'I take it an official Overlord will be elected then?'

'Indeed,' Gerant nodded, looking from Jorrun to Osun and back again. 'I'd heard rumour that those who had taken the seat here were Dunhams, is it so?'

Osun raised a hand to point behind him. 'We are the Raven Coven. I'm Osun Raven, these are Jorrun, Kesta, and Calayna Raven.'

The man lowered his head to look at them from under heavy eyebrows. 'So that rumour is also true, you have women in your coven. You break the laws of Chem!'

Osun shrugged. 'I'm writing new ones.'

'You can't do that. What you're doing is unnatural.' The skin of his face reddened.

'That depends on your point of view,' Kesta said, her voice calm and reasonable. 'In my land it's perfectly natural for women to lead and use magic, the only reason it isn't so here is because fearful men decided to make it so. Now men of courage will change it.'

'Over my dead body.' Gerant showed his teeth.

'Careful, Gerant,' Jorrun said quietly. 'We can grant that wish. Every Dunham we have met is dead.'

'Come now.' Osun stood quickly and Gerant took a step back. 'We have gotten off to a bad start. We have different ways here but there is no need for us to be enemies. Will you remain as our guest tonight and eat with us? We can show you our trade plans and how adapting in Navere and opening up our harbour will benefit Chem, especially in our present economic climate. I'm sure Feren would like to hear what we're doing and why we have made our little changes. Perhaps you could tell us more about your lord and his own plans so we can consider Navere's vote at the full moon?'

Gerant's mouth opened and closed several times before he stuttered, 'Well, yes, that's a very reasonable offer, but … but can I trust that a coven who so flouts the laws of Chem will hold to the laws of hospitality?'

'I swear by the gods none will harm you under this roof so long as you yourself harm none,' Osun said without missing a beat.

Gerant gave a bow. 'Then I accept.'

'Captain Rece here will escort you to a guest room.'

Rece's eyes widened a little, but he nodded. Osun would have to trust the captain to arrange a room at short notice that would keep Gerant suitably out of the way.

'Someone will escort you to dinner in about an hour.' Osun smiled.

Gerant gave a slight bow of his head, his eyes darting to Kesta and Calayna again, before he followed the captain out.

As soon as the door closed, Calayna turned to him. 'Osun, you really are good! You defused that so deftly.'

Osun gave a slight shake of his head, not able to meet her eyes. 'We need him to think us friends when we arrive in Arkoom, or we are doomed before we set out.'

'We're going then?' The skin above Kesta's nose and around her eyes crinkled in concern. 'In a month?' She turned to look at Jorrun who also avoided her gaze. 'We're not ready.'

'Ready or not,' Jorrun replied. 'We have to go.'

'But the women can't shield yet, let alone fight.'

'They would have to stay here.' Osun plucked up the courage to meet her mis-matched eyes. 'With you. To protect the palace and Navere.'

'No!' Kesta spun about to look down at Jorrun. 'I need to go, to fight with you to take Arkoom.'

Jorrun stood and touched her cheek gently with three fingers. 'One of us has to stay to defend the women, we can't take them with us to Arkoom with things as they are. You stay, or I stay.'

Osun swallowed and held his breath, Kesta turned to look at him and he could almost see the thoughts that stormed behind her eyes.

Her voice was barely a whisper, 'I'll have to stay.'

Chapter Twenty-Two

Dia; Fulmer Island

Dia sat bolt upright, gasping for air. Her heart pounded against her ribs and sweat ran down over her collarbone.

'Dia?' Arrus stirred sleepily at her side. 'What is it?'

She breathed out slowly through her mouth, calling flames to her fingers and looking quickly around her familiar bedroom.

'Dia?' Arrus propped himself up on an elbow.

She shook her head. 'I was having a nightmare.' Her throat was still raw from crying, the skin around her eyes sore. It was several hours since she'd received news that Larissa was dead and that Temerran was being held for it. She still couldn't believe it, it made no sense. How had things gone so wrong?

'Did you dream of Larissa?' Arrus prompted.

'No.' She frowned, lighting a candle from a distance and settling back against her pillow. 'I don't think so. I dreamt of Fulmer Island, only there were Eldemen warriors everywhere and ...'

'And?'

She swallowed, looking up at the wooden beams. 'They were hanging people; I think they were *walkers*.'

Arrus leaned over to kiss her cheek and then took her hand in his larger one to stroke her fingers. 'It's hardly surprising you're so unsettled. Have you decided what to do?'

'I must go to Taurmaline and look into this myself, what else can I do? Bractius can't even tell me how she died.'

'I don't like i—'

'I know.' She reached over and placed her free hand on his stomach, feeling it rise as he breathed in. 'But she was a *walker*, and this threatens the fledgling peace between Elden, the Fulmers, and the Borrows. I'd normally say you should stay here and Worvig should come with me as he knows Taurmaline, but I think you should come.'

'Of course I'm coming,' he replied.

'It's Everlyn I'm torn about.' She sighed. 'With Larissa dead and Kesta still in Chem it's Everlyn I'd turn to next to look after the Fulmers with Pirelle in my absence, yet she's the one I'll most need with me in Elden.'

Arrus grunted. 'We need to train more *walkers* for fighting, ironic since we are supposed to be at peace.'

Dia stretched her legs, reaching a cold spot in the sheets with her toes.

'Perhaps it will be enough to leave Heara here to run things with Worvig and Pirelle?' Arrus suggested.

Dia laughed. 'You can tell Heara she is staying behind if you like.'

Arrus chuckled. 'Fair point. I'm not that brave a man. For what it's worth, I think take someone other than Everlyn and leave her here. It means someone else gets the experience of dealing with Elden and shadowing you, while Everlyn remains here ... just in case.'

Dia nodded, rolling over and letting Arrus snuggle her against him in a hug. 'That makes sense. I might take Mimeth, she's young but quite strong. I can practice some battle magic with her on our crossing over.'

She kissed Arrus and then pulled away from him to get up.

'Where are you going?' He sat up.

Dia pulled on her trousers and buttoned a jacket over her night shift. 'To send a messenger to Fox Hold to get Mimeth here as soon as possible. We need to be on our way to Taurmaline.'

Arrus lay back down with a groan. 'You're right, of course. Give me a moment and I'll come with you, I need to sort which warriors to take with us, anyway.'

***

A sick feeling settled in Dia's stomach as she sighted castle Taurmaline across the lake. She pulled her long cloak more tightly around her body, the strong wind making her blink rapidly to save her eyes from stinging.

'It's so big, Icante.' Mimeth spoke beside her. The young *walker* had skin darker than most, shoulder length black hair, one brown eye and one hazel.

Dia nodded. 'It does seem intimidating. So many people will be confusing and overwhelming to your *knowing* until you learn to filter it out.'

'Catya, slow down!'

Dia turned around at Heara's exasperated shout. The young girl was climbing down the main mast with the confidence of a squirrel. She wished Heara had left the girl behind, but she could understand why she hadn't. Heara had come to love Catya as fiercely as though she were her daughter, but somehow lacked a mother's paranoid fear for her safety, not checking the girl near often enough for Dia's liking.

They were drawing close to the dock and Dia moved out of the way, remaining on the deck so she could keep a watchful eye on the castle and the city. It looked much the same as when she'd left it, which felt somehow obscene considering the death of a beautiful young *walker*. She sighted Temerran's glossy ship, the Undine, bobbing at anchor among the comparatively ungainly Elden ships. It hurt somehow, to see it captive there, as though a wild bird had been chained.

They were met by one of the King's advisor's, Merkis Dalton, and Dia realised that the King had sent the most important person he could other than meeting her himself. Merkis Vilnue fell in beside his countryman as they were escorted to the castle. The newly made Elden Ambassador had insisted on coming and Dia was glad. She trusted the man and didn't doubt his friendship and even loyalty to the Fulmers. She couldn't help but wonder, though, if there was trouble, which side would Vilnue take?

The King met them on the steps to the castle. He looked older to Dia, more lines about his eyes and the skin of his face seemed greyer and less taut. He kissed Dia's cheek and shook Arrus's hand in both of his, holding it a moment longer after shaking it.

'My deepest condolences to you both, and to the Fulmers,' he said. 'I still don't know how this happened under my roof.'

Dia forced herself to thank him. From her *knowing* she felt his genuine grief, his confusion and a deep, underlying exhaustion. Larissa had said something about him not sleeping, hadn't she?

'Please, come within.' The King gestured for them to walk beside him. Merkis Dalton set about directing the warriors they'd brought with them. Only Mimeth, Heara, and Catya remained with Dia and Arrus. 'As your young warrior, Dorthai, requested, poor Larissa is laying down in the dungeons. It didn't seem at all fitting, but it's cold there and the best we could do to keep ...'

'It's all right.' Dia felt sorry for the man and touched his arm. 'We in the Fulmers believe when the spirit is fled, the body matters not except to return to nourish the land that once nourished it. It's important to us Larissa comes back to the Fulmers, but we are not offended at where you've had to put her. Tell me, do you still hold Temerran under guard?'

294

Bractius pressed his lips together into a thin line. 'I do. I've been as fair as I could about it, he's under guard in his rooms, but his men are in the dungeon. He still protests his innocence, but I didn't want him going anywhere until we get to the bottom of this, or at least until you have had a chance to speak to him yourself.'

'I would like to do so as soon as possible. And Dorthai?'

'He and your other man insist on guarding Larissa's room and keeping it untouched until you can see it.' He barked a humourless laugh. 'I try not to be offended that they don't trust me!'

'It is the situation, not you personally, that they don't trust.'

Bractius nodded his head and glanced at her, his eyes looked red. He really had liked Larissa very much. A cold hand reached in to grab her heart; what had the young queen thought of that?

'I feel like I should be putting on some show, some fancy dinner.' Bractius rubbed at his forehead with his fingers. 'But I'm sure you'd much rather get to seeing your people? You remember the way to my private audience chamber?'

Dia nodded.

'I'll see you there when you're ready.' Bractius turned and strode away down the corridor.

Behind her, Merkis Dalton cleared his throat. 'I'll show you to Larissa's room.'

He led them toward the wing of the castle where Dia and Arrus had previously stayed. Larissa had been given the room which Kesta had occupied in her time in Taurmaline. Dorthai straightened up on seeing her, his eyes widening.

'Icante! Arrus Silene, I'm so sorry, I failed you!'

'Don't be foolish, Dorthai, you failed no one,' Arrus interjected.

Dia wanted to say the same, but she couldn't yet, not without knowing the truth. 'Tell me what you know,' she asked.

Dorthai swallowed, looking down at his feet and then meeting her eyes. 'I could see no sign of injury on *walker* Larissa and I thought perhaps she might be lost in the flame, as I heard could happen but ...'

'But?' Dia prompted gently.

'Well, the bed was soiled, so I knew she was dead.'

It was Dia's turn to look away. 'I see. And you examined the room?'

'Only a little,' he replied quickly. 'I didn't touch anything, but did ... well, I smelt a few things in case there were any odours that might fade.'

Heara grunted.

'You did well.' Dia forced a smile and turned to Heara. 'Take a look, the rest of you wait outside.'

Dorthai unlocked the door and Heara stepped in, Dia pausing just inside the doorway. The smell was awful, stale, musty, with the scent of old excrement. It was gloomy, the shutters closed fast with only a small shaft of light squeezing through the join. Heara circled the room, looking down at the carpet, before going to the bed and lifting the sheet. She examined the pillows, then held each to her face, breathing in hard to scent the fabric. She looked over the bedside table, then the central table, picking up a glass to sniff it. Dia drew in a sharp breath and opened her mouth to protest when Heara touched the inside of the glass with the tip of her tongue.

'Elderflower,' Heara said.

She crouched before the fireplace and stirred the ashes with the poker. She stood up, placing her hands on her hips and looking around the room again.

'Anything?' Dia asked.

Heara shook her head with a frown. 'I can't see any sign that anyone else was in here with her, though several people have tramped in and out over that carpet so it's hard to be sure. I'll go over it, inch by inch, just to be certain. Let's take a look at Larissa, then I'll come back after.'

Dia nodded her agreement.

They went back out into the hall and Dia looked from Catya to Mimeth and back again. 'We're going to look at Larissa's body. It will be distressing and unpleasant, but you'll learn things. I'll leave it up to you if you'd like to come or not.'

'I've dressed bodies for burial,' Mimeth said. 'Although never a fellow *walker*. I'll come.'

Dia turned to Catya, Heara also regarded the young girl, shifting her weight from one foot to the other.

Catya chewed at her thumb, her blue eyes not leaving Dia's. 'I'll come. I want to learn.'

'Are you sure?' Dia leaned forward a little to bring herself a little closer to the girl's height.

Catya glanced at Heara and nodded.

'Should I come?' Dorthai asked.

'No, guard Larissa's room just a little longer.' Dia touched his arm. 'Until Heara has finished with it.'

'This way, then, please.' Merkis Dalton gestured for them to follow.

They left the bright corridors and went down into passages with bare stone walls and a few, widely interspersed torches. Merkis Dalton held up a hand. 'Wait a moment.' His voice echoed.

He went ahead of them to a gate that barred their way and spoke to a man who stood in the doorway of a room off to the right. Arrus shifted beside Dia, glancing back over his shoulder. The man came out, using a large, dark key to unlock the gate.

'It's just in here.' Dalton gestured with his head.

As soon as they were all through the gate, it was closed and locked behind them. A shudder went through Dia.

'Okay, be warned.' Dia caught all of their attention. 'This will be really bad.'

Dalton took in a deep breath and opened the door.

They were hit at once by the horrendous smell, sulphurous, like rotting eggs. All of them automatically put their hands to their faces, Merkis Dalton pulling his tunic up over his nose. Catya retched.

'No one has to come in.' Dia regarded them all. 'Try not to think of this as Larissa.' Gritting her teeth and steeling herself, she stepped into the room and slowly approached the bench on which a covered body lay. Glancing over her shoulder she saw everyone had followed her, pride over sense. Dia stood near the head, meeting Heara's eyes. The scout took hold of the blanket and pulled it away.

Catya ran out of the room, Arrus following her more slowly, his face almost grey. Merkis Dalton stood completely still, facing toward the wall with his head bowed.

'Okay.' Heara drew in a deep breath. Dia herself was breathing as little as possible. Heara stepped forward to study Larissa's face, gently prizing open her mouth and moving aside the bloated tongue to look inside. Dia had to turn away, bile rising from her stomach, as Heara prodded at the skin below Larissa's protruding eyes. She studied the body's fingers and nails next,

298

Mimeth finding the courage to step up beside her. As Heara lifted the purple-hued hand some of the skin came away and Dia couldn't help but let out a groan.

She heard movement behind her and saw Catya had crept back into the room, holding tight to Arrus's hand.

'If I turn her over, I'm likely to cause damage,' Heara said.

Dia swallowed. 'What's your conclusion so far?'

Heara gave a shrug. 'As Bractius said, no sign of any wounds and no obvious sign of poisoning. The decomposition makes it much harder to judge on that count though.'

Dia sighed and rubbed at the bridge of her nose. 'Okay, let's leave it. My *knowing* tells me Bractius is telling the truth, as far as he knows it.' She turned to Dalton who was still looking away, his nose covered. 'Can you take us to Temerran now, please?'

'At once.' He hadn't even finished his words before he spun on his heels and led them out of the room. Heara and Mimeth quickly covered Larissa again before following. Some of Larissa's red hair spilled out over the bench and Dia froze, feeling a sob rise up from her chest.

It was a relief to get back to the brightly lit, carpeted hallways, the smell of the wax and lavender polish that was used on the wood was comforting.

There were six guards outside the door of Temerran's room, Dia frowned and glanced at Merkis Dalton. The guards stood up straighter but moved aside at once, Dalton grabbed the doorknob and pushed the door open.

Inside the room Temerran halted, his fingers caught in his copper curls, his eyes widening as he saw Dia.

'Icante!' He took two steps toward her, then glanced at Dalton, his hand falling to his side.

'You'll wait outside, Merkis.' Dia turned to look at the Eldeman, holding his gaze.

Merkis Dalton bowed and withdrew from the room. The others crowded in, Arrus closed the door behind him.

'Dia.' Temerran's shoulders sagged, he seemed somehow much younger. 'I'm so sorry about Larissa. Have you any news of my men?'

Dia's mouth opened and her hand went to her throat. 'I was told some of your warriors are being held in the dungeons, but I haven't seen them.'

Temerran turned, and moving slowly, went to sit in a chair. Dia opened up her *knowing* but didn't need it to recognise the Bard's fear. 'You'd better tell us what happened,' Dia said.

Temerran looked up. 'There's not much I can tell you. We arrived and were welcomed, treated as guests and allies. There was a feast at which I sang, it went on until the early hours. I was awoken from sleep by Eldemen bursting into my room, I was told Larissa had been murdered and that I was suspected!'

Dia exchanged a glance with Mimeth, knowing that her fellow *walker* would also be monitoring the man's emotions. As far as she could tell he was completely innocent.

'I was questioned by several men, including the one who just let you in, Dalton? I've asked so many times for an audience with King Bractius, but he has refused to see me. Dia.' He reached a hand across the table towards her. 'There is something very wrong here.' He looked around the room at the others.

300

'You may speak with confidence in front of everyone here,' Dia reassured him.

His voice dropped almost to a whisper. 'There's a darkness here in Taurmaline. I feel the nip and stab of poisoned words. Do you feel the fear, the jealousy, the paranoia? They follow the Queen like ghostly dogs and eat the King from the inside.'

Arrus cleared his throat. Dia felt as though a weight had settled on her shoulders and a snake wrapped around her ribs to squeeze. Her own arms went about her waist. 'I'll speak to Bractius and do what I can. You have no idea what killed Larissa?'

'None,' Temerran shook his head, his brows drawing in tight. 'Save that to me she felt like the only light in this black castle.'

'Is there anything else?'

'I ...' Temerran stared down at his hand on the table, the pale-red hairs on his arm were standing up. 'There is something ... but ...' He shook his head and breathed out loudly in frustration. 'It's like something won't let me remember.'

'Convenient,' Arrus muttered.

'No, there is something ... foggy, about this place,' Mimeth agreed with the Bard.

Dia drew in a deep breath. 'Okay. Heara, you and Catya go back to Larissa's room and check every inch. Temerran, I'll do my best to get you and your men out.'

She opened the door to find Merkis Dalton pacing the hallway. He glanced past her at Temerran.

'Arrus Silene and I will see the King now.' Dia didn't give Dalton any time but immediately set off toward the private audience room. Heara,

Mimeth, and Catya started off in the opposite direction to go back toward Larissa's room and Dia smiled as she heard Dalton swear under his breath. He grabbed one of the guards by the arm.

'Escort those ladies!' he barked, then hurried to catch up with Dia and Arrus.

***

A page was waiting outside Bractius's room, as were two guards in armour far more ornate than that of the others in the castle. They stepped aside for Merkis Dalton who knocked and then tentatively opened the door. Bractius was seated at his desk in the corner, playing with a glass filled with a dark-red liquid with his left hand. His right lay on an open scroll.

He stood up on seeing Dia, his brown eyes widening. 'Did you find anything?'

She raised a hand, opening up her *knowing* to send calm toward him. Arrus pulled out a chair for her as Dalton closed the door, remaining in the room with his arms folded. Dia sat, taking in a deep breath before looking up at the King. 'We haven't found much more than you, your majesty. As you say, the cause of her death is hard to tell. It could be poison, it could be some natural cause. Had we seen her earlier it might have been easier to find an answer.'

'I can tell you something.' Bractius sat slowly, leaning across the table toward her and glancing at Dalton. 'When I saw her, lying in that bed … it was … it was terrifying. Her eyes were so wide, her mouth contorted as though in a scream, but her body …' His voice became hoarse. 'It was calmly composed in comparison, her hands on her chest.'

Dia realised she was staring at the Elden king.

'Could it be magic?' Bractius whispered.

302

Dia opened her mouth, biting her lower lip before replying. 'Not any magic I know, but I'm starting to find there are more types of magic than I ever knew. One thing I can tell you, although I understand if my word is not enough, Temerran of the Borrows is innocent. If you're holding him on my behalf, then I ask you to please release him and his men. He is not the culprit.'

'Not?' Bractius tilted his head and leaned back in his seat. 'But if not him, then who? You have no enemies here in Elden.'

Dia decided to bite her tongue for the moment. 'As I said, we can't even be sure the cause wasn't something natural. My scout, Heara, is still looking, she may find something yet.'

'Well.' Bractius shrugged, slumped in his seat. 'I'll let the Borrowmen go, although I'd rather they left Elden immediately.' He looked at Dalton, who nodded.

'I can understand that, although it's a shame to mar the peace we have established.'

Bractius just wrinkled his nose and shook his head. 'Until we are sure, I'll take no risk.' He grabbed up a scroll and crushed it in his fist. 'I don't suppose you've heard any more from your daughter and Jorrun?'

'Not since your ship came back,' Arrus said. 'You?'

He shook his head. 'I intend to send Teliff back very soon with more trade goods. I keep intending to order Jorrun back, but then I tell myself I'm being paranoid. He is doing more good where he is. At least I hope so.'

'Kesta seems to think so,' Dia said quietly. She didn't add that she felt the task her daughter and Jorrun had set themselves seemed almost impossible.

'I have something to ask.' Bractius shifted in his seat. 'I won't expect you to send me another *walker* ambassador, not after what's happened. It's a shame Worvig didn't stay, I liked him, although he didn't say much. But ... would you both stay a while? A week, maybe two, just until things settle a bit?'

Dia realised the king was afraid. He felt incredibly vulnerable without Jorrun, and Larissa's death had shaken his nerves as well as hurt his heart. Bractius had realised for the first time in his life that he was alone. He trusted no one, not even herself and Arrus, but he desperately wanted to.

'I need to get Larissa's body home as soon as possible,' Dia replied.

The King's face fell.

'Would you perhaps be able to get her taken to the Fulmers?' Arrus suggested to Bractius. 'Perhaps Dorthai and Mimeth can escort her?'

A smile lit Bractius's face for the first time. 'An excellent idea, Silene!'

Dia bowed her head but said nothing. She should really be the one to escort Larissa home, but the state of Elden and Temerran's startling words had her deeply troubled. As much as she wanted to return to the isolated sanctuary of the Fulmers, she had a horrible feeling this wasn't something to dismiss.

'Is that Elden wine?' Arrus nodded toward the King's glass.

'Oh! Forgive me, I'm so rude,' Bractius stood. 'It's port, would you like a glass?' He looked from Bractius to Dia.

'Oh, no thank you.' Dia held up her hands. 'I'd like to see how Heara is getting on.'

'I'd love to join you for a glass.' Arrus grinned.

Bractius grabbed up a decanter. 'Dalton, please see the Icante back to Larissa's room.'

Merkis Dalton hesitated, looking meaningfully at Arrus.

Bractius almost growled. 'Just do as I say, Merkis!'

The man coloured slightly, but gave a terse bow and opened the door for Dia.

As they walked along the corridor, Dia turned to the Merkis. 'You did a lot of the interviewing and investigation, what were your conclusions, honestly?'

Dalton was silent for a while, studying her face before answering. 'If I'm honest, were it not for the incongruity between body and face and her relative youth, I'd have said natural causes. As for the Borrowman, he could be a marvellous actor I suppose, but he seemed as totally shocked by all this as the rest of us.'

'Is there anyone else who might have had reason to hate Larissa?'

Dalton didn't answer, keeping his gaze on the carpet. Dia's eyes narrowed.

'Not to worry,' she said after a while. 'Would it be possible for me to speak with Temerran again before he departs Elden? I want to be sure there is no ill will between the Borrows and the Fulmers after all I did to create a truce.'

Dalton sighed, his mouth turned down in disapproval. 'I suppose that would be all right. After I tell him he may leave, I'll mention your request.'

'Thank you,' Dia raised an eyebrow. She understood the king's advisor being protective, but something really did seem to have put a hornet in the man's trousers. Her *knowing* gave her his emotions, but not the cause. She sighed. Not for the first time, she wished her daughter were not so far away.

***

She'd been back in her allocated room with Heara, Mimeth, and Catya for almost two hours when Arrus came stumbling in, his cheeks flushed and his hair standing up a little as though he'd run his fingers through it several times.

'Sorry,' he mumbled. 'I was just making friends with the King.'

Dia laughed and shook her head. 'It's fine.' She held out her hand toward him. 'Did you learn anything?'

Arrus winced. 'Only his changing opinion of Jorrun. He seems ... I don't know, ill almost. Exhausted, manic at times. He is not the secretive and controlled man I've met on other occasions. What of you?' He looked from Dia to Heara.

'We found these.' Heara stood up from where she sat on the table and lifted up three pieces of parchment. 'Letters Larissa had begun but not sent. Strangely they were hidden under her mattress.'

'What do they say?' Arrus asked as he reached out to take them.

'That Bractius's nightmares are so severe they are disturbing his waking mind,' Dia told him. 'And that she'd also begun to have frightening dreams.'

'Jorrun used to fix my bad dreams,' Catya told Arrus, her blue eyes wide. 'He taught me how to make them go away.'

'But nothing Larissa tried, worked,' Dia took the letters from Bractius and waved them in the air. 'She was also concerned about sending these, even though they were written using the code we agreed.'

'So, she suspected someone is somehow behind this?' Arrus looked around at the women.

Dia jumped as someone knocked at the door. Heara went to answer, her hand on her dagger hilt. She moved aside to let Temerran in. There were two Elden guards with him, but she shut the door in their faces.

'Icante, Silene! Thank you for clearing my name.'

'It's no more than you deserve,' Dia replied.

'So, did you discover anything?' He looked around at them all.

'Some hidden letters,' Dia told him. 'What magics do you know of that can manipulate dreams?'

'Dreams?' Temerran frowned. 'I can help induce sleep and encourage calmer dreams with my songs, is that the sort of thing you mean?'

'Maybe.' Dia tapped at one of her teeth with her thumbnail. 'Can you give someone nightmares?'

Temerran breathed out loudly. 'Possibly, I've never tried. There are no songs I know of for such. Is there someone you want me to try it on?'

'No,' Dia sighed and looked up at the ceiling. 'The magic of dreams is an ancient Elden magic. As far as I know only Jorrun can dream-walk.'

'Dream-walk?' Temerran's eyebrows shot up.

'Not a myth,' Dia confirmed.

'Listen, there's something else,' Temerran said urgently. 'You remember there was something that deeply concerned me, a hazy memory of danger? I've been wracking my brain. I've recalled something, but it's all but useless. Green eyes, and a sense of danger.'

Dia leapt to her feet and the others looked at her in shock. 'Green eyes?'

'Yes.' Temerran looked her up and down with a worried frown. 'I remember seeing green eyes over the Queen's shoulder and that's when I knew something evil dogged her steps.'

Dia glanced at Heara. 'I too have seen green eyes and felt a dire warning, although I dismissed it as imagination.'

'When?' Arrus demanded.

'In a water bowl. Weeks ago.'

Temerran drew in a deep breath. 'Someone has been watching you.'

A shiver ran down Dia's spine.

'Listen, under these circumstances I don't feel happy leavin—'

Dia opened her mouth to protest but he held up a hand and continued.

'I've no choice but to leave Taurmaline on the Undine, but I don't intend to leave Elden until you're safely away, Icante.'

Dia thought for a moment. Fear was walking about the inside of her ribs on tiptoes. 'I don't want you to get into any trouble, nor for anyone else to get involved really, but you could go to the Raven Tower at Northold. We have friends there, Merkis Tantony and Rosa. They might shelter you for a while. Be honest with them – completely.'

Temerran nodded.

'There are ravens there, they know me. If you find a way to communicate with them, you might be able to send a message.'

'Is there a quill and ink here?' Temerran looked around the room.

Heara grabbed some from behind her and handed them to him. He held his hand out toward Dia. 'Give me one of them.'

She handed him one of Larissa's unfinished letters and, turning it over, he drew several strange runes. Under each he then wrote a letter and handed it back to Dia.

'If I write to you, I'll use the old Borrow runes,' he said. 'No one here should be able to read them.'

'Thank you.'

Temerran hesitated, then stepped forward to hug Dia, and then shook Arrus's hand. 'No matter what, I'll try to be near in case you need me.' With a nod, he headed toward the door.

'Wait!' Catya called out.

Temerran halted and they all turned to look at her in surprise.

'I should go.'

'What?' Heara looked down at the girl, her hands on her hips.

Catya rolled her eyes. 'I'm from Northold. Rosa and Tantony know me and I know the Raven Tower. We can look there for books on dream-walking.'

Arrus grunted in surprised approval.

Heara shook her head, 'I can't let yo—'

'Yeah, you can.' Catya mirrored Heara's stance. 'I don't trust many men, you know that. I trust Tem. This will probably be a safer mission for me than staying here with green eyes.' She glanced at Temerran and noted the Bard's own emerald eyes. 'No offense.'

'None taken.' A spark of amusement lit his face.

'You may go,' Dia said, above Heara's protest.

Temerran regarded them all slowly before holding a hand out for Catya. 'Look after yourselves.'

'You too,' Dia murmured.

Chapter Twenty-Three

Kesta; Covenet of Chem

'But what if they attack you?'

Kesta, Jorrun, and Osun had taken their conversation into the library. Jorrun had barely said a word and was avoiding her eyes.

'That's why it's important to win Gerant over,' Osun told her. 'Make him believe that despite our differences we're not planning on causing trouble – at least for a while.'

'Is Feren likely to win a vote to be Overlord?' Kesta looked from Osun to Jorrun.

'Probably more likely than anyone else.' Osun sighed. 'The Dunham name is still feared and from my intelligence he has the support of four seats compared to our one. We always knew this could happen. We'll have to hope diplomacy or Jorrun's greater strength will be enough to buy us time.'

'You need me to go with you.'

Neither Jorrun nor Osun disagreed, though she knew they hadn't changed their minds.

'I'll try to walk Gerant's dreams tonight,' Jorrun said quietly.

'What?' Both Kesta and Osun replied at once.

'I may find something of Feren's intentions, possibly even learn more of the Seats Gerant has already visited.' Jorrun leaned back in his chair to look at them both. 'Gerant is nowhere near as strong as me.'

'But he might have better training at dream-walking.' Kesta turned to Osun for support.

'No, look.' Jorrun stood and bending over the table moved some books aside to pick up a plain bound ledger. 'Dryn kept a record of everyone's bloodlines. I remember seeing Gerant Irren.' He opened the ledger and leafed through the pages. 'Here. There is almost no Elden blood in Gerant's line, but if you look at Karinna's, he had strong Elden hereditary, like me.'

Osun looked at his brother with wide eyes. 'This ledger is invaluable!'

'Indeed.' Jorrun displayed no emotion on his face and Kesta immediately felt concerned he was withdrawing again.

'Are we in there?' Osun moved around the table to look over Jorrun's shoulder.

Pain flickered in Jorrun's eyes, 'I am. You … you were.' He turned the pages and came to one with Osun's name at the top. The page had been scored through with several heavy lines.

Osun shrugged. 'It's of no matter, we know I have no magic in my blood. What of Feren?'

'He is here.' Jorrun closed the book and placed his hand on it. 'We should all study this, get some idea of what to expect of those we might come up against.'

'What of Jagna?' Kesta asked.

'His bloodlines are also mostly Chemman, with a little of both Elden and Fulmer,' Jorrun told her.

'I meant should he learn this also.' Kesta shook her head. 'And will he go with you or stay here with me?'

'I'm sorry, Kesta,' Osun said with genuine concern. 'He is the only other magic user we have. We'll need him in Arkoom.'

She nodded. Untrained as they were, she'd at least have the other women. 'What of Azrael?'

'With us,' Osun replied.

'With you,' Jorrun said at the same time.

'He must go with the two of you.' Kesta held Jorrun's gaze. 'Your mother gave her life so he could be here to protect you both.'

Jorrun looked away, Osun stared at her and then nodded.

Jorrun sighed. 'We should get ready to entertain Gerant.'

'I don't think all of the women should come.' Kesta's hand went to her throat. 'Let him see we are strong, but not how strong.'

'Agreed.' Osun nodded firmly. 'I'll see you shortly.' He gave Jorrun's forearm a squeeze as he went past.

As soon as the door closed behind Osun, Jorrun spun about and grabbed Kesta's hand. 'I don't want to leave you here, but I can't see another way, not ye—'

'It's okay, I know.' She squeezed his fingers. 'We have a little time yet. I wouldn't normally try this early, but I'll begin getting the women to start learning to shield. Some of the Drakes that helped us before might be prepared to help us again for a while.' She laughed nervously. 'I'm almost tempted to ask my mother to come!'

Jorrun narrowed his eyes, becoming very still.

'What?' Kesta demanded.

'Loathe as I am to drag the Fulmers into this, it might be worth seeing if the Icante can spare a trained *walker* to help you. In the meantime, you've given me another idea. I'll send a pidgeon to Bractius and see if he can schedule Teliff's next trade visit for when Osun and I head to Arkoom. It will give you some support without it looking like an Elden invasion of the palace.'

Kesta felt some of the tension go from her shoulders. 'That would help so much.'

He hugged her tightly, leaning his cheek on the top of her head. She breathed in the scent of him, drawing in his warmth. 'It's going to be okay.'

I hope so, Kesta thought.

***

The evening with Gerant wasn't as fraught as Kesta had expected. The Chemman sorcerer did seem uncomfortable at first with the women talking freely around the table, he made little or no eye contact with them and spoke to none of them directly, however he wasn't rude or antagonistic. Mostly they talked of the difficulties that faced Chem after the downfall of Dryn and the fights between the remaining covens that had followed.

'I'd be interested to know what Feren plans for Chem's recovery,' Osun said, putting down his fork and playing with the stem of his wineglass. 'After all we can't support someone if our vision for Chem's future is too different.'

Gerant gave a snort and Kesta stiffened. 'I don't think anyone's vision for Chem's future matches yours.' His eyes travelled over the women.

Kesta opened her mouth but Jorrun squeezed her leg under the table.

Osun took a sip of his wine. 'I imagine this does seem very strange and after years of the same traditions, a little frightening, even. But with most magic users here dead, it seems prudent to make use of those with good blood. How many sorcerers are there left in Chem with trained power exactly?' He held Gerant's gaze.

Gerant shifted in his seat. 'Lord Feren only seeks stability, to restore law back to the land and ensure our defences.'

'You need not worry about attacks from Elden or the Fulmers,' Jorrun told him, his eyes were narrowed as he regarded the Chemmen. 'Our links with those countries and the trade we are establishing ensures peace. As long as we are here in Navere, there will be no attacks from our neighbours.'

Gerant leaned back in his chair and regarded Jorrun. 'I see.'

'I hope you do.' Jorrun didn't blink.

'Peace and stability suit us very well.' Osun leaned forward to pour more wine into Gerant's glass. 'And if that's what Feren is aiming for we have no reason not to vote him in as Overlord.'

Gerant lifted his chin a little. 'That's good to hear,' he said eventually.

They went back to eating, Kesta made an effort to try to get a comfortable conversation started again. She missed her father, getting people relaxed and talking was something he was always good at. She noticed Gerant was staring at one of the female servants who waited on them and she went cold inside. The woman was young and quite pretty, she'd already had to ask Captain Rece to warn his guards to stop harassing her when she'd seen two of them try to corner her in a hallway. She called the woman over and discreetly asked her to stay and help in the kitchens. From her expression, Kesta knew she understood and was grateful.

'I don't suppose that one will be available tonight?' Gerant pointed toward the servant's back with his knife, as she left through the door. The whole room grew silent, most eyes turned toward Kesta. 'Or is she used by one of you?' Gerant grinned at Jorrun and Osun.

Osun looked quickly down at the table but Kesta saw his jaw clench and his face redden. Jorrun went to stand, but it was Kesta's turn to stop him.

'That doesn't happen here,' she said, forcing her voice to be calm, although her hands shook beneath the table. 'No man in this palace can lay with a woman without her consent.'

'I don't suppose you would consent?' His grin widened.

Jorrun's hands clenched into fists.

Kesta laughed, although it sounded hollow even to her. 'I'm married to Jorrun, as you know full well, Gerant.'

He raised his hand in a shrug and winked at Jorrun. 'Ah, you can't blame me for trying!'

Osun cleared his throat and deftly changed the subject. 'So where are you off to next?'

'West to Letniv.'

Jorrun reached for Kesta's hand under the table and didn't let go until dinner was finished and Osun suggested they move to a receiving room along the hall. Several of the women took the opportunity to slip away, escorted by Cassien and Captain Rece. Only Calayna and Estre remained with them, the latter standing very close to Jagna. To their dismay, Gerant drunkenly regaled them with the tale of the grizzly part he'd played in the destruction of the Borrows. Kesta found herself feeling sick and looking around she realised no one else was speaking.

Gerant's story came to a faltering halt and he drained his glass.

'Fascinating,' Osun said through gritted teeth. 'Thank you for sharing that.' He looked toward the door where Captain Rece had returned to wait with one of the other guards. 'Captain, perhaps you would be so good as to assist our guest to his room?'

Rece stepped forward at once. Gerant waved a hand lazily. 'I suppose I'm about ready to sleep.' He pushed himself up from the chair and followed Rece out of the room without a backward glance.

The moment the door closed, Azrael shot out of one of the lanterns, making himself big and contorting his face to the most demonic expression he could muster. 'I wanted to burn him!'

'Yes, it was very tempting,' Jorrun agreed.

Osun sighed and slumped into one of the chairs. 'Hopefully we have done enough to warn them off attacking Navere or murdering us in Arkoom.'

'I thought everyone did really well,' Calayna said.

'We'll see.' Jorrun gave a slight shake of his head before turning to Kesta. 'Come on, we have more work to do tonight.'

Kesta said her goodnights and followed Jorrun out into the hallway, Azrael bobbed along ahead of them. Jorrun stopped.

'Azrael, sneak into that man's room and see if he scries to Feren.'

Azrael darted about in a big loop. 'Good idea!' The fire-spirit darted into one of the lamps and vanished.

'You're very quiet again,' Kesta said as the went up the stairs to the library.

'Am I?' He glanced down at her with a frown. 'I guess I'm worried. And I don't want to leave you.'

Kesta smiled briefly. Although she didn't doubt how much he loved her, it was still good to hear it sometimes. 'I envy you getting to leave the palace and travelling for a while. Thank the spirits for the gardens here.'

'Kesta.' He turned toward her outside the library door, he glanced down at the carpet before capturing her eyes and asked without blinking. 'Would you consent to swapping some vials of each other's blood so we can scry? I know it's blood magic bu—'

'Yes.' She placed a hand on his chest and stood on her tiptoes to kiss him. 'Absolutely, yes!'

His shoulders and back relaxed a little and he pushed the library doors open. 'Under the circumstances I think it will be wise for me to enhance my power and protect myself and set out an elemental star. I'll have to do my dream-walk down here, there's no room up on the balcony.'

He strode about the room, gathering up his items. Kesta built and lit the fire and then waited in one of the chairs, glancing through Dryn's ledger of magical ability. She found Jorrun's page, but hesitated to read it. It felt like too much of an invasion of his privacy.

'Have you read about yourself?' she asked him.

He glanced up from where he knelt on the floor setting out his items. 'Yes. There is Borrow blood in my ancestry, too.' He sat back on his heels. 'I thought that was strange considering how ...' He winced. 'How carefully I was bred. Take a look at the next page.'

Kesta turned the paper and had only just started reading the name when she noticed the jagged remains of a torn-out page. 'Something has been removed. Was it Osun, do you think?'

He came to stand beside her. 'No, his page was crossed out, remember. I have no idea who could have been removed, I'm surprised it wasn't mine. It might be worth discovering, though.'

She nodded, staring at the torn paper as though to force it to give up its secrets.

Azrael melted slowly out of the fireplace so as not to startle them.

'Anything?' Jorrun asked.

Azrael made himself small. 'He fell asleep almost at once.'

Jorrun sighed. 'I suppose that's a good thing. Okay, let's get started.'

Jorrun lit his candles and with a thin-lipped smile at Kesta, threw some herbs onto the fire and lay down in the centre of his symbolic star.

Kesta watched him breathing for a while, it was some time before the muscles in his body relaxed. The wood in the fireplace snapped, making her jump, and she quietly moved Dryn's ledger and opened it, looking for any names she knew. She stopped when she got to Feren, running her finger down the words and leaning closer to the page. Out of the corner of her eyes she saw Azrael move over to one of the lamps to drink the oil. Feren seemed to be of pure Chem blood. She flicked through to Dryn himself, feeling a sense of revulsion as she touched the page. Dryn's mother had been of Fulmer descent. Another stolen woman. She shuddered.

She jumped up as Jorrun stirred, going to the nearest candle on the carpet and kneeling down. His eyes moved beneath his closed lids and the fingers of one hand twitched before he sat up with a gasp, his blue eyes going straight to Kesta's.

'You're all right?'

He nodded, a frown on his face. 'I need to think a moment, that dream was somewhat ... foggy.'

She fetched him a glass of water and he waved at her to step inside the star set out on the carpet. Kesta sat beside him and Azrael hovered closer.

'Anything?' Kesta prompted, her concern growing.

'Yes, actually.' Jorrun tapped at her leg. 'Our guest has a certain amount of loyalty to Feren, but there is no friendship there. His mission is actually as he says, to give a personal invitation to Arkoom, but he has his own motivation to look out for a Seat he can steal for himself. Thankfully he has decided we are much too strong and has taken our threat of Elden and Fulmer support seriously.' He glanced at Kesta, his fingers clenching and uncurling. 'He is disgusted, furious even, at our giving women power and protection. I ... I won't tell you of his thoughts, he has been wise in keeping them to himself.'

'Sadly, I'm sure he isn't the only one thinking them.' She sighed. 'This is going to take a very long time.'

He touched her jaw with two fingers to turn her head to face him. He kissed her, then took her hand to pull her to her feet. 'But it's not impossible. Come on, let's try to get some sleep.'

***

318

Thankfully Gerant left before midday and Kesta selfishly left Osun and Jorrun to deal with him, sticking to her usual routine of getting the women to practice their magic. Five of them could now quickly call fire and a further two had just opened up their minds to let in magic, including Kussim. The young woman was still somewhat reserved but had begun to speak more when there were no men about. Kesta could see how much her reticence hurt both Jorrun and Osun, but she knew that rushing her would do no good.

Kesta got them to start trying to summon wind so they could form protective shields. Normally a *walker* wouldn't start such training for months after developing magical ability, but they didn't have the time to refine each small skill to perfection. It was a frustrating time for all of them. Jorrun came in to help with the lessons on a couple of occasions, but his presence proved to be more disruptive than helpful.

Farkle lost his battle against his illness on the same day a letter arrived from his son to say it wouldn't be safe for him to travel to Navere. Osun locked himself away in his room that day, leaving Jorrun and Kesta to run things with Calayna and Jagna. Twice Kesta went to Osun's door and raised her hand to knock, but both times she stopped, her disgust at the man's past behaviour getting the better of her. Osun emerged the next day, quiet but composed. He made swift arrangements to have his friend buried in Navere. Kesta wondered what Osun wrote in the letter he sent to Farkle's son.

The time of Jorrun's departure came painfully quickly. Osun arranged an elaborate dinner the evening before to which even Captain Rece and two of his sergeants were invited; it was strange to see them out of their uniforms and looking so human. Kesta could understand Osun's reasoning, however she couldn't help but feel some resentment that her precious last hours with

Jorrun were being shared with others. She forced herself to smile through the meal, but her stomach tightened with every minute that passed.

Osun stood and tapped at his glass with a spoon. He grinned, making him look so much younger. 'I have a surprise for everyone. Follow me, please.'

Kesta looked at Jorrun but he took her hand without saying a word and they followed Osun down the hall to the largest room in the palace. Music spilled out through the open double doors and the curious murmurs increased in volume. When she looked at Jorrun again, a slight smile played about his lips and she glowered at him in annoyance.

'What are you up to?' She demanded.

He squeezed her hand tighter, but still said nothing.

When they entered the room, Kesta saw nearly all of the servants and a few of the guards were clustered around tables on which lay food and carafes of alcohol. The far doors stood open into the starlit garden, but fires blazed in the two fireplaces. In one corner musicians played a lively melody that Kesta didn't recognise.

'Come in, everyone!' Osun turned to face them with his arms open wide. 'My people of the Raven Coven!'

Kesta stared at Osun wide-eyed as people pushed past them into the room. It was a brilliant move, one that would bring the palace together, inspire loyalty, despite their strange and foreign ways.

'It was his idea,' Jorrun said, seeming to read her thoughts. 'To keep you safer. Will you dance with me?'

'Dance?' She stared up at him in shock.

'You know, moving your feet to the music? You Fulmer heathens do dance, don't you?'

She punched him in the shoulder. 'Of course, we do! Just not to boring Elden music.'

'Boring Elden music?' He tilted his head and narrowed his eyes at her. 'You barbarian women have no refinement.'

'Luckily for you.' She took a step forward, not breaking eye contact even to blink. She saw his pupils dilate and his skin flush, she grinned.

'Witch,' he said, grabbing her right hand and putting his other to the small of her back to pull her into a dance.

'I didn't know you danced,' she said seriously.

'I haven't in a long time.' He frowned. 'But Osun thought it would be important we did. Look around.'

Kesta did so and realised most of the people in the room had stopped to watch them, there was little conversation above the music. She immediately blushed scarlet and missed a step to stand on Jorrun's foot.

'Why are they staring at us?' she hissed.

'Dance is a rare thing in Chem.' He leaned forward to speak softly in her ear, his breath tickled the corner of her jaw. 'And men and women don't dance together. Look again.'

She did so and saw Osun was now also dancing with his young niece, Kussim. With them were Jagna and Estre and Calayna with young Cassien.

'They've been learning.' Jorrun grinned down at her. 'Small steps, but meaningful.'

Kesta swallowed, letting Jorrun lead her as she peered past him to try to watch the others. Calayna stepped away from Cassien to invite Captain Rece to try, Cassien in turn held out his hand to Rey.

Without warning a sob broke up from Kesta's chest and escaped from her. She turned to hide her face against Jorrun's neck and shoulder; his skin was warm and soft.

'Come on, let's go.'

She looked up at him, wiping one cheek with her fingers. 'What abou—'

'They are happy, the don't need us.' Keeping hold of her hand he led her along the hall and up the stairs to the library.

***

She awoke slowly, feeling Jorrun's chest rise and fall beneath her cheek, his arms still wrapped around her. He must have felt her eyelashes against his skin as she opened her eyes as he spoke at once.

'I was just thinking of waking you. I didn't want to, but I have to go soon.'

Sitting up a little, she realised it was light in the library despite the fact the stained-glass window faced westward. They hadn't slept until very late – or very early. She smiled to herself, stretching slowly, but her smile quickly faded and a frightened feeling, close to grief, gripped her heart. She sat up to look down at Jorrun.

'I'm so sorry,' he said. 'Sorry to put you through this, sorry to leave you with this burden.'

'Jorrun.' She touched his lips with the tips of her fingers. 'We went through all this last night. We chose to be here, to do this.'

He placed a hand on her chest, just below her throat. 'If anything goes wrong, take my ship and get yourself safely to Fulmer. Save as many of the women as you can. Don't try to hold Navere; it's the people that are important, not the place.'

She nodded, not able to take her eyes from his beautiful blue ones.

She gave a shriek as he pulled at her arm, causing her to fall across him. He hugged her so hard she could barely breath. 'Promise me you won't risk yourself.'

'Only if you do the same.'

She felt him nod. 'I'll scry to you as often as I can, but it might not be every night, I'll have to be careful.'

She found she'd lost her own voice. Her throat was painfully tight and pressure built behind her eyes, but she blinked rapidly to stop herself from crying. 'I finally understand why you shut yourself away in the Raven Tower that day you made me leave. It wasn't because you didn't care, it was because you loved me so much.'

She felt his chest still as he held his breath. Despite her best efforts, tears escaped from her soul.

'It took all the willpower I had not to give in and go down,' he said quietly. 'But I did give in.'

'What do you mean?' She sat up to look at him.

'You didn't see then?' He searched her eyes.

She shook her head.

'I lit every candle in the Raven Tower.' His voice broke. Kesta lay back down, holding him tightly and kissing his neck. She felt him swallow. Without a word he slowly untangled himself from her to get dressed. She didn't move, couldn't move, as he picked up the small bag he'd packed.

'No risks, Kesta,' he said in a hoarse whisper. 'I'll come back to you.'

She listened as he made his way down the steps and out of the secret door to the library. She heard the soft tread of his boots across the thin carpet and the click as the library door closed behind him. She waited until her heart hurt too much to bear it, then she jumped up and got dressed, running from the library and up the stairs to one of the old coven members' rooms that overlooked the gardens. She was in time to see Jorrun, Osun, Cassien, and Jagna ride away out of sight.

She'd never felt so alone, so vulnerable, in all her life.

Chapter Twenty-Four

Ayline; Kingdom of Elden

Ayline shifted in her seat. Her back ached abominably. Beside her, Bractius barely said a word, in fact there was little conversation at all in the King's private dining room. Adrin didn't seem to notice the mood of the others, his arms making large gestures in the air as he told of a sea skirmish he'd fought against Borrowmen. The witch queen, Dia, scowled down into her plate. Ayline supposed Dia was offended, having demanded the freedom of Temerran and allowing his escape, she obviously still considered the Borrowmen allies. She snorted to herself. Temerran was quite handsome she supposed, although some ten years younger than the witch, knowing Fulmer women Dia had probably seduced the Bard to do her bidding.

'Something wrong?' Bractius glared up at her from under his reddish eyebrows.

She glanced about quickly to see if anyone else had noticed her indiscretion. 'No, my love, it's just difficult to get comfortable. I can't wait for our child to be born.'

She smiled, but he barely looked at her, pushing some chicken through the gravy on his plate and then stabbing it several times with his fork. His eyes were red and bloodshot, and he hunched over the table.

'Your majesty, something troubles you?' Dia asked.

Ayline gritted her teeth, it was hard not to snarl.

Bractius sighed. 'My stupid nightmares have come back.'

'I thought they'd gone?' Ayline demanded. 'When did they come back?'

Bractius dropped his fork and leaned back in his chair. 'About a week.'

A week! Ayline stared at Dia. Inari had been right. She'd refused to see or even acknowledge the young servant since Larissa's death and his awful behaviour. She didn't want to admit he'd really frightened her.

Bractius shook his head and picked up his wine goblet. 'It's hardly surprising since I got that letter from Jorrun requesting a 'discreet' ship full of warriors to guard his palace while he goes gallivanting off to secure his power in Chem. I should never have let him go, he is needed here.'

'Have you told him about your nightmares?' Dia asked.

'I'm a grown man!' Bractius snapped at her. It was hard for Ayline not to grin. She saw Arrus stiffen defensively.

'He is a dream-walker though,' Dia replied gently, totally unphased by his uncharacteristic temper.

'I'm fed up with advice.' Bractius stood up and stormed out of the room.

Ayline glared at Dia before standing and dropping her napkin on the table. 'Excuse me,' she said.

She followed her husband, the ungainly bulk of her body making it difficult for her to hurry.

'Bractius! Wait a moment. Please.' She stopped to lean with a hand against the wall. Surprisingly enough he turned to wait for her. 'I don't mean to offend you,' she panted. 'But I am worried about you.'

Bractius gestured almost violently toward the young page who had followed him, and the young boy darted away. He stared at her for a moment, his eyes almost going straight through her to the empty corridor beyond. Ayline shivered, wondering if he saw the ghost of dead Larissa.

He seemed to shake himself and rubbed at his face. 'Let's talk in my room.'

Ayline straightened her spine and hurried to catch up with him. As soon as they entered, Bractius poured himself a drink. 'I'm sure these dreams will drive me insane,' he muttered.

'What do you dream of?' Ayline sat carefully in one of the chairs.

'Different things, each time worse than before.' He swallowed the honey-coloured spirit back in one gulp and poured some more before sitting down. 'I've dreamt of Jorrun, of blood pouring from his mouth as he speaks to me of his plans for Chem. I dreamt of Temerran, of snakes wriggling free from the end of his flute, another after another, until the castle was full of them and they wound about my body and neck.' Ayline stared at him in growing horror, wrapping her arms about her stomach. 'I dreamt our child was born a monster with no head and arms like waving tentacles.'

Ayline gasped, her hand going to her mouth as nausea gripped her.

'Last night,' Bractius went on in a whisper, feeling his way around his desk as though he were blind, to slump in his chair. 'Last night I dreamt that birds filled the air, hundreds, thousands, turning the day to night. The sun cracked like an egg, bleeding into the sea and Taurmaline castle turned to dust.'

Ayline sat completely frozen, her heart beating loud and fast in her ears. 'I had no idea it was so bad.'

Bractius shook his head and took another sip of his drink. 'Sometimes I think the only way to escape would be to die.'

'No!' Ayline cried out. 'You can't let them beat you.'

Bractius sat up straight and glared at her. 'Them?'

She swallowed. 'Don't you think it strange your nightmares came when Larissa was here, stopped when she died and then started again when Dia arrive—'

He slammed his glass down. 'Nonsense!'

But she could see the doubt in his eyes.

'Think about it though,' she urged. 'Who else could do this to you? It was happening before Temerran came.'

Bractius rubbed at his beard and throat, his eyes narrowed, but he shook his head. 'No. No, that makes no sense. If it's the *walkers* doing this to me, why would they kill Larissa?'

Ayline opened her mouth, but she couldn't think of an answer. She sighed. 'We must think of this some more, husband. Be careful.'

He surprised her with a smile and reached across the table to hold his hand out for hers. 'Thank you, Ayline.'

She let him squeeze her fingers, his palm was warm and clammy.

'I should check on our guests and get myself to bed.' She pulled her hand free to stand. 'I'll see you tomorrow.'

He nodded, his eyes already distant.

She stepped out into the hall and found the King's young page waiting patiently outside, he gave her a polite bow. She hesitated, considering fetching some guards to stand outside her husband's room. On the one hand there was no point, this vile magic couldn't be stopped by any guards. On the other, it might improve her husband's view of her still further. She nodded to herself. Instead of returning to the private dining room, she found a guard and ordered him to ensure at least two men stood watch outside whatever room the King was in from now on.

She returned to her own rooms and was relieved, though hardly surprised, to find none of her ladies were present. Lerra's mattress was empty though and there was no sign of the girl. Ayline frowned in annoyance and pushed open the door to her bedchamber. She let out a gasp. Inari was sprawled out on her bed, one side of his mouth pulled up in an impertinent smile.

'What are you doing here?' she demanded, glancing around quickly. 'How dare you!'

Inari tutted and rolled over to prop himself up on one elbow. 'You can do better than that for the man who is offering you a throne.'

She stepped slowly into her room, jumping as the door slammed shut behind her. Inari pushed himself up with fluid ease to sit cross-legged.

'So, does the King suspect the Icante yet?' he asked.

She edged slowly around toward the window, although there was a twinge of longing in her muscles, something about Inari had started to make her hands shake with nerves. 'He doesn't want to believe it,' she told him. 'He says if the *walkers* were against him, why would the Icante kill Larissa?'

Inari snorted. 'Because Larissa loved your husband and refused to continue the Icante's bidding, so she got her sycophant, Temerran, to kill her before she revealed the truth.'

Ayline stared at him with her mouth open. 'Really?'

Very briefly, his nose creased in distaste. 'Of course, it's obvious. You need to get that idiot husband of yours to have the Icante arrested and put in the dungeons.'

Ayline shook her head. 'She would never allow that, what about her powers?'

'Have her husband arrested first and put him somewhere she doesn't know. If she doesn't cooperate, he'll die. In fact, if she doesn't cooperate then there will be war against the Fulmers, and all the witches will be hung – or burned.'

'I'm not sur—'

'Oh, for the gods' sake!' He jumped off the bed and stalked toward her, she shrank back against the wall. 'Tell him it will be a test. He will set her and her people free if she stops the dreams. Only, if the dreams stop, he'll know it's her and can charge her with witchcraft.'

It kind of made sense, but Ayline shuddered under the young man's angry gaze. She forced herself to nod.

'Good.' He stepped back to look her up and down. 'Now come to bed.'

'It's a bit uncomfortable now the baby is s—'

He grabbed her wrist and crushed it in his long fingers. 'Do as I say.'

***

Ayline woke with a scream, she clutched at her pillow, sobbing into it as she rolled from her back onto her side. The nightmare had been unbearable, worse than anything Bractius had described. In her dreams she'd given birth to a creature more like an eel with teeth longer than her fingers. The blood had just poured and poured from her body. Hot and shaking, she looked around the room to find she was alone. She padded to the door and opened it a crack, then wider. There was still no sign of Lerra. She drew in a deep breath as she heard women's voices. Clenching her fists to still her shaking body, she thrust open the door to her parlour and raised her chin to look around at the women there. There were only three, including Sonay, but even so relief swept through her and her knees weakened.

'Your majesty?' Sonay asked in concern, leaping to her feet to take her arm. 'Are you ill?'

'Send word to the king,' she gasped. 'The dream curse has fallen on me and his child now too!'

One of the other women leapt to her feet and scurried out of the door while Sonay helped Ayline back to her bed. Sonay snugged the blankets around her and then fetched her a glass of water which she gulped down thirstily.

'Where is Lerra?' Ayline asked anxiously.

Sonay bit her lower lip. 'No one has seen her, your majesty. Do you think you could eat?'

Ayline retched at the thought of it. 'Just some tea please! Chamomil—' A shudder ran through her. 'No, thyme tea, please, with rosemary.'

'I'll see to it.' Sonay's eyes ran over her face. 'I won't be long.'

As Sonay left the room, Ayline found herself suddenly remembering Rosa and a desperate longing for the older woman burst open in her chest. She screwed her face up and tensed all of her muscles. The baby moved.

'It's all right.' She rubbed at her stomach, speaking soothingly despite her own anxiety.

There was a bustle of activity outside the door and it was flung back against the wall as Bractius burst in.

'Ayline! Are you hurt? Is the baby okay?' He sat on the bed, his weight making the mattress sag and creak.

She held out her arms and he hugged her for the first time in months, rubbing her back with one hand and kissing her hair above her ear.

'I'm all right.' She sniffed. 'But, oh my love!' She pushed him back to look into his brown eyes. 'I understand now. The dream I had last night.' She let tears leak from her eyes. 'I'm so scared for our baby.'

'I'll write to Jorrun at once.' Bractius stood and began to pace around the room. 'He must forget Chem and come back here to sort this out.'

Ayline sat up. 'Oh, but that might be too late. You must listen to me, my love. I know you don't want to believe it …'

He stopped his pacing to glare at her.

'But I'm certain it's those witches from the Fulmers.'

'I told yo—'

'No, listen.' She slapped the blankets hard with one hand. 'We can test them, to be sure. Have Arrus arrested discreetly and locked away somewhere to ensure Dia's co-operation. Arrest her then on suspicion of witchcraft. Tell her if she stops the dreams, we will let her husband go and leave the Fulmers alone. If she refuses to stop the dreams, then we will declare war on the Fulmers and hang every last witch.'

Bractius opened his mouth and he shook his head slowly. 'This doesn't fee—'

'They are killing our child!' Ayline shrieked.

Bractius raised his hands and then covered his face with them. 'All right. All right, we will try. I hope the Fulmers will forgive me if you're wrong. Are you well enough to meet me in my private audience room shortly? I'll have the Icante summoned there.'

She nodded eagerly. 'I can meet you there.'

Bractius's shoulders sagged and his head was bowed as he silently left the room.

Ayline leapt out of bed and snatched up a dress, feeling excitement quicken her pulse. She yelled for her dwindled following of ladies to come and help her and she quickly washed her face and neck while they laced her into a dress and pinned up her chestnut hair. She didn't want to think about what she was doing. She was protecting her baby, protecting her future, taking the power she was owed. The respect she was owed.

Taking in a deep breath she raised her chin and set out from her rooms to her husband's private audience chamber. Her three ladies tried to follow but she turned and waved them away. 'Thank you for your loyalty, but please wait for me in my rooms.'

She didn't wait for their responses but continued through the corridor. She stopped dead in her tracks when she saw Inari, changing candles in the sconces. He didn't so much as glance at her as she sidled past. Turning her back on him made her skin crawl, but she forced herself to walk on. Two guards stood outside the King's room and she didn't bother to acknowledge them or knock, before turning the handle to step in. Bractius made to stand, but on seeing her settled back in his chair. Merkis Dalton was also in the room, along with the chief of the King's guards. All three men stared at her for a moment, before Dalton darted forward to pull a chair out for her.

They waited in awkward silence for several minutes before someone knocked lightly at the door and Dia came in. She glanced at those in the room before addressing Bractius without a curtsey or any reference to his title. Ayline found herself frowning as she watched the older Fulmer woman from under her lowered brows. She couldn't deny that despite her age Dia Icante was a striking woman, there was something very elegant, poised, and warm about her despite her odd brown and blue eyes. With her hair pinned up but softly loose about her face, the Icante's swan-like neck was all the more prominent.

'Icante.' Bractius cleared his throat, standing and straightening his shirt. 'As you know I've been plagued by evil dreams. Last night my wife was attacked also.'

Dia turned to look at Ayline, her eyebrows raised. 'Really? Is your majesty all right?'

Ayline refused to reply but turned to regard her husband. He cleared his throat again. 'I don't understand why you have done this to us, but I want you to stop your magic.'

'What?' Dia almost laughed, she looked around at them all. 'You think this is me? Seriously? Dream-walking is the magic of Elden, not the Fulmers. This isn't something I can do.'

Bractius stood, but he looked down at his desk rather than at the Icante. 'Nevertheless, it's a strange coincidence that my nightmares happened when Larissa was here, ceased with her death, and then started again with your presence. And now, after my wife has brought her suspicions to me, she and my child have been attacked.'

'Attacked how?' Dia demanded, looking Ayline up and down.

'To secure your co-operation, Arrus has been placed under arres—'

'What?' Dia's eyes widened and she took a step forward. Both Ayline and Bractius flinched, the guard put a hand to the hilt of his sword. 'This is ludicrous. We saved you from the Chemme—'

'How do we know that wasn't part of your plan?' Bractius's face reddened and spittle flew across the table as he spoke. Ayline put a hand to her throat and leaned back against her chair. 'Your daughter seduced and stole Jorrun to use him to conquer Chem. You yourself would take Elden but I won't let you!'

'No!' Dia shook her head, her brows creased together. She looked appealingly from Bractius to Dalton's unrelenting stare. 'This is madness. The Fulmers are a land of peace!'

'Prove it then!' Bractius spat, his eyes bulging. 'Go willingly to the dungeons and allow us to complete our investigation. Better still, cease this cowardly attack on us in our sleep! If our nightmares end, we will leave the

Fulmers alone, but if they do not, I will have every last witch hanged, and the Fulmers burned into the sea!'

Dia took several staggered steps back toward the door, shaking her head. 'Bractius, please believe me, I would never do you harm. Let me find out who is behind thi—'

'Silence!' Bractius bellowed, his cheeks almost purple, the veins standing out in his neck. 'Go with my guard to the dungeons and I will spare your husband's life.'

Dia clasped her hands together before her stomach as though to comfort herself, she glanced toward Ayline and her eyes narrowed.

'I trust the truth,' she said firmly. 'I'll go along with this charade for the moment for Arrus's sake. You are ill advised, your majesty, and ill-used. Don't let them take my protection from you.'

'Protection?'

Ayline thought Bractius would have a fit there and then.

'Take this creature away!'

The guard made no eye contact as he opened the door for the Icante. Her shoulders fell but she held her long neck still straight as she followed him out. As soon as the door closed, Ayline leapt up to run to her husband who had collapsed against his desk.

'Oh, my poor dear,' she said, cradling his head. 'We will be safe now, thanks to you.'

Outside in the hall, Inari slowly, meticulously, changed the candles, a whistle on his lips and a smile in his green eyes.

Chapter Twenty-Five

Jorrun; Covenet of Chem

'Azrael's coming!' Cassien shouted.

Both brothers reined in their horses and turned to see where the young man was pointing. A bright light came hurtling toward them, Jorrun's horse snorted and tried to pull its head free. He leaned forward to stroke its neck. Azrael slowed and made himself smaller and more human in shape. He regarded them both for a while, his colours softening to yellows.

'Well?' Osun demanded.

'No Drakess will come with uss to Arkoom.' Azrael told them. 'They are afraid of the city!'

'Why?' Osun glanced at Jorrun. 'They came in numbers when we fought Dryn and there is no one who is anywhere near a match for him there now.'

Azrael shifted his shape to become vaguer in appearance and Jorrun narrowed his eyes at his elemental friend, suspicion creeping through his mind, turning to fear as it reached his heart.

'What are they afraid of?' Jorrun demanded.

'None of them would ssay.' Azrael dropped low, close to the ground. 'Kesta and I felt something though, in Navere, a presence.'

Osun scowled impatiently. 'Is there actually something to fear or not?'

Azrael made himself some fiery shoulders and shrugged, looking mournfully at Jorrun. 'The best I can do is go ahead and sspy for you.'

'Do so, then,' Osun replied at once.

Jorrun opened his mouth, drawing in a deep breath to protest. 'We don't have much choice but to go to Arkoom, but there is no point walking
336

straight into a noose, and that includes Azrael. If he is to spy, then it should be when we are closer and not too far away to aid him if anything goes wrong.'

'But surely the further in advance we get any information, the better,' Jagna spoke up.

'Exactly.' Osun nodded firmly.

Cassien glanced at Jorrun briefly, but said nothing.

Jorrun clenched his teeth and his nostrils flared a little as he looked at his brother. It was rare for Osun to go against him, was he letting his feelings for the fire-spirit cloud his judgement? 'It's up to Azra, I guess, although I would prefer him to stay with us.'

'I'll be very careful.' Azrael moved closer to Jorrun's eye-level. 'And not stay there long.'

Jorrun closed his eyes, opening them again to see the dark mountains before him. 'Only if you're sure, bug,' he said at last. 'Don't risk yourself unnecessarily.'

'I won't!'

'And keep an eye out for Tembre,' Osun added. 'I'm not happy that he didn't wait for us.'

'It's possible he didn't get your message,' Jagna said.

Osun grunted. Jorrun had to agree with his brother on that point, it seemed more likely that the Chemman had decided to disassociate himself from them.

Azrael bobbed up and down before shooting away eastward.

Without looking at any of the others, Jorrun started his horse forward.

***

Jorrun sat up, fighting his blanket for a moment before gasping in air. In the darkness of the tent he heard Osun snore. Pain stabbed through his skull and he leaned forward, cradling his head. He could taste blood in his mouth, and he ran his tongue around his teeth and the inside of his cheeks to see if he had bitten anything in his sleep. He had such an overwhelming desire to breathe in the open air he didn't wait to put on his boots, snatching them up to stumble outside.

He drew in several deep breaths that didn't seem to satisfy his lungs, leaving him feeling dizzy.

'Everything all right?' Jagna called out softly. It was the young Chemman's turn to keep watch and he was perched atop a boulder that had been rolled down the mountain many years ago by snow.

Jorrun rubbed at the bridge of his nose and then put on his boots, struggling to keep his balance.

'I can't seem to sleep,' he said quietly, his pulse was still loud in his ears. 'Why don't you get to bed? I'll take the watch.'

'You're sure?' Jagna slipped down from the rock, pulling back his fur hood. His breath misted before him, picked out by the bright moon.

'Go on.' Jorrun indicated the tent with his head.

Jagna had only been gone moments before Jorrun regretted having not picked up his coat. His teeth chattered and his body shook. He ached to call Kesta again although he'd already scryed to her before going to bed. Even out here in the open he had an unrelenting fear some trap was about to close in around him.

Calling flames to his fingers, he re-lit their dead cooking fire, risking the light and the smoke. He didn't fear attack from bandits and robbers, they'd already been attacked on the road and he and Jagna had seen them off easily. But there was something else out there in the dark – or maybe not out there, maybe …

'Jorrun!'

The voice came from within the flame, a voice that made his heart skip and his muscles sag in relief.

'Azra! You're safe?'

Azrael detached himself from the fire and hovered close to him, his heat a relief to Jorrun's freezing skin.

'I am ssafe, and glad to be back.' Azrael altered his shape so he looked like an inverse teardrop with dark-blue eyes. 'Jorrun, Feren intends to eliminate all of his rivals by drawing the strongest to Arkoom, but you know that.'

'I suspected, yes.' He looked down at the burning wood, watching the edges turn slowly to ash. 'But we always knew we'd have to confront the last of my family.'

Azrael puffed himself out larger. 'I saw Tembre on my way back. He is a day ahead of you.'

Jorrun continued to stare into the fire. 'Tembre will die.'

'I could make him wait?'

Jorrun was surprised to find himself considering it. Tembre might have offered them limited support in return for Osun's clever planning, but the man would probably never really support the freedom of Chem's women.

'Jorrun?'

He sighed and sparks flew up from the fire. 'I'm not sure I like the sound of the man but see if he will change his mind and wait. Advise him if he goes alone, he will likely die.'

'I will, Jorrun.' Azrael crackled.

'Azrael.' He looked up into the fire-spirits swirling eyes. 'Are you hiding anything from me?'

'No, Jorrun!' Azrael made himself large.

Jorrun let out a silent sigh, standing to move away from the fire to better see out into the night. He wanted to believe the fire-spirit, but every nerve in his body was screaming to him that something was wrong.

***

They were attacked twice more on the road before they caught up with Tembre. The first group of men fled at the first fireball thrown by Jagna, the second group had been larger and more desperate. Over a dozen men, all well-armed and equipped with serviceable armour had lain an ambush across the main road. Cassien had been thrown from his horse before quickly rolling to his feet to defend himself with his sword. Even with all his power, Jorrun had been hard pressed to defeat the desperate men, especially with his terrified horse trying to unseat him to escape his magic.

It had taken Cassien over an hour to retrieve his mount, but eventually they found themselves above the forested valley, overlooking the capital city of Chem, Arkoom. It was a breathtaking sight, the high-walled city stood at the fork of a silver river, backed by high, dark mountains. A steady stream of people came and went along the black paved road, tiny and insignificant in the vastness of nature.

Jorrun saw Cassien looking over Tembre and his men with narrowed eyes. He didn't blame the young man for his distrust. The Chemmen sorcerer hadn't seemed particularly pleased to see them despite Azrael's warning. He'd been polite enough to Osun, but wary with Jorrun. Jorrun assumed the man had his own agenda that didn't coincide with Osun's. For the first time Jorrun found himself having serious doubts about what he was doing. The majority of those used to power would never accept the changes they wanted to make. It would be easier to just take those who wanted a new life back with him to Elden, or to the Fulmers. But that would mean abandoning the rest.

He sighed.

'Brother?' Osun looked at him in concern.

Jorrun gritted his teeth. 'Let's get this done.'

He urged his horse forward, and they followed the long road beneath the dark boughs of the evergreen forest, the pine needles dampening the sound of their horses' hooves. When they reached the city, the queue of people waiting to get in was wary and subdued. Many furtive glances were thrown their way and one man visibly startled when he met Jorrun's eyes. He realised he had automatically slipped back into his guise of the Dark Man. Perhaps that wasn't a bad thing.

Both Osun and Tembre produced the official invitations they'd been given by Gerant and were ushered through, their two parties mingling as they passed under the portcullis, but spreading apart again on reaching the start of the main street.

'Will you head straight to the palace, or find lodgings first?' Tembre asked Osun.

Osun chewed at the edge of his thumb.

Jorrun watched his brother intently. He didn't like the idea of handing their horses and gear over to the palace, but neither did he want to give Tembre a chance to get there first and strike a deal with Feren behind their backs. He had to bite his tongue and stop himself speaking for Osun.

His brother drew in a breath. 'We'll stop briefly at Arkoom inn, it's on the way. Have you ever stayed there, Tembre? I'd recommend it.'

Tembre's huge eyebrows lowered in a frown and he glanced at one of his sorcerous companions. 'I haven't, but I'll take your recommendation.'

Jorrun relaxed a little, it seemed the Chemman didn't want to split up either.

They left their horse and gear in the care of the lodging manager and continued on foot toward the temple district. After his time back in Elden and their achievements in the palace of Navere, Arkoom seemed even more shocking than the last time Jorrun had been here. Chem's instability had caused an increase in poverty and slaves were crammed into small, stinking pens. Several shops were boarded up and the burned-out temple stood like a looming reprimand. Most of the outer walls still stood, but the roof had collapsed inward and little remained of the once impressive doors.

The priests were unperturbed. They stood outside like a flock of carrion birds squabbling over the remnants of the population that hurried past with bowed heads. Their gaudy coloured robes were obscene against the sooty stone, their laughter a false and sickening sound in the miserable city. Jorrun realised with shock that the only god represented there was Hacren, the god of death. He glanced around, trying to see if there was any sign of any other priests. As he looked back, he saw a woman being dragged out of the derelict building, the priest that had her by the hair was so rough she couldn't scramble onto her feet. She was dropped and her face hit the cobbles.

Jorrun drew in a sharp breath, power coming instinctively to his fingers.

'Jorrun!' Osun warned him sharply, grabbing his arm.

The priest lifted the woman's head, she was younger than she'd first appeared, perhaps still a teenager under all the dirt. Without hesitation the priest drew a knife across her throat, his eyes meeting Jorrun's with a grin.

Jorrun froze, his eyes painfully wide. He could taste blood in his mouth.

'Jorrun!' Osun gripped his arm hard.

'Kesta would have stopped him.' Despair washed up from his stomach with his nausea. 'Why didn't I? What's wrong with me, Osun?'

'Too many years in this damned country,' Osun snapped. 'Come on, brother.'

Jorrun swallowed and managed to tear his eyes away from the priest's.

The others had moved on ahead, only Cassien looking back to ensure all was well. When Jorrun glanced back briefly he saw all the priests had now stopped to watch him, a shudder went through his body from his shoulders to his feet. He put his hand up over his nose at the cloying smell from one of the incense shops. He kept his eyes on the muddy cobbles, following Osun's feet and not daring to look into the windows of the skin shops. He swore to himself that when he got back to Navere, he would close every last one whether the owner had found a new trade or not.

His mood darkened further when he saw they'd reached the gates to the palace. Cassien had fallen back to walk beside Osun, his hand on his sword hilt. They showed their invitations and were allowed through, one of the guards hurrying ahead to warn of their arrival. Jorrun couldn't help exchanging a nervous glance with his brother. Their plan was to try to keep the peace a while longer to buy themselves more time. What he wanted to do was tear the city to the ground.

The palace gardens, once immaculate and brightly lit, were dreary, untamed, and buried beneath mud and fallen leaves. A part of him felt satisfaction, a garden should be a natural place, not all straight edges and invisible cages. A smile pulled at his lips when he saw a whole wing of the palace was still in ruins. He wondered if his father were still buried somewhere beneath it.

They were taken to the main entrance and Jorrun's heart skipped a beat when the doors banged shut behind them. Several guardsmen lined the walls of the corridor they were taken down, eyes downcast but for nervous glances. Jorrun wished he had Kesta's *knowing*. He wished he had Kesta. Other than his brother and Cassien, he was still uncertain of everyone's loyalty. This confrontation would be won or lost by Osun's acting skills, or his own power.

Some gilded double doors were thrown open and Jorrun saw that beyond them was a room with white marble pillars and a blood-red carpet running down the middle. On a raised dais stood a circle of fifteen seats, one of them taller and higher than the others. Six of the seats were occupied including the Seat of the Overlord. Several warriors stood at the edges of the room, all armed for battle. The hairs rose on the back of Jorrun's neck.

'Welcome!'

The man in the Overlord's seat stood. He would have been as tall as Osun, maybe even Jorrun, but he had developed a slight stoop. His lined face was still unmistakably Dunham, although his eyes were more grey than blue and his long hair, tied back in a tail, was almost white.

'I believe the two of you are my great-nephews?' He looked from Jorrun to Osun and back again.

'We are, and pleased to meet with you at last.' Osun gave a slight bow and smiled warmly.

344

Jorrun saw several of those seated exchange glances. The warriors around the room shifted their feet, their eyes mostly firmly on Feren, and on his hands.

Jorrun immediately drew up a shield and Osun turned to him wide eyed. Cassien had seen it too, felt it instinctively as only one who had faced death every day could have.

'Trap!' Cassien yelled as he drew his sword.

Tembre and his party moved away from them as Feren's sorcerers sprang to their feet, calling their own power. Feren lowered his head and grinned at Jorrun even as Osun raised his hands, shaking his head. 'No, this is some misunderstandin—'

'Tembre!' Jorrun turned to their supposed ally who had backed toward a corner, shielding his own men. Jagna stepped forward into a fighter's crouch, his eyes darting from one person to another as he anxiously protected Osun and Cassien alone.

'Tembre, are you with us?' Jorrun demanded, heat rising to the surface of his skin and his muscles tensed in anger. 'Tembre!' he bellowed, calling flames to his hands.

Tembre tore his eyes away from Feren and straightened up, stalking slowly forward to stand beside Jorrun, who turned back to his uncle just in time to meet the flames he hurled at him.

Cassien grabbed Osun, pulling him behind him, Jagna groaned, his face reddening as he strained to hold his shield against the combined attacks of the Arkoom sorcerers. Jorrun passed them, letting his anger consume him, he drew power through his body and wrenched the seats from the stone that held them. As the heavy, metal chairs bowled Chemmen off their feet, Azrael launched himself from a lantern to consume those whose shields had faltered. The smell of burning flesh made Jorrun want to vomit, but he forced himself to draw air in through his flaring nostrils. Feren was battering Jagna but Tembre still held back, waiting to see which way the tide would turn. His cowardice drove Jorrun's fury and he had to force himself to unclench his fists and allow the magic to flow.

A roar burst from Jorrun and he hurled Feren off his feet, the old man hit the marble floor hard. Jagna took the moment of reprieve to strike out at one of the other sorcerers, breaking the man's shield. Cassien cried out in alarm as Osun ran forward to finish the man off with his sword, Cassien threw his own body between Osun and a fireball that sped toward him; Jagna deflected it just in time, breathing hard, his power waning. Several of the Arkoom warriors that had been circling the edges of the battle saw Jagna's weakness and took the opportunity to go for Osun and Cassien.

They hadn't expected them to be such ferocious swordsmen.

Osun and Cassien fought back to back, slicing the Arkoom men down. Almost spent, Jagna stumbled, wildly casting out wind to turn aside a blast of flame that came from one of the remaining sorcerers. As the robed man raised his hands to strike again, Azrael wrapped him in a fiery embrace. Jorrun tensed at the sound of the screams.

Feren threw fire and then the broken chairs at him, scrambling backward to get to his feet. Out of the corner of his eye, Jorrun saw that Tembre and his men had finally stepped in, attacking the remainder of the Arkoom warriors. Feren managed to stand and with a growl he launched himself toward Jorrun. Jorrun braced himself against his uncle's whirling tornado, pushing back with all his strength. Taking in a deep breath he stepped aside, dropping his shield. Feren went stumbling past him and Jorrun struck him from behind, pinning him to the floor with magic. He drew a dagger and grabbed a handful of Feren's coarse, greying hair, lifting his head to expose his neck. Jorrun hesitated, his pulse rushing loudly in his ears. With one swift movement he slit his great-uncle's throat. Hot, sticky blood spilled over his hand and he dropped the dagger, swallowing and breathing hard.

He straightened up to survey the room, but had no time to move or speak. Unbearable pain split his skull and a fog seemed to force itself down through his brain, pressing into his eyes and choking him. He tried to cry out, but the force building in his throat was too strong. Sight was torn from him, he reached out blindly, feeling heat against his skin before he collapsed to the blood-red carpet.

Chapter Twenty-Six

Osun; Covenet of Chem

'Jorrun?' Osun watched in horror as his brother crumpled to the ground. He looked around quickly, seeing that all of Feren's men were dead. 'Get those doors secure!'

Instead of obeying, Cassien leapt over the body of a fallen enemy to stand at Osun's side, his sword ready. Jagna stumbled over to join them, eyes wide.

'There's not enough of us to Hold Arkoom,' Tembre panted, wiping blood from his mouth with the back of his sleeve.

Azrael shot toward the Margith Chemman, making himself huge. Several of Tembre's men staggered back, crying out in fear. The fire-spirit hissed. 'If you betray uss, Tembre, every Drake in Shem will force their way through your melted eyess and burn through your blood slowly until you are asshes!'

Tembre swallowed and held up his hand. 'I won't betray anyone.' He gestured at his men and they split up to check the doors.

Osun quickly knelt beside Jorrun, relieved to see the slow rise of his chest.

'Did he try to channel too much power?' Jagna asked.

'I wouldn't know.' Osun glanced up at him with a shrug. He checked Jorrun's pulse, it was rapid, as rapid as Osun's own.

'What do we do?' Cassien asked in a whisper.

Osun drew in a deep breath and stood up. Only one of the fifteen Arkoom seats still stood in its original place. He spotted Gerant's broken body and felt not an ounce of sympathy for the man. 'Okay. Does anyone know what Seats those men held?'

'Well, Feren held Harva of course,' Jagna said.

'I recognise Veron there.' Tembre pointed. 'He held Letniv, and Backra there held Darva.'

'So, there's ten seats we're not sure of.' Dread made Osun's skin feel icy cold. 'They could be on their way, they might have been defeated already before we got here.' He looked down at Jorrun. 'Why didn't he let me tr—'

'It *was* a trap.' Cassien jumped to Jorrun's defence. 'I don't think any amount of talking would have worked.'

'Too many people know you kill Dunhams.' Tembre looked Osun in the eye. 'Too many people fear your changes in Navere.'

Jagna snorted. 'Whatever you think, Tembre, those changes are working.'

Tembre held up his hands placatingly and gave his head a slight shake.

Osun placed his hands on his hips. 'We bluff it out, like we did in Navere. Get me a guard in here, a servant, anyone!' He waved a hand toward the door.

Tembre's men looked startled, but one of them opened the door and shouted, 'Hey, you! Come here!'

A moment later a worried looking guard slipped through the partially open door, his mouth falling open at the state of the room.

'You!'

The man jumped at the sound of Osun's voice.

'Don't stand there like an idiot!' Osun frowned at him. 'Get these bodies cleared away and disposed of, then get these chairs fixed. And we want something to eat and drink.'

'Y–yes, master!' The guard bowed and backed out of the door. Moments later he appeared with some of his fellows and two male slaves. They hurriedly picked up the dead Chemmen and carried them away. Tembre and his men seemed to relax a little, Tembre even sitting in the one good chair. Osun's own tension refused to alleviate, his stomach a tight knot of apprehension. Azrael's frantic fluttering above Jorrun wasn't helping. Osun took off his cloak and laid it over his brother. Taking his cue, Cassien also unclasped his cloak and folded it up to place carefully under Jorrun's head.

'Do we hole up and make our stand here?' Jagna asked quietly, indicating the room before running his hand over his stubbled head.

'No,' Osun replied just as quietly. 'That will seem too desperate.' He rubbed at the bridge of his nose, trying to think. 'We use Jorrun as an excuse. There are two towers in the palace, I believe they are both used as living quarters. We pick one to defend, although it will also mean we are trapped there.'

Jagna winced, but he nodded.

Someone knocked at the main doors and, with a nod from Osun, Tembre's men opened it. A wide-eyed and well-dressed servant entered and gave a low bow. He looked around at them all, his eyes finally settling on Osun, despite Tembre being sat in a Seat.

'We have refreshments, master,' the man said. 'May we bring them in?'

'Of course!' Osun feigned impatience. 'And my brother is injured. Where are the best rooms in this palace?'

'The Overlord's rooms overlook the gardens at the centr—'

'What about the towers?'

'Well.' The poor servant shifted his feet and rubbed his hands together. 'They haven't been used in a while, but the western tower was always given over to the favoured guests.'

'Good.' Osun smiled at him. 'Have them made ready and bring in those refreshments.'

As the man moved away to beckon in his fellows, Cassien whispered urgently, 'Should we get a healer for Jorrun?'

Osun swallowed and shook his head. 'We can't trust them and must hide every weakness.'

Osun tried to relax his muscles and look comfortable and confident as the servants walked in with trepidation, some of them veiled women. After being in Navere he had to bite his tongue and stop himself from thanking anyone as he took a glass of wine and some bread with ham and melted cheese on it. He winced and shoved at Cassien when the young man made eye contact with a servant and opened his mouth to speak to him.

'Who is your Captain?' Osun asked one of the guards.

'Capsen, master.' The guard gave a hasty bow.

'Why hasn't he presented himself?' Osun glared at the man. 'Go and get him!'

The guard gave a frantic nod, backing up and almost running from the room. Osun turned to see Cassien grinning at him.

'Cass! Wipe that smile off your face!'

Cassien blinked at him, his face reddening a little, but the young man straightened up and gave a slight nod.

Osun could feel the tension in the room but, unlike Navere, he doubted kindness or explanations would get him anywhere, not in the short term. They had to establish dominance and control, and quickly too. Jagna looked pale and swayed a little on his feet, Jorrun still hadn't stirred. He watched Tembre for a moment, lounging in his chair. He had Cassien, and he had Azrael, not much against the whole of Chem.

The guard he'd sent out came scurrying back in, following after an overweight man in an ornate but impractical uniform.

'I am Captai—'

Osun dropped his glass and punched the man hard in the face, breaking his nose and sending him sprawling back against the carpet.

'Why were you not here at once?' Osun roared, feeling an artery pulse in his neck and his face warm with the rush of his blood.

The captain dragged himself back a bit, stuttering a reply, 'I … I stay out of the business of masters!'

'What's the point of guards who don't guard? I might as well have you all killed! Get up!' He waved a hand at him, aware of the complete silence in the room. 'Ensure the palace is secure, no one but servants bringing essential supplies gets in without my say so. How many other masters have come here recently? How many did Feren kill?'

The captain's mouth flopped open.

The other guard stepped forward, his eyes wide. 'Master, there have been two other parties. Both were all killed. I believe they were from the Seats of Caergard and Darkhall.'

'Thank you.' Osun gave the man a polite nod, his voice now icy calm. 'Stay here a moment.'

The guard bowed, glancing at his grovelling captain who was now on his feet.

'Don't just stand there, go and carry out my commands!' Osun flicked his fingers at the captain as though dismissing a slave. The captain didn't need telling twice.

Osun turned back to the other man. 'What's your name?'

'Embry, master.'

'Embry, do you think you can find thirty guards who can actually do their job?'

'Yes, master.'

Osun snorted. 'Glad to hear it. Find them and arrange a rotation to guard the western tower. If anyone gets past them and I find myself having to do any killing, I'll hold you responsible.'

'Understood, master.'

Osun nodded, looking him up and down. 'You may carry out my command.'

The man bowed and hurried away. Osun saw the servant who'd arranged their refreshments was hanging back and seeming to want his attention.

'What is it?' Osun asked, his voice polite and even.

The servant gave a low bow. 'Master, your rooms are ready.'

'Very good. Find someone to carry my brother up and then lead the way.'

***

Osun sat with his head in his hands, he leaned back and rubbed at his aching temples and groaned. The palace's account books were a mess. After Dryn's death, several hands had penned sporadic entries, none of which seemed to be accurate or make any sense. Messages had piled up and spilled off the desk and onto the floor despite Cassien and Jagna's best efforts to help. His eyes stung, he'd barely slept in the five days they'd held their tentative occupation of Arkoom Palace, and not because of the paperwork. He jumped as a door banged somewhere down the hall, he strained his ears to listen but he could hear no footsteps. His eyes fell on the door handle and he held his breath. Nothing. He breathed out, forcing his spine to relax.

Twice the palace guards had turned away Chemmen sorcerers who had come at Feren's summons. One group of three from Farport and a larger group from Gysed. Thankfully they'd heeded Osun's instructions to go back and see to the running of their own cities and districts. It seemed hearing the last of the once great Dunhams had been defeated was enough to give them pause and prevent any thoughts of their own attempts at the Overlord's Seat. Osun made sure they were informed he had no intent of taking the Seat himself but would wait until things had settled to call a genuine vote.

If it bought him some time, it would be something.

He let out a cry of alarm as Azrael squeezed out of the candle on his desk.

'Ssorry, Ossun.' Azrael darted about in a big loop. 'Come quick, though, I think Jorrun is waking!'

Osun leapt up, knocking back his chair and almost running for the door. His brother had shown no sign of consciousness since they'd taken him up to his tower room days ago. For a while he'd lain completely still, his temperature high and his breathing shallow. Then two days had followed of violent tossing where Jorrun had murmured or yelled out unintelligible words that had terrified Osun. He'd been tempted to send a message to Kesta, to see if she could help, but he didn't want to risk leaving the women of Navere vulnerable. Knowing they were still safe, that back in Navere things were different, was what kept him going.

He burst into Jorrun's room, it was dark but for a single lantern hung up on the wall. The body on the bed was completely still, making a long shape beneath the blankets. Osun's heart fell, his pulse still fast. Azrael must have been mistaken.

'Are you sure, Azra?'

The fire-spirit flew in over his shoulder and went to hover over the bed, illuminating Jorrun's still face and giving it life.

'I ... I wasss,' Azrael buzzed.

Slowly, Jorrun's eyes opened, seeming almost a golden colour in the light of Azrael's flame. He didn't blink.

Something made Osun freeze, held his mouth firmly closed.

'Jorrun?' Azrael sounded anxious.

Jorrun smiled and sat up slowly, his eyes not leaving the fire-spirit.

'Jorrun?' Azrael backed away toward the lantern, making a keening sound that made Osun catch his breath. His eyes widened, going from the fire-spirit to his brother. Jorrun grinned, showing his teeth, and Azrael squealed, darting into the lantern and vanishing.

Osun found his feet rooted to the spot as his brother turned to look at him. Jorrun laughed and Osun felt as though his bones wanted to crawl out of his body.

Chapter Twenty-Seven

Catya; Kingdom of Elden

The two Borrowmen warriors shipped their oars and tied their rowing boat to Northold's small wharf. Catya jumped out, looking across the grass to the familiar row of small houses and beyond them the trees that partially hid the Hold's walls. She smiled at the sight, feeling her heart beat just a little faster. She hadn't been born here, but it was her home, every tree, every rock, every stone as familiar as her own hand. Her gaze travelled upward, the Raven Tower itself appeared dark and empty and Catya wrapped her arms about her body, feeling suddenly cold.

'Should we wait here?' Temerran asked.

Catya shook her head. 'No, come on.'

She led them along the path, she could hear Kurghan sawing in his large boatshed, but no one came out to see them. As soon as they neared the walls though, a shout of alarm went up. Catya felt her apprehension build, but she held her head high and straightened her back, keeping her stride swift, but not hurried. She waved up at the defensive wall, not waiting to see if she was recognised, but continuing around to the main road from the north-west and the gates to Northold.

'Halt!' One of the warriors stepped forward to bar their way. There were four Eldemen, dressed in warm woollen cloaks over their leather armour. Catya recognised Rosa's touch and smiled to herself.

'You know me.' Catya placed her hands on her hips. 'I'm come home to see Rosa and Merkis Tantony.'

'Aye, I know who you are, Catya.' The warrior indicated over her shoulder with his head. 'But those men don't 'alf look like Borrowmen to me.'

'It's because they are.' Catya frowned at him, shifting her feet impatiently. 'Just get the Merkis, will you?'

The man glanced back at his comrades, none of whom seemed eager to take the decision off his shoulders.

'Oh, for goodness' sake!' Catya clenched her fists. 'This is really important! Do we look like we're here to conquer Northold?'

The warrior opened his mouth, but before he could think of what to say, the gates opened up and Merkis Tantony stepped out followed by two of his men. Without thinking, Catya darted forward and launched herself at Tantony to hug him, making him stagger back a step. She had grown since she'd been away, her head came up almost to his shoulder now.

Merkis Tantony gingerly patted her back before peeling her arms away. She looked up to see him regarding Temerran with his wise grey eyes.

'Who is this?' he asked.

'Tantony, this is Temerran, Bard of the Borrows and friend of Dia Icante.'

'I see.' Tantony looked from Catya to the red-headed Borrowman. 'And is it just the three of you?' He looked past them toward the road.

'It is,' Temerran gave a slight bow. 'My ship, the Undine, is on its way to the Fulmers. I have reason to need to stay.'

'Have you?' Tantony's bushy eyebrows lowered over his eyes. 'Well you had better come in and explain yourselves.'

The other warriors begrudgingly gave way and Catya skipped forward to walk at Tantony's side as he made his way through the homes of the outer circle and waved a hand to command that they be allowed through the inner gate. Tantony's limp seemed more pronounced than usual and Catya felt a twinge of sadness.

She found herself holding her breath as she looked around her former home. It seemed somehow smaller. She smiled when she saw how much the herb and vegetable beds were flourishing and that the construction of the storage barn was well under way. Her feet faltered when she saw a familiar figure kneeling on the grass, weeding with a small trowel. She was taken aback by how much her heart ached at the sight of the older woman.

'Rosa!' Catya tore across the grass, giving Rosa barely enough time to get to her feet. Rosa felt somehow softer than Catya remembered as they collided, and the scent of her lavender soap brought tears streaming from her eyes. She lowered her head to hide her face, forgetting she now tied her hair back in a neat plait, like Heara. Rosa lifted her skirt and used the material to dab at Catya's face as though she were a much younger child and not a young warrior. Catya was surprised to find she didn't mind.

'Catya, oh I'm so pleased to see you!' Rosa exclaimed breathlessly. 'What brings you here, are you with Kesta?' She looked around at the others.

Catya shook her head. 'We're about to explain to Tantony, you'd better hear it too.'

Rosa nodded, narrowing her eyes. 'Who's that handsome fellow you're with?'

Catya found herself blushing a little, which annoyed her. 'He's much too old to be handsome.'

Rosa snorted. 'Is he indeed?'

Catya bit her bottom lip and glanced up at Rosa, worried she'd offended her, Rosa was at least ten years older than Temerran. Rosa was smiling though, so Catya relaxed.

'Your study?' Rosa suggested to Tantony.

'I think so,' he replied.

'I'll arrange refreshments.' Rosa lifted the hem of her long skirt and hurried ahead of them into the keep.

Tantony turned to Temerran. 'Would your men like to wait in the great hall?'

Rather than be offended, the Bard smiled at Tantony, his green eyes sparkling with humour. 'I'm sure they'd be delighted to.' He turned and nodded to his men, who found themselves seats near to the door.

'This way.' Tantony led them up the tower steps to his study. Catya found herself longing to go to the Ivy Tower and take a look at her old room. She wondered if it were indeed still hers, or if it had been given to someone else.

Tantony sat behind his desk, pulling at his greying beard as he looked Temerran up and down. 'Sit, please.'

Temerran did so and Catya pushed the door closed before pulling out a seat to sit beside the Borrowman. They sat in uncomfortable silence, Tantony frowning at Temerran with his shoulders tensed, his face softening every time he glanced toward Catya. The Borrowman Bard in contrast sat back against his chair with a relaxed smile on his face.

Catya broke the silence. 'Have you heard anything from Kesta and Jorrun?'

Tantony cleared his throat. 'Not for a while, not since the King's ship returned from Chem. You?'

'The same.' Catya sagged a little in her chair.

There was a soft knock and all of them sat up as Rosa came in, balancing a tray on which were four mugs of blended-herb tea and a few oatcakes. Temerran immediately stood to help her which made Tantony scowl.

'I'll get it,' he barked, knocking the table with his leg as he hurried around to take the tray.

'Thank you,' Rosa said breathlessly as she sat down beside Tantony. 'So, what's all this about?'

Catya looked at Temerran and he nodded for her to go ahead. Catya explained first everything that had happened in Taurmaline before having to backtrack and start her tale again from when Temerran had arrived at the Fulmers. Rosa watched her with wide eyes, but Tantony became more and more restless, shifting in his chair and scratching at his beard.

As soon as Catya finished, Rosa turned to Tantony. 'What can we do?'

Tantony continued to study Temerran a while longer before replying. 'The one person who could solve this is miles away in Chem. I can try to get a message to Jorrun. I imagine, for the King's sake, he would return, but it would take time.' He sat back in his chair, turning his mug around on the table with one hand. 'I'll send some men by boat to Navere. It's a while since I've been to Taurmaline, I had no idea things were so bad there. You really think the King is in danger, Borrowman?'

Temerran nodded. 'The Queen also. My most immediate fear is for the Icante though. I'm not sure what I can do to help, but …' He shrugged. 'I couldn't just leave and do nothing. It was the Icante's suggestion that I come to you.'

'I have no real influence over the King.' Tantony sighed. 'But keep your head down and be discreet here and you can stay.' He turned to Rosa. 'We'll have to think about this.'

She nodded, playing with her fingers in her lap. 'There is the Raven Tower.'

'What do you mean?'

She drew in a breath. 'Jorrun's library. We might find something there about dream magic that might aid us.'

'Just as I suggested!' Catya sat bolt upright in her chair.

'Just us, though, Catya.' Rosa raised a finger. 'No strangers in The Tower, no offense, Temerran.'

He smiled and waved a hand at her. Catya grinned, not long ago it had been she who'd been custodian of The Tower and had tried to deny Dia entry. 'Shall we start now?'

Rosa stood and reached out a hand toward Catya. 'Let's get to it. I'm sure Tantony can sort out finding somewhere for our guests to stay.'

Tantony sighed silently, but nodded.

'So, how have you been?' Rosa gave Catya's hand a squeeze before letting it go so they could make their way down thestairs single file.

'The Fulmers are amazing!' Catya took the uneven stairs as nimbly as a rat. 'I feel so free there – safe. No one laughs at me being a warrior although there's this one stupid boy who keeps challenging me.'

'Really.'

Catya glanced around to see Rosa was smiling.

'He's an idiot. But Dia explained that just because he's stronger, it doesn't mean I can't learn to be a better warrior, that women should rely on their heads not their muscles. Anyway, Heara is tough. But I'm learning so much.'

When they reached the great hall Catya went straight to the two Borrowmen and placed a hand on the shoulder of one. 'You're staying. Tem will be down shortly.'

The Borrowman looked up at her and smiled. 'Thanks, Cat.'

She looked around for Rosa and saw her friend had halted and was looking from the Borrowman to her with a startled expression on her face. Catya frowned but continued outside. When they were alone again, she said to Rosa, 'You don't need to worry about the Borrowmen. Temerran really is on our side now.'

'Yes, but who is on the other side,' Rosa replied.

Catya felt an icy chill in her stomach. Rosa was right. They'd made peace with the Borrows thanks to Dia and Temerran. Kesta and Jorrun had ensured that Chem was no longer a threat. So, who exactly was their enemy?

'I mean ... there has to be someone?' She looked up at Rosa. 'Unless ...'

'Unless the King is just ill.' Rosa frowned. She pushed open the door to the Raven Tower. A single lantern stood lit on the table and Rosa picked up a taper to light the others that hung along the length of the wall. They entered the first library and Rosa put her lantern down. With no window in the room it was still hard to see. Rosa put her hands on her hips and looked around.

'Well, let's get started.'

***

They spent seven days searching through the libraries, making notes, and slipping lengths of string in books to mark the pages. It was Rosa who discovered the most useful book while going up to feed the ravens. She noticed a few books on Jorrun's table, buried beneath maps and scrolls. One of them contained chapters on dream-walking. With Temerran being the only one of them that had any knowledge of magic, Tantony reluctantly agreed to bring him into their research. They sat together in Tantony's study, Temerran leaning over the book with a frown on his face, his chin resting on his hand.

'It seems to imply distance isn't a barrier.'

Catya sat up straighter as Temerran finally spoke, his eyes still firmly on the page.

'Providing there is some blood link. Otherwise the dream-walker must be within a few yards of the dreamer.'

'Jorrun can't help the King from Chem then.' Tantony sagged in his chair.

'It also means they can't accuse Jorrun,' Rosa said meaningfully.

Temerran winced. 'This book wouldn't prevent a determined witch hunt. Do you know what close blood relatives the King has?' He looked from Rosa to Tantony.

'No one particularly close.' Tantoney frowned. 'His father had a cousin who I believe has two daughters.'

'Daughters.' Temerran sat back in his chair to regard Tantony. 'That might be worth looking into. A dream-walker, according to your research, would need to have Elden blood.'

'But it could be someone closer to the King with no blood connection,' Catya pointed out. 'It could be anyone at court. Is there any way to know if someone is using magic? I know Jorrun used to feel it if someone did, as does Dia.'

'I don't have that ability.' Temerran pressed his lips together into a thin line. 'Dia might have learned something. Larissa left some notes, but nothing of a particular enemy.'

Catya tried to go back over everything she'd witnessed in the castle at Taurmaline. There had been a tension about the place that she'd attributed to Larissa's death, but now she wondered.

'Temerran.' She tilted her head to look at the Bard. 'You said there was a darkness following the Queen. Could it be magic you sensed? Could the Queen be a witch?'

He shook his head slowly and opened his mouth to reply, but he hesitated. 'My magic is in words, in tone, inflection, music. I can hear in someone's voice when something's wrong. With the Queen though, it was something more instinctive. A feeling of dread I couldn't put my finger on, a stain on her aura. It was as though … as though she willingly embraced darkness, dark words and dark thoughts.'

Catya shuddered and wriggled in her chair to hide her discomfort.

'She has never spoken of magic as far as I can recall.' Rosa frowned. 'Except to speculate about Jorrun and what he did in his tower along with all the other young ladies. I've never seen her possess any books on magic, in fact she was not over-fond of reading. Or studying.' She sighed. 'No, I cannot see it, but I might be wrong.'

'I'm not sure what we can do about this. We won't hear back from Jorrun in a long while. We may just have to leave it in Dia's capable hand—'

There was a loud knock on the door.

'Come!' Tantony called out.

The door opened and Kurghan stuck his head through the gap. 'Excuse me, Merkis.' He glanced around at the others in the room, his gaze laying longest on Temerran before he looked back to Tantony. 'May I speak freely?'

'Please do.'

He stepped in and closed the door behind him. 'My niece has just come back from Taurmaline. It's not good, Merkis.' Kurghan swallowed. 'Dia has been arrested for witchcraft against the King.'

'No!' Catya leapt up, her heart leaping to her throat. 'That's nonsense!'

Temerran stood more slowly, placing a hand on her shoulder. 'It is indeed.'

'What do we do?' Rosa looked around at them all.

'Nothing in a rush,' Tantony said sternly. He gestured for Catya and Temerran to sit back down. He drew in a deep breath. 'Right. We need to go to Taurmaline to see for ourselves what's going on. Rosa, write to the Queen and ask if you can visit with her.'

'No.' Rosa shook her head, looking down at her hands before turning to meet her husband's eyes. 'That will give her the chance to say no. We turn up and act surprised we're not expected. It's not unknown for a letter to go astray.'

Tantony nodded. 'We'll do that. Catya ... Catya we'll need you to stay and look after the Raven—'

'No!' She protested 'I need t—'

'You need to stay here with Temerran,' Tantony emphasised. 'And you're the only one to go into Jorrun's Tower. We need to take someone we trust with us to Taurmaline to get word back to you if we need you to join us.' He looked from Temerran to Catya. 'Someone who can hole up in an inn or something with a raven to send back.'

'I'll do it.' Kurghan offered at once. 'I have family in Taurmaline, I can stay with them. It wouldn't be the first time I've run off on a quest with you.'

Tantony grinned. 'Very well. We'll need to make a few preparations, but we'll get going as soon as may be.'

'If things get bad, if you can't get Dia out,' Temerran said. 'Let me know sooner rather than later. My magic has its limits, but it might be enough.'

Tantony nodded, then reached his hand across the table. Temerran took it and they shook.

Catya wrapped her arms about herself and looked at Rosa across the desk. The older woman wasn't Kesta, but she remembered Kesta's words that Rosa was wiser than the both of them. Anxiety was a storm in her belly, but there was hope there too.

Chapter Twenty-Eight

Kesta; Covenet of Chem

Kesta turned the page, running her finger down it as her eyes devoured the words hungrily. She drew in a sharp breath, then bit at the end of her thumb, before releasing it to turn the next page. She sat back in her chair, rubbing at the back of her neck. The large volume on the table in front of her she'd found on the shelves, up on the balcony, one night as she lay unable to sleep. It contained instructions on magics she'd never heard of before, including how to briefly alter the structure of some objects so that you could pass something living through them. She recalled the two times Jorrun had tricked her with that very magic, including their wedding day. She grinned to herself, she couldn't wait to surprise him and pay him back somehow.

Her smile fell away, and she looked back down at the book. There was some other incredibly powerful stuff in this book, some of which she'd witnessed Dryn Dunham doing. Could she do any of these things? Was she strong enough?

A knock at the door made her flinch and she quickly closed the book.

'Come in!'

Captain Rece stepped into the library, glancing around before giving her a polite bow. 'Master, may I speak to you about something ... about something a bit delicate?'

'You can always speak to me about anything.' She gestured to the chair beside her.

Rece glanced at her, his shoulders were hunched up, he sat on the edge of the chair. 'Today I had to discipline two of my men.'

Kesta straightened, her stomach tightening.

Rece swallowed before going on. 'They'd been fighting, they'd knocked the hells out of each other. It seems … it seems the fight was over one of the Raven Sisters. Vilai. I questioned them both and it turns out that one of them has been seeking to win, um, favours from the young sister, by bringing her gifts. He discovered she was … well, she has been lying with the other.' Rece could barely meet her eyes. 'I thought you should know.'

Kesta rubbed at her temple. This was going to be tricky, but at least the men had attacked each other rather than Vilai.

'Take your helmet off, Rece.'

He stared at her as though she'd asked him to strip naked.

'Go on.' She nodded toward it.

Reluctantly he reached up and undid the strap, placing the helmet on the table. There were flecks of grey in his brown hair, especially above his ears.

'Good.' She smiled. 'Now, I want you to listen to me, but wait until I finish before you react.'

He nodded.

'Okay.' She thought for a moment, looking up at the stained-glass window before turning back to him. 'Explain it like this to your men. In the past, when it was considered women here were property, the man who owned a woman gave permission about who could lie with his women – including giving permission to himself. Now, in this palace, and soon in Navere, women own themselves, just as a man owns himself. A woman grants the permission about who can lie with her and a man grants the permission about who can lie with him. If Vilai has made no promises, then she may deny permission to the first of your men and grant it to the other at any point she chooses. However.' She held up her hand, seeing that Rece was itching to speak. 'I will speak with Vilai and explain to her that she needs to make her intentions clear, especially now when things are so new and delicate.

'In my land, the Fulmers, men and women have sex with whomever they wish without commitment, but they generally make it known to each other if they are looking for something permanent. It saves misunderstanding and the chance of someone being hurt. If they fall in love and wish to make a promise to be exclusive with each other, then a *walker* will perform a hand fasting ceremony – a marriage. Please explain that to your men, and I will have a talk with the women.'

Rece nodded, he'd gone a little red in the face.

'I'll do that, master.'

'Just Kesta, when you're not wearing your helmet.'

His eyes widened and he glanced toward his helmet. He nodded slowly and met her eyes. 'So, you have no objection to, um, relations between men and women of the palace?'

'Of course not. As long as it's consensual on both parts. In fact, if, in time, anyone wished to make a permanent arrangement I'd be delighted to perform a hand fasting ceremony.'

Was she mistaken or had Rece's face reddened a little more? Was there someone the captain was thinking of? She decided not to pry.

'You've given me a great idea, actually. I might see if anyone from the Rowen Order is brave enough to get married here at the palace.'

'Maybe if we did it in a subtle way,' Rece agreed reluctantly.

She called up her *knowing* and felt his concern.

'Yes, I think subtle would be best too.' She sighed. 'Has the Elden ship arrived yet?'

Rece shook his head. 'We are not expecting Merkis Teliff until later today.'

'Is there anyone waiting for an audience with me this morning?'

'Yes,' Rece frowned deeply. 'There are two priests demanding to speak to a master.'

Kesta screwed her face up in disgust, then stood so quickly she made Rece jump. She patted his shoulder. 'Come on, let's get this over with.'

There were two guards waiting outside the library and they fell in behind Kesta and Rece. The captain opened the door to the audience room and checked it before holding the door open to let Kesta precede him. Calayna was waiting, pacing nervously, her shoulders sagged on seeing Kesta and she hurried over.

'Some priests have come.'

'I know.' Kesta still had her *knowing* open and she sent reassurance toward the tattooed woman. She put an arm about Calayna's shoulders and steered her back toward the chairs. Looking over her shoulder, she addressed Rece also. 'In reality, how much control do the priests of Chem have?'

'In terms of this life, of political and financial influence, quite a lot,' Rece replied. 'As conduits to the Gods, the priests can own your soul. Which god you choose can determine the path of your life. Although they have no voice in the Seats, they can certainly manipulate those that do.'

Kesta nodded. 'Is it rude for me to ask which god you chose as your patron?'

Rece looked down at the floor, bringing his heels together. 'I've always followed Seveda, the god of healing.'

Kesta opened her mouth, but closed her teeth quickly down tight. For a guard to follow the god of healing rather than the god of war seemed …

well, a contradiction. Yet … for the man that stood in front of her, it somehow made sense. She turned to Calayna who was watching the captain, her mismatched eyes unblinking. Realising she was staring, Calayna shook herself.

'For women the priests mean nothing,' she said. 'Mostly. There are times when women are sent to the priests as gifts, as payment. To be used and ultimatel—'

'No.' Kesta raised both her hands. 'I don't want to know more or I'm likely to kill them the moment they step in.'

Rece stepped toward her in alarm. 'Killing a priest condemns your soul to hell.'

'Yes, I'm sure they tell you that.' She clenched her fists and realised she was breathing fast. She forced herself to relax. 'Calayna, come sit to my left. Rece, when you're ready, let them in.'

The poor captain looked from her to Calayna, his mouth open and his eyes wide, but he gave a quick bow and strode across to the main doors. He instructed one of his men to let the priests in, himself standing to one side, staring straight ahead and as stiff as a broom, though his right hand rested on his sword hilt.

The doors opened and two men crept in, both with shaven heads and wearing blood-red robes. The taller of the two wore a necklace made of rat skulls dipped in gold, the shorter a simple black pendant with a large red stone set in it. It wasn't hard for Kesta to guess these were priests of the death god, Hacren.

'What is this abomination!' Spittle flew from the tall one's mouth. His eyes bulged and his face reddened.

Kesta feigned confusion, she looked behind her and then up at the raven banner. 'What? This?' She pointed. 'I rather like it, actually. We did stitch it rather quickly, but it's not that bad a job.'

'How dare you speak, creature!' The priest's face was almost purple.

Kesta shrugged. 'Well, you're talking to me. It would be rude not to answer.'

'You will be flogged! Burned! Where is your master?'

Kesta stood. Calayna shrank back in her chair. Rece glanced at her but otherwise didn't move; he knew what was coming.

'I have no master,' Kesta said quietly, lowering her head but keeping her eyes fixed on the priests.

'Then it's true!' The priest hissed, spitting on the floor. 'This palace is a nest of demons!'

Kesta placed her hand behind her back, feeling her power flow to her fingertips. As furious as she was, she had to stay in control of her emotions. 'No, this is just a place of truth, where men and women understand they are equal upon the earth and under the sky. Your old masters destroyed themselves with greed and arrogance, not understanding that power is a fragile thing that can be taken away with little warning. Cruelty only rules for so long before the oppressed will fight back, all it takes is someone to lead the way.'

The priest turned his head sideways to regard her with one eye. He reminded her of a bird trying to sight its prey to strike at, it made her feel sick. 'You are right that the old masters destroyed themselves, but it's not you who will rule in their place. The time of the gods is coming. Hacren is coming. Weak pretenders like you, abominations like you, will be his slaves!'

Fear gripped Kesta's heart but she tried to keep it from her voice. 'Send your god.' She brought her hands around in front of her, flames leaping up from her fingers. The priests staggered back, the shorter raising his arms in front of his face. 'And I'll discuss my "weakness" with him.'

She heard Calayna gasp and Rece flinched.

Kesta called up wind and hurled the two priests down the hall to thud against the doors. Rece tensed, drawing his shoulders in, but he stood firm. Kesta strolled toward the two fallen men as they dragged themselves up, recalling the fire to her hands. 'Like it or not,' she said. 'I'm a master and Navere is under my protection. I won't interfere with your business if you don't interfere with mine. Understand I do not fear you. If a god claims my soul then it's between me and *her*. Hurt any of my people, threaten any of my people, and you will see your hell very soon!'

She stood over the two priests and they cowed away from the fire in her hands.

She withdrew her power and the fire went out. With a cheerful smile she waved at the guards either side of the door. 'Kindly see these men out.'

The guards hesitated for a moment, eyes wide, before scrambling quickly to obey. Kesta sauntered slowly back toward Calayna, but she didn't smile, she felt deeply troubled.

'You shouldn't have challenged the gods.' Calayna stared at her. Rece hurried over to join them, his eyes wide and his face pale.

Kesta sighed. 'We *walkers* don't worry much about gods, we've never met one. We believe it's your actions, your deeds, every day that count, not what some deity dictates. Being good because you're afraid of the consequences is … insincere. Choosing to be a good person, to do the right thing, because your soul knows it should be so ...that's the measure of a truly good person.'

Calayna clasped her hands together under her chin, her eyes still wide. 'Your words make sense, bu—'

'But what god has ever helped the women of Chem?' Kesta said angrily. 'What god cares for their souls?' She clenched her teeth, her face flushed, and she had to stop her fingers curling into fists. She looked at their frightened faces and exhaustion rushed through her body. Frustrated, angry tears pressed at her eyes and she blinked them back in annoyance. 'Calayna, Rece, you're both good people and it has nothing to do with gods and priests. You just know right from wrong. Please excuse me.'

She hurried from the room, heading back to the sanctuary of the library. She wished so, so much that Jorrun was there, or Rosa, or her mother. She had to content herself with hugging the blanket that still smelt a little of her husband. For some reason she couldn't put her finger on, the priests had shaken her far more than she wanted to admit.

***

Kesta woke. The small vial of Jorrun's blood she wore around her neck stung her skin with its heat. She sat up quickly, pulling the scrying bowl toward her and tipping water into it. Her heart was racing and she almost dropped the larger container of Jorrun's blood as she grabbed for it to spill three drops in the bowl. Jorrun had already called her once this evening, what could be wrong?

His image formed in the water, she could see bare tree limbs moving beyond his head in the darkness. His face was shadowed, his eyes dark, but his mouth moved upward into a smile on seeing her.

'Jorrun, are you safe? Why are you calling again?' She curled her hand around the vial that hung from her neck, waiting for the vibration of his voice through her fingers.

'I'm safe. I need you to come to Arkoom. I need you to bring the women.'

She stared at him, blinking twice with her mouth open before she shook herself. 'Arkoom? But ... what of Navere? Is it saf—'

'Navere isn't important now.' Jorrun frowned. 'I need you in Arkoom.'

His image faded and the vial in her hand cooled rapidly. She sat back on her heels, her pulse still rapid. Arkoom? Perhaps Jorrun had defeated Feren and needed her to help hold the capital. Still, to bring all the women and leave Navere undefended, that was ... strange. She bit at her thumbnail.

'He must have his reasons.'

Too disturbed to sleep, she called up her magic to light a lamp and went down the narrow stairs to the main floor of the library. In the days since the priests had visited, she'd begun to learn and practice two of the more powerful magics she'd found in Dryn's books, as well as pushing the Raven Sisters harder in learning to shield with wind and control fire. They still had a long way to go, but if they continued their lessons on their way to Arkoom, they might at least be able to defend themselves.

She slammed her hand down on the table.

'No. No, Jorrun, I'm not happy with this.'

She sat at the table, watching the lantern flame dance as she formulated her plan, considering her options and their possible outcomes. As light began to illuminate the coloured glass of the window, she went to find Calayna and Rece.

'Is this a *helmet off* kind of meeting?' Rece asked, as he slumped, bleary-eyed, in one of the chairs.

Kesta waved a hand at him. 'It's not a good meeting, that's for sure. Jorrun has asked me to go to Arkoom.'

Rece sat up and Calayna gasped.

'Wait,' Rece frowned. 'It's been, what, eight days?'

Kesta nodded.

'Well, I guess it's feasible they've made it there by now, but Arkoom is a nine- or ten-day journey.' He glanced at Calayna, who shrugged. 'Did he say why?'

She shook her head. 'It seemed like he couldn't talk for long. He was outside though.'

Rece regarded her. 'What will you do?'

She sighed. 'Well, I must go, but I'm not leaving Navere undefended. I'll ask Merkis Teliff if he can postpone sailing back to Elden for a few days. I'll also not take all the women. Beth must stay of course, her baby is due soon. Sirelle should also stay with little Ursaith being so young. Kussim is strong, but behind the others in her magic learning as she came to us later. Of the others I'll ask for two more to stay and for the rest to come with me. Calayna, Rece, I wish to leave the two of you in charge of Navere.'

'Me?' Rece stared at her in surprise.

'Of course, you.' Kesta tutted. 'I trust you.'

Rece glanced at Calayna, colouring slightly.

'I will appoint you a member of the coven,' Kesta went on. 'Is there someone you can rely on to replace you as Captain?'

He nodded.

'I don't like this,' Calayna admitted.

Kesta shook her head. 'Neither do I. I want you to promise me something though. If things go bad, you'll evacuate as many good people as you can from Navere and sail for the Fulmers.'

'Agreed,' Rece said at once.

Calayna nodded slowly. 'When will you go?'

'Tonight,' Kesta narrowed her eyes. 'Even if it's urgent for us to get to Arkoom, it will do no good to rush off unprepared with only half the things we need for the journey, and we need to put things in place here. We'll leave when it's dark and try to keep quiet that I've gone for as long as we can.'

***

Kesta had to shush the women several times before they set off from the palace. Her first plan of securing good horses and riding swiftly to Arkoom had been foiled by the fact that, of course, none of the women but her could ride. She'd had to make do with two wagons and a horse for herself and the eight palace guards who would accompany them. Merkis Teliff had kindly lent her four of his Elden warriors and it was they who drove the wagon teams. All Kesta could do to speed their journey was to purchase spare horses from the poor pickings at the Navere market so they could change teams when needed.

Kesta led the way out of the palace gates and through the cobbled streets of the city. She wore a green cloak with the deep hood pulled up over her head, a small green veil covered the lower part of her face. All the women wore similar uniforms of pine-green trousers and tunic below a lighter green cloak, with their raven emblem sewn above their hearts. Apparently, it had been Kussim's idea that the Raven Sisters wear something to distinguish themselves and the women had been working on the clothing for several days. Even Rece had worn a green satin shirt with his baggy black Chemmen-style trousers as he waved them off beside Calayna.

Kesta drew in a deep breath and held it. She knew she was leaving Navere in good hands, but there was no way of knowing for sure if those hands would be strong enough.

She let her breath out, focusing on the way ahead.

She had only made the journey to and from Arkoom once, and most of her return journey she'd spent sleeping in a wagon as she recovered from serious injury. Captain Rece had furnished her with maps and two of the eight guards knew the way well. With the wagons they had no choice but to stick to the roads. Kesta used her *knowing* as often as she could without draining herself, to warn them of any potential trouble. Her horse also helped her, its sharper senses able to pick out trouble before her magic. It was a young horse, curious and fearless as only the young can be. Kesta found herself missing Griffon which in turn took her thoughts to Northold and Rosa. She prayed all was well with her friend, at least she'd be safe back in Elden.

Only two days from Navere, Kesta's mare smelt an ambush. Kesta got her guards to slow down and she jumped from her mare's back, leaving the path to sneak ahead. She was no Heara, but her Fulmer training meant she was able to approach the men undetected. She used her *knowing* to judge their character and strength. With a snort she stood, hurling fireballs at the hidden men on the ground before blasting two more out of a tree with wind. The men fled and Kesta watched them go with her hands on her hips.

'Thanks for the extra horses.' She grinned.

Her smile quickly faded. They had a long way to go yet and she'd been unable to get hold of Jorrun since his instruction to come to Arkoom. Worse still, when she'd tried to *fire-walk* she'd been unable to. It was as though the fire-spirits had fled Chem and the realm of fire through which she tried to *walk* was empty of life. Her uneasiness was growing. What had happened? What if she arrived too late? But if there'd been no hope, if he'd thought she wouldn't make it in time, Jorrun would never have asked her to follow him and risk the other women.

***

Five days into their journey they lost one of their guards. Despite the mare's warning, they had little time to prepare as a group of twenty well-equipped and mounted men struck them. Kesta used her *knowing* to get several of their attacker's horses to throw their riders, but their attack was ferocious. The Raven Sisters had their first experience of fighting, coming out of their wagons to form two circles, most shielding as Kesta had taught them, while two in each group hurled out flames. It worked well, but their guard was struck down by a well-aimed arrow. Kesta insisted on staying to bury him before they moved on.

There was still no word from Jorrun.

As they sighted Arkoom in the late afternoon of their ninth day of travelling, a cold dread settled in Kesta's stomach. Hatred surged through her body to clench her fists as she looked down into the valley, at the city nestled in the mountains. Smoke rose from a distant volcano and from the fires of the charcoal burners in the forest between her and Arkoom. Her mare fidgeted beneath her and Kesta absently stroked its neck.

'I'll call you Destiny,' she whispered to the horse, her eyes still on the city. 'Wish us luck, Destiny.'

She urged the horse forward down the long road to Arkoom.

***

She'd expected resistance at the gates, but as soon as one of their guards declared them to be of the Raven Coven, they were ushered through, the Arkoom guards even clearing others out of their way.

'It seems we're expected,' Kesta said, more to herself than to the others.

'What's happening?' Estre had pulled aside the canvas to look out past the Eldemen who drove her wagon.

Kesta waved at her to get back inside. Every instinct was telling Kesta to flee, but she couldn't put her finger on why. She tried to put her anxiety down to her previous experience of this dreadful city, but as much as her head tried to convince her, her heart was screaming otherwise.

'Let's find somewhere to keep the wagons and horses,' she told her guards, her voice muffled by her veil. 'I'd rather keep them in the outer circle of the city and near the gates, just in case.'

'There's a hostler just here.' One of the guards nodded to a street off the main road to the right.

'That will do for now,' Kesta agreed. Her nerves were so on edge she was beginning to make herself feel nauseous.

They paid for two days keep for the wagons and horses in advance and arranged for the sale of the bandits' horses. Kesta stroked Destiny's nose and kissed her warm cheek before replacing her veil and hurrying to join the others. A small group of curious onlookers had already gathered. Even veiled the women of the Raven Coven stood out like swans among ducks.

'Let's get to the palace, quickly,' she said.

The seven guards led the way and the Eldemen brought up the rear. Several people stopped to watch them pass, but no one challenged them. Every muscle in Kesta's body tensed as they reached the gate to the inner circle of the city, the vile temple district. She didn't need to warn the women that followed her, they knew better than she – hopefully – ever would, what life was in the capital of Chem.

Once again, they were allowed straight through, this time with the words, 'The Overlord is waiting for you.'

Overlord. So there had been an election?

She kept her head down, resisting the temptation to look up at the higher-market slave shops and the skin houses that sold temporary rights to the bodies of women. Movement caught her eye, and a stone whizzed toward them. Estre cried out as it struck her on the arm. Kesta called flame to her hands immediately, her eyes searching the wide street as she growled, 'Keep walking.'

Several people ran at the sight of her magic, some stood, wide-eyed and dumfounded as they looked her up and down. Kesta made her flames dance higher. 'That's right,' she snarled. 'Women have power here now.'

She spotted the ruin of the great temple and stopped abruptly. She couldn't help it, she laughed. She lowered her hands to better see it through the heat haze of her fire. Azrael had told her the fire-spirits had destroyed the temple, but she'd never thought to see it for herself. She narrowed her eyes. Oh, how she longed to burn this whole city down!

'We'd best get to the palace,' one of the guards urged nervously.

She nodded, letting her flames subside, with a last glare at those who hadn't run away. As they passed the temple, she realised it was totally empty, with any luck, she thought, all the vile priests were dead.

Word had obviously gone ahead to the palace as a servant was waiting to take them directly up to where the Overlord waited. Kesta's pulse hammered in her throat, she couldn't wait to see Jorrun, but at the same time her fear had become intense. She realised she was beginning to feel light-headed and she forced herself to breathe more deeply. They were taken along a corridor to a small, plain, door outside which stood two guards.

'Just you.' The servant looked at Kesta. 'The others are to wait here a moment.'

Vilai let out a small whimper.

'It will be fine.' Kesta looked at them all. 'Just stay together and remember what I taught you.'

The servant knocked and opened the door a little, looking in before widening it and indicating Kesta should go in. Her eyes immediately found Jorrun and relief made the muscles of her knees go weak.

'You're all right!' She grabbed for a table to steady herself.

'Kesta?' Osun's eyes were huge as he stared at her, glancing at Jorrun. 'Why are you here? Why have you come?' He stood frozen, he looked … terrified.

'You … Jorrun didn't tell you he'd called me?' She tilted her head to look at Jorrun who was grinning at Osun.

Jorrun snorted. 'Osun doesn't know much, do you Osun?'

Osun looked down at the floor and didn't respond.

Jorrun turned to her and held out a hand, looking her up and down. 'Welcome, my love.'

She rushed forward around the table, wrapping her arms around him to hold him tightly. His right hand travelled down her back and she tensed, stepping back a little. He smelt wrong. She looked up into his eyes and he quickly looked away.

'You brought the women?' he asked.

'I did,' she replied.

'Good.'

Someone knocked at the door and Osun opened it, Kesta could see from Osun's expression he wasn't happy to see whoever it was. 'It's Garva,' he said to Jorrun.

Jorrun nodded and reached out to touch the side of Kesta's face with his right hand, stroking her lower lip with his thumb. 'Please excuse us, Kesta, I have some things that must be attended to. The women will be taken to their rooms, but you should wait for me in mine. Someone will show you the way.'

She nodded, fighting her annoyance at being dismissed. She glanced at Osun who was still holding the door slightly ajar and staring at the floor. She decided not to protest, after all, she had no idea yet what the situation was here and she didn't want to cause Jorrun any unnecessary trouble.

'All right, I hope I'll see you soon, though.'

He smiled. 'I hope so too.'

Osun opened the door wider to let her out, his eyes still on the ground.

'All right, Osun?' she asked.

He nodded, glancing at Jorrun.

She froze, coming face to face with two priests in the red robes of Hacren. Instinctively she drew power to her hands, but they barely gave her a glance as they passed her and went into the room.

'Everything all right?' Estre asked anxiously.

Kesta nodded, although she wasn't so sure. 'We're to be shown to our rooms for now. Make sure none of you is alone, try to stay in groups of three and don't wander from your rooms except to gather in each other's.'

They all nodded, including the guards and Eldemen.

They were led by the servant to some guest quarters, Kesta waiting to ensure they were settled and obeying her instructions before allowing herself to be led away to Jorrun's room. She smiled to herself, it was up in a tower.

She sat on the edge of the bed and looked around, it appeared to have hardly been used. His small travel bag still sat on a chair and a single shirt hung over the back of it. She spotted a familiar shape on the desk and walked over to pick it up, running a finger down the green book and feeling the dents of the embossed letters, the jagged edge of the hole that ran through it where it had caught the dagger aimed at her heart.

She jumped when someone knocked lightly at the door. She opened it and was disappointed to find it was Osun and not Jorrun standing there. He looked around the room, even glancing under the desk.

'You're alone?'

She nodded, watching in puzzlement as he closed the door and slid the bolt across. 'Kesta, something's really wrong with Jorrun.'

'What?'

'I mean …' Osun clenched his teeth, seeming to struggle to find the words. He was breathing hard and his fingers were curled into fists. 'Sit down.'

He grabbed the bag off the chair and turned it so he could sit and face her. She sat slowly on the bed.

'Kesta, when we got here, we found it was a trap, as we feared. But we won. We defeated Feren. The moment Feren fell, though, Jorrun collapsed. He was unconscious for several days. When he woke … when he woke, he seemed different. Very different. Azrael … Azrael fled.'

'What do you mean Azrael fled?' She stood up, her breath caught in her throat, her heart racing.

'I mean he took one look at Jorrun, flew into a lantern and hasn't been seen since.' Osun reached out a hand toward her. 'Kesta, I had no idea you were coming here, if I had I'd have tried to warn you to turn back and get yourselves the hells out of Chem.'

Goosebumps rose on her arms. 'But ... it's Jorrun.'

Osun leaned toward her. 'Kesta, after he awoke two covens arrived here. He slaughtered them all. All. He didn't speak to them, not even to ask their names. He just killed them. I persuaded Tembre to return to Margith, I feared Jorrun would kill him too.'

'No.' She shook her head, sitting back on the bed and nearly missing the edge. 'He must have had a reason.'

'I don't know, Kesta.' He regarded her unblinking. 'I don't know. But please, Kesta, don't be alone with him. Please. Please, Kesta.'

'All right.' She realised she was shaking and pulled her arms in tightly around herself.

Osun stood and reached out a hand to briefly touch her arm. 'I have to go, he'll wonder where I am. I'll try to think of something.'

She nodded. Osun went to the door and un-bolted it, glancing at her once before slipping out.

She stood at once and began to pace up and down the small room. She didn't want to believe Osun and she knew he was a brilliant actor, a brilliant liar. She cursed herself that she hadn't used her *knowing*, but deep down, she knew she hadn't needed to. She'd sensed a wrongness about Jorrun herself, but she'd been so happy to see him she'd dismissed it.

Unable to keep still, she opened the door and hurried down the steps. She went straight to the rooms where she'd left the women and checked with her Navere guardsmen that all was well. Rather than frighten the women, she decided to tell them nothing for the moment and do a little investigating of her own. She feared she wouldn't be allowed the same freedom here she'd had in Navere, but no one she saw tried to stop her, they just threw frightened looks in her direction and hurried on their way.

'Is there a library here?' she asked one of the palace guards. He nodded and gave her directions without looking at her, her *knowing* brought her his fear, his resignation, and deep sadness.

She shook herself and hurried on.

When she came to the library doors, she hesitated only a moment before pushing them open. What she saw froze her to the core and welded her feet to the stone ground.

Jorrun stood in the centre of the library with his arms around Vilai, his head bent to kiss her passionately. He paused, sensing Kesta there, and looked up, a smile slowly spread from his lips to his eyes. Kesta's heart stopped, the floor seeming to rush away from beneath her feet.

She couldn't speak, couldn't tear her eyes away.

He'd betrayed her.

Chapter Twenty-Nine

Dia; Kingdom of Elden

'Dia?'

She drew in a sharp breath, standing up from the hard-wooden plank that served as a bed and flinging herself against the bars.

'Heara?'

After three days of silence it was shocking to hear a voice, let alone one she'd so longed to hear. For the first two days of her imprisonment Merkis Dalton had questioned her endlessly, asking the same things over and over again until she'd finally lost her temper. Demands to see the King had been ignored, as had requests for news about her husband. Every night she'd endured the same nightmare, Fulmer Hold burned to the ground, *walkers* hanging from trees like hideous vine-fruit. Worst of all were the dreams of her kneeling over Arrus's grave, her fingers that dug in the dirt to get to him covered in tattoos. She'd tried not to sleep, but it somehow made the dreams worse, as though her weakness left her more vulnerable to their grip.

Heara appeared before her in the darkness and she grabbed Dia's hands in her strong fingers. 'Dia! Are you hurt? Have they mistreated you?'

'No. No, not really. Heara, how are you here?'

Heara grinned, showing her even teeth. 'I finally managed to sneak in! I'm going to see if I can break you ou—'

'No!' Dia gasped. 'What about Arrus? Where are they holding him?'

'I haven't found that stupid lump yet.' Heara frowned. 'But I will.'

'I can't go until he's safe.'

'Dia.' Heara bent her head to look her in the eyes. 'You are the Icante. If it comes down to it, you have to get out without him.'

Dia pulled her hands free and looked away. Heara was right, but she didn't want to even think about it, not yet.

'Heara, try to find him. It's not just about Arrus though, Bractius is threatening the Fulmers.'

Heara snorted. 'Let him threaten. They saw what you can do, Elden would be conquered by Chem if it wasn't for you. I don't understand why you don't just walk out of here.' There was both anger and sadness in Heara's voice.

Dia thought of her dreams and shuddered.

'There is more going on than we know, Heara. I could walk out, I could probably blow this castle apart, but what would it achieve? Whoever is behind this will still be here. I don't dare leave Elden as our enemy too. What's going on out there? Is there any news?'

'Yes.' Heara gripped the bars. 'Tantony and Rosa have come from the Raven Tower to see if they can find out anything and help. Cat and Temerran are still at the Tower trying to find answers from Jorrun's library. Vilnue is doing his best to try to calm the King and reason with Dalton, but he isn't getting far.'

'What of the Queen?'

Heara's eyes narrowed. 'She barely leaves the King's side; the bitch is putting on a great act of the doting wife at the moment. If you ask me, I think the both of them are moon-touched.'

Dia moved back to the bars and held out a hand for Heara's. 'Try to find Arrus. If he's safe, I might risk letting myself out. Get Rosa to watch the Queen, I think she's the key. See who she meets with, who she talks to.'

Heara nodded. 'Is there anything I can bring you? Have you eaten? Are you warm?'

Dia nodded. 'Just bring me news if you can.'

Heara pulled Dia's hand through the bars and turned it to kiss her palm. 'I won't let them hurt you, I promise.'

'I know.' Dia nodded, feeling tears push at her eyes and make her nose sting. 'Don't take any foolish risks, we have to think of the Fulmers.'

Heara nodded, holding her eyes for a moment before vanishing into the darkness of the corridor.

***

The heavy tread and scuff of feet warned her she had visitors, too loud and too many to be Heara. She sighed, not moving from her position on the bench, legs crossed beneath her long skirt, head leaning back against the rough wall.

Light spilled down the corridor and shadows appeared first before the men. Merkis Dalton regarded her briefly before gesturing for a guard to open the cell. The guard fumbled with the keys, glancing at her several times although she didn't move. She looked around at the men, glad to see the vile chieftain, Adrin, hadn't come to gloat and grin at her with them this time.

'How is the King?' she asked.

'Better now you've stopped sending him nightmares!' Dalton stepped into the cell and the guard with the torch reluctantly followed.

'I wish I did have the power you attribute to me, perhaps then I wouldn't be having such harrowing dreams myself.'

He narrowed his eyes. 'Are you claiming *you* are being attacked?' He searched her face. With her dry stinging eyes and the heaviness of the skin beneath she imagined she must look at least ten years beyond her age.

'I don't imagine it will matter what I say, you will believe what you want.'

'I'll believe what's true!' His face reddened. 'The King has sent me to give you one last chance to explain yourself. Why have you turned on his friendship? Why have you attacked the King?'

Dia leaned forward. She didn't raise her voice but Dalton flinched back. 'I risked my life and that of my people to save Elden from Chem, despite what your King did to my daughter. The only reason I'm even here is because someone in your castle killed Larissa. Have you found her murderer yet, by the way?'

Dalton shuffled his feet. She knew from their previous conversations he doubted the Queen's story.

'I'm here to ask questions, not answer them.'

'But you refuse to listen to the answers.'

'Your answers are lies, witch!'

Dia drew flame to her fingers and Dalton cried out, staggering back to the bars. 'And again, as I've told you, I'm a *fire-walker*, not a witch.' She let her flames die out. Dia stood and both men almost fell over each other to get out of her cell.

'That was your last chance,' Dalton warned as the guard hurried to lock the door.

Dia sat back down. She couldn't put one man before the Fulmers, she knew that, not even Arrus. But she couldn't ignore the threat of war against the Fulmers. It was many years since Elden had murdered all of its people who could use magic. Were the Fulmers strong enough to prevent the same thing happening in her own land? Could a nation without magic defeat the few *walkers* that lived on the islands? It was possible. If only Jorrun hadn't gone off to Chem.

She got quickly to her feet and looked around her cell, there was nothing there but her thin blanket that she could burn. Calling her power, she blasted open the door, it swung open but remained on its hinges. Checking the hallway, she saw an unlit torch in a bracket on the wall. She pulled it down and returned to her cell, calling up her flame to light the wood. She waited until it burned steadily and then sat on the damp floor. It took a while for her to focus through her tiredness and the throbbing headache that never quite left, but eventually she slipped into a trance and triggered the part of her brain that allowed her to *walk*. Nothing happened. She tried again, pushing away the fear that crept through her bones.

Nothing.

There was nothing there, no life, no welcoming vortex, no Drake to carry her through the fire realm to see through a window of flame. The fire-spirits had abandoned them.

***

Dia landed with a thud on the hard flagstones, she could still feel the dirt of her husband's grave beneath her fingernails. She drew a fist to her chest, trying to hold back the pain in her heart, barely able to breathe. Her body shook, and she squeezed her eyes tightly closed, welcoming the coldness that seeped up from the floor into her bruised shoulder and hip. She couldn't help it, she curled up into a ball and sobbed, giving in to her exhaustion.

Laughter seeped into her thoughts, it was a moment before she realised the sound was real. Shame washed through her and she reluctantly uncurled and turned over, dreading to see who had witnessed her weakness.

Ayline stood grinning through the bars, a guard standing back against the wall with a torch in his hand.

'Your majesty,' Dia said through gritted teeth. She pushed herself up onto her knees and then slowly stood. 'Can I help you?'

Ayline looked her up and down, a sneer making her mouth crooked. 'I shouldn't think so.'

Dia called flame to her fingers and Ayline shrieked, staggering back from the bars. Dia immediately let her fire die, the guard drew his sword and moved to stand between her and the Queen.

'I'm only here because I agree to be,' Dia said. 'You should remember that, Ayline.'

'Your husband is only alive because I say he can be!' Ayline spat, pushing the guard aside.

Her words bit deep. Dia froze, watching the Queen as though she were a snake deciding whether to strike. Her face had gone red, and she folded her hands protectively across her unborn baby.

'We know you're trying to kill the King with your magic,' Ayline hissed.

Dia scowled and shook her head. 'A lie, Ayline. You know it isn't me. How many times do I have to tell you *walkers* can't dream-walk. It's an Elden magic, ask Jorrun!'

'We did.' Ayline screwed up her small, pretty nose. 'He wrote back to say *walkers* are witches and witches can poison dreams.'

'No.' Dia shook her head in denial. She took two steps forward, her eyes not leaving the Queen's, Ayline shrank back. 'He can't have. He would never say that. You can't have heard from him.'

Ayline's face broke into a grin. 'You are to hang.'

Dia felt the ground fall away from beneath her, but somehow, she was still standing.

'If you try to escape, if you try to fight us,' Ayline went on. 'We will execute Arrus in your place, we will burn him at the stake. If you don't let the hangman place the noose about your neck, we will destroy the Fulmers and burn every last *walker*. Jorrun himself said he will burn Kesta.'

Her hand flew to her stomach. This couldn't be real, it had to be one of her nightmares. She staggered, reaching out a hand to hold herself up against the wall. It was some time before she realised she was standing in darkness. Ayline and the guard had gone. She felt her way back to the wooden bed and sat staring at the floor, she didn't move except to blink, and then only when her eyes stung. Her breath came only when her lungs forced her to inhale. Eventually she slept and the nightmares tore her soul apart.

***

It was a while before she realised there were people in her cell. She stared blankly at Merkis Dalton for almost two minutes before she blinked and focused on his face.

'Icante? Icante, I'm sorry, you must come with us.'

She sat up slowly, her muscles stiff and her limbs cold. 'Where?'

Dalton pursed his lips and flexed the muscles of his jaw before answering. 'Out into the courtyard.'

'Where is Arrus?'

'He is safe, as long as you do as you're told.' The Merkis didn't look at her as he spoke.

She breathed in and out. Dalton took hold of her arm, his fingers surprisingly gentle. He led her out of the cell and along the corridor. She tripped on the first step she reached until she recalled from her foggy memories what stairs were and lifted her knees. She heard Dalton curse under his breath. They came out into an open area and she gasped, lifting her face to feel the cold wind against her skin. The light hurt her eyes, but she couldn't close them. There were people there, she was aware of their emotions like pecks of a bird against a window, not actually feeling them.

They came to some wooden steps and Dalton stopped, she tried to continue but the man held her back. His grip on her arm tightened and released, tightened and released.

'This is wrong,' he said through gritted teeth.

She felt the deep breath he drew in and he finally started up the stairs, his feet loud on the planks. Dia's own steps were silent until they reached level ground, then her footfalls seemed to echo. Dalton held her arm a moment longer, then let go and walked away.

Dia shivered.

She felt the vibration of someone else approaching and a large presence behind her. Something was slipped over her head, it was rough against her throat. She hadn't realised there had been voices until they ceased their murmuring. There was a tension in the air; expectation.

The wind blew her hair back from her face and for a moment she remembered touch. She blinked.

A single voice spoke, deep, angry, full of fear. The words bounced off her.

But there was another sound. Someone was singing. Dia fought not to hear it, but it dug in deep, the pain was excruciating, and she cried out, tears blurring her vision.

She could see!

Her eyes were rainbows, splitting and splitting again. The song filled her soul, her heart swelled and burst against her ribs. She looked up at the blue, blue sky. Small clouds hurried past like strands of lace and a single raven flew overhead. She watched it glide, strong in its elegance, a glint in its intelligent eyes where the light caught them. The wind caressed her skin, lifting her hair to tickle her cheek, the sun was a warm blessing that eased her bruises.

Beside her, the hangman reached out his hand to pull the lever.

Chapter Thirty

Kesta; Covenet of Chem

Jorrun's smile turned into a grin, his eyes travelled across Kesta's body. He let go of Vilai and she collapsed to the floor. Kesta drew in a sharp breath and stepped back, her heel hitting the solid library door. Her heart stopped. A knife jutted out from Vilai's spine and her dress was stained a dark red. Kesta forced herself to look back up at Jorrun, he was wiping a spot of blood from the corner of his mouth with the tip of one finger, his eyes still fixed on hers. He placed his finger in his mouth and sucked at it noisily. Nausea rushed up from her stomach to her throat.

'Well, that's a shame.' He took several sauntering steps closer. 'I was looking forward to spending some time with you.'

Kesta pressed her back up against the solid door, shock rendering her speechless, she could barely breath, she felt hot, the air stinging her skin so that she shivered convulsively. Jorrun frowned at her. 'I was hoping for a little more fight.'

She forced her mouth to open. 'I … I don't understand. I know you. I felt what you were feeling …'

He tutted, taking another step closer. 'Oh, and of course no one can fool a *walker*. By the way, thank you for my throne.'

She stared at him, her breath coming hard and fast.

'You made it so much easier for me to take Chem. Of course, I'll have to destroy everyone who helped me get here, everyone with power. I'm tempted to keep you, though.' He looked her up and down, his eyes lingering on her mouth.

'Jorrun.' His name came out in a whisper, hurting the muscles of her chest. Even with the truth standing right before her, she didn't want to believe it. He was so close now she could smell him, the metallic scent of blood.

Light flared before her and she raised her arm to shield her eyes. Azrael made himself huge and Jorrun staggered back.

'Don't you touch her!' Azrael hissed. He flipped himself about. 'Kessta! Run!'

She didn't need telling twice, she grabbed at the door handle and wrenched it open, sprinting out into the hall. Azrael shot out of a lantern ahead of her and she kept running as she yelled, 'Tell the women to get out! Warn Osun!'

Her heart hammered against her ribs, she turned one corner and then another, but her senses told her Jorrun was just behind her. She needed to buy the others time to get out but fear kept her feet moving. Two guards moved to stop her and she created a blast of air to throw them out of the way. She halted, chest heaving, her pulse loud in her ears. For a moment she heard nothing, then the sound of firm, steady steps. He wasn't hurrying, he was confident he could catch her. He stepped out into the hall and the sight of him made her heart catch.

For a moment panic rushed through her veins, he was so much stronger than her. Then grief doubled her over, tearing every raw nerve from her body. This couldn't be true! It couldn't be happening! Jorrun was a gentle, honourable, and caring man, he loved her, she knew he did! Jorrun would never betray her or hurt Vilai.

He tilted his head slightly. 'Do you want me to catch you, Kesta?'

Her stomach churned, anger cut through her fear and she sent a blast of flames down the hall toward him. Instead of running she pressed forward, ducking into a room and finding some stairs. The sound of his laughter followed her down. She stumbled, feeling dizzy, and had to force herself to breathe properly. The stairs came out into a large room with a polished marble floor, her steps echoed as she sprinted for the door at the other end. She heard the handle turn behind her and spun on her heels, shielding just in time as a strong blast of air knocked her off her feet.

'You belong to me, you know you do.'

She growled, scrambling onto her feet. 'Even when I loved you, I didn't *belong* to you, Jorrun!'

'Your heart has put you in a cage, foolish one.' His eyes seemed to darken and Kesta tensed. 'Even now, when you know I'll hurt you, you can't run.'

Kesta gritted her teeth. 'I'm not running because I'm going to kill you!'

He laughed. Cold fingers wrapped around Kesta's spine and the strength seemed to go from her muscles, but she drew power. She created a wall of flame before her, at the same time as shattering the door at her back. It took only seconds for Jorrun to sweep aside her flames, but by then she was already racing down another hallway.

Azrael shot out of a lantern to her right. 'Ruun, Kessta! The others are out!'

She gasped in a breath and ran to keep up with the fire-spirit. Azrael blasted open some double doors and then shattered the windows of the room beyond.

'Keep going, Kessta! Don't sstop! I'll protect the others.'

'Azra!'

But the spirit was already gone.

Kesta fled across the room. The broken window before her still held sharp and jagged glass, beyond it was darkness. She jumped up onto a table and sprang across to the stone sill of the window. She waited, her fists clenched, the roaring blood in her ears making it hard to listen out for the sound of his boots. She wanted to be sure the others were far enough away.

She jumped at the sound of his voice, turning about on the precarious ledge to face him. She'd forgotten how quietly the tall man could move.

'At least make it a challenge for me, Kesta,' he pouted. 'I thought you were stronger tha—'

She threw a blast of air, ripping glass free from the window to hurl with it. Using the blast to give her more momentum she launched herself off the ledge, landing on her hands and springing up onto her feet and straight into a sprint across the grass.

'Kesta!'

She halted, looking back at the figure standing in the window, even in the deep night with little light to see by, his shape was unmistakable to her.

'I'll give you a ten-minute head start, my love, then I'm coming for you!'

His laughter followed her as she raced across the lawn to the gates and the temperature of the air around her seemed to drop dramatically. Several guards lay dead there, signs of burns on some, the rest cut down by swords.

'Kesta!'

She shrieked, immediately flushing scarlet with embarrassment. It wasn't Jorrun, but his brother who was waiting for her. 'This way, quickly,' he urged.

She nodded and followed him, their boots loud on the cobbles. 'Where are the others?'

'As safe as they can be.' He glanced over his shoulder at her. 'Azrael's with them. What happened?'

She swallowed and shook her head. She couldn't bring herself to talk about it. She felt sick as she forced out, 'Jorrun is evil.'

He grabbed her arm and pulled her off the main street, taking off his cloak and handing it to her.

She looked at it in confusion.

'Put it on and pull up the hood.' Osun's dark-blue eyes were wide in the darkness. 'The temple district is very busy even this time of night.'

She nodded, doing up the clasp.

'All right, this way.'

He hurried down some steps, taking them two at a time. When he reached the bottom, he checked both ways before stepping out onto a main street. He'd been right, there were still a lot of men about, many of them unsteady and bleary-eyed from alcohol or the intoxicating incense. The street was brightly lit with coloured lanterns hanging from the eaves of the places still open for business. Osun didn't stay on the street long before turning off and squeezing down a very narrow gap between two buildings. They came out to a barely wider muddy path strewn with discarded rubbish, it stank of urine. High walls either side made it impossible to tell where they were.

Osun stopped at a door. His shoulders rose as he seemed to take in a deep breath. He tried the door handle and then forced it open. Light flared up, making Kesta raise her arm against the glare, instinctively she shielded both herself and Osun.

'Osun!' Jagna let his flames die. 'Kesta! You made it!'

'Is everyone here?' Osun demanded.

'We couldn't find Vilai.' Jagna glanced at Kesta. 'The women said she'd gone off with Jorrun.'

'Vilai's dead,' Kesta said, surprised at the venom in her voice. The girl had been tricked, just as she had, this was certainly no time for jealousy. 'Where are we?'

Osun indicated for her to go in. 'I'll show you.'

Jagna stepped aside and Osun led her further into the building. As her eyes adjusted, she realised they were in a corridor, but above them there were holes in the ceiling and beyond that she could make out stars. There was a strong smell of burned wood and she drew in a sharp breath.

'This is the temple.'

Osun nodded over his shoulder. 'Most of the priests moved out to start temporary shrines elsewhere straight after the fire, but the priests of Hacren stayed. Until recently, that is, they've moved into the palace with Jorrun now. I was never privy to their conversations but I didn't imagine they were good. Anyway, since they took the palace, I thought we might as well make use of their temple.'

As they approached a large gap in the wall ahead of them that she guessed had once held a door, she began to hear the quiet whispering of women's voices. Light flickered, making Osun's shadow dance.

'Did you find Kesta?'

She recognised Estre's voice.

Osun nodded, gesturing over his shoulder. As soon as she stepped into the room, Jollen ran over and grabbed Kesta's hands. 'We're so glad to see you! Oh, but your hands are freezing!' Jollen's brown eyes narrowed in concern.

'She's shaking,' Estre added, coming over to put her arm around her. 'I think she's in shock.'

'Nonsense!' Kesta snatched her hands back and shrugged away from Estre. 'Right, we don't have time to mess about.' She looked around the room. Cassien was standing guard further down the hall with two of the Eldemen. 'Where's Azrael?'

'Keeping an eye on Jorrun's progress,' Jagna told her.

She realised there were women sat together in the room that she didn't recognise. Osun saw her expression. 'Jagna and Cass have been smuggling out Arkoom women for the last few days. At first Jorrun didn't even mention them, but then he asked where they were and after tha—'

'Don't tell me.' She closed her eyes tight for a moment. 'All right.' Kesta nodded. Realising her hands really were shaking, she quickly clasped them together. 'You need to get out of here quickly. Get to the horses and make for Navere. Jorrun will expect it but it's your fastest route to the Fulmers and safety. He isn't concerned about any of you at the moment, but eventually he will be. Go now.'

She turned and headed back the way she'd come. There were several cries of protest behind her and Osun ran to catch her up, grabbing her arm.

'What are you doing?' he demanded.

'I'm going to kill Jorrun,' she snarled, pulling her arm free.

Osun took a step back. 'But he's much stronger than you, and he knows you.'

'He knows my love, Osun, he doesn't know my hate!'

He stared at her, his mouth opened and closed before he spoke. 'Kesta.' He reached a hand out tentatively toward her and she saw he was shaking too. 'I know you're angry and really hurt, but please don't throw your life away. The women need you. I need you. We won't make it back to Navere without you.'

She looked away and swallowed. She didn't want to admit it, but right now she really didn't care if she died, the only thing that was keeping her standing was the overwhelming anger surging against her reason. 'He is coming for *me*, Osun.' She looked up at him and held his gaze. 'Anyone who is with me will die. If you run, you might make it.'

He shook his head, making a snorting sound through his nose, and clenching his fists. Without a word he darted away back toward the others.

Kesta strode through the broken corridor and kicked open the door at the end. A headache gripped the base of her skull but she ignored it, focusing all of her attention on her need for revenge. She heard shouting and a man's scream.

So, Jorrun was in the temple district.

She heard the squelch of someone running in the mud behind her and turned to see Osun catching up with her. He wasn't alone. Jollen, Rey, and three of the other Raven Sisters were with him. 'What are you doing?' she demanded.

'Coming with you!' He retorted angrily. 'Did you think we wouldn't? I've given the others my instructions. Jagna and Estre will take a few of the horses and ride straight for Navere and try to warn them to evacuate. Cass will lead the rest with the wagons.'

'You all have to go!' Kesta gritted her teeth. 'Go on!'

Osun raised his chin. 'No.'

She wanted to punch him, she wanted to call up her magic and hurl him down the alley. 'Osun!'

'You're not the only one who's angry and hurt and betrayed, Kesta!' His face reddened, and he blinked rapidly. The veins stood out on his forehead. 'I tried so hard to be like him, to be a better man, but it was all a lie! All of it! Naderra ...' His voice broke, he stood there panting, unable to speak.

Pain leaked from Kesta's heart, seeping into her anger. She buried it, clinging to her rage. 'Come on, then. Sisters, try to stay hidden, only fight if you have to and like I taught you.'

She didn't wait for a reply but hurried as best she could down the narrow gap and out into the main street.

Jorrun was waiting for her. He grinned, moving his feet into a fighter's stance. 'I didn't think it was in your nature to run.'

She didn't bother to reply, she had no interest in anything he had to say. She called fire to her right hand and wind ready to shield herself with her left, stepping out into the street to draw his eyes away from the gap between the buildings.

Jorrun gave a slight shake of his head. 'Very well. You know, of all the mortals under this sky, I would have chosen you to be my queen. A pity. Perhaps I'll give you one last chance to consider it before I kill you.'

As he called his own flames to dance above his right hand, Kesta spotted Azrael moving slowly toward him. Kesta didn't take her gaze off Jorrun, there was a sheen of sweat on his face and his skin was flushed. His wide blue eyes didn't blink and a part of Kesta's soul cried out at her loss, at his betrayal, that those beautiful eyes hid evil.

She threw her fire at him at the same time as Azrael, but Jorrun raised his shield and easily deflected them both. The wall of fire he sent back was almost lazy, there was little power behind it. He was playing with her, he wanted the fight to last, to enjoy it.

He watched her, barely acknowledging Azrael who battered at his shield like a frenzied giant wasp. She couldn't bear to look into those eyes.

Drawing up a huge surge of power she sent a tornado spinning toward him. He tore it apart, sending an answering blast that threw her down the street to land hard on the cobbles. He advanced toward her, a frown on his face, he knew she was also holding back on her power. Azrael made himself so large that for a moment the fire-spirit completely engulfed Jorrun. With a shriek, Azrael went spinning back, pinned against the broken wall of the temple.

Kesta scrambled to her feet. 'Let him go!'

Jorrun grinned. 'What do I get in return?'

Kesta drew up more power, ripping up cobbles to pelt him with. His concentration wavered as he focused on defending himself and Azrael managed to wriggle free. Kesta didn't stop her attack, swapping wind for flame. Jorrun continued walking toward her, his shield barely troubled. She was breathing hard, her headache now gripping most of her skull. He struck out and her own shield collapsed, she staggered, but managed to keep her feet.

'Jorrun!' Osun roared.

Jorrun turned slowly. 'There you are, *brother*.'

Osun stood in the middle of the street, his feet planted in a fighter's stance, his sword drawn.

Jorrun shook his head. 'Well this is rather futile, *brother*.'

Osun raised his sword and ran at him.

Jorrun gave a surprised grunt and called a small fireball to throw, it never hit Osun. Azrael swooped down and pulled it out of the air, at the same time the Raven Sisters threw their own weak flames toward Jorrun, quickly shielding as he turned on them. Gasping for breath, Kesta called up every last ounce of her power. She pushed it down into the earth, burrowing deep beneath the street. As Jorrun called up flames to obliterate the terrified sisters, Kesta pulled upward, her muscles strained and blood burst from her nose.

The ground heaved.

Jorrun spun around to look at her in shock, his flames spraying across the cobbles. The street split below him and the walls of several buildings cracked. Huge black rocks burst upward around Jorrun, showering him in dirt. He rose into the air, his shield powerless to stop his ascent as a jagged rock propelled him upward. He waved his arms, trying to keep his balance. Kesta collapsed onto her knees, blood trickling from the corner of one eye. Jorrun fell, landing hard on the ground. Kesta pushed herself onto her feet and ran, drawing her dagger as she leapt over the chasm her magic had left. She landed at Jorrun's side and plunged her dagger down toward his heart.

Chapter Thirty-One

Dia; Kingdom of Elden

The hangman gave a grunt. Dia turned to see an arrow protruding from his chest. Her eyes widened and she searched the crowd, finding Rosa standing beside Tantony, a bow in her hand. Several warriors, led by Adrin, were pushing through the gathered people to seize them.

'Hang the witch!' Ayline shrieked. 'Quickly!'

One of the guards reacted, darting forward to grab for the lever, but he fell backward as a ball of flame seared past his face and settled on the rope to burn through it above Dia's head.

'Doroquael? How are you in Elden?'

'No time!' The Drake hissed. 'Fight, Dia!' He formed a fiery arm and pointed.

She followed his direction, crying out when she saw the hooded form of Arrus, standing in the crowd beside Heara.

Dia didn't need telling twice, she drew up her power.

The sky went dark. Ayline screamed. Dia turned to see ravens and a host of other corvids flocking in such numbers they blocked out the intensity of the sun. Tantony had drawn his sword, holding Rosa behind him as the guards came to grab her. Tantony wasn't alone, Dia's heart leapt when she saw Worvig push his way to the Merkis' side along with several other island men. Worvig grinned as he engaged Adrin with his broadsword. At their back was Everlyn, power ready at her fingers.

'Dia!'

Something tugged at the bonds that held her hands tight behind her back. Her fingers stung as the blood flowed back into them and she turned to see brilliant green eyes.

'Temerran!'

He lifted her chin with one finger to look intently at her face. 'Dia, are you all right? Are you back with us?'

'Yes.' She nodded, feeling the remainder of the fog slowly lift from her mind. 'Yes, I'm back!' She looked around at the courtyard below the scaffolding on which she stood, at the frightened upturned faces of strangers. There was another raised construction opposite her, a dais on which stood the King, Queen, and Merkis Dalton. Several warriors had made a ring around them to protect them. The KKing cowered like a powerless old man and she sucked in air, recalling her own state of mind just a few moments ago.

She grabbed Temerran's arm and ran down the steps, Heara and Catya were there to meet her, weapons ready. Arrus collided with her, lifting her off her feet and kissing her face over and over.

'Arrus!' She tried to untangle herself. 'Later! What's happening? Do we know who's behind this yet?'

'Not yet.' It was Temerran who replied. 'But it revolves around the Queen.'

Dia snarled. 'Let's get her.'

Dia called flames to her fingers and the crowd parted with shrieks and screams, many running for the gates. The Eldemen guards and islanders were still fighting, Everlyn pulling Rosa out of the way and shielding her with magic. Worvig had smashed Adrin's sword from his grip, blood soaked the Elden Chieftain's shoulder as he backed away behind his men. Dia ran for the dais, several archers fired at her, but the arrows were turned aside by her shield.

Glancing up at the battlement, she saw Merkis Vilnue yelling at the archers to cease. 'Stop. She's saving us again, you imbeciles! Look!'

Ayline saw her coming and her eyes widened in terror. 'Guards! Guards, stop her!'

Dia focused her power and swept most of the guards off the dais with ease. Heara and Catya overtook her, leaping up onto the wooden planks and engaging the remaining men with their short-swords and daggers. They were breathtaking to watch, the woman and girl so fast and graceful it was like they performed a deadly dance. Arrus took the stairs slowly, his eyes fixed on Merkis Dalton who had drawn his own sword.

Dia halted, looking up at Ayline.

'Mercy,' the Queen whimpered. 'Mercy for my baby.'

'Your baby is the only reason you're alive,' Dia growled. 'Now, tell me! Who is behind this? Who is destroying the King?'

'You are,' Ayline spat.

Dia took a step closer and Ayline staggered back. Arrus and Dalton still faced each other, Bractius looked like a heap of rags discarded on the ground. Dia became aware the courtyard had quieted but she didn't look around. In her peripheral vision she saw the ravens come to rest on any available perch.

'Ayline, you know it isn't me,' Dia said patiently. 'But you do know who it is.'

Ayline's eyes darted briefly to somewhere past Dia's shoulder. Beside her, Temerran turned to look.

'One last chance,' Dia said, calling flame to her hands.

'Inari!' Ayline screamed. 'Inari, help me!'

Temerran drew in a sharp breath and Dia turned around. The courtyard had emptied, most of the people having fled. Everlyn and Rosa

409

stood guard over some disarmed and injured Elden warriors while Tantony, Worvig, and his men secured the gates. A servant had remained, standing alone beside the scaffold. He was young, about seventeen, the short stubble uneven on his face. It was his eyes that made Dia freeze, she'd seen them before.

'It's "Quinari," actually.' The boy shrugged. 'I think you might have met my brothers.'

Dia stared at him, tensing as he straightened up.

'No? I must admit I don't look as much like a Dunham as they do, it's probably because I don't have much vile Fulmer blood. I'm mostly Elden.'

'You're Jorrun's brother?' Rosa asked in surprise.

'Apparently so.' Inari's smile vanished. 'Not that I ever met them, my father raised me to destroy Jorrun and Elden after my brothers fled here like traitorous cowards. I can't wait to sit on the throne to welcome them home. Well. It seems I'm going to have to do this myself.' He called on his power and Dia sucked air in sharply through her mouth when she realised what he was doing; he was summoning a storm.

With a raucous cry the ravens took to the air, some of them attempted to dive at the young Chemman, but Inari's wind battered them away. Dia took in a long, slow breath and stilled the air around her, trying to chill it and prevent the thunderhead forming. It was a risk, it meant she had no shield and Inari didn't hesitate to take advantage. He increased the heat of his magic, sending a ball of flame larger than himself toward her. Everlyn stepped in, blocking the blast, staggering back at the force of the attack.

A loud thud shook the gates as the city's warriors tried to break in to get to their king. Ayline made a run for the castle door, but Rosa ran after her and grabbed her by the arm. Everlyn ducked as Dia sent an inferno of her own

410

back at Inari, their flames met curling upwards and wide across the courtyard. The scaffolding on which Dia was to be hung ignited, both Arrus and Dalton turned their bodies to shield the prostrate Elden king. Dia raised her left arm, increasing the power behind her attack at the same time as preparing a vortex of wind with her right. Everlyn realised at once Dia was going to attempt the same trick she'd used against Relta months ago back in Fulmer. The younger *walker* prepared to take over Dia's attack. Dia cloaked herself in air and ran straight through the flames, grabbing the dagger Everlyn held out for her.

A force like a charging bull hit Dia full in the chest and she was thrown back, landing hard on the scorched ground. She rolled onto her knees, coughing hard to re-open her crushed lungs. Somehow, she managed to retain her shield, Everlyn backing toward her as she scrambled to her feet. The conflagration dissipated and through the heat haze, and smoke Dia glimpsed the young Chemman, he seemed totally unscathed, above them the storm continued to build, the ravens circled high above the castle. Dia gestured for Everlyn to move to the left, while she circled around to the right. Doroquael slowly slipped out of the fire that consumed the gallows, moving silently toward Inari.

Dia raised her hands, forming a tornado around herself that ripped stone and earth up from the courtyard. She advanced on Inari, the air around her picking up speed and ferocity. Doroquael blasted him from behind, tearing burning wood from the gallows to hurl like jagged spears. Everlyn called all the power she could muster to attack his right side. Inari didn't flinch, but for a moment his storm faltered in its growth. His smile had gone, and he frowned, his lip curling upward a little on one side. He turned his attention to Everlyn and Dia felt a stab of fear. Everlyn was no fool, though, she dropped her attack immediately to shield. It was enough to save her, barely. She was thrown across the courtyard to hit the castle wall. Dia held her breath, eyes wide. Everlyn moved her arm, she was alive.

Doroquael made himself huge and Dia increased the speed of her approach, carefully balancing the air around her at the same time as trying to reach for the gathering storm. Inari batted the fire-spirit away, but his frown increased, and he staggered a little. Dia let go of her tornado, stepping out of it to blast Inari with an intense blue flame at the same time as drawing lightning down toward him. He shielded, the lightning caressing the shell of it and sparking off the stone on the ground. The tornado hit him, and she heard him cry out, but he ripped it apart. He was little more than a boy, but he was stronger than anyone Dia had ever faced before.

She was breathing hard, her vision beginning to blur. She didn't have much left.

Temerran moved around to help Rosa hold onto the Queen, who spat, scratched, and wailed like a child. Tantony and Worvig were using their bodies to brace the gates. Vilnue was halfway down the stairs from the battlement, Heara guarding the door to the castle although her wide eyes were on Dia. On the broken dais, Arrus and Dalton now stood side by side between the King and the magical battle.

Dia drew power, but Inari yelled, 'Stop!'

Dia held but didn't let her magic dissipate.

'Look to your king!' Inari snarled.

Both Arrus and Dalton glanced behind them.

'Your majesty!' Dalton threw himself to the ground. The King was fitting, his muscles convulsing and his eyes bulging.

'I have his mind.' Inari smiled, his green eyes hard. 'I can control his body. You will surrender, or he dies!'

Dia turned back to the boy, her eyes barely flickered as a small figure stepped out from behind the burning gallows.

'He isn't my king.' Dia shrugged.

'Icante!' Vilnue cried out in shock.

Dia felt the boy draw power, saw the flames begin to form at his fingers, she used the last of her power to shield herself, ducking instinctively.

Inari cried out, his mouth stayed frozen open as he stared at Dia, he tried to send his blast of flames, tried to reach up for his storm, but his knees gave way and he fell forward onto his face.

Catya stood behind him, her hands on her hips. Her small dagger protruded from Inari's back.

'Hmph.' Catya looked up at Rosa and grinned. 'Better than letters, just like I always said!'

With a cry, Rosa let go of the queen and dashed across the courtyard to grab Catya and smother her face in kisses. Dia let herself sink to the muddy ground, both Temerran and Arrus rushing over to assist her. Ayline made a run for the castle but stopped dead in her tracks when she saw the expression on Heara's face.

'Bractius?' Dia demanded, trying to see past her husband.

'Alive,' Dalton called out.

Dia narrowed her eyes at the Merkis, she'd deal with him later, but for now … 'Tell your warriors to stand down!' she commanded. 'Let's get the King to his bed and find a healer!'

Dalton glanced at Ayline. 'What abou—'

'Secure her in her room for now,' Dia suggested.

'Come on, love.' Arrus put his hands under her shoulders and lifted her to her feet. 'We can sort them out later. Sleep first.'

She didn't argue but leaned on his arm as he led her inside the castle.

Catya placed her foot on Inari's back and pulled out her dagger, cleaning it on his shirt before placing it back in its sheath on her belt. Rosa tutted and shook her head, but she grinned when she held out her hand to the girl.

***

Dia woke slowly, her head too heavy to lift off the pillow and her eyes were gritty and dry. She could hear soft voices and she forced herself to roll over onto her side.

'Dia!' Arrus got up from his chair and came to sit on the edge of the bed. She looked around the room and saw Heara was sitting in front of the door. 'How are you feeling?'

'Tired.' She smiled. 'But I didn't have a nightmare for the first time in days. What's happening?'

'Well.' Arrus raised his eyebrows. 'Tantony and Rosa have pretty much taken over running everything, I think that idiot Dalton is too ashamed of his mistakes to argue much. The Queen is protesting that she was as bewitched as the King and is a poor, innocent victim.'

Dia sighed. 'To some extent, I imagine she is, but there is jealousy, ambition, and greed in her heart. What of Bractius?'

'He sleeps.' Arrus shifted on the bed. 'Worvig is guarding him along with Dalton.'

She nodded. 'Everlyn?'

'Resting, she is well but for bruises.'

'And Catya?' She closed her eyes and smiled.

Heara barked a laugh. 'Running the castle with Rosa. There'll be no controlling her after this.'

414

'I don't know,' Dia said quietly. 'I think perhaps she has exchanged one defence for another.'

Heara leaned forward, resting her chin on her hand. 'I'll watch her, but right now what she seems to need is a mother, and that mother, whether they know it or not, seems to be Rosa.'

'It was Rosa who found me.' A shadow passed across Arrus' face and his eyes grew distant. 'They had me locked in a wine cellar with four guards on the door.' He grinned suddenly. 'A very nice vintage it was too!'

Dia closed her eyes and shook her head, but she couldn't help smiling.

Dia pulled herself up and Arrus moved out of her way so she could stand. 'Get everyone together in the King's private audience room, including Dalton.'

Heara nodded and quietly left the room.

'Can I ask what you're planning, Icante?' Arrus reached out and took her hand.

She glanced down at him and squeezed his fingers. 'Not revenge, as much as I'd like it. Sadly, we'll have to forgive some of what was done to secure the future of the islands, but trust me, we will never forget.'

She got dressed, the smell of her clean change of clothes was pure bliss after being in the same dress for days. She chose trousers and a tunic, Arrus buckled her short sword around her waist. She kissed him, then headed for the door.

The King's room seemed uncomfortably small with so many people crowded into it. Dalton had taken up position behind the King's desk, he struggled to meet Dia's eyes as she entered the room. Catya was perched on the desk beside Rosa who'd been given one of the chairs, everyone else had chosen to stand. Heara and Vilnue stood together beside the door, Temerran and Tantony flanked Merkis Dalton. Arrus was the last to enter and he closed the door behind him.

'Worvig?' Dia asked her husband.

'Still with the King,' he replied.

'I have to ask.' Dalton looked around at them all, his fingers twitching into fists when his eyes rested on Dia. 'Is the King your prisoner? Because—'

'Don't be ridiculous, Merkis.' She frowned at him. 'As always, the Fulmers protects your king, not threatens him, I would have hoped you understood the difference by now.'

Dalton's face reddened. 'What do you propose?'

'Once I'm satisfied Bractius is out of danger, we will return to the Fulmers. Sadly, I will not be leaving an ambassador here. Your king will have to do more than apologise before any *walker* ever sets foot here to help him again. As for your queen, I will leave her for Bractius to deal with. Quite frankly, I think they deserve each other.'

Dalton opened his mouth to speak but closed it again quickly as she continued.

'Merkis Tantony and Rosa know how to run a Hold well, I suggest you let them take care of Taurmaline until the King is properly back on his feet. In the meantime, we'll try to get hold of Jorrun and Kesta, see if they know anything of Inari and if he was working alone or for Chem.'

Rosa's eyes were shining, but Tantony shifted his feet and glanced at Dalton.

'Merkis Dalton, you may leave,' Dia said.

'What?' Dalton stared at her. 'You can't dismiss me!'

She tapped at her lip with one finger. 'Let me see ... as I recall it, you allowed yourself to be influenced by an enemy of Elden and collaborated with a plot to kill your king. You imprisoned me – the person most able to defend your king – and threatened war against Elden's greatest ally. Shall I go on?'

'It wasn't like that,' Dalton protested.

Tantony cleared his throat. 'Looked like it to me.'

Dalton shook his head. 'Tanton—'

Tantony roared, making nearly everyone in the room jump. 'You are dismissed!'

Dalton glared at them all but strode toward the door.

'Vilnue,' Tantony said. 'You will head the investigation into Dalton's innocence – or guilt.'

'What?' Dalton spun about to look at Tantony, but he unclenched his fists and nodded. 'I'll cooperate fully, Merkis.'

Heara opened the door for him with a grin, then pushed it shut behind him with her foot.

'Do you think it was just that Chemman boy?' Tantony asked Dia.

'I hope so,' she replied. 'But it will be as well to be cautious. As for the Queen, I don't think she poses any danger on her own, not now anyway, but she will bear watching in future if Bractius lets her live.'

Rosa's hand went to her mouth.

'When will yo—'

'Icante!' A sibilant voice filled the room before Doroquael squeezed through the keyhole and shot across the room, making himself bigger. 'Icante! Dire news from the fire realm! No Drake dares leave the realm to come to the land under the ssky, the god of death walks in Shem!'

'What do you mean, god of death?' Heara demanded.

'Hacren! The preissts raised him! He … he walks in Jorrun's body!'

Dia froze, even her lungs stilled. She looked from the darting fire-spirit to Temerran.

'I'll recall the Undine,' the Bard said.

'Are we going to Chem?' Catya asked timidly, her eyes wide.

'Yes,' Dia said. 'Yes, we are.'

Chapter Thirty-Two

Jorrun; Covenet of Chem

The darkness was complete. He could feel nothing, neither cold nor heat nor the ache of his body.

Am I dead?

Had someone in the throne room of Arkoom slain him and left his soul to linger, trapped, with no way of knowing how to escape? His first thought was of Kesta, was there any way he could get to her, tell her he was sorry, sorry he had let her down again? Was there any way to know she was safe?

He felt something at the edge of his senses and hope surged through him. It was … it was emotion; but not his. He cautiously reached for it, trying not to hope, trying to keep his own feelings in check. It felt a little like dream-walking, although as far as he knew he hadn't entered someone else's mind. He tried to go over what had happened but his memory resisted. He'd killed Feren. As far as he recalled nothing had touched him, neither magic nor weapon.

The emotion fluttered close, stronger than before. It didn't feel quite right, like a note that was off key, as though there was a buzz within it. There was triumph there, but wariness, suspicion.

Jorrun edged a little closer, pausing as his own fear tried to emerge. It had been panic, terror, his inability to keep control that had allowed Karinna to trap him months ago. He had to be careful this time, much more careful. It was time to be the Dark Man again.

He moved closer.

Light.

He steadied himself. The emotions he could sense barely flickered and Jorrun suppressed his own relief. He crept closer still, the light suddenly filled his mind and he could see. Not clearly though, it was like scrying without using blood to reach a specific person. Everything seemed far away, blurred, but there was Osun's face before him, distant, lined with worry. He was talking but Jorrun couldn't hear him. His brother left the room and the perspective changed, whoever he was within had sat down.

The emotions intensified, veering toward anger and lust. Something brushed Jorrun like a single thread of web across his face, a thought.

Jorrun retreated, worried his excitement might give him away. He needed to do much better at stilling his own mind and heart. He needed to assess what was happening, judge the strength of the one who seemingly held him captive. Was this his own body, or someone else's? He couldn't be sure.

It was hard to tell what time was passing, but it seemed like long moments between his attempts to gather information as though for some moments he ceased to exist. He established he was still in the palace. Osun was there from time to time but he didn't look at all happy, more importantly, from the movement of his brother's lips, whoever he was inside of was being addressed as 'Jorrun'. He considered fighting, but without being sure he could win it seemed too big a risk at present. As far as he knew, the other presence didn't know he was there, if he gave himself away, there was every chance he could be destroyed.

From the change of the light outside the palace windows, he judged that two days passed. During that time, whoever had his body didn't seem to sleep. He was shocked when he felt a surge of power, it flashed past him, through him, but he wasn't able to grasp it. He rushed at the light, fearful of what he would see, and sound exploded around him. He froze, trying desperately hard not to feel anything, not to think. The words seemed to come from far away.

'Jorrun, Wait!' Osun yelled.

There was a snort, closer, the voice that came out was his own. 'Why, brother? You won't be safe while these sorcerers live.'

Magic surged past him again and he saw fire through the window of light. There were screams and he saw two men trying to shield themselves. They were Chemmen and no one he recognised. He couldn't see Osun. Another blast of fire and both Chemmen were engulfed. Osun's horrified voice came from behind him.

'I might have been able to reason with them. They may have joined us.'

'What, like that traitorous idiot Tembre? Don't be a fool, Osun.'

His brother came into view as Jorrun's errant body turned toward him. There was such sadness on Osun's face that Jorrun retreated rapidly, afraid of giving himself away.

Who, or what, was it that controlled his body? How could such a thing even happen? He needed his books. He thought desperately for a long time, but the closest thing he could think of that matched his situation was the necromancy that raised the dead, or dream-walking. As far as he knew, you could only control a mind through dream-walking, not a body, although you could convince someone to harm themselves. Necromancy though, a powerful necromancer could possess a body, make it do what he wanted, even see and hear through it, just as he was now. Only he was no necromancer, and as far as he knew, his body wasn't dead.

Could someone, something, possess a body that was still alive, one with its soul still intact?

Apparently so.

The key seemed to be going into the light, but could he take control? He wanted desperately to try. He wondered if he could do it subtly, carefully, like manipulating a dream without the dreamer being aware. He took a chance. He moved slowly, using every ounce of his patience.

Jorrun's body seemed to be eating, for a moment he tasted the salt and fat of the meat on his tongue. There was a glass of wine. He imagined picking it up, letting the liquid trickle down his throat. Just like dream-walking, he pressed the suggestion forward.

His body reached out and took the wine, taking a big gulp.

Jorrun froze. Was it just coincidence?

Only one way to know. He waited and tried it again, only this time it was water he imagined wetting his mouth. He pushed a little further forward until sound came flooding into him.

'You!' his voice shouted. 'Bring me water.'

Jorrun withdrew, slowly, slowly, trying not to rush back to allow himself to feel excitement in the safety of the darkness. It worked, but how could he best use it?

He found the answer to that the next evening. He felt the emotions of his cohabiter rise, there was anger and a strong flavour of fear. He crept into the light to look. He was in a dark room, possibly a tower. Other than a bed, a table, and chair, there was little in it. The fireplace was stacked ready, but unlit. Two others were in the room, their heads shaven and wearing robes of a startling red. Priests.

One of them held something in his hand. Jorrun struggled to retain control when he realised what it was, his book, his gift from Kesta that had saved her life.

'Give that to me!' his voice said, he saw his own hand reach out to snatch the book from the priest. He threw it on the desk. 'If you need to learn the words in it, then I'll teach you.'

He listened in growing horror when the stupid priests revealed everything they knew. He could feel the hatred around him grow, they didn't know it, but when their use ran out, those priests would die, and not in a pleasant way.

'Shall we put the book in the library?' One of the priests tried. 'It is an ancient text and extremely valuable.'

'Get out!'

'Yes, mighty Hacren.'

Hacren!

No, it couldn't be true.

Could it? But from the conversation he'd just heard, whatever shared his body was at the very least a very powerful spirit and there was no doubt now it possessed him. But did it know he was still alive?

His view changed and power flowed past him as the fire was lit. Without thinking, Jorrun created an image of the book burning on the logs, even adding the sound and the smell. He let it seep into the light as he would have into the mind of a dreamer, he felt the being's satisfaction with its strange, alien buzz. His view changed again as his body moved them out of the room. He didn't see if the book really was still on the desk, he prayed it was.

***

The emotions that brought him back to awareness made him feel sick with fear. There was desire, hunger, and a covetous lust that would have made Jorrun's skin crawl had it still been his. As much as he needed to hurry, he forced himself to hold back, to keep calm. He edged toward the light but had to dart back almost at once. He'd glimpsed one of the priests holding the arms of a woman he didn't know. Blood spilled from a neat wound in her throat and her mouth had moved as she tried desperately to breathe. Power rushed past him and it was tempting to draw it in, to make himself stronger, but he repulsed it even as the Chemman god drew it in. Even without a stomach he felt sickened.

Twice more over the next few hours he felt the same euphoric rush of power. Jorrun tried to make himself smaller, to remain unnoticed, as he crept forward to see. He felt guilt at the relief that again they were women he didn't know, even as he knew he couldn't continue to sit back and let it happen. Hacren was getting stronger. There had been no sign of Osun at any of the sacrifices. Did his brother know? And if he did, would he ignore it, thinking Hacren was still him, still Jorrun?

Was Osun still even alive?

He got his answer not long after.

Jorrun felt the familiar mixture of dreadful, sickening emotions. He edged closer to the light, seriously contemplating whether he should make a grab for some of the power, use it somehow to take back his body and defeat Hacren. What he saw sent him hurtling back in shock.

No! It can't be!

More than ever, it was imperative that he keep calm, keep control, but never had he been so terrified in his life. He inched closer, stopped, closer, paused. He slipped into the light. His body was in a study and before him were

Kesta and Osun. Osun's face had gone deathly pale as he asked Kesta how she came to be there. Hacren was delighted, a cat playing with a mouse.

Get her out of there, brother, get her out!

If his body had still been his, he wouldn't have been able to breathe. It took more will power than he'd used in his life when Hacren embraced Kesta, every part of his being screamed for the god's death.

He retreated, he had to, to gather himself.

There was no choice now, win or lose, the moment Hacren threatened Kesta, he would have to strike, even if it meant his own destruction.

He moved forward and felt relief as he saw Osun and Kesta leaving the room. Priests appeared before Hacren and Jorrun crept closer to try to listen to their conversation.

'She is dangerous, master.'

'Not to me, you fool!' Jorrun's voice replied. 'Why do you think I called them here? Osun's dear 'sisters' are my best source of power. As for her ...'

Jorrun shuddered, barely able to contain his rage.

'... she is the only one left in Chem who is even remotely a threat to me, but I'll deal with her, and I'll enjoy i—'

Hacren stilled.

'Master?'

Jorrun felt Hacren's suspicion, carefully, slowly, he drew back.

His rage was such he no longer cared about preserving his own life, all that mattered now was getting Kesta away from this so-called god.

Please, Osun, you must *know! Get her away.*

He hovered anxiously at the edge of the light for the next three hours, watching as Hacren plotted with the priests and set up the foundations for his dictatorship of Chem. It was pitch-black outside the windows when Hacren used Jorrun's body to stalk down the corridors, heading for the guest quarters. Hacren barely knocked at one of the doors before opening it, three women sat on one of the beds and Jorrun recognised them at once, Rey, Vilai, and Jollen.

'Jorrun!' Vilai stood up at once, her brown eyes wide and a flush on her cheeks.

'I need your help with something,' Jorrun's voice said. 'This way.'

It was Rey who protested. 'But Kesta sai—'

'You know she is safe with me.'

Jorrun would have killed Hacren then and there if he'd known how, if they'd been two mortal men. Vilai stood up at once and followed him into the hall, the light turned away from the anxious faces of Rey and Jollen.

'I used to dread the thought of coming to Arkoom.' Vilai chattered as they made their way back through the corridors. 'But this is different. Where are we going?'

'The library.'

Jorrun's mind was filled with images of his own safe, beloved library back in Northold, and of the small sanctuary he had made with Kesta on the balcony back in Navere, the place he carried scars on his back for. A creeping dread swept through him like a cold wind, he knew very well what Hacren intended for this naïve Chem woman. Could he hold back and let it happen? Could he watch Vilai die in order to wait to help Kesta? He knew his best hope of seeing the god destroyed was to aid his wife to defeat him, but could he live with such a choice?

The chances were, he wouldn't live.

They entered the library, Jorrun heard the doors close behind them.

'You are a beautiful girl, Vilai.' Hacren reached out a hand, running his fingers around the back of Vilai's neck. The girl's eyes widened, Jorrun could see his body's reflection in her dark pupils.

'But … but what about Kesta?'

'This is Chem.' Hacren shrugged. 'And I make the rules.'

Hacren pressed Jorrun's body up against the girl, forcing her lips open with his tongue. Jorrun tasted the blood as Hacren bit down hard on her lower lip. Jorrun could bear it no longer, he gathered himself to attack.

The library door opened.

Jorrun froze, the look on Kesta's face burned his soul.

Hacren forced a dagger up and into Vilai's lung.

Power surged through Jorrun's body and this time he snatched at it, not caring about his own damnation, forcing aside the paralysing guilt.

Kesta backed away.

Jorrun gathered himself on the edge of the light, preparing to pounce…

Then Kesta said his name in a way that shattered him into a million pieces.

No, Kesta, it isn't me! I'd never betray you!

Fire blazed before them as Azrael placed himself between the god of death and his prey. Joy leapt through Jorrun, he'd never been so pleased to see his dearest friend.

Kesta ran and Azrael followed.

'Hello, Jorrun, I wondered if you were still here!'

Jorrun froze, dread filling him, but there was no point hiding any longer. *Leave her alone!*

'Or what?'

Jorrun surged into the light, trying desperately to fill his own limbs, to move his own muscles. He tried to attack, but the power he'd grasped refused to materialise into magic of any substance.

I'll destroy you!

Hacren laughed again. 'Empty words from a ghost. I'm glad you're here, not that you'll survive for much longer. Shall we catch up with Kesta?'

Jorrun tore at the light, trying to grasp at something physical, trying to force his way back. Memories of his capture by Karinna hit him like stones and he calmed himself immediately. If his fear won, he would lose. If his anger took control, he couldn't help Kesta.

The hallways of the palace flashed by before him. A thrill of excitement ran through Hacren as well as an intoxicating shiver of fear. Part of the creature was exhilarated to be hunting something that would pose a threat, be a genuine challenge to its power. The fact that its quarry was female added fuel to that desire.

Strength, power, wasn't working. Jorrun had to be clever, had to use what he did have. He needed to dream-walk in a mind that was awake, trick a soul that knew he was there.

He could only stare in shock when they easily caught up with Kesta, twice she turned to face Hacren, only to flee again, before they found her waiting on the sill of a high window. Why hadn't she just run? But of course, she wouldn't, she would fight. More importantly she would protect; like a mother playing lame to save its young, she was luring Hacren away from the others.

His admiration was marred by Hacren's as she dived out the window and was away across the grass as fast as a hare. Instead of hiding his emotions he let them flood into the light, let Hacren feel his pride.

428

'Kesta!'

She stopped and turned to look back at him.

'I'll give you a ten-minute head start, my love, then I'm coming for you.'

Without bothering to respond, Kesta ran on, disappearing through the gates. Hacren steered Jorrun's body back out into the hall and headed straight for the doors.

You said you'd give her ten minutes!

'I lied.'

Coward! You have no honour.

Jorrun's body chuckled quietly. 'Chem is mine now, Jorrun. I make the rules and I can change them. As for Kesta, the moment she stops amusing me, she'll die.'

Hacren stepped on the bodies strewn about the gate as though they were no more than discarded rags and headed down the main street toward the temple district.

Jorrun had to slow him down.

Using his skill as a dream-walker, he created a perfect image of Kesta, not forgetting the spark of her soul and the fire of betrayal that had been in her eyes – it was something he would never forget. What hurt the most was the fact she might never know it wasn't true, that he would never betray her. The thought was unbearable, but if he could help her destroy the supposed god, or at least help her get away, that was all that mattered.

He set the image in the doorway of a shop, even showing the blossoming of flames in her hand. Hacren spun about to blast fire at the illusion, slowing when he felt no magical resistance. Hacren ceased, staring at the blackened space that contained nothing but a burning empty doorway.

Jorrun tried to contain his hope; if nothing else he might be able to get Hacren to waste power. He created another image, and another, putting every beloved detail of his wife into each creation he subtly slipped into the light. Again, and again Hacren struck, setting fire to the temple district, sending its residents fleeing in panic.

'What are you doing, Jorrun?' Hacren demanded.

He didn't reply, he couldn't, a figure had stepped out from a narrow gap between two buildings. It wasn't grief, confusion, or hurt on her face, but something he'd never seen before. Savage hatred.

Hacren saw her too and delight shivered through Jorrun's stolen body. 'I didn't think it was in your nature to run.'

Kesta didn't reply but called up her power at once, flame cupped in one hand.

Hacren gave a slight shake of his head. 'Very well. You know, of all the mortals under this sky, I would have chosen you to be my queen. A pity. Perhaps I'll give you one last chance to consider it before I kill you.'

Jorrun didn't see Azrael's attack from behind, but he felt Hacren's shield shudder. Jorrun moved all the way into the light, drinking in the sound, trying to reach for his other senses, grabbing at his body with the futility of snatching at air. He could do nothing but watch helplessly as Kesta was hurled down the street. For a moment flames obscured his vision, but Hacren tore Azrael off him and pinned him against a wall.

'Let him go!' There was no fear in Kesta's voice, only the confidence of someone who believed in herself completely. Did Hacren sense it? Or did he dismiss her in his arrogance?

You can do this, Kesta!

Jorrun poured all of his love, all his pride in her, into the light, but the god of death didn't feel it that way, interpreting it only into a great need to possess her.

'What do I get in return?'

Jorrun loved that she didn't waste her time with words but responded with a fierce attack. He desperately needed to help, he couldn't afford to wait for an opportunity, he had to make one.

Then the unthinkable happened. Hacren drew a huge amount of power and shattered Kesta's shield. Triumph consumed the god, but a new challenger made him turn.

Oh, brother, be careful! Jorrun thought, even as he thanked Osun with all his soul.

Hacren gave a feral growl and launched a ball of fire at Osun, almost howling in frustration as Azrael swooped in to smash it aside. The window of light moved and Jorrun saw five of the Raven Sisters huddled together. They sent a weak blast of power at Hacren and the god gathered his own to strike back. Without thinking Jorrun jerked the attack aside.

He recoiled in shock.

How did I do that?

Then the ground heaved. The window of light moved rapidly, and he saw Kesta sitting in the street, her fingers splayed across the cobbles. Her eyes were wide but her dark brows drawn down in fierce concentration, blood trickled from her nose. The street cracked apart and massive rocks surged upward. Jorrun felt almost euphoric, delighting at Hacren's shock.

She was amazing.

The ground gave way beneath them, then they were launched upward. Hacren gathered all of his power, preparing to decimate the woman he' so badly underestimated. Jorrun relaxed, giving a bodiless smile. Without even trying he moved one of his legs back and Hacren toppled from the ascending rock.

Kesta might never know he hadn't betrayed her. He hoped she would. But she was alive.

It was enough.

The light spun away from him.

Jorrun let go.

Chapter Thirty-Three

Kesta; Covenet of Chem

Kesta's hand jerked, and her dagger hit the cobbles beside Jorrun, making an awful, screeching sound against the stone. Jorrun's shirt was open at the top; there was no sign of the amulet his mother had given him.

'Kesta!' Osun ran to join her. 'Is he dead?'

Blood was slowly oozing from beneath his head, but she knew he was still alive, his chest slowly rose and fell.

'We have to kill him!' Osun said, although he didn't move.

Slowly, Kesta reached out her hand, sliding her fingers beneath the fabric of Jorrun's shirt to lay her hand across his collar bone. She reached out her *knowing*, expecting there to be nothing, but what she felt were two distinct personalities, two lives.

She snatched her hand back, almost losing her balance before sliding her legs out to sit on the wet ground. She doubled over, her arms tight about her body as tears forced themselves from her eyes. Her anger fled, leaving her chilled to the bone. The pain of her fear, of her grief, knocked the breath from her. She blinked up at Osun, trying to clear her vision.

'Kesta? What is it?' Osun crouched, placing his hand on her shoulder and looking from her to Jorrun. 'If … if you can't do it, then I'll kill him.'

'No!' She shook her head, forcing out the word. Tears dripped from her chin. 'He's still there! Jorrun's still there!'

'You're not making any sens—'

She raised a hand to bid him wait while she tried to gather herself. Azrael flew over to join them and Kesta closed her eyes, gratefully drawing in the warmth of the fire-spirit. She swallowed, clearing her painful throat. 'Whatever awoke in this body a few days ago wasn't Jorrun.'

Azrael became completely still.

'There are two lives in this body.' She pointed. 'Jorrun is still there.'

Osun started to shake his head, but he stopped, holding her gaze. 'You're sure?'

'I'm very sure.' She grabbed Osun's hand and crushed it in her own. 'I don't know how, but something has taken over Jorrun's body. He's still there, though, I can feel him.'

As she turned to place her hand on Jorrun's chest again, she noticed Azrael back away.

'Azra?' She scrambled up onto her knees. 'What do you know?'

The fire-spirit crackled and spat and made himself smaller.

Osun stood. 'You ran the moment he woke, Azra.'

'I went for help! The other Drakess wouldn't ansswer me! They were too afraid of him.' He darted about erratically. 'I didn't know you were coming here, Kessta! I thought you were ssafe in Navere! I came back here to sspy, to see if I could sstil trust you, Osun, or if you were one of them.'

'One of who?' Kesta demanded. 'Calm down, Azra, and tell us what's going on.'

'All of the blood magic, all of the death, the priessts ussed it to summon him!'

'Summon who?' Osun growled.

'Hacren!'

'What?' Osun shook his head. 'You're telling me Jorrun is possessed by the god of death?'

'Yeeessssss!' Azrael wailed.

'No.' Kesta shook her head violently. 'The gods of Chem aren't real, they can't be! Anyway, how could I have defeated a god?'

Osun tensed, glancing around. Kesta looked up to see a few people had crept back into the street.

'We've got to get out of the open,' Osun said. He gestured toward the raven women who hovered nearby. 'Help us get Jorrun into the temple.'

'What's happening?' Rey demanded as she bent to pick up one of Jorrun's legs.

'Let's get inside.' Osun grunted as he took the weight of Jorrun's torso.

Blood was still oozing slowly from the wound on Jorrun's head. They carried him toward the back of the vast building, laying him down carefully.

'I need to see to that.' Kesta tried to push past Osun, but he stopped her.

'A moment, Kesta.' He looked into her eyes, he looked as though he was going to cry again. 'If we save him, we save Hacren too.'

Kesta opened her mouth, but no sound came out. They couldn't just let Jorrun die!

Osun tore his eyes away from hers. 'Azra! The rest, now.'

'Hacren is still weak, the spell issn't complete! I don't know if he isss a god! Fire-spiritss are ancient but we have never met one. Whatever Hacren isss, he is powerful, but he can't manifessst his full strength until he absorbs sufficient blood sacrifices of those with magic or the priessts bind his soul to Jorrun's body.'

'How do you know that?' Osun demanded.

'SSpying, Ossun.'

'Is there a way to banish Hacren, save Jorrun?' Kesta demanded.

Azrael made himself large and then small again. 'There *might* be something in the book.'

'What book?' Kesta and Osun demanded at once.

'Jorrun's green book. The preissts got all excited about it, they could read it. One of them saw it when they went to his room. They ssaid it had ancient magics from long, long ago. Hacren wouldn't let them have it. Hacren was going to burn it, but for ssome reason he didn't.'

Kesta sprang onto her feet, clenching her fists and letting out a cry of frustration. 'Damn it all!'

'What?' Osun stared at her.

'The book is still in the palace!'

She paced up and down for a moment, wiping the drying blood away from her nose with her sleeve. 'Okay. So. We need to treat Jorrun's wound in case he can still be saved, but we don't want him waking in case it's Hacren that comes out. There are drugs to keep very sick people in deep sleep, is there anywhere we can get some?'

Osun nodded, a frown on his face. 'You can buy anything in Arkoom.'

'See to it quickly.' She pointed at him. 'Azrael, catch up with Cass and tell him not to leave yet, we'll need him and the wagons. I need to recover my strength,' she muttered, clenching her fists.

'For what?' Osun narrowed his eyes.

'To go back for the book. Was there anyone left at the palace with power?'

Osun shook his head.

'Good, then as soon as I can, I'm going back to tear it down.'

***

Kesta looked around at the women, some of them were sleeping, but most sat quietly talking. Rey was seated at Jorrun's head, watching for any sign of him – or Hacren – waking. Beside her was a small, dark bottle.

'Be very careful,' Osun warned. 'Too little and he'll wake, too much and he'll die.'

He looked at Kesta. They both knew prolonged use of the drug would eventually kill him, anyway.

They'd moved from the temple, breaking into an abandoned incense shop further along the street, too many people had seen them carrying Jorrun into the ruined hall of the gods. Cassien had luckily not yet left the city and had now moved all their horses to an inn nearer to the temple district, leaving the women he'd been trying to smuggle out in the care of the Navere guards and Elden warriors. Kesta felt uneasy that their party was so split, but for the moment it was the best they could do.

She tested her power, reaching for it carefully. It came, but reluctantly, and brought an instant headache. It would have to do.

She knelt on one knee and slowly reached out to touch Jorrun's cheek. His skin was warm, soft beneath the rough hairs of his short beard. She breathed in slowly, her eyes drinking in his face. 'This really had better be the last time I have to rescue you.'

She stood and headed for the back of the shop.

'Kesta?' Osun scrambled to his feet. 'What are you doing?'

'I'm going for the book like I said I would.'

Azrael darted about above their heads. 'No, be careful, Kessta.'

'He's right.' Osun hurried to put himself between her and the door. 'And we need you to get us to Navere. What if ... what if Hacren wakes when you're gone?'

'Azrael will have to deal with him.' She glared angrily at the fire-spirit who shrank back.

'I should go with you at least.'

'And me.' Cassien stood up straight.

Kesta shook her head. 'As much as it galls me, the women can't leave here without a man.'

'Stay, Cass.' Osun waved a hand at him. 'Azra, get to the others in the inn, have two of the men bring a wagon here along with our horses.' He indicated himself, Kesta, and Cassien. 'I want us all ready to get out of here as soon as we get back from the palace.'

Kesta clenched her teeth, but she didn't protest as Osun followed her out into the stinking alley.

They avoided the main street as much as possible, Osun directing her until they came within sight of the palace's high walls. The gates were firmly closed and two very nervous guards stood before it.

Kesta didn't hesitate. 'I want to get into the palace.'

The two men stared at her in wide-eyed shock and Kesta clenched her fists. She'd completely forgotten about being a woman.

'Who's in charge in there now?' Osun demanded.

'The Overlord,' one of the guards replied quickly.

'There is no Overlord.' Osun scowled. 'The priests have taken over, you idiot.'

The guards exchanged glances.

'Oh, we don't have time for this!' Kesta drew on her power and sent a formidable blast toward the gates, they burst open, hanging precariously off of their huge iron hinges.

'Come on.' She glanced at Osun before striding through. 'And you men had best get a long way from Arkoom if you know what's good for you!'

'Slow down, Kesta,' Osun called after her. 'Even you can't take on every guard in the palace! Let's go around to a servant's entrance and see if w—'

She looked back at him over her shoulder. 'There were only two guards on the main gate, this place is almost empty, look.' She dared to stretch out her *knowing* for a few seconds, she could feel lives, but nothing like the amount there should be in a building this size.

Osun grunted. 'Even so, w—'

'We'll try the window I escaped out of.'

Osun raised his eyebrows but said nothing, lengthening his long stride to keep up with her as she left the main path to cut across the gardens.

The window was unguarded, the glass still scattered across the grass below. She had to jump to catch the ledge, straining to pull herself up. Osun followed her more easily.

They stepped cautiously across the room, listening for any sounds of people. A door opened and closed further down the hall and Kesta found herself holding her breath. Osun leaned his back up against the door frame and opened the door slowly, peering through the crack.

'Looks clear,' he whispered. 'This way.'

He walked quickly up the hall, pausing at one of the doors. 'I have an idea, stay back and trust me for a moment.'

She nodded, watching as he squared his shoulders and forced the lines of worry from his face. He turned the handle and pushed it forcefully open.

'Master!' Someone gasped.

'Get everyone out of the palace,' Osun ordered. 'Everyone, quickly! The Overlord is dead, and a powerful sorcerer has come to destroy us all. There is no one to defend us. Out. Get out!'

A portly man in a fancy guard's uniform came hurrying out, his face red and his eyes bulging. He barely glanced at Kesta as he scuttled past, calling out several names in a terrified squeak. Moments later a bell started to ring in a clarion of alarm.

Osun turned to look at her, one eyebrow raised.

'I thought you wanted to be subtle?' She couldn't help it, she smiled.

'Well, I figured that, knowing you, you really do intend to tear this place down and I doubted you'd want any innocent people caught up in it.'

She regarded him for a moment. His eyes were darker than Jorrun's, but beneath the long curling hair and fuller beard they were so much alike physically it hurt.

'Come on.' He turned his back on her and hurried up the hall. A group of veiled women, led by a male servant, rushed past towards one of the exits.

Only one guard stopped on their way to the tower, hastily bowing to Osun.

'Forgive me, master, what's happening? May I assist you?'

'Just get everyone out!' He snapped.

'A shame we can't tell them to make the priests stay.' Kesta growled.

They hurried up the tower steps and Osun made sure Jorrun's room was clear before opening the door wide to let Kesta in. She unclasped Osun's cloak and handed it to him, grabbing up her own green one she'd left behind. Osun had picked up Jorrun's small travel bag, slinging it over his shoulder as she ran her fingers over the familiar green book.

'Kesta?'

She picked it up. 'Can you see Jorrun's amulet anywhere?'

They made a quick search of the room, but whatever Hacren had done with it, it didn't seem to be there. Kesta's heart sank, it was all Jorrun had of his mother.

Osun regarded her sympathetically. 'Let's get out of here.'

She nodded and led the way back down the winding steps. A noise startled her and a priest darted out of one of the rooms, his arms laden down with scrolls and several items made of gold. His eyes goggled when he saw Osun and he nearly dropped everything. Kesta didn't hesitate, she called up wind and pushed him down the stairs, running after him and drawing her dagger.

'Kesta!' Osun called in alarm.

She grabbed the priest by the front of his tunic, placing one knee on his chest to hold him down with her weight and pushing the edge of her blade into his neck just below his jaw. She applied just enough pressure to draw blood.

'You're going to answer my questions,' she hissed. 'If you don't answer quickly, you'll die.' She stared down into his watering brown eyes. 'Now, first, how did you summon Hacren?'

The priest glanced at Osun who'd stepped up behind her. 'The—there's a summoning spell carved into the back of his shrine. Priests have t—tried before, b—but there was never enough blood. The—the war against Elden brought enough death for it to succeed this time!'

'But why in the Gods' name would you do something so stupid as to summon the death god?' Osun demanded.

'Revenge.' The priest showed his teeth, spittle on his lips. 'You burned his holy temple!'

'Hells.' Osun cursed.

'And abominations walk our beloved land.' His nose creased in disgust as he glared at Kesta. 'Hacren will devour them!'

Kesta pushed the blade harder against his skin and pulled it a little to her right. The priest squealed and tried to get up as Kesta opened up a small wound.

'Why Jorrun?'

'Because a good heart is sweater to devour and Hacren wanted a strong and pleasing body.'

'How do we stop him?' she asked.

The priest grinned, his eyes lighting up. 'You can't!'

She cut deeper. 'How?'

'You can't!' The priest grabbed at her wrist, but Osun snatched his hand away, holding it in a white-knuckled grip. 'If you kill the one he inhabits, Hacren will just move to another host! He is earth-bound now.'

'How do we kill him?' Kesta roared, her face going red.

'A binding spell.' The priest spluttered, trying to pull away from the dagger. 'Bind Hacren to a man of this realm to give him mortal weakness. But it will also draw through all of his power from the heavens.'

Kesta slowly lifted the knife, she couldn't breathe. 'Then ...'

'Whatever you do.' The priest's mouth twisted up into a grin again, although it quickly vanished at the expression on Kesta's face. 'Whatever you do, Jorrun dies.'

Kesta slit his throat, Osun leaping back with a cry of disgust as blood splashed him.

'Damn it, Kesta, he might have known the binding spell!'

She turned on him with a growl. 'We are not killing Jorrun!'

She scrambled to her feet and began pulling open the scrolls, Osun grabbed her wrist and she growled at him again.

'Kesta, didn't Azrael say what we need is in the green book?'

She pulled her wrist free and stared at him. 'Yes.'

She stood and strode off through the hall, not waiting for Osun to follow.

Kesta tried not to think about what the priest had said, but his words burned into her soul. She pushed her body harder, sprinting for the palace doors, not caring if Osun was keeping up. Cold air hit her face and gravel crunched under her feet, changing to softer grass. She spun around, anger and despair rising through her body to blacken her sight. She drew up power, taking in everything she could until her skin felt as though it would split, then with a roar she reached beneath the palace to rip and lift the rock on which it stood. Blood burst from her nose and blurred her vision further as it trickled from her eyes. Her knees gave way and her palms hit the ground hard, but she still strained to make the rocks rise.

'Kesta! Kesta, stop it!'

She could barely hear him above the roar of blood in her ears and the thunder of the collapsing palace. She reached deeper, the pain in in her head so excruciating that her vision went white.

Osun threw himself to the ground beside her. 'Kesta! You're killing yourself, stop it!'

She drew air into her lungs, yelling with all of her remaining strength. 'I don't care!'

Osun grabbed her face between his hands, forcing her to look into his eyes. 'Well I care! And so does everyone else whose lives you've touched!'

The strength went out of her and Osun had to grab her arms to keep her from collapsing to the ground.

'But you heard him!' she said. 'Jorrun i—'

Osun let go of her to put his arms around her. She grabbed at the fabric of his tunic, holding it in her fists as her body shook. She leaned her head against his collarbone, barely able to draw breath through the spasms of her sobs. She could feel Osun's own body shaking, but he didn't make a sound. When he let her go and looked down at her, his eyes were very red but his skin pale, wet tracks marked the dust on his face from the fallen palace.

She could only stare at him as he took the edge of his cloak and wiped the blood and tears from her eyes and nose with a gentleness that made her hold her breath.

'We have to move,' he said.

She tried to stand, but her knees wouldn't work. She shrieked in protest when Osun picked her up. She tried to wriggle free, but she had no strength left.

'Pack it in,' Osun said sternly. 'You're too weak to walk and we need to go. Let someone else help you for once in your life!'

She glowered over his shoulder but stopped trying to fight and let him adjust his grip. He smelt surprisingly clean despite their recent exertion. His long hair tickled her cheek. He strode across the grass and through the abandoned main gates, following the main street. Eventually Kesta relaxed, letting her chin rest on his shoulder as she kept her eye out for any danger behind them.

Arkoom city was in chaos. The alarm bells and fleeing palace staff had unsettled people enough but seeing the palace crumple had sent people running in terror. Most people were heading for the gates, but some had stopped to grab what they could from the abandoned shops and stalls. Kesta saw a group of men had gathered around their wagon and Cassien was having a hard time keeping them from stealing the horses.

Azrael flew out of the wagon, making himself huge, and the men staggered back, turned tail and ran.

'Put me down,' Kesta snarled, her eyes not leaving Azrael. She would never have imagined being really angry with the fire-spirit, but her fury bordered on hate at that moment.

'Azra!' she shouted as Osun set her on her feet. 'Did you know? Did you already know we can't save him?'

Azrael completely lost his shape, becoming no more than a flickering yellow teardrop with tiny blue eyes. 'The only thing we can ssave him from iss torment, Kessta. You know how he fears to be trapped. I'm sorry, Kessta, but I couldn't let you know he wass there. I knew you couldn't kill Hacren if you did and he needs to be destroyed before he gets sstronger. You understand don't you, Kessta? Please? Jorrun would rather die than live in torment. He would rather die than let Hacren loose. You know that's true. Poison him while you can, sset Jorrun free.'

Kesta's heart hurt so much she had to press the heel of her hand hard into her chest. Azrael's words tore at her soul. Then realisation hit her and her eyes widened. She glanced at Osun and then turned back to Azrael. 'You don't know, do you?'

Azrael pulsed briefly larger. 'What, Kessta?'

'The priest said Hacren is now earth-bound, like you. If we kill Jorrun, Hacren will just move to a new host.'

Azrael shot upward with a wail and darted about like a mad thing. 'I didn't know, Kessta. I didn't know! What do we do?'

'Calm down for a start,' Osun said. 'Cass, let's get going, it's going to be hell trying to get out the gates.'

'I'll clear the way,' Azrael offered.

'When we join the other wagon,' Kesta told the fire-spirit. 'You'll travel in that one.'

Azrael wailed, but bobbed in agreement. Kesta immediately felt guilty at her angry punishment, she knew keeping him from Jorrun would hurt the little Drake. She knew already she would relent but for the moment she climbed up into the wagon, not protesting as Osun helped her.

The frightened women who huddled inside moved to let her past, Rey giving up her place at Jorrun's head.

'He seems comfortable, for the moment,' the raven sister told her.

Kesta looked down at Jorrun's face. It was easier to hold on to her anger than let grief slip in. Was he aware as he had been when caught by Karinna in his dream? She shuddered. Was there any way to reach him, to let him know she was there, or would it be Hacren she roused and shared her heart with? She managed to find enough space to curl up into a tight ball. Her eyes were sore and her chest felt as though someone were standing on it. She couldn't help it, she reached out her hand and touched his face with the tips of three fingers.

I'm here, Jorrun.

Chapter Thirty-Four

Kesta; Covenet of Chem

The road out of Arkoom was a tangle of terrified refugees, most on foot but a few with carts and wagons. It took nearly two days to leave most of them behind and by the time they reached the pass that forked west to Margith or south toward Navere, they were almost alone upon the road.

'I wish I had time to warn Tembre about what's going on.' Osun looked toward the setting sun.

Cassien grunted. 'He was never really on our side, I'd not trust him to help us now.'

Kesta followed Osun's gaze, but she had to agree with Cassien. She'd realised soon after they'd left Arkoom that they had no actual reason to head to Navere, they were no more likely to find an answer there than in the ruins of the palace she'd left behind. But Navere was the closest thing they had to a safe place.

Destiny pricked up her ears and lifted her head. Automatically Kesta reached out her *knowing*. 'Men on horses,' she said. 'A large number!'

'I'll look.' Azrael didn't wait for agreement but shot ahead of them. The fire-spirit had done its best to get back into Kesta's good books. She hadn't quite forgiven him even though she understood why Azrael had wanted her to kill Jorrun. Even thinking about it hurt. She glanced back at the wagon, he still slept deeply but his pulse had slowed and his hands and feet were cold to touch. It wouldn't be long until the poison that kept Hacren sleeping took any choice from her hands.

'Kesta!' Osun brought her mind back with a start and she looked to where he was pointing. Azrael was hurtling back, but he wasn't alone, another

447

fire-spirit was with him and the two of them where flying rapid loops around each other as they came.

'It's Doroquael.' Azrael buzzed and hummed in pure delight, his colour going an intense blue with yellow flickers at the edges.

'Doroquael?' Kesta sat straight in her saddle. 'How are you here? How did you cross the sea?'

'Kessta! I came on the Undine.'

'Horsemen.' Cassien warned, drawing his sword.

'They are friends.' Doroquael flipped over and made himself more human-shaped. 'See?'

Kesta watched as the horsemen came into view, there were a dozen and the men were dressed in clothing that made her catch her breath. 'Islanders!' Her eyes widened as she recognised the man at their head, her eyes stung and she urged Destiny into a gallop, her heart in her mouth. The rider saw her and spurred his own horse forward. He barely had time to dismount and catch her as she threw herself from Destiny's back.

'Uncle Worvig! Why are you here? Why are you in Chem?' She clutched at his wide ribcage, letting herself sag against the familiar safety of her uncle, letting her tears fall unashamedly at the comforting feel of his strong arms.

'Hey now.' Worvig rubbed her back. 'We're here because you needed us.'

His words pierced through her wall of anger and her throat tightened painfully. Her nostrils flared and she blinked rapidly, clenching her teeth to keep control. 'How did you know?'

'Doroquael heard from the other fire-spirits.'

'Azra?' Kesta turned to the Drake.

'I told you, Kessta. I tried to get help, I really did.' He made himself small.

'Siverael.' Doroquael crackled. 'He heard Azra had been trying to get into the fire realm and why. He travelled through the realm all the way to Elden to find me.'

Kesta's chest muscles clenched, then she froze. 'But wait, you were in Elden, Doroquael?'

Osun and Cassien had caught up to them, Osun dismounting.

'There's a lot to tell you,' Worvig said, looking Osun and Cassien up and down.

'We'll set camp here for the night,' Osun said, turning to Cassien who nodded and turned his horse back to give instructions to the others.

'Osun,' Kesta said. 'This is my uncle, Worvig Silene. Worvig, this is Jorrun's brother, Osun.'

'And Jorrun?' Worvig frowned at her in concern.

'We have a long story to tell, too,' she said quietly.

They set the camp and several of Worvig's men agreed to stand the watch. They shared their rations and Kesta gestured Osun and Cassien over to sit with her uncle. Azrael approached slowly, making himself tiny.

'Kessta? May I watch Jorrun and Hacren for you?'

She nodded. 'Go on, Azra.'

The fire-spirit shot away to the wagon, but Doroquael remained.

Kesta turned to Worvig. 'Go on, you go first.'

They exchanged stories and Kesta had to stand up and pace around their camp for a while to calm herself down as Worvig told of her mother's imprisonment. She returned to sit beside him slowly, her eyes not leaving his face as his tale came to an end.

'So, Temerran brought us to Navere and your mother sent us out to look for you.'

'How is Navere?' Osun asked, leaning forward.

'Things seem well there.' Worvig reassured him. 'Your captain did tell us the only real trouble they've had is from the priests.'

Kesta growled.

'There were letters there for Jorrun, from King Bractius and messengers from Merkis Tantony, they obviously never reached him.'

'Had a man named Jagna and a lady, Estre, made it back there?' Osun asked. 'They rode ahead of us.'

'Not that I know of.' Worvig frowned. 'But we did pass a man and a woman riding fast in that direction with spare horses, maybe three days ago.'

'Let's hope it's them.' Osun looked from Cassien to Kesta.

'So.' Worvig regarded Kesta. 'What of you?'

She swallowed and began her own tale. Osun occasionally shifted beside her but he didn't interrupt. Worvig took her hand but also said nothing.

Kesta finished with a sigh. 'That is where we are.'

Doroquael hovered closer to her. 'Kessta, I will go at once to your mother and carry your tale. And perhapss Temerran the Bard may know ssomething of help.'

'Go with my blessing.' She smiled at the spirit although the muscles of her chest ached. 'Please take care.'

Doroquael bobbed and was away at once.

Osun stood. 'Let's sleep and then start out early.'

Kesta looked up at him, but his gaze was somewhere far away. She wondered if, like her, he was too afraid to feel any hope her mother could somehow help. A part of her wanted to reach out to him, to be close to someone who understood how she felt, but she couldn't quite let go of her disgust at his past. Osun stood and quietly walked away alone.

***

Her pulse quickened at the sight of Navere and, sensing it, Destiny quickened her pace. Osun moved forward to join her and she gave him a nod, neither of them could bring themselves to smile. Jorrun's pulse was now barely a flutter, the movement of his lungs so slight that the rise of his chest was hardly perceptible.

At the gates to the city they were greeted by salutes from the guards, one of them running ahead to let the palace know of their arrival. Kesta pulled her hood forward and bowed her head to hide her face, her shoulder muscles were so tight her neck hurt. She tried to push the tingling leap of the butterflies of hope away, so scared there would be no solution she felt physically sick. The cobbled road that led through the city to the palace seemed infinitely long and she had to fight the urge to push Destiny into a gallop.

They were met by several of the Raven Sisters the instant they reached the palace gardens. Kussim looked hopefully from Osun to Kesta, her puffy eyes then travelling over the canvas of the wagons. Kesta couldn't look at her.

'Welcome home!' Beth enthused, she held a small bundle in her arms that Kesta assumed was a baby. She wanted to be glad for the former slave, but she didn't dare let herself feel anything.

'Let us get inside a moment,' Osun said gently. 'It is good to see you though, sisters.'

They rode toward the stables, Kesta glanced toward the main doors of the palace and was both relived and disappointed her parents hadn't met her there. Servants came out to take the horses from them and Kesta rubbed Destiny's neck and shoulder.

'Do you want to help me carry Jorrun in?' Osun asked her.

She nodded without turning and followed him to the wagon.

Cassien and Worvig also came to assist, and they took the edges of the blanket on which Jorrun lay and used it to convey him. Rey hurried forward to open the doors and the others followed. Kesta looked around at them all. 'Go and get some rest. Thank you for everything you've done. You were amazing.'

The Raven Sisters dispersed reluctantly, all of them wanting to know what would happen with Jorrun. Kesta shut her *knowing* down as tightly as she could, the last thing she needed was other people's grief and pity.

'Where?' Osun turned to ask Kesta.

She laughed, but without humour. 'The library, of course!'

'I'll let the Icante know.' Azrael whizzed off along the hall.

When they reached the library doors, Worvig took hold of Kesta's corner of the blanket so she could dart forward and open them. They placed Jorrun carefully on the carpet. Kesta couldn't look at his face as she checked for his pulse.

She snorted. 'I guess we would know already if he'd died.'

She started as the door opened and she drew in a sharp breath at the sight of her mother. Kesta covered her mouth with her hands and gritted her teeth hard to try to hold her emotions in check. Her vision blurred as she stood and she ran blindly into her mother's arms. When she opened her eyes, she saw a man of about Osun's age with curling red hair and bright green eyes watching her. He gave her a slight bow as she stepped away from her mother.

Dia followed the direction of her gaze. 'Kesta, this is Temerran of the Borrows.'

'Oh!' She exclaimed, reaching into the pocket inside her cloak for the green book, the weave of its hard cover as familiar as her own skin. She thrust it toward him. 'Can you read this?'

Kesta held her breath as Temerran examined and then opened the small book. Osun stepped up beside her with a polite nod at Dia.

Temerran looked up. 'I can.'

Kesta drew in air and bit hard at her lower lip.

'It is a book on spirits, of their nature and how to deal with them.' He looked back down at the broken pages, leafing through them slowly. Kesta folded her arms tightly around her body. Dia walked over to the fireplace and ignited the wood stacked within. Almost at once, Azrael and Doroquael climbed out, staying near to the stone chimney breast as though fearful of getting in the way.

Temerran frowned and the muscles of Kesta's chest clenched.

'There is nothing in here of gods.'

The floor swam away from Kesta and Osun darted forward to grab her about the waist and hold her up.

'Kesta?' Dia stared at her opened mouthed for a moment, before pulling out a chair for Osun to help her into.

'Lady.' Temerran took several swift strides across the room to kneel on one knee beside Kesta. 'Lady, there is something though. There is mention of demons; that they are powerful spirits of an ancient kind with a vicious nature. It says they can be called through to this realm and inhabit the body of a mortal.' He made a gesture of annoyance with his hand. 'The next part is damaged but I think it suggests the demon needs to be bound in some way in order to fully manifest in this realm with its powers. Killing the host merely frees the spirit to find a new host. Binding it to the host allows you to kill the demon, but they are so powerful it's near impossible.'

Kesta growled. 'We know this already.'

'I think I can perform the binding.'

'What?' Kesta shot to her feet. 'What did you say?'

Temerran looked from her to Dia. 'I'm a bard, my power is in my voice. I think I can perform the binding. The words are right here.' He pointed at the page.

'We can kill the demon?' Cassien asked excitedly.

Kesta's heart slowed, she felt every beat against her ribs. She turned to look down at Jorrun, at his pale face, the long lashes of his closed eyes. 'And we kill Jorrun.'

Dia drew herself up. 'Leave us a moment.'

Temerran bowed and made his way to the door, holding it open for Cassien and Worvig. Osun followed reluctantly, exchanging a glance with Kesta. The two fire-spirits melted into the fire. Kesta sat slowly back down in the chair, her eyes not leaving Jorrun.

She didn't look up as her mother picked up another chair and placed it beside her. 'Kesta, I'm so sorr—'

Kesta raised a hand and turned away.

Dia drew in a deep breath and continued softly. 'I wish there was another way. One way or another, Jorrun will die. Doroquael told me what Azrael did. That little spirit loves Jorrun with all its fiery heart. You are going to have to make the same choice as Azrael did. To save Jorrun, to sav—'

'Enough!' Kesta couldn't help it, she called her power, an instinctive and overriding need to defend herself. Her eyes were tightly shut, her hands clenched into fists.

'Kesta, it will hurt. It will hurt more than anything you've ever known, but you have to do this. You won't want to hear my words now, but in time life will go on. There are people who love you and need you, and there are other people for you to lov—'

She stood so quickly her chair fell back. 'Not like him!' she yelled, pointing at the prone body on the floor.

'No, not like him.' Dia shook her head. 'Love like that comes to too few of us. Souls like that often burn intensely but far too briefly.' Dia bit her lower lip and looked down at the floor, glancing at her daughter. 'Souls that change the world are too often taken from us early.'

'We didn't have any time.' Kesta's body shook as tears burst from her eyes. She let her power go, static played around her arms. She sank to the floor next to the chair, leaning her forehead against her folded arms. Her temperature seemed to rise and she pulled at the neck of her tunic, her breaths coming in gasps. She wanted to break the world.

'But look how much you did in the time you had together.' Dia reached out to stroke her hair. 'You brought such changes to the land beneath our sky.'

Kesta needed to scream that it wasn't fair, but she knew how naïve and childish such a thought was. There had to be a way. This couldn't be how it ended.

She moved her arms and let her forehead rest against the wood of the chair, running her fingers though her hair to grab clumps of it tightly close to her scalp. 'I can't do it. I can't kill him.'

Dia rubbed her back. 'Do you want me to do it?'

Kesta covered her head with her arms, her throat and lungs so tight she could barely breathe, let alone reply. Sweat trickled down her back. She breathed in and out, part of her wanting her lungs to stop. Her blood rushed loudly in her ears and she tasted blood as she bit hard on the inside of her lower lip. No time. Time was at and end. Everything spun around her so quickly she thought she'd vomit. Had Azrael been right? Was this the only way to save Jorrun, to save them all?

She tensed her muscles and forced her head to move. She nodded.

'All right.' Dia kissed the top of her head. 'I'll give you some time.'

Kesta didn't hear her mother's steps but she heard the library doors click closed. She called her power back and with a roar threw fire at the chimney. She turned and blasted air at the stained-glass window, coloured shards shattering outwards. She grabbed her chair and smashed it hard against the table. Only one leg broke so she brought it down again and again until every leg was off and the muscles of her arms screamed in pain.

'Kessta.' Azrael and Doroquael came shooting out of the fireplace. 'Kessta. Dire news.'

She raised her head, the bright light of the fire-spirits stabbing into her eyes. 'How can things be worse?'

'Kessta.' Azrael's shape changed so rapidly she could barely focus on the frantic spirit. 'Temerran has been reading more of the book to prepare for the binding. He says the demon, Hacren, cannot be bound to someone with magical blood. It's why they chose Jorrun, he is the most powerful sorcerer under the sky, so Hacren could still be strong without his own powers, without risking the mortality of being bound.'

Kesta sat on the floor so hard she bruised her coccyx, sending jarring pain up her spine. She stared up at the fire-spirit. 'So … so when Jorrun dies, he dies for nothing, Hacren just moves on?'

Azrael and Doroquael both started wailing, she placed her hands over her ears and clenched her teeth. 'Stop that!' She bit hard at her thumb.

No. This can't be!

The library door opened.

She spun around and moved into a crouch, breathing hard, her fists clenched at her sides. Osun stood in the doorway, his dark curly hair hung across his eyes as though he had been running his fingers constantly through it. He stepped in, closing the door behind him, his eyes on the floor.

'Kesta, I've been talking to Temerran.'

She was too exhausted to reply, too beaten.

'I think there's a way.'

She lifted her chin, her eyes ached as she tried to focus on him.

'Temerran says he's seen men drown in the sea, he's seen the life go from their eyes, but if you breathe air back into their lungs, force the beat back into their hearts, you can bring them back.'

Kesta stood slowly. 'What are you saying?'

'If we drown Jorrun in the sea, drive Hacren out, Temerran thinks we might be able to save Jorrun.'

'Might?' She was breathing hard, each exhale loud through her nose.

Osun nodded and took another step forward. 'Isn't it worth a try?'

'But …' Kesta looked into his bloodshot blue eyes. 'But if Hacren leaves Jorrun he will move to a new body. To destroy him, we will have to try to bind Hacren to that new body. And it will have to be someone without power.'

Osun swallowed and looked down at the floor. 'I know.' He looked up and met her eyes. 'Kesta. Do you forgive me? Do you forgive me for what I did to Milaiya?'

She caught her breath. She opened her mouth. She wanted to say yes, but she couldn't.

'Neither do I.' Osun forced a humourless smile. 'I'll do it. I'll drown my brother and let Hacren take me.'

'No!' Kesta took two swift steps forward to stand before him.

He bowed his head and closed his eyes. 'I would have given anything to know how it felt to love – and to be loved.' He opened his eyes to look at her, slowly reaching out a hand to touch her face with the tip of two fingers. 'My brother is everything to me. I want to do this, Kesta. And, I want to be someone you're both proud of.'

'You already are!' His image blurred and Kesta had to clench her teeth hard to stop her jaw from shaking.

He shook his head, not meeting her eyes. 'You know what kind of man I am, Kesta.'

She went to protest, but he stopped her.

'Do you know why I came back to Chem? It wasn't for the reason you and Jorrun did. I came here because I wanted to prove *you* wrong. I came here to force you to forgive me. I came here because ...' He drew in a breath. 'I needed you to think better of me. Because ... because what you think of me matters.'

She swallowed, staring at him. She couldn't find her voice. His image blurred before her, split by rainbows.

'Two boys,' Azrael darted toward them. 'Two boys I ssaw through the flame. Both loved by our dearest Naderra, both with special blood and great

458

hearts. We made a sacrifice, Naderra and I, to get them away from Chem sso that they might find the potential for great good, insstead of great evil. Now … I will lose one – or both.' Azrael started wailing again.

'It's worth a try, isn't it?' Osun looked at her.

She turned away, rubbing at the back of her neck with one hand. She turned slowly and looked him in the eyes. He seemed somehow younger, vulnerable, his dark-blue eyes wide and desperate. She recalled the first time she'd met him, how affronted he'd been by her behaviour, then his shy smile, his clumsy attempts at friendship. He'd known she'd hated him, but he'd never stopped trying and he'd always tried to protect her, even against Jorrun.

'Just because I can't forgive what you did, it doesn't mean I don't c … It doesn't mean I don't love you, Osun.' Guilt chewed at her heart. She took two steps toward him, lifting a hand to touch his bearded cheek. She closed her eyes and leaned forward to kiss him gently on the lips.

His eyes widened, but he shook himself and squeezed her hand tightly. 'Just promise me something. No matter what happens, you must live, Kesta. Don't let Hacren defeat you. If you have to, then run, save yourself to fight another day. As long as you live then I can have hope you'll defeat him. As long as you live, I know you'll save me. Promise me, Kesta.'

She couldn't tear her eyes away from his, as much as his intensity burned her heart.

'I promise.'

'Then let's do this.'

'Are you sure, brother?'

Osun nodded. 'I'm sure, my dearest sister.'

Chapter Thirty-Five

Kesta; Covenet of Chem

'Osun, let it be me!' Cassien almost ran to keep up with Osun's long strides as they hurried down the hall.

'Don't be stupid,' Osun snapped.

Kesta wiped at her eyes with the heel of her hand, trying to force her lungs to steady. She glanced at Osun but couldn't meet his eyes.

'But, maste—'

Osun rounded on the boy. 'What have I told you? You don't call anyone master! You *are* a 'master' now, Cass.'

Cassien halted, his mouth open, his cheeks were wet. 'Well at least let me come and fight.'

'Cassien,' Osun said more gently. 'I told you, no men must come but me and Temerran.'

'How can you be sure he'll only go for a man's body?'

It was Kesta who answered. 'Because we have seen enough of the creature's nature to know that's so.'

Osun sighed. 'Cassien, your friendship and loyalty mean more to me than you'll ever know. I need to do this, I want to deserve your loyalty.' He didn't wait for a reply, but continued into the audience hall.

The Raven Coven had gathered in their seats, the three central chairs remained empty and Osun headed straight for them. Kesta took the seat to his right. Instead of taking the other seat, Cassien went to sit among the sisters. Dia, Temerran, and Arrus were also there with Heara and Catya.

Worvig had remained with the fire-spirits to watch over Jorrun. Captain Rece was the only one who stood.

'I'm sure you have already heard our situation.' Osun looked around at them all. 'We don't have time for long farewells. I wanted to thank you all for everything you've done, without your courage we'd have had no chance to change Navere. Without your faith, we could never have held it. Stand by each other and you will do more than survive, you will put in place a foundation to secure the safety of the women – and men – of Chem for generations to come. Our plan was for me to be Lord of Navere Coven, perhaps even Overlord. You don't need a lord. Chem doesn't need an Overlord. You are the Raven Coven, share your wisdom and run Navere together. There are fifteen ruling Seats, vote on every major decision and there will always be a yes or a no with no need for one person to dictate. Arkoom Palace is in ruins, Navere is the most stable and prosperous city in Chem, you have a chance to make it the centre of this land. Take it.

'Calayna, Rece, Jagna, and Estre, I've left plans, ideas, detailed laws that I would like you to consider. It's all in my study. I leave them in your capable hands.'

He stood and there were several cries of protest. Dia and the others from the Fulmers headed straight for the door.

'Jorrun doesn't have much time.' Osun raised his voice to be heard. 'Those who will fight, please come with me now.' He turned to Jagna and they clasped wrists. Rece gave him a salute before doing the same. Calayna hugged him, kissing his cheek before stepping away. Kesta couldn't help but notice how much Osun tensed at such close contact. Osun searched the crowd with his eyes and spotted Cassien sitting with his head bowed. Kesta held her breath as Osun made his way over.

'Cassien,' he said. 'It was worth coming back to Chem just to free you.'

Kesta choked back a sob, swallowing hard and rubbing at her forehead to hide her tears.

Cassien stood slowly and Osun hugged him, Kesta could see the boy was shaking and she had to look away. She hurried to catch up with her mother.

'How are you doing?' Dia slipped her arm around Kesta's.

'I'm terrified,' she admitted. 'I'm sorry you got dragged into thi—'

'Kesta.' Her mother squeezed her arm. 'We were all dragged into this. I'm glad I'm here to fight at your side this time.'

'I wish we didn't have to risk the others.'

Dia glanced over her shoulder. Their plan was simple, but there was so much that could go wrong.

Arrus went ahead of them with Worvig and two other warriors, bearing Jorrun away from the city and toward the beach. Rece and his guards had to chase away several curious onlookers. They placed their stretcher down and the men who wouldn't be staying started back toward the city. Arrus and Worvig lingered, Kesta wished they would just go, it was hard to see the sadness and fear on their faces and their anger that they couldn't stay to fight. They both hugged her, but she pulled herself away from them quickly. She needed to get it over, she needed to fight Hacren.

When they were all in position, Osun took hold of Jorrun's shoulders and dragged him backward into the water. Kesta's breathing was so rapid she felt dizzy. She couldn't bear it, but she couldn't look away. Osun glanced at her as the water reached his knees, Jorrun's long legs floated up, moved by the waves. Osun's own shoulders rose and fell as he looked down at his brother. A small sound escaped from Kesta's lips. It felt like forever before

Osun tensed and stopped supporting Jorrun to force him down below the water. Kesta wanted to scream, but she couldn't move, couldn't even call her power. Was she losing him? Was she watching Jorrun's life leave him forever?

There was no struggle, but Osun's face had reddened. He looked up and as his eyes caught Kesta's it felt as though lightning had struck her heart.

Osun let go of Jorrun.

He arched backward, his body spasmed. Osun's hands flew to his temples to hold his head. He staggered. Kesta instinctively stepped forward, but her mother grabbed her arm. Both Azrael and Doroquael wailed like keening seabirds.

Osun looked up but it was no longer he.

Hacren regarded all of those on the beach. The gathered Raven Sisters had already been shielding and Temerran began his clear-voiced chanting.

Hacren walked slowly up out of the water, his eyes on Kesta and Dia. He completely ignored Jorrun's lifeless body. He didn't move like Osun, he moved like a hunter, placing each foot carefully on the wet sand. 'So, this is your plan.'

Neither Kesta nor Dia replied, they moved apart, backing a little way up the beach. Doroquael flew to Dia's shoulder and Azrael to Kesta's. Kesta could see Heara waiting, her knees bent, watching for Hacren to be far enough away for her to run for Jorrun's body.

'I've beaten you before,' Kesta said, letting her voice tremble. She backed up a little more. Hacren followed, glancing at the Raven Sisters.

'I only had the feeble powers of a mortal, then, and I didn't know a *fire-walker* knew the magics of the gods. Now I do. Don't worry, I still won't kill you too quickly.'

Dia called her power and Hacren's eyes flashed open wider; Osun's eyes. He turned to face the Icante.

'So, who might you be?'

Heara made a dash along the shoreline, Catya on her heels.

'The Icante of the Fulmers,' Dia replied, her head held high, her breathing steady. 'And we know you are no god.'

Hacren laughed, so different to Osun's shy laugh. He grinned. 'Oh, I've been a god. It was long ago, but I rather liked it.'

Temerran continued to sing his chant. Kesta didn't dare look toward the water, didn't dare hope, she couldn't afford to let herself be distracted. She called up her *knowing*, watching for any warning of when Hacren's body was bound and his powers were his. She could feel emotion, but like Azrael it was different, hard to pin down. It reminded her of touching something metal that had been struck and still vibrated.

'You are just a spirit.' Dia continued to keep his attention.

Hacren's face darkened, his smile fading slowly. 'Be careful, woman, there's a reason why I was named the God of Death.'

'Because you've gotten used to dying?' Dia raised an eyebrow.

Hacren growled, his fists tensed, but he drew no power. Kesta's eyed flickered past him to the sea, Heara had pulled Jorrun out of the water and Catya was breathing into his mouth. Hacren glanced behind him.

'You creatures are so stupidly sentimental.' He turned to head back toward Jorrun, he had no weapons, Osun had made sure of that. Heara leapt up from pushing at Jorrun's heart, drawing her short sword. With a glance at her mother, Kesta called up power and swept Hacren off his feet, throwing him onto his back and tumbling him along the wet sand. Everlyn broke free

464

from the circle of the Raven Sisters to form a shield around Catya, Heara, and Jorrun's still body.

Hacren got slowly to his feet, trying to retain some dignity. His face had reddened and his blue eyes had darkened, seeming more a slate-grey than blue. Kesta glanced at Temerran; was the binding even working? Azrael made an anxious loop in the air.

'That wasn't wise, Kesta,' Hacren snarled.

She didn't respond, forcing herself to relax her power a little and not waste it.

She stepped back, drawing in air sharply as flames blazed in Hacren's hands. He went straight for Kesta, the force of his attack driving her to her knees, she raised her arms above her head, straining to keep her shield. Azrael flew in front of her, giving her strength, but even with the two of them her muscles screamed and sweat beaded her skin.

She fell back as Hacren's attack broke off without warning. A huge tornado surrounded Hacren flinging stinging sand and stones as it dug into the beach. Dia held it balanced with one hand at the same time as starting to build a thunderhead. Kesta scrambled to her feet.

The tornado dissipated, sand and debris rained down on the beach and Dia staggered back, fighting to retain control of her storm. Waves of fire rolled toward Dia and for a moment Kesta lost sight of her mother. Kesta gathered power, bracing herself to reach below the sand for the rock below. She heaved upward, feeling a vein burst in her nostril and the warm tickle of blood. Her muscles screamed at her to stop but she kept going, trying to find a weakness in the unrelenting rock. With a gasp she let go, staggering back and blinking at the red and black that flashed behind her eyes. A small dip appeared in the sand, but that was all. Despair washed through Kesta, the rock was too hard, too solid, she'd wasted all that power for nothing.

Taking in a deep breath she sent a gale toward Hacren, turning aside his flames to give her mother a moment of relief. From the corner of her eye she saw Everlyn stalking closer, her shield raised.

What of Jorrun?

Kesta added flame to the wind, both Azrael and Doroquael swooped in to attack Hacren, battering against his shield. Everlyn added a blast of her own and finally Hacren's attack on Dia faltered. Kesta felt pride straighten her spine, the Icante was still on her feet, still building her storm.

Hacren turned his attention to Everlyn, he glanced at Kesta, showing his teeth, before tearing up sand to form a molten ball to hurl at the *walker*. Kesta did her best to turn it aside but it still took out Everlyn's shield. The Raven Sisters hurried forward, keeping formation, all of them shielding. Everlyn got onto her feet, retreating backward toward the safety of the sisters. Lightning lashed out from Hacren, leaving sharp after-images on Kesta's retinas. She spun around, expecting to see Everlyn dead, but the *walker* had somehow drawn enough power to shield again. The Raven Sisters reached her, Jollen stepping in front of Everlyn.

Kesta turned to look at her mother and their eyes met. How had he called lightning without first creating a storm?

Dia gave Kesta a single sharp nod and they both sent a blast of fire at Hacren. The Sisters and the two fire-spirits all joined in. Hacren's shield held, his face – Osun's face – showing little strain as the fire shifted to reveal him.

They'd feared he would be much stronger, they'd been right to be afraid. It was obvious that even with the Icante here they didn't have the power to defeat him. They'd have to rely on being smarter, in catching him out in some way. Kesta felt a fool for having banked on her ability to raise rock, in choosing a place where they might save Jorrun, she'd unwittingly sacrificed that exceptional power. There had to be something else she could try.

Lightning flashed within the clouds up ahead and thunder left Kesta's ears ringing. Dia reached up to aim the lightning, but Hacren was quicker, somehow manifesting the elemental magic within himself and hurling it at the Icante. The sharp smell of ozone filled Kesta's lungs and she had to blink several times before her vision cleared enough for her to see her mother was still alive. She moved toward her, intending to shield and allow her mother to concentrate on attacking, but Hacren turned instead to hurl his next bolt of lightning at the Raven Sisters. Several of them screamed as their shields failed, but some held, protecting the rest.

Kesta turned back to Hacren, the creature was laughing. Fury stiffened every muscle in Kesta's body, he was still playing with her, making her choose between the Sisters and her mother.

She stepped back toward the Chem women and Hacren grinned, sending blinding light lashing toward Dia.

'Fight *me*!' Kesta yelled. She drew up her power and threw everything she could at Hacren. Azrael and Doroquael flew to her shoulders creating a fiery barrier to protect her, but they were both hurled aside by icy winds.

Three times Dia called lightning down, but Hacren's shield held. Ignoring Kesta, the demon began a continuous attack on the Icante, each time Kesta moved toward her, Hacren blasted the Raven Sisters. Heat left Kesta's blood and she was suddenly chilled to the bone despite the flames. She was panting, her leg muscles straining to keep her steady, the pathways in her body that channelled power so raw and swollen she could barely pull anything through.

Dia collapsed onto one knee, blood tracked down her sand spattered face. Kesta glanced at the Raven Sisters, huddled together, exhausted Everlyn at their head. The fire-spirits rejoined her, but their flame was a dull yellow.

Hacren called power to his hands.

She had to do something, now before he killed them all. She looked at his face, seeing past the contorted features to remember the surly, selfish, shy, incredibly brave man she'd not allowed herself to know.

Promise me, Kesta.

'Wait!' Kesta stepped forward.

Hacren lowered his hands, tilting his head to one side as he regarded her.

'Let them go, let them all get safely to the Fulmers and … and I'll stay with you. I'll obey you for as long as you leave them alone.'

'Kesta, no!' Dia got to her feet. 'Don't you dare!'

Hacren grinned, his eyes travelled over Kesta before he took a few, considered steps closer. Kesta felt sick, she clenched her fists to stop her hands from shaking.

Hacren grunted. 'I'm not sure you're worth that many lives, Kesta, much as I'd enjoy torturing you. Choose five.'

Her mouth opened but she couldn't speak, couldn't breathe. How could she choose? She couldn't!

Behind her both fire-spirits were making an angry, buzzing sound. Somewhere, Temerran was singing. Dia stiffened.

Kesta glanced around at the others, shaking her head, gripping the fabric of her tunic hard in one fist. It would have to be those that had the most chance of defeating Hacren in the future, the strongest magic users, but that would mea–

Hacren took another two steps forward. 'Choose now, or the deal is off.'

'Get. Away. From. Her.'

Kesta's heart smashed against her ribs and she spun around, gasping in air. Jorrun leaned against Heara, barely able to stand, his face as pale as the foam of the sea.

Hacren laughed. 'Well, well. You're determined, I'll give you that, Jorrun. A bit selfish though, forcing your wife to watch you die for a third time.'

Jorrun called power to his free hand as Heara adjusted her grip to hold him up.

Hacren's eyes widened and he stepped back.

Jorrun sent fire streaming toward the demon as he moved around to place himself between Hacren and the Raven Sisters. Dia tore lightning down from the sky, circling to be closer to Kesta, the lightning hit the sand before Hacren's feet, spraying it up against his shield.

'The ssea, Kessta,' Azrael hissed excitedly in her ear.

Kesta didn't understand what the fire-spirit wanted, but she drew the last of her power, sending a steady stream of weak flames toward Hacren. Dia and Jorrun continued to close in on either side of her, Jorrun's attack ferocious, her mother's waning. They came together, the Raven Sisters shielding with the last of their strength, Kesta and Dia joining them as Jorrun began to press forward toward Hacren, Heara all but carrying him.

Lightning flashed and sparked around them, Kesta closed her eyes, concentrating only on drawing the dregs of her strength through her shredded and raw nerves.

A shocked cry forced her eyes open. Jorrun ceased his attack. Kesta moved forward, her breath ragged in her throat, her heart pounding with exhaustion.

Hacren was in the sea, lightning lit it from the inside and steam rose as Hacren's body jerked, his arms flailing as he struggled to get free. Creatures as clear as crystal whose skin seemed to flow continuously had him in their grasp and were pulling him out and under. The demon's fire and lightning were futile, air no more than an inconvenience to these liquid beings.

Rey gasped. 'What are they?'

'Old friends,' Dia replied. 'Of a sort.'

Kesta moved from the shelter of the Sisters and stepped down to the wetter sand. Hacren was below the water now, a dark shape. She flinched as he burst to the surface, but there was no life in his wide, reddened eyes. The sea spirits came up for a moment, not looking toward the larger group, but to Catya and Temerran who stood alone further down the beach. Temerran raised a hand and the spirits faded into the sea.

Kesta drew in a breath, her eyes falling on the floating body that was already moving out on the tide. Hope bloomed painfully in her chest. She broke into a run.

Someone called her name but she ignored it, wading out into the sea. She took hold of Osun's arm and dragged him back toward the shore.

'Kesta!' Her mother was hurrying toward her.

Kesta pulled Osun up onto the sand, looking around for help. 'Heara! Temerran! Quickly, bring him back!' She couldn't understand why they were just standing there, why no one would help Osun.

'No, Kesta.' Her mother was shaking her head. 'They are bound remember, if we revive him, it will be Hacren who comes back. Osun is gone.'

She stared at her mother, glancing around at the others. She looked back down at Osun, at the wet, black curls that clung to his face, at the water trickling slowly from his mouth. At the dark-blue eyes that'd had the chance to smile too rarely. The blood seemed to leave her limbs, leaving them cold and weightless. Grief welled up deep inside her chest, exploding out and up, streaming from her eyes.

Something heavy landed in the sand beside her and she turned to see eyes of a lighter blue. She reached up a shaking hand to touch his sandy face and pressed her forehead against his.

'Jorrun.'

Chapter Thirty-Six

Kesta; The Free City of Navere

The lantern flickered, sending her shadow dancing up the wall. She held her breath, listening for the sound of the door or the soft tread of feet. Shaking her head, she forced herself to relax, putting down her book to look at the man who slept beside her on the balcony floor. His skin was still pale and looked bruised beneath his closed eyes, his short beard untidy where Hacren hadn't trimmed it. Jorrun had vomited several times on their way back to the city, eventually having to sit and wait until Temerran had come back with Rece and a wagon. Osun's body had travelled with them, Kesta insisting only a green cloak of the Raven Sisters be used to cover him. Kesta and Jorrun had huddled together, chilled and stiff from the salt water of the sea, his lips icy when she kissed him.

She shivered. They'd boarded up the library window she'd destroyed but there was still a draught. Dia had tried to get Jorrun to use a smaller room where he could sleep next to a fire, but of course he'd refused.

'Kesta?'

'I'm here.' She shifted down under the blanket, laying her head on his chest and finding his right hand with her left. His heart was racing and he still felt much too cold.

'I'm sorry. I'm sorry I let you down.'

His chest moved and she realised he was crying.

'No, no you didn't.' She pushed herself up to look down at him. He wouldn't meet her eyes at first but when he did Kesta felt pain lance through to her own heart. She remembered he no longer had his mother's amulet, but she didn't call up her *knowing*. 'Why would you think that?'

'I brought us to Chem. I couldn't stop Hacren.'

'None of us could have stopped him on our own.' She stroked his hair. 'And if we hadn't come here Chem would now be ruled by a powerful and evil spirit, not to mention those dreadful priests.' She shuddered. 'Sleep, please, you're still fighting that poison.'

He nodded, but his eyes were still wide and almost desperate. She kissed him and lay her head back on his chest. His arms went around her, uncomfortably tight, it was a while until he slowly relaxed his hold on her.

'I've been thinking about what to do with Osun,' he said quietly.

Kesta bit her lower lip, feeling pressure build at once behind her eyes. 'He should stay here, where he was loved, where … where people knew what a great man he was.'

She felt Jorrun's lungs still.

'You really mean that.'

She nodded against his chest, feeling the grief build up again inside her. 'I do. I still hate what he did to Milaiya, I always will, but he wasn't the selfish man he thought he was, not deep down. It makes me so angry that he won't get to be the person he could have been.' She rubbed hard at her eyes with the heel of her hand. 'I'm angry at myself that I didn't start to get to know him until it was too late but at the same time my morality couldn't have let me do anything differently. Although when you look at what he's done for Naver—'

'Kes.'

She swallowed, waiting for him to find the courage to say what he needed to.

'We need to think about what we're going to do about Chem.'

'We'll have to stay,' she replied without hesitation.

His chest rose and fell beneath her cheek. 'Not forever.'

'No, not forever.'

***

Kesta knocked softly at the door, steeling herself to enter the room that had so very much been Osun's. It was Jorrun who took the handle and pushed it open.

Dia smiled to see them, handing the parchment she was holding to Arrus. Jagna was sat at the desk and quickly stood, but Jorrun waved at him to relax. Dia searched Jorrun's face, frowning a little at what she saw.

'I'm fine.' He sighed. 'I need to talk to you about what happened in Elden.'

Dia nodded. 'Of course.'

'I'll leave you,' Jagna offered.

'We also need to discuss what we will do about Navere, and Chem,' Kesta said. 'Could you get the coven to meet?'

'Of course.' Jagna hurried off at once.

'Perhaps you should consider losing the name "Coven" for the city's ruling body for a start.' Dia raised her eyebrows. 'Anyway.' She frowned down at the paperwork on the desk. 'I've been looking through all of Osun's plans and his proposed laws for Navere, they really are rather brilliant. He has put a lot of consideration into consequences.'

Kesta and Jorrun looked at each other but said nothing.

'Anyway. Elden.'

Jorrun didn't protest when he was offered a chair. Kesta and Arrus also sat while Dia perched on the edge of the desk. She went over everything that had happened in greater detail than Kesta had heard from Worvig. When she finished, Jorrun sat silently looking down at the floor. He took in a deep breath.

'I had another brother.'

'One that hadn't been taken away from Chem and Dryn Dunham,' Dia said slowly.

Kesta watched Jorrun's face and with a sharp intake of breath she recalled the torn page in Dryn's book. 'Do you think Inari was bred to be stronger than you, to be able to conquer Elden?'

'Undoubtably. We will probably never know the whole story. He may have always been intended to go to Elden to defeat me and take the country, or perhaps he went of his own accord to take revenge.' Jorrun glanced at her. 'I'll have to go to Taurmaline.'

Kesta felt panic hit her. If he went to Elden, then she'd have to stay here without him to take care of things in Chem. The thought of being separated from him again so soon filled her with dread.

'Yes, you should both go to Elden.'

Kesta stared at her mother.

'Deal with Bractius and then spend some time with Tantony and Rosa at Northold, give yourselves some time to rest and recover.'

'Bu—'

Dia raised a hand to stop Jorrun. 'Arrus and I will stay to help here, for a month after you leave, no longer. Calayna and Jagna both seem very capable, as are Rece and Estre, but they'll need guidance and protection for a while longer. I'll send Worvig and Everlyn back to the Fulmers.'

'You'll really do that?' Kesta looked from her father to her mother. 'But after everything you went through in Elde—'

'We need Jorrun to sort out Elden,' Dia said. 'And he can't go if people aren't protected here.'

Jorrun nodded, his eyes seemed distant.

'Thank you.' Kesta jumped up to kiss her father's cheek and hug her mother.

'Temerran has already agreed to take you on the Undine in a week,' Dia told them.

'Actually, I have my own ship,' Jorrun said.

'Actually, you're still sick.' Dia looked him up and down from under her lashes. She grabbed up a handful of the papers on the desk. 'And there are a lot of things that need sorting before you go.'

Jorrun sighed and nodded. 'Very well, a week.' He reached out for Kesta's hand. 'We had better let the Raven Cove—' He glanced at Dia. 'We had better let the Ravens know our plans.'

They made their way to the audience room. Nearly everyone seemed to be there, very few sitting, most standing in small groups to talk. Kesta looked around, a frown in her face.

'Where's Cassien?'

'He's up in his room,' Beth replied, overhearing, her baby snugged in a sling against her chest. 'He won't come down.'

Kesta turned to Jorrun and he nodded. 'Go on, I'll let everyone know what's happening. Join us when you can.'

Kesta touched his arm and then hurried back out into the hall. She took the stairs up to what had been the coven's quarters two at a time. Cassien wasn't in his own room, but it wasn't hard to guess where he'd be. She knocked at the door to Osun's old chambers and opened it without waiting. She found Cassien curled up in a chair.

'Oh, Cass.'

He sniffed loudly, wiping his nose with the back of his sleeve. He didn't look up. Kesta walked over to the chair and crouched beside it, reaching out a hand to rub his shoulder. She used her *knowing* to send him comfort, knowing that it would never fill the hollow ache of the boy's grief.

'I never knew who my father was,' Cassien said quietly.

Kesta waited.

'Never even thought about it. As far as I know I was born a slave, all I had were masters. I spent so many years wishing I was dead, and yet I couldn't stop fighting to live. Crazy eh?' He looked up at her, his eyes bright. 'Then Osun came and bought me and I found I had something to really fight for and someone who …'

Kesta squeezed his shoulder, trying to hold back the wave of pain that tried to break free from her own chest.

'You can still fight for him, Cass, for what he believed in, for what he died to protect. It will be harder for you to do it without him, but you can do it. Osun was so proud of you, Cass, he saw something special in you the moment he spotted you in the slave pen. Come here.'

Cassien sat up and fell into her hug; shaking against her as she rubbed his back.

'Jorrun and I will be sailing for Elden in a few days, would you like to come?'

'Me? Me, sail over the sea to another land?'

'If you want to.'

'I want to.'

'Come on, your sisters need you downstairs.'

He nodded, slowly sitting back and wiping at his face with his sleeves, a flush on his cheeks. Kesta stood and led the way back down to the audience room. He paused outside to straighten his clothing and flatten down his hair.

'You look fine.' Kesta smiled at him.

They slipped into the room quietly, everyone was silent and still but for servants who were handing out drinks and Jorrun who was mid-flow in a speech. Kesta touched Cassien's arm and they moved through the others to be closer to Jorrun.

'It isn't going to be easy, there will be a huge amount of resistance and no doubt many setbacks, but we can do this, for Osun and for ourselves. The Fulmers are with u—'

There was a cheer from Arrus, which made several people laugh.

'—s and Elden too. Soon, through Osun's careful planning, we will have other city provinces with us also. We will only trade with provinces that prove they are making efforts to give freedom to women, we will only offer aid to help those covens that do the same. When they see our stability, when they see our prosperity, they will join us.

'But what they won't join is a coven.' He drew in a deep breath, looking around at them all. 'We are not a coven, brothers and sisters, we are a family. We are The Ravens, protectors of what is right, defenders of our land. And our land ...'

He paused, Kesta found herself holding her breath, her heart beating faster. This wasn't the Dark Man, this was her Jorrun, the man he always should have been had he been free of Chem and Bractius. The type of man Osun too, could have been. His eyes met hers.

'Brothers and sisters, where we stand, what we defend, is the Free City of Navere.'

478

Kesta choked, her hand going to her mouth as she blinked rapidly. There were several gasps in the room, then applause and cheers rang out. Kesta had to shut down her *knowing*, the emotions overwhelming. Some people, men and women, broke down and cried. She found herself grabbing Cassien's hand.

Jorrun raised his glass, his cheeks a little red.

'Raise your glasses, my family. To the Free City of Navere!'

'To the Ravens!' Arrus bellowed.

***

'What's happened?' Jorrun asked before they even got through the door to what they would always think of as Osun's old study. Their few belongings had been packed alongside a whole crate of books and taken down to the ships already. They were supposed to be saying their farewells, but Captain Rece had warned them of a disturbance in the audience room.

Dia breathed out loudly through her mouth, glancing at Calayna and Jagna. 'Three men came in to complain that the women they'd bought for breeding had run away here to the palace. They demanded to know what we were going to do about the loss of their property and how they were expected to have heirs.'

'What did you do?' Kesta demanded. Jorrun tensed beside her.

Calayna grinned and Jagna gave a snort.

Dia raised her hands at her daughter's worried face. 'Oh, don't worry, I didn't incinerate them! Much as I wanted to. I told them they'd have to get married in a consensual relationship, the same as everyone else. It got me thinking though, perhaps we should draw up contracts, instead of a man buying a woman from a merchant, he pays her an ... an independence fee, so she can escape if she needs to. It would mean a man would have to consent to treating her well.'

'I don't know.' Jorrun looked down at the floor. 'That could be complicated, but it's worth considering. I certainly wish I'd put more consideration into my marriage contract.'

Kesta's eyes widened and she looked up at him.

He grinned and she punched him in the arm.

'See?' Jorrun turned to Dia, his grin not fading.

Dia sighed and shook her head at them. Kesta felt warmth flowing from her heart, it was the first time she'd seen Jorrun really smile since his brother's death.

'It's had us talking about a difficult subject also.' Jagna frowned, not looking up at them. 'We want to close the skin houses but fear it will increase attacks on women. We …' He looked at Dia for help.

'It makes me feel sick to say it,' Dia said. 'But it seems the best way forward might be to see if there are any women who would work voluntarily in skin houses, run themselves. They would be paid, have strict rules of conduct.'

'They would likely be richer than any merchant in Navere,' Jagna added.

Kesta felt Jorrun tense beside her.

'They would need to pay guards to protect them,' Kesta said quickly. 'And it would have to be strictly monitored by the Ravens to ensure no one was there against their will.' She shuddered. 'Though I couldn't imagine anyone choosing such a life.'

'Small steps, subtlety,' Dia said, looking around at them all. 'Just as Osun suggested.'

Jorrun closed his eyes, his fists clenched. 'I don't like it, but it makes sense.'

Kesta rubbed at her temples, it was still too awful to contemplate, but they had to think of the stability and long-term future of their province.

She drew in a sharp breath and bit her lower lip, since when had Navere been hers?

'Come on,' Dia said. 'You two were meant to be going.'

Jorrun nodded and took Kesta's hand.

There were so many people waiting to see them off that it took some time to leave the palace. Kesta kissed Jagna and Rece on the cheek, hugging every woman of the Ravens. Jorrun held Kussim for a long time, promising he would be back soon. Kesta went to her parents last, her fingers clutching the fabric of her mother's cloak.

'Go on,' Dia said.

'Thank you.' Kesta's eyes were screwed tightly shut. She felt Jorrun's light touch on her back and she stepped away from her mother.

They were just a small group gathered to walk down to the docks. Temerran had two of his men with him, Azrael and Doroquael had both insisted on braving another sea crossing. Catya was also coming, sniffing back an embarrassed tear at leaving Heara, but wanting to visit Rosa. Cassien held the halter of a horse, a black mare with one white sock.

'We're taking a horse?' Jorrun asked.

Kesta grinned. 'Yes, it's your horse.'

'Mine?'

'She's called Destiny.' She looked up into his blue eyes. 'You said you wanted a horse that would enjoy a friendship with a human.'

He opened his mouth and shook his head, regarding her for a long time before bending down to kiss her. 'In the middle of all this, you found me a horse.'

Kesta shrugged. 'My mother has an affinity for birds, for me it seems to be horses.'

'Thank you.'

Kesta looked around, her eyes falling on the road that led through the palace gate. 'There is one last thing I need to do though.'

'What?' He frowned at her.

'Walk through Navere to the docks on my own.'

'Now that I've got to see!' Jagna said. Several people surged forward, but Kesta raised her hands.

'If you all follow, I won't be alone!'

'We'll be five minutes behind,' Jorrun said. He looked worried, and proud.

Kesta smiled, taking in a deep breath. She took a last look at her family, that of blood and those of choice, then set off toward the city. She was wearing her green raven cloak, hood down, her face bare. On her tunic was the raven emblem the sisters had designed and sewn. The guards saluted her as she passed and she raised a hand to acknowledge them. The city was busy, everyday life, trade, survival, went on. There were women on the street, but none of them alone and nearly every group still had a male escort. Most people stopped to stare at her and she smiled, holding her head high.

One man spat on the road in front of her. Kesta laughed, calling up her power and throwing the man down the street. There were several cries and gasps. Kesta ignored them, feeling a sense of peace grow inside her. She called up fire and made three small balls of flame. She juggled them all the way down to the docks, smiling to herself as men fell over themselves to get out of her way and women stopped to watch, wide-eyed. When she reached the waterside, she sent her fireballs to hiss and steam in the sea water.

The Free City of Navere. Still a dream, but oh so much closer to truth.

The others caught up with her quickly, but instead of following Temerran toward the Undine, Jorrun placed his hand against Kesta's back and turned her toward his much smaller but achingly familiar ship.

'Are you not coming on the Undine?' Temerran asked them.

'We love to sail,' Jorrun replied.

'Ah.' Temerran folded his arms and leaned back, looking from Jorrun to Kesta. 'Well, when you have other things to do than sail, come alongside and I'll throw you a tow rope.'

Heat rose to Kesta's cheeks.

Jorrun smiled. 'We'll do that.'

'What about ussss?' Azrael turned a backflip.

'You go with Catya and Cass on the Undine until we get to Northold,' Jorrun replied. 'You'll have more room on the Undine and Catya will tell both of you bugs as many stories as you want to hear, no doubt very bloodthirsty ones.'

'I know lots of stories.' Catya nodded.

Azrael didn't seem at all pleased, but he and Doroquael bobbed off after the others.

Kesta turned to Jorrun. 'Sailing.'

'Well, it's true.' He looked down at her, a spark of mischief in his eyes.

'You're still recovering from that poiso—'

He put a finger over her lips. 'I guess we'll see about that.'

***

The Undine was a magnificent ship, her lines so sharp she seemed to be made of wind. Jorrun and Kesta had to use their magic to keep up with her, but they both revelled in the challenge. At night they drew up alongside, taking the tow rope and shutting themselves in the cabin away from the rest of the world.

They sailed down the Taur together, stopping at the small wharf of Northold only long enough for the fire-spirits, Catya, and Cassien to disembark with Destiny. They exchanged news, learning from Kurghan that Tantony and Rosa were still at Taurmaline. Kesta and Jorrun both thanked Temerran profusely, promising to stay in close contact. The Undine turned about in the lake, heading back up the Taur to return Everlyn and Worvig safely back to the Fulmers.

'What now?' Kesta asked Jorrun.

Jorrun untied the rope from the post and shoved them away from the wharf with his boot. 'Now, we sort out Bractius.'

***

Kesta stood at the prow, watching as the castle of Taurmaline grew larger on the horizon. It was hard to tell if the butterflies in her stomach were anxiety or excitement, perhaps a little of both. Jorrun's eyes were firmly fixed on the harbour, watching for directions from the harbourmaster. She jumped out of the ship to tie up; the wharves were busy. Jorrun turned to her with a grin as he drew himself up and took on the demeanour of the Dark Man, even calling flames to his fingers as he cleared a way for them through the startled crowd. The castle guards straightened as they passed and Jorrun headed directly to the audience room. He didn't knock, blasting the doors open as the herald and two guards scrambled out of the way.

484

The room appeared empty, only two torches burning on the walls. Movement caught Kesta's eye and she realised there was a man seated on one of the benches at the side of the room, the very place she'd first sat many months before with her father to speak to Bractius.

Adrin looked pale, his eyes wide. His right arm was strapped against his left shoulder and stubble grew on his cheeks and chin.

'Thane!'

Jorrun narrowed his eyes. 'Where's the King?'

'In his private study.'

Jorrun turned to go and Adrin scrambled to his feet. 'None of this was my fault, I couldn't d—'

Jorrun spun around and pointed a finger at the chieftain who shrank back against the wall. 'That had better be so.'

He didn't waste any more time but headed back out into the hall. Kesta spared a glance for the cowering Adrin, how had she ever felt any fear of the pathetic man?

Kesta looked up at her husband as they marched toward the King's private room.

'Jorrun?'

He glanced at her, his eyes hard, but he placed a hand against her back and ran a lock of her long, black hair, gently through his fingers.

As before, he didn't knock. The King wasn't alone, Tantony leapt to his feet, his eyes wide.

'Jorrun! Kesta.'

Kesta only had time to give him a brief smile. Bractius stood slowly, moving to the edge of his ornate desk. His eyes flickered from her to Jorrun.

'Jorru—'

Jorrun didn't stop, he strode straight up to the King, punching him hard in the face and knocking him off his feet to sprawl against the wall.

Kesta covered her mouth with both hands, staring at her husband in shock. Tantony edged around to her, his skin reddening.

Jorrun glared down at the King, his fists still clenched. 'If you *ever* threaten my wife or her family again, king or no, I will end your reign!'

'Jorrun!' Bractius spluttered, pulling himself up against the wall. 'I was bewitche—'

'I should have knocked you on your arse a long time ago!' Jorrun snarled. 'Instead of making excuses for you. I should have spoken up every time you were wrong!'

Bractius stared up at him with his mouth open.

Tantony touched Kesta's arm. 'Come on, let's leave them to sort this out.'

'Bu—'

'Come on.' Tantony pushed the door open. Kesta left reluctantly, not because she was worried about Jorrun, but because she dearly wanted to see Bractius get what he deserved.

'Rosa will be glad to see you.' Tantony looked her up and down. 'I'm glad to see you too, strangely enough.'

Kesta turned and grinned at him, then flustered him with a bear hug. 'I'm glad to see you too. What's been happening?'

Tantony sighed and shook his head. 'Things are settling but Bractius is still all over the place. He refuses to admit Ayline had any part in this and has pretty much shut himself away. I've been doing the best I can with Teliff and the Huscarls, but running a kingdom is a bit over my head.'

Kesta slipped her arm through his. 'Oh, I doubt that, Merkis.'

'I'm telling you, without Rosa's sensible head I'd have drowned in paperwork and hung every idiot who comes here with a petty petition by now!'

Kesta grinned. 'That would be one way to stop petty petitions.'

He glanced around at her and snorted. 'I miss the quiet of Northold.'

'Me too,' Kesta replied, her heart clenching and all humour fleeing.

Rosa was seated in the Queen's parlour and she dropped her sewing, leaping to her feet as soon as she saw Kesta. She gave a startled cry, then threw herself across the room to hug her.

There were four other ladies in the room and they all politely got to their feet.

'Kesta!' Rosa looked her up and down. 'You look well, but ... what has happened?' She regarded Kesta's eyes intently.

'A lot.' Grief pushed at Kesta's throat. 'But we'll tell you both soon. For the moment,' she looked across to the closed door. 'I think I need to speak to the Queen.'

Rosa's smile faded and she glanced at Tantony.

'I won't hurt her,' Kesta said. 'You know that.'

Rosa rubbed at her forehead. 'Well, I'm not sure I couldn't say that she'd deserve it, but it's not up to me.'

Tantony hung back as Rosa knocked softly and then entered the Queen's private rooms. Ayline was in bed, propped up against pillows, a young girl who was reading to her from a book stopped as they came in. Ayline's eyes widened and she fought her bedding to sit up straighter.

'You!'

Kesta's eyes narrowed as she regarded the queen. Her hair was perfectly pinned up and there was a flush to her pale cheeks.

'Yes, me. Don't worry, I haven't come to kill you.'

'I was enchanted!' Ayline fluttered her eyelashes. 'Bewitched by evil dreams!'

Kesta drew up her *knowing*. 'No doubt, but the darkness in your heart is yours alone. You see enemies where you could have had friends. I imagine that has been so all of your life. Is the loneliness worth it, Ayline? Is the shadow of power worth the fear and the paranoia?'

All pretence fell away from Ayline's face and she glared at Kesta with open hatred. 'I have power!'

'Hmmm.' Kesta raised her hand and looked down at her palm, she called flames there and Ayline shrank back. 'What is power? I imagine you see it as something needed to dominate, to control. Luckily for you.' Kesta let her flames die and looked her in the eyes. 'I believe power is having the strength to stand up against what is wrong, to protect those you love. Perhaps you'll understand when your child is born. Perhaps you won't. But I'll be watching you, Ayline.'

'Watch away,' Ayline snarled.

'Oh, I will.' With a nod at Rosa, Kesta left the room, closing it slowly behind her.

Rosa and Tantony walked with her to Jorrun's quarters.

'Are you all right?' Rosa asked.

Kesta realised they hadn't said a word in quite some time.

'Yes, I'm fine.' She forced a smile. 'I fear Ayline will be trouble, and yet I can't quite hate her.'

'Elden isn't Chem,' Rosa replied. 'But it's hard enough for a woman with a sharp mind. Unless she is lucky.' She turned to smile at Tantony and the gruff Merkis blushed beneath his beard.

'I see that.' Kesta sighed. 'Catya is back at The Tower waiting to see you.'

'She is?' Rosa's eyes lit and she looked at her husband.

'We'll go as soon as Jorrun has finished with the king,' he reassured her.

***

They stayed for five days, Kesta anxiously feeling their short break away from Chem slipping by. Although she knew the Drakes, Catya, and Cassien were all safe back at Northold, she itched to be there with them too. On the fourth and fifth night they dined with Bractius, Ayline making excuses that she was too tired and due to have her child at any moment.

As much as she wanted to remain angry at Bractius, Kesta's heart eased as she saw the friendship between Jorrun and Bractius relax and then blossom again. Jorrun had told the King of Elden he would always be his friend, that he would always protect him, but that he was a Raven now, bound to defend anyone in need on the land beneath their sky. In a quiet moment, his face flushed by wine, Bractius said, 'I abused your friendship, Jorrun, took advantage of your conditioning in Chem, just as my father did.'

'I know.' Jorrun looked down at his hands. 'But you're still my friend. As long as you understand, you will never take advantage of me again. There is a bigger worl—'

'You belong to the world. It makes me feel jealous.' Bractius sniffed, wiping his nose with the back of his hand and grabbing for his goblet. He took a big gulp of wine. 'You and Kesta. Ravens. I'd be obliged if you could visit me now and again. I'll miss you.'

Kesta had reached for her own wine with one hand, finding Jorrun's long fingers with the other. He squeezed her hand tightly.

'I'll miss you also,' Jorrun replied. 'Northol—'

Bractius banged his goblet down on the table. 'Northold is yours forever, your home.' Bractius's words slurred but his eyes were intense. 'Always. Your home. Whenever you need it. No conditions.'

Jorrun drew in a breath, his eyes fixed on his empty plate. He turned to look at Kesta and she placed a hand on his chest. He leaned in to kiss her.

***

As they stepped through the inner gates of Northold the next day, they became aware of the sound of swords clashing, the ring and shriek of metal on metal occasionally drowned out by a cheer or a collective gasp.

'What in the Gods' name?' Tantony exclaimed.

They rounded the keep to see a large gathering of folk not far from the Raven Tower. The ravens themselves were unsettled, circling the high tower and uttering deep throated cries.

Jorrun pushed his way through the crowd, holding out his hand for Kesta. When they got to the front, Kesta shook her head and groaned. Cassien and Catya were fighting, the girl moving with breathtaking speed but the young man totally unphased, calm, thoughtful, careful. It was exciting, inspirational to watch, but Kesta found her heart in her throat.

'Children!' Rosa stepped forward, clapping her hands together.

Both Cassien and Catya stopped. Cassien lowered his sword and Catya dropped hers, running to throw her arms around Rosa.

'Hmmm,' Kesta leaned against Jorrun. 'That's something to watch I hadn't considered.'

'Catya is just a girl.' Jorrun frowned. 'There's three years between them.'

'There's ten years between us, old man.' She looked up at him and grinned.

He pulled her round and kissed her, biting her lower lip. 'I'll show you who's old.'

She slapped his thigh hard. 'Seriously though, we'd better watch them.'

Jorrun nodded. 'Yes, Silene.'

She narrowed her eyes at him, her pulse beating faster.

Kesta turned to Tantony. 'We expect an exceptional welcome home feast, Merkis. I'm sure you can see to it.'

Tantony gave a bow. 'It will be dealt with at once, Raven Kesta.'

Kesta startled, staring at Tantony wide-eyed. She bowed her head, raising her hand to her forehead to hide her eyes, why had that title hurt so much?

'Kes?' Jorrun took her hand.

She squeezed his fingers and headed for the Raven Tower.

The door closed behind them and they paused on the stairs, her hands tangling in his thick, dark hair. Like a cold wind, memories of Osun's curly hair and dark-blue eyes struck her and she wrapped her arms tightly around Jorrun, her face tucked against his warm neck, feeling the pulse of his veins.

'Kes?'

'Let's go up,' she said.

Her heart caught at the sight of the familiar room at the top of The Tower, the mess on the table. The scrabbling and reptilian smell of the ravens in the loft above. The small, unmade bed pushed up below the window, the books lain everywhere with feathers, paper, ribbons, anything thin enough to use as a bookmark.

The fire sparked and Azrael came leaping out, followed by Doroquael.

'You're home!' Azrael flew crazy loops around the room.

Jorrun turned to look down at her.

She reached up to touch the side of his face, relishing the familiar feel of his neatly trimmed beard. Kesta looked into his blue eyes, recalling the day she'd been forced to marry this man against her will to save her people. 'From this day we are bound together, pledged to work together to make our lives a better one; a happy one.'

His eyes widened and he smiled. 'We will listen to each other, respect each other, and support each other, being patient with each other's differences and imperfections.'

'We will remain truthful, loyal, and faithful to each other in all aspects of life. Do you agree to these terms?'

Jorrun looked away, his eyes narrowing in a frown. He drew in a deep breath and rubbed at his bearded chin. Kesta growled at him, giving his chest a light shove, although she couldn't help laughing.

He turned back to her, his eyes sparkling with amusement. 'For all the lands beneath the sky, I agree.'

Epilogue

The Free City of Navere

Kesta wrapped her arms around herself and shivered. White fog surrounded her, its dampness seeping into her clothing and hanging in her hair. Dark shapes loomed and muffled voices came in snatches.

'Just a little to port!' she called back over her shoulder.

Jorrun adjusted the rudder and they turned slightly, hitting a wave. Kesta felt her stomach lurch and her hand went to her mouth. She swallowed several times, trying to quell the nausea. She forced her breathing to slow, feeling relief wash through her as they bumped against the wharf. She sprang up onto the rail, leaping across and catching the rope that Jorrun threw to her. It took a moment for her body to register that she was on still land and she held onto the post around which she wound the rope. The winter sea had been rough, but even so it was unusual for her to feel so sick.

Jorrun placed a hand against her back, his eyebrows drawn down in concern. 'You look very pale, Kesta.'

She forced a smile. 'I'll be all right in a bit.'

He placed a lantern down on the wooden planks and both Azrael and Doroquael came shooting out, spinning away into the fog. Jorrun tutted, then handed over her small travel bag and they headed along the wharf toward the main street that led to Navere's palace.

'The Undine is here.' Jorrun indicated with his head and Kesta followed his gaze.

'Good, we didn't get much chance to get to know the Borrowman. Do you … do you think there really might be peace between the lands now?'

493

Jorrun was silent for a while, then sighed. 'Between the lands, yes. In Chem, sadly, not yet.'

The fog thinned as they moved away from the water and they saw glimpses of the building that Dia had commanded be converted into a guard house. Two men stood to attention outside, the eyes of one widening on seeing them and their green cloaks. Kesta's hand moved unconsciously toward the raven crest sewn onto the front of her tunic. The guard said something to his companion, and they stepped forward, giving a smart salute.

'Masters, may we know your names?'

Kesta placed a hand on her hip and opened her mouth, but Jorrun quickly raised a hand. 'We are Jorrun and Kesta Raven. You're obviously new.'

Kesta narrowed her eyes, fighting the temptation to call her power and show them exactly who she was! Then she drew in a sharp breath. The two men had shown no surprise, no objection, to the fact that she walked Navere without a veil and dressed in trousers. Had things changed so much in just a month?

'I've served the city for five years,' the guard replied. 'But I didn't have the honour of seeing you, masters, when you were here before. And ... um ... master Icante insisted that we challenge anyone who arrives at the docks.'

Kesta gave a snort of laughter, wondering what her mother made of being called '*master Icante*.' Jorrun flashed her a look of annoyance and she quickly straightened her face.

'Have you had any trouble?' Jorrun asked the man.

He frowned. 'A few men have tried to leave the city by sea and force their women to go with them. We let the men go but made them leave the women.'

'What became of the women?' Kesta asked quickly.

494

'I believe they were given employment at the palace.' The guard shrugged. 'There ... um ... have been a lot of instances of men leaving the city because of the new laws.'

Jorrun nodded. 'We won't interrupt you any longer.' He glanced at Kesta and set off toward the palace. She had to hurry to keep up with his long stride.

'Jorrun?'

It was a while before he responded, he seemed to shake himself. 'Sorry, Kesta.' He slowed his pace and she slipped her arm through his.

'You're worried.' She looked up at him.

He drew in a deep breath and sighed it out. 'Of course, I am.'

She looked around at the city as they passed through it. It did seem quieter than the last time she'd been here. Several guards patrolled the streets in pairs and her feet faltered when she realised that small groups of women moved together in the open without a man to escort them. The market was busy, and she couldn't help but squeeze Jorrun's arm and stop to stare when she saw a section of stalls being run purely by women. Her chest tightened and she chewed at her bottom lip, barely blinking as she watched.

'Come on,' Jorrun gave her arm a gentle pull.

The guards at the gate to the temple district seemed to recognise them and they were invited through at once, a runner went ahead of them, presumably to warn the palace of their arrival. Kesta's eyes immediately sought out the temple. Scaffolding had been set up around the scorched ruins although she could see no one working there. More than half of the shops were boarded up and Kesta felt her stomach tighten into a cold knot. As much as she reviled the trade of the temple district, without commerce, the city would die and their hopes of reforming Chem with it.

'This doesn't look good,' Jorrun murmured.

Kesta swallowed, wanting to reassure him but unable to find the words.

A familiar figure waited for them at the gates of the palace and Kesta let go of Jorrun's arm to hurry toward him.

'Captain!'

Rece took two steps back, his eyes widening as Kesta grabbed him in a hug. The poor man turned bright red and stared wide-eyed at Jorrun.

'Kes,' Jorrun sighed. 'Don't give the poor man a heart attack.'

She scowled at Jorrun and turned to smile at Rece. 'I thought you were used to my barbarian ways. How are you?'

Rece straightened his uniform. 'I am very well, maste—'

She punched him in the arm. 'My name's Kesta. Anyway, aren't you a Raven too?'

Rece glanced down at the crest on the front of his tabard.

'Where's the Icante?' Jorrun asked.

Rece seemed to sag in relief. 'This way.'

He led them across the garden, here and there a little snow rested in the shadows. They had barely entered the building before they were surrounded by the Raven Sisters. They were reserved with Jorrun, giving polite greetings, but one after another pushed forward to hug Kesta, both Estre and Rey squeezing her particularly hard. They were bombarded with questions with little time to actually answer.

'Did Cassien not come with you?' Kussim asked.

'He stayed in Elden,' Kesta told her. 'He couldn't face coming back here yet.'

The women hushed and Kesta found she couldn't meet their eyes. A tingling pain started to rise in her chest, and she tried to push it back down. It was hard not to think of Osun, of how his presence had somehow suffused the palace, changed its very essence.

Jorrun cleared his throat. 'The Icante?'

'This way.' Rece politely pushed through the women.

A feeling of dread rose in Kesta, her pulse just a little faster as they headed toward the room that Osun had used for his study. She glanced at Jorrun, knowing that his grief was so much larger than her own. Rece didn't stop at the room though, instead taking them to the library. It was quite dark inside, the stained-glass window still boarded up and just a little low, winter sunlight, streaming in from two smaller windows. The room was busy with several conversations seeming to be happening at once. People turned at the sound of the door being opened, one of them Arrus.

'My urchin!' He almost ran, crushing Kesta in his arms and lifting her up off the floor.

'Ow!' Kesta laughed.

Arrus dumped her back on her feet and grabbed Jorrun's hand, thumping him hard on the back. 'We weren't sure if we'd see you today or tomorrow.' The big man beamed at them.

'The crossing wasn't too rough in the end,' Jorrun told him.

Kesta looked around the room, spotting Calayna and Jagna. She met her mother's eyes and a feeling of peace and relief swept through her.

'What's happening?' Jorrun asked.

'Well.' Arrus's eyebrows shot up. 'You have interrupted an informal guild gathering.'

'Guild?' Kesta frowned.

'One of Osun's brilliant ideas,' Dia said as she walked toward them.

Kesta glanced at Jorrun.

'Welcome back.' Dia hugged Kesta gently and kissed Jorrun on the cheek. 'Come on, I'll excuse myself for a moment and we can catch up.' Dia caught Calayna's eye, and the tattooed woman raised a hand in acknowledgement. 'How are you both? How are things in Elden?'

They left the library and Dia headed along the corridor.

Jorrun drew in a breath. 'Elden is good. Repairs are close to complete at Taurmouth and the river settlements are starting to recover. Taurmaline is somewhat subdued, like its king. It's settled though and I think all will be well. Elden has an heir now, Ayline had her baby shortly before we left.'

'A boy,' Kesta added.

Dia nodded. 'I'll send Bractius a letter. And the two of you?'

'We are well.' Kesta smiled, although her heart felt heavy and her stomach still fluttered.

'Did Catya not come with you?'

'She and Cass are staying with Tantony and Rosa a little longer,' Jorrun told her. 'They'll meet you in the Fulmers. It will do Cassien good to spend time in the islands.'

Dia smiled at that. 'And the Drakes?'

Jorrun snorted and rolled his eyes. 'They came with us, no doubt they'll turn up when they've finished gossiping with the Chem spirits.'

'And here?' Kesta asked. 'What's happening here?' She held her breath.

'Come this way.' Dia took them to the east wing and opened the door to a room Kesta had never been in before. It was small but had two large windows. Shelves had been newly built up against one wall and filled with books. The only other furniture was a bed, a desk, and an old dark-stained wardrobe. Dia looked at them both, her eyes lingering on Jorrun's face. 'The library is rather busy these days. I had this room prepared for you. It seems to have been just a small reading room or parlour, I have no idea who used it. Will you be all right in here?'

Kesta held her breath and looked at Jorrun. He'd become very still. He swallowed and turned away from Dia to look around the room. His voice was very quiet when he spoke. 'I'm sure it will be fine, thank you.'

Kesta breathed out.

'Well, then,' Dia walked across to the window, gazing out over the gardens. 'It hasn't been easy, but we're getting there. Some people have left Navere and we let them. We started the guilds to give the tradespeople a little power and some say in the running of the city, it's been tough and there has been plenty of resistance to changes, but on the whole it's working. The foreign market is prospering, and we've started to have visitors from other provinces to take a look at the goods from Elden and the Fulmers. We even have visitors coming purely out of curiosity at the city that has women with magic!

'Despite our funds being strained, I've started repairs to the templ—'

Kesta opened her mouth to protest but Dia stopped her. 'Their faith is fundamental to Chem. Rebuilding the temple and showing respect to the gods of Chem will reassure people and win us supporters. I did put a condition in place though. We will also build a small women's temple where women can enter and visit the gods.'

Jorrun sat on the desk, his eyes on his hands as he picked at his thumbnail. He nodded slowly. 'Yes, that was a good move.'

Kesta and Dia both watched him for a moment.

'Settle yourselves in,' Dia said. 'We'll go over the books and reports this afternoon, but there's no rush, I'll stay a week or until you've had a chance to get your bearings and settle back in. Do you feel up to a welcome meal tonight? The Ravens are excited to have you back.'

Kesta anxiously waited for Jorrun to reply.

He looked up and forced a smile. 'That's fine.'

Dia squeezed Kesta's arm as she passed, leaving the room.

'Are you all right?'

Jorrun hopped down off the desk and slid his arms around her, leaning his cheek against the top of her head. 'I'm okay. I'm just missing Osun.'

She nodded. *I miss him too.*

***

Their welcome dinner that night started off as a quiet affair with Kesta and Jorrun listening in as the Ravens chattered around them. Jagna and Estre had been married by Dia using a Fulmer ceremony only a week before and their wedding was still a favourite subject for conversation. The room hushed when Temerran began a tale about a woman who was half fish and could lure sailors into rocks with her voice. Beside Kesta, Rece cleared his throat and spoke quietly.

'Kesta. I, well, Calayna and I have a favour to ask you.'

Kesta turned to give him her full attention. It was the first time she could recall that he'd ever used her name.

The Chemman swallowed, glancing about to make sure no one was watching. 'Would you perform mine and Calayna's wedding ceremony?'

She opened her mouth, her hand going to her throat. It was a moment before she could find her voice. 'Of course I will!'

There was a shriek and Kesta spun around to see Azrael darting out of one of the lanterns, Doroquael following more sedately. Azrael flew loops around the room, seeming to brighten at the stir he was causing.

'The Drakess are coming back!' He crackled. 'The Drakes are coming back to Shem!'

Jorrun took her hand and squeezed it.

They moved on from the dining room to the larger room where Osun had arranged his farewell gathering. To Kesta it felt like another lifetime ago but at the same time still somehow painfully close. Temerran sang for them and Heara insisted on dragging poor Vilnue up to dance. Kesta laughed, but her heart ached. She turned to Jorrun, knowing how much harder it must be for him.

'Do you want to leave?' She took his hand in both of hers.

His eyes travelled over the room. 'Not yet. I need to see this.'

She swallowed, her grief blossoming painfully in her chest at the same time as hope warmed her soul. She wondered if Osun were somehow watching over them all; if he knew that his sisters were safe.

***

Kesta was awoken by the churning of her stomach, she felt hot and slipped out of the bed to pour herself a glass of water. She walked over to the window, placing a hand on the cold glass, taking in a deep breath and breathing out slowly.

She jumped as a hand rested on her shoulder and she turned to scowl up at Jorrun. He laughed and bent to kiss her cheek. They stood for a moment in silence, gazing out across the garden. A light sprinkling of snow covered the grass.

'It's going to be all right, isn't it,' she said.

Jorrun nodded. 'I think so. I hope so.'

Nausea gripped Kesta again and she rubbed at her stomach, squirming uncomfortably.

'You're unwell again?' he asked in concern.

Kesta frowned. 'I didn't think I'd drunk that much wine. Perhaps I ate something bad.'

Jorrun examined her face, his eyes travelling down to the hand that lay over her stomach. His face suddenly lit with a grin and he laughed.

'What?' she demanded, giving him a shove. 'I'm glad you find my illness so amusing!'

He placed a hand to the side of her face and kissed her before moving behind her and wrapping his arms about her. She leaned back against him, absorbing his warmth as they watched out the window again.

Kesta took in a deep breath. 'I used to worry about where my home would be, but I don't anymore. My home is with you. My people are anyone who needs me.'

Jorrun squeezed her tighter.

'Do you really think we'll be all right?' She looked up at his reflection in the window.

He smiled. 'I do. All three of us.'

Acknowledgements

Thank you as always to you, dear reader, for taking the time to read The Raven Coven, I really hope you enjoyed it. If you did, you'll be pleased to know there will be more, I plan for there to be at least another two books in the series. I'll have to ask you to please be patient though, as I have a fulltime job and need to sleep, I sadly can't write as often as I'd like.

Please come and say hello on twitter @EmmaMilesShadow
Or on Facebook www.facebook.com/EmmaMilesShadow

A big thank you to my editor, Emma Mitchell of Creating Perfection. Also, to my blog tour organiser, Rachel Gilbey and Sarah Anderson who put together the cover.
Thank you to my three beta readers, Katrina Hay, Maria Sinclair and Kirsty Chricton for their support and invaluable feedback.

One of the most powerful things you can do in your life is to surround yourself with positive like-minded people. People who love what you love, understand you and support you. So a mention again to Katrina and Maria, so glad I met you. And also to the amazing Fiction Cafe and all its wonderful admins and members. Wendy, you change people's lives.

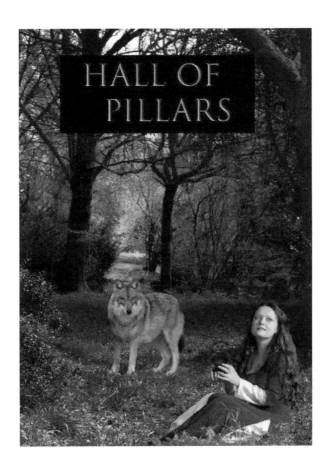

HALL OF PILLARS

Life on the edge of the wilds where the fey roamed free was hard, but Mya did her best to protect and raise her nephew. The time of his coming of age was drawing close and as proud as she was of him, she was afraid to let him go, afraid that the truth of his mother's death would come back to haunt them. A chance meeting strikes up an unusual friendship that will sustain her through the hardest of times and of those, for Mya and her unexpected allies, there will be many; for a traitor arrives at the village, destroying everything she believes to be true and they must flee, or die

Printed in Great Britain
by Amazon